Annie Bea...   ...e

Mink Elliott

hera

First published in the United Kingdom in 2020 by Hera

Hera Books
28b Cricketfield Road
London, E5 8NS
United Kingdom

Print ISBN 978 1 78863 982 8
Ebook ISBN 978 1 912973 38 5

Printed and bound in Great Britain by Clays Ltd, Elcograf S.p.A.

Annie Beaton's Year of Positive Thinking

For Sam and Max with all my love xxx

The Wisdom of Kintsukuroi

Kintsukuroi is a kind of Japanese ceramic style. The word *Kintsukuroi* means 'to repair with gold'. In the *Kintsukuroi* tradition, when a ceramic piece breaks, an artisan will fuse the pieces back together using liquid gold or gold-dusted lacquer. So rather than being covered up, the breaks become more obvious and a new piece of art emerges from the brokenness.

Kintsukuroi embraces flaws and imperfection, but it also teaches the essence of resilience. Every crack in a ceramic piece is part of its history and each piece becomes more beautiful because it has been broken.

Cyndie Spiegel, *A Year of Positive Thinking*

Chapter One

November

November 11 – Crappy Birthday!

I suppose I should've known it was going to be a bad day when I hobbled into the office kitchen and discovered we'd completely run out of Canderel. *And* skimmed milk.

I mean, really. How's a girl – sorry, *woman* – sorry, fifty-year-old, frumpy, completely *knackered* woman – supposed to lose any lard when all those impossibly young, ridiculously skinny cows scoff your diet food before you've even made it into work?

With great difficulty, let me tell you.

Still, I suppose you just have to get on with it – when in Rome and all that. So I put six teaspoons of sparkly white sugar in my full-fat milky tea and slosh it all over myself as I limp to my desk, wondering how the hell everyone else manages to walk with cups of tea without getting wet and whether my colleagues have bought me the standard caterpillar birthday cake from M&S.

'Oh, you guys!' I put my palm to my throat in exaggerated surprise when I see said cake sitting on my desk. 'You remembered!'

Maeve, on the other side of the desk divider, tuts in mock annoyance, rolls her eyes and mutters something about not being *allowed* to forget, thanks to my calling her voicemail every day for the past two weeks to helpfully remind her.

At least I think it was mock annoyance.

'Who even *leaves* voicemail messages these days?' she says, 'I mean, if you want to *talk* to someone, *text* them.'

'I know, right?' nod all the other twelve-year-olds, as they continue tippety-tap typing, staring at their screens stony-faced.

They don't even look at their fingers whizzing about on their keyboards – just straight at the screen. I suppose it's because they all learned to touch-type by the time they were three – probably round about the same time Amelie and I were standing on pub tables in crop tops and low-slung combat trousers, pissed as newts and raising our pints in celebration of an England goal as we watched Euro '96.

God, those were the days. When I was able to wear a crop top without angry mobs calling the Environmental Agency and getting offended by the wodges of fat mushrooming over the tops of my elasticated pants. Not that I *want* to wear crop tops anymore – nor do I wear elasticated pants... yet. It's just that it'd be nice not to feel like Fred Flintstone stuffing himself into a size zero sabre-tooth tiger frock every morning when I get dressed.

But anyway, back to the work thing. So I smile weakly and instantly feel like I'm somebody's visiting great-grandmother, like Maggie Smith on *Downton Abbey*, pretending not to be able to hear them, when in all honesty, I just can't for the life of me *understand* them. And I've left my ear trumpet at home.

Bloody youngsters – they just don't know how to have a laugh at work, do they? It's all heads down, get on with the job, eat a vegan salad at your desk (no pub for three-hour lunches like the good old days), don't bother me with your idle chit-chat – particularly if you're wont to offend – and leave at five *on the dot* so I don't upset my delicate work/life balance.

Not that there's anything *wrong* with that, per se, it's just… oh, I dunno. It's just not how we did it back in my day. In *my* day? God! Can I *sound* any more like a bitter old fart?

I squeeze my bum into my chair and fire off a not-too-shabby piece (soz, *post*) about how to tell kids about terrorist attacks without scaring the bejesus out of them, pinging it over to the Ed for her approval before it goes live.

As I wait for her response, I scarf some more cake.

'Hmm… that's not really what I asked for,' Suzette says seconds later, screwing up her face. 'Far too… *journalistic*.'

She virtually spits out the last word, like I've just written an ISIS recruitment pamphlet or something and follows it up with a harrumph that would register on the Richter scale. If I hadn't been wedged in so tight, I would've fallen off my chair – in the thirty-odd years I've been writing for magazines and newspapers, no one's *ever* accused me of being even *remotely* journalistic before, let alone *too* journalistic.

'Can I have a quick word, Annie?' Suzette swivels her chair round to face mine in such a characteristic no-nonsense way that by the time I've put down my cake, grabbed a pen and notebook and dutifully waddled after her towards a small, empty room, I've pretty much already figured out that the word she wants to have with me isn't 'promotion'.

Suzette sits down with a curt efficiency reminiscent of Miss Trunchbull and I close the door behind me, gritting my teeth in anticipation and inadvertently grinding down on a stray sliver of maraschino cherry.

'So,' she begins, a lightning-fast smile flashing across her face, the fluoro strip-light refracting menacingly off her Hollywood-white fangs. 'How are you finding it here so far?'

Her eyes bore into mine. I look away, my heart sinking at the realisation that my considerable bulk is blocking the one and only exit from this shark tank. I sit on my hands and feel my thighs spilling over the side of the chair. And just for a nanosecond, I'm transported back to when I was seven years old, getting told off for nicking a strawberry Mivvi from the local shop.

'Good, good,' I say. 'I think?'

'Really?' she sounds surprised.

'Well, it's only been a few weeks and I'm sure it won't be too much longer before I've got the hang of the... what's it called? The thingy, you know, the M&Ms? No. The M&S?'

In an attempt to give her a clue, I air-type and peer into an invisible computer screen.

She sighs and looks down at her notepad. 'Do you mean *the content management system*? The CMS?'

'That's it! Not the M&S, the CMS! You can see why I thought it—' I cut myself off when it becomes clear Suzette doesn't think the mix up is even the slightest bit amusing. 'So anyway, once I know how to find and actually put up photos—'

'You mean *source* and *upload images*.'

'I do? Yes, I do! Once I can do that properly—'

'Look,' she says, getting flustered, 'what I need now is a really good ROI.'

'Is that a kind of coffee?' I manage, always keen to nail the new lingo. 'Much more into tea, me. You just can't beat a hot, sweet cup of Yorkshire—'

Suzette closes her eyes and shakes her head slowly.

'Return on investment,' she says flatly.

'Oh?' I raise my eyebrows as if this is almost interesting.

'And I haven't been getting that from you. The pressure's on me to really deliver and if any part of our machine isn't pulling its weight, I have to swiftly isolate, then jettison that defective part.'

I'm nodding like the Churchill dog, trying to give the impression I have a clue what she's burbling on about, when it slowly occurs to me that when she says 'defective part', she means *me* and that by 'jettison' she means she's giving me the sack.

Not a great feeling, let me tell you – especially considering it's my birthday. Fifty years old today. Yup – fifty, fat and now fired, too. Imagine – it's the first job since you had kids, you're there for three weeks, you hit the big five-oh and then BANG! The job is gone.

'I'm sorry, Annie,' Suzette says, trying to sound almost sympathetic or human or something. 'You're just too slow and the other websites keep pipping us at the post with the news – not to mention the celebrity mum exclusives.'

I suck on my bottom lip, inadvertently making a squeaking sound and hang my head, looking at the blue carpet beneath our feet. It's a rather nondescript blue – neither navy nor duck egg, but somewhere in between – and it suddenly matches my mood perfectly.

6

'I mean,' she goes on, 'you don't even know who half the celebrity mums are! *Any* of the celebrity mums. You're just too out of the loop. Not current enough, too old-school, too technologically challenged, not with-it enough, too *old*—'

'All right, all right.' I put my hand up in the universal sign for I get the picture.

'I don't mean too old, I mean – oh, you do understand, don't you Annie?'

I nod and nearly manage a smile. Because I do. Finally I understand something someone is saying in this strange place. I'm not just too old, I'm *waaaaay* too old.

'Thanks for being a good sport about it all,' she says, like she's about to chuck me on the chin, buddy-style, as she stretches her lips into a sharp-toothed Cruella De Vil smile.

She stands up.

'Er, so is that it? Am I fired? No verbal warning? No written warning? How about a notice period? Will I get severance pay? Am I officially on gardening leave?'

Straws? Clutching? *Moi?*

'You haven't even passed your month's trial yet, Annie,' Suzette sneers. 'I think it would be best for all concerned if we kept this civil, just between us, and you went quickly and quietly. Today. As in *now.*'

She raises both her voice and her eyebrow at this, as though I'm deaf and dumb.

I briefly consider up-ending the table in a brilliant gesture of cool, anti-authoritarian, heroic defiance while some Clash or Jam song strikes up and my colleagues all get to their feet and applaud me – me, the only one to ever have the guts, the chutzpah, the *cojones* to actually stand up to Suzette and her despotic, robotic boss behaviour.

But then I remember my dodgy knee. And that sharp crick in my neck that spikes me every time I make any sudden moves. I glance down at the Boots standard issue knee support I've stretched over my leggings and wince at the sight of my muffin-top hanging over the waistband.

'Right you are,' I say, in a sing-song, completely non-threatening, not remotely rebellious way. And then I apologise meekly for loitering in the doorway, standing aside to let her leave the room first.

When I get back to my chair, no one looks up from their screens or acknowledges my presence in any way, so I make short work of gathering my stuff and get the hell out of there.

Bugger. Joe's going to kill me. I wasn't getting paid much to work at the website, but, as he once so eloquently put it, 'it was a hundred times more than I'd been contributing to the family coffers for the past nine years.'

Which had really pissed me off, to tell the truth. I mean, I may not have been in paid or appreciated employment in an office, like I was BK (before kids) – able to have a loo or lunch break, dick about on the internet for hours and maybe even get to drink a whole, hot cup of tea – but I was working hard twenty-four/seven looking after two recalcitrant kids, exhausted by teaching them how to be half-way decent human beings while simultaneously keeping them alive every day. Which is no easy task when you have the attention span of a gnat, the organisational skills of a lentil and your culinary prowess is limited to taking fish fingers out of the freezer and having Domino's on speed dial.

8

Joe's always had little understanding of and even less respect for what a woman goes through when she has children. Or at least no understanding or respect for *me*.

So anyway, on the plus side (which I clearly am these days – I simply must give up sugar or carbs or food altogether soon), I won't have to spend half my weekly wage on the nanny who picks the kids up in the afternoon, now that I can do it myself again.

The thought of this puts a little spring in my step as I get off the train at Teddington. And when someone walks past me smoking, I make up my mind to head into the Londis and grab a packet of cigarettes. Better than a pack of Quavers and a Twix, right?

I haven't had any fags for nigh on five years, now. I only ever had the odd one after Izzy was born and when I saw the blue line on the pregnancy test (which would turn out to be Ben), I axed them entirely. But I feel strangely liberated and almost free, now, like I was in my twenties, leaving work in a magazine office and going freelance with nothing but a head full of ideas, everything to play for and no one to answer to.

Except Joe.

When I get to the school gates, drenched in perfume (Fidji, my fave since 1985), reeking of deodorant (Mitchum For Men ever since I had kids and started sweating and fretting profusely) and still stuffing a whole packet of Extra sugar-free chewing gum into my mouth to disguise the disgusting smell of smoke, Izzy spies me immediately.

'Mummy!' She lets her usual cool demeanour drop for a second. 'What are you doing here? Where's Becca?'

I bend down slightly to give her a hug (she's only nine, but nearly as tall as me) and tell her I wasn't happy about not seeing her enough, so I left my job.

She nods in a *well, you're only human* kind of way and as we move to the junior part of the school, I tell her to follow me, but keep quiet, careful not to let Ben see her as I dart to hide behind a wall. Izzy lets out a squeal and then quick as a flash covers her mouth.

I see Ben standing in the playground, looking around for Becca, so I tiptoe over towards his back, motioning for Izzy to follow and silently, stealthily put my hands over his eyes, saying in my deepest, gruffest fee-fi-fo-fum giant's voice:

'Guess who?'

I feel his cheeks rise and imagine him grinning his little face off. His fingers feel my hands and then pat my arms all the way up to my shoulders and neck. I suck in the double chin and try not to giggle while his fingers search my face for clues. He feels my chins, my cheeks, then my upper lip, his touch lingering on my jawline.

'DADDY!' he shrieks, delighted. 'I can feel your beard!'

–

On the walk home, I explain to the kids that I have neither the time, nor indeed, the pain threshold that threading requires, and we make excited plans about what we're going to scoff tonight, given that it's Mummy's birthday.

'Daddy's made the cake!' Ben yelps.

'Your favourite one, Mummy,' Izzy chimes in.

'But I have so many favourites! Is it Red Velvet? Pavlova! Oh I know – Death By Chocolate, with all that cream cheese in it!'

'I get the first slice,' says Ben, who doesn't give a rat's soggy bottom about what kind of cake it is, as long as it's cake.

A boy after my own heart.

Once Joe's home, we've had our special birthday meal (Slimming World Hunter's Chicken and chips, made by Joe) and each had a slice of the best cake in the world ever (it was Death by Chocolate by the way), I put the kids to bed and gird my loins to tell Joe about the job.

'Come up here!' I bellow down the stairs. 'I've got something to tell you!'

I'm sitting on our bed upstairs, eating the rest of the cake, and finally, after what seems like an eternity, I hear Joe slowly climbing up the stairs.

As soon as he's in our doorway and clocks me, something about him changes – his expression, the way he's holding himself, the way he's breathing – everything.

He closes the door silently and his mouth twitches, exactly the way it did when we said our wedding vows. He was so nervous then, I thought he was going to burst into tears or faint or spontaneously combust in front of the registrar.

He makes his way towards me and I see tiny beads of sweat on his forehead and upper lip.

'I've got something to s-s-say, too,' he stutters.

'You first.' I give him a nod of encouragement and pat the space beside me with one hand while I feed my face a gargantuan bite of cake with the other.

'I don't know how to say this,' he says, staring at the floorboards and shaking his head at my offer of a seat. 'But, well, I—'

'You what?' I gurgle.

'It's... I... there's...'

Suddenly his eyes lift and he's transfixed by my boobs. Naturally, I feel a bit self-conscious and brush some crumbs off my cleavage. Then I have what I believe is called an *aha!* moment (as opposed to an 'oops' moment, like they have in the Tena Lady ads). He's getting all randy and doesn't know how to ask me for a quick bunk-up! He never really was any good with words, especially when it comes to the saucy stuff. He's a lover, you see, not a talker. All trousers and no mouth. No wonder he's nervous – we haven't had sex for, ooh, let's see... Ben will be six soon, so that's five add nine months of preg – jeez, it's nearly been six years now. Six years? Oh. My. God.

Thinking of it like that pulls me up short a bit and in that instant I realise that the closest I've come to seeing any action lately was a pap smear I had two years ago. Honestly, I was so excited, I even shaved my bikini line and put make-up on for my appointment.

'I... I'd like...'

'Go on,' I say, putting on my best Mae West. 'Out with it, big boy.'

'I want a divorce,' he says slowly but surely.

'Would you mind awfully if we didn't tonight, babe, it's just that I've got a bit of a tummy ache and— wait. What? Did you just say *divorce*?'

He nods and nearly collapses with relief, smiling nervously, rubbing his hands over his shiny pate and looking anywhere but at me. I feel my sugary smile fading fast, morphing into the 'O' of shock as I watch him turn his back on me, yank open the door and fairly skip out of the room.

I inhale slowly, carefully, lest I actually choke on cake crumbs and we're literally left with a case of death by chocolate.

'Oh,' Joe pops his head back round the door jamb, 'and let's not get lawyers involved, eh? I'm sure we can sort this all out by ourselves. Keep it amicable. Like Gwyneth Paltrow and whatshisname – that guy in Coldplay – a nice, friendly "conscious uncoupling", yeah?'

He drums his fingers and knocks on the door frame decisively, wandering off, whistling 'Happy' by Pharrell Williams. I even hear him clapping his hands and picture him spinning around in a circle in some lame attempt at a victory dance.

Then my eyes fall onto what's left of the cake and I come over all queasy.

–

November 12 – At First I Was Afraid...

Obviously I didn't get any sleep last night, what with trying to process the shittest birthday since records began and a stomach ache no amount of Tums could soothe.

I keep going over the phrase he used to soften the blow – 'a conscious uncoupling'. A conscious *un*coupling. A conscious un*coupling*? Sounds like we're two train carriages getting unhitched. Which is sort of what we are, I suppose. And it's kind of a neat tying-up of loose ends in a way, our relationship coming full circle, considering that when we got together at a mutual friend's boozy wedding, we were so drunk, it was more an *un*conscious coupling than anything else.

What's left of my birthday cake is on the floor next to the bed and I'm still lying prostrate in said bed – in the exact same position I've been in for the past ten hours. It feels strange, but rather than wallowing in self-pity (an activity to which I am no stranger) or raging against the injustice of it all (ditto), I think I'm actually a bit *relieved*.

And not just because he didn't want sex last night (although, let's face it, *phew)* – but because someone finally came out and said what needed to be said.

Which is quite sad, really. I mean, it all started so well, fifteen years ago. It was all love's young(ish) dream, full of promise and potential…

I think back to when our kids were born and Joe just about burst with joy. Both times, I was too busy being stitched up to even entertain the idea of bursting, but I was so chuffed that he was so excited – so into it. This was going to be our magical journey, an adventure we were all going on together, as a family.

But that was then. I look down at two softly snoring small heads, one under each arm. They both snuck in here in the middle of the night and look at them now – angelic in their sleep, beautiful in their innocence with not even the vaguest idea of how their lives are about to change beyond all recognition.

I gaze at them for a few moments, lost in the heartbreak of it all. And then I remember they've got school and I've got to get a shift on, too.

'Right, that's it!' I put on my best Sergeant Major boot camp voice. 'Snooze time's over – every little body up, up UP!'

Ben stays stock still, ignoring me. But Izzy, who's been acting like an adolescent ever since she was four years old, huffs, puffs and nearly blows the house down with the torrent of abuse she hurls at me.

'Why do you always have to YELL IN MY EAR like that? I WAS ASLEEEEEP! Do you get that? ASLEEP! No one else's mum does that – GOD! WHY DO YOU ALWAYS HAVE TO BE SO WEIRD?'

And so a new day dawns, full of sunshine, lollipops and kind words to send you on your merry way.

'I'm sorry, sweet—' I try feebly to apologise.

'Just FORGET IT!' She screams and tries to kick off the duvet – but her feet get caught up in the cover, making her exit from the bed nowhere near as smooth and dramatic as she'd no doubt hoped.

Ben's eyes flip open at this and he starts up his contagious giggle.

'Foot fight!' he screeches and farts an audible exclamation mark.

'ARGH!' Izzy shoots both me and Ben daggers as she falls out of the bed.

'Ooh – are you all right?' I leap (Okay, okay – slope) out of my side of the bed and scurry (schlep) around to my darling daughter lying on the floor on Joe's side.

'What do *you* care?' she pouts and picks herself up off the floor, batting my helping hand away in the process. 'You fat *cow*!'

Did I mention Izzy's only nine years old?

I suppose it's just a taste of things to come, really. I mean, everyone knows that kids from broken homes are traumatised beyond redemption, have mouths like sewers and end up either in prison or on *The Jeremy Kyle Show*. Or both.

I feel my breath catch in my throat and hot, minuscule sweat bubbles stinging my upper lip. My thighs start to tingle, the way they do when I'm driving, trying to join the M4 from a slip road and cars are whizzing by me and trucks are monstering me from behind and all I want to do is pull over and stop but I can't because I'll cause an almighty pile-up and Jesus, why can't I just *breathe* and what if this is it, the final moment where I have a stroke, pass out, write the car off and kill us all as well as a hundred other innocent bystanders with no one to blame but myself—?

'*Mummy!*' Izzy and Ben are right up in my grill, looking worried.

'Er, right. Now. Where was I? Yes, yes, time for the up and soon thereafter, the off. Let's move it and—'

'A-groove it!' Ben's heard this annoying order of mine so many times, he has no trouble finishing it for me.

'Are you all right?' Izzy seems concerned.

'Yup, fine,' I reply in my best reassuring tones. 'Why wouldn't I be? I am woman, after all – hear me roar!'

I find my phone and put 'I Am Woman' by Helen Reddy on YouTube, the first stirring song on this morning's soundtrack.

'Durgh – not this again.' Izzy runs upstairs to get her uniform on and I sing along with Helen while I get Ben ready.

'Please stop,' he looks at me, imploringly. 'Stop singing, Mummy – you're making my ears sad.'

He puts his hands over his ears and looks like he's about to burst into tears, so I dive onto my phone and frantically search for the theme from *Black Beauty*. But the opening bars make *me* well up – just as they used to when I was a kid – so I put the decision in my little boy's hands.

'What do you want to hear, then?'

'*Rocky, Rocky, ROCKY!*' he beams.

'Okay, okay – heard you the first time.'

Ba ba ba buh-ba buh-ba baa buh-ba ba; the trumpets herald their famous refrain.

And as I help Ben get his little school trousers on and his pixie-sized school fleece, I feel as though I'm having an out-of-body experience, looking down on myself and my little boy, suddenly acutely aware of our respective fragility.

And then I get mad. Just for a moment, granted – but mad nonetheless. How *dare* Joe put us in this position? How *dare* he announce that he's leaving me as though it's no big deal, like he's just nipping out for loo roll? How *dare* he pull the rug out from under us so that we're free falling, riding the clutch down a Devil's Elbow kind of curved slip road onto the Highway To Hell?

This vision of me and the kids careening into oblivion makes me sit up super straight, unintentionally bumping Ben off my lap. He laughs as he hits the soft shag pile and eagerly puts his shoes on while I silently vow that from now on the kids will only see their mum as strong, capable, loving, caring and totally in control.

They completely depend on me and I can't fall apart in front of them. So I'd better start getting some decent sleep in, then, if I want to stop being quite so cranky. And these panic attacks can bugger off and all. Oh yes! No longer shall I inadvertently teach the fruit of my loins the fine arts of shouting, swearing and tantrumming, for I am a soon-to-be Divorcée With Kids – a Proud Single Mum, solely in charge, winging it on her own and well-worthy of capital letters!

It's going to be a whole new life for me and my brood. Imagine not getting disappointed/confused/pissed off with Joe every five minutes! Truly putting the kids first in both thought and deed! And not having to hear his extraordinarily loud peeing every night!

I yelp a little bit in excitement – I can't wait to get this party started. And start it I shall – today, this minute, right here, right now, from this moment forth and forever more!

Just as soon as I've dropped the kids off and had a quick kip on the couch. Well, how can I be a one-woman powerhouse if I'm totally knackered?

–

Once I've woken up from my power nap on the couch (it was lovely, thanks for asking; diaphanous dreams of me in a size twelve Wonder Woman outfit with American tan tights, a nifty neon-yellow lasso and a gold crown atop my full, lustrous, wavy-not-frizzy barnet), I wander into the kitchen and fire up my laptop.

Because it's all well and good banging on about how brilliant you're going to be at this whole Divorcée With Kids lark, but where exactly do you start? And how do you know what pitfalls to avoid and which ones are worth diving into and struggling through because they'll make you stronger in the end?

First stop, Google.

Now this is interesting. Turns out, according to the Citizens Advice website, if you and your soon-to-be ex can quite amicably sort out who the kids will live with and how much maintenance is fair, you can fill out some forms and £550 later, hey presto! You're out of contract. No blood-sucking parasites (sorry, solicitors) needed.

But then I remember Joe saying he explicitly didn't *want* to get lawyers involved in our divorce. And I wonder why. I mean, I know he's as tight as a gnat's chuff, but maybe he's got something to hide. A secret worth a fortune? Or a whole other family living a few short miles away from us? A secret girlfriend? A secret boyfriend! Maybe he's just trying to rip me off – he *does* earn £600 a day as an IT contractor doing... whatever it is IT contractors do.

I've asked him loads of times, but at the mere mention of 'IT', my eyes glaze over and I suddenly feel the irresistible urge to catch up on my 678-episode *Cash In The Attic* box set.

Come to think of it, I can't even remember the last time we talked about anything other than who was the most tired or who deserved a lie-in more or who was taking Izzy to a birthday party and Annie, will you bloody well stop spending so much on the weekly shop because John West tuna is fine, no need for poncey and exorbitant Ortiz...

He's been sleeping on the couch for months, *years*, now. In fact, I think the last time we slept together was probably the last time we ever had sex with each other, six years ago. I remember the date exactly, because it was Izzy's third birthday. And that was the night Ben was conceived.

I shake my head at these unmissable signs of crisis and wonder why I didn't do something to try to save our marriage before, when it was disintegrating in front of our very eyes? Of course, I must've known we were on a slippery slope – but maybe I was too consumed by the kids and that new mum world – even though 'new' is pushing it, really, considering I was well past it when I had Izzy (forty-one), let alone Ben (forty-fucking-five).

I must have been exhausted and unable to think beyond my latest epic mummy fail to spare a thought for Joe and our rotting relationship.

And I *did* try. I'd leave Jilly Cooper's jolly super classic, *How To Stay Married* on the keyboard in his home office, hoping he'd have a read and see the funny side of our – and probably every other married couple's – foibles.

Somehow, it would always mysteriously find its way back to the top of my bookshelf in the bedroom, come to think of it.

I even borrowed Mum's *Fear of Flying* by Erica Jong and tried to figure out whether I had any sexy fantasies that maybe Joe and I could live out. But I couldn't find any. I was a sexual desert and I wasn't even thirsty. I mean, sex is so *unseemly* when you're over *un certain âge*, isn't it?

And before you start to think I'm asexual or something, I'll have you know I was quite the unstoppable sex machine in my twenties. And when Joe and I first got together, we were at it like rabbits. But after we had the kids, getting Joe to undo a jar of Dolmio's was about as saucy as we ever got.

I suggested we go to counselling, too, sporadically. Joe, of course, was never up for it, though – and in his case, you can't even lead a horse to water, let alone make him drink.

Ah. The Drink.

Joe's clear and ever-present preference for beer (or meths, or Bach Rescue Remedies – whatever's going, really) over me and the kids can really get a girl down sometimes, you know. All times, actually.

Speaking of the kids, they'll obviously come with me – or does he think he'll have them? And where will we live? We can't stay here unless Joe pays our rent and the rent on somewhere for himself... But this is ridiculous! I don't know what his plans are or how he sees any of this playing out. And I can't make any decisions about our future until I know what he wants to do.

Or can I?

Why do I have to wait for him to tell me what to do? I don't!

Do I?

He's always wittering on about how he does everything round here – works his fingers to the bone in an office he hates, does all the hoovering because I obviously don't know what a Dyson *is for*, for Christ's sake etc, so maybe now's the perfect time to get proactive and do something without checking with him first.

An image of him saying: 'What the hell do you *do* all day?' pops into my mind's eye and I puff my cheeks out as I exhale.

At this point, I can practically hear the familiar dull thud of my self-esteem falling to the floor. The gorgeous, stripped oak floor of this, the rented London house we could never afford to buy on one salary, as Joe is a tad overly-fond of pointing out to me. But instead of cringing at the thought of his supercilious face spitting his bile into mine, today it spurs me into action.

I ring around several local solicitors to get the gen on a) how expensive they are (ooh – that much? Just for a *chat*?), b) whether getting a divorce without lawyers is a valid thing (it is) and c) would I qualify as a pro bono case (with how much your husband earns? Don't be bloody ridiculous).

Figuring it's time I let my nearest and dearest know what's going on, I text my oldest and bestest friends Aisling and Amelie:

> Am getting divorced! From Joe.
> How you? Xxx

And despite the fact I appear to be Getting On With Things, sounding bright and breezy, I suddenly give myself away big time and collapse into a sobbing heap.

I mean, apart from the big questions, like: how are the kids going to react, where are we going to live and how on earth am I ever going to cope all on my own, I can't believe it's all over. Fifteen years of being a couple, able to rely on each other for a shoulder to cry on or a warm, strong hand to hold in a crisis… And now? Pfft. Now it's just me.

No one to talk to about the funny thing Ben said or the insightful thing Izzy came out with; no one to fall asleep to *Midsomer Murders* with; no one to whinge to when I've waited in all day for the gas man and he bowls up at five to five… Oh, God! It's all a terrible, horrible mess. What the hell am I going to do?

November 15 – ...I Was Petrified

After three days checking out Rightmove, hyperventilating at the cost of renting in London, and not getting even so much as a returned text from Joe, I decide I can't suffer in silence on my own anymore, so I give Mum and Dad a ring.

Without even a nod to the normal social pleasantries, Mum tells me that *sans* job, the kids and I have no other choice but to move into her sister's, my maiden aunt Audrey's, rundown cottage in the Chilterns. Turns out my self-help–addicted Auntie Aud's just about to go off on yet another journey of self-discovery (this time to the Amazon), so the house'll be empty for, ooh – let's just say the foreseeable.

'But it's so *boring* there!' I squeal. Just because I'm fifty, it doesn't mean my ungrateful, whingeing inner child is ever far from the surface.

'Only the boring are bored,' Mum tuts back at me. 'And anyway, the kids come first, they'll love it. There is no other option. Apart from all three of you coming to live with us in our tiny London basement flat—'

'Which is never going to bloody well happen!' Dad barks, snatching the phone. 'You can't afford to rent in London, there's a perfectly good house in the country waiting for you – get out of that ludicrous marriage and hotfoot it to the hills.'

'I don't know if I'd call it *a perfectly good house*...'

'It's got a roof and walls, hasn't it? It's never going to make it onto *Grand Designs*, obviously, but it's good enough for you and the grandkids. Now let that be an end to it.'

'Can't say I'm surprised you're finally getting shot of each other – he was never good enough for you, darling.' Mum's back on the line now. 'Nice enough bloke, I suppose, but you could do so much better. Lose a bit of weight, get some highlights, maybe think about wearing a little bit of lippie every now and again…'

'Mum!' I'm aghast. 'What would Germaine say if she could hear you talk like that? Single-handedly setting feminism back several decades in one sentence?'

'If she could see *you*, she'd probably agree with me!'

I grunt and curse my straight-talking mother. Mum and Germaine Greer are old pals from Sydney Uni in the sixties, you see, where they caroused and shocked and banged on about female eunuchs in smoke-filled, late-night Sydney coffee shops.

She's never said as much, but I often wonder whether Mum's envious of the celebrity and notoriety Germaine has or whether she's not remotely bothered.

'I taught her everything she knows, after all…'

Good old Mum. She's in her late seventies now and still giving the academic world hell. If only I had half the chutzpah Mum has, I'd be happy. At that thought, I get off the phone, gird my loins and get going.

I call Auntie Audey (the 'r' in Audrey was far too difficult for any three-year-old to wrap their laughing gear around, so it's stuck) and give her the goss.

'Well, can't say I'm surprised,' she says, sounding just like Mum. 'He was a nice enough chap, I suppose – you just weren't particularly well suited is all. I mean, Aquarius wasn't he?' 'Yeah, I think so,' I reply, momentarily wondering what the hell that has to do with anything. 'Too emotionally cold and distant for you, Scorpio. It's like I've always told you – you need a Virgo or Cancer, someone in touch with, not frightened of and actually *keen* to explore their emotional side. I've always said it, you need a slightly older man. One who's secure, confident and financially solvent. Preferably with a full head of hair. And all his own teeth.' 'Ever the romantic,' I tease. 'Well it's true! You have to be physically attracted to him or else what's the point? You need emotional and physical love, my girl.' I screw up my nose at the mention of physical love and squirm a little. It's like watching a sex scene on TV while you're sitting on the sofa with your parents when you're a teenager. Talk about *awks*, as Izzy would say. 'No use pussyfooting around the issue – we all have our needs,' she ploughs on. 'Now. I imagine you're looking for a charming, bijou two-bedroomed cottage in the heart of a Chilterns village with a fabulous southerly aspect, close to all amenities and with lovely, friendly neighbours, to stay in till you get back on your feet, right?'

We both take a desperate breath in. Charming? Bijou? Bombsite, more like. Books strewn about over every available surface – and up the walls. Self-help, tarot, astrology, wicca – if there's a book about it, she'll have it. I thought it was fascinating and cosy when I was a kid, but last time we were there, Joe went on and on about how chaotic and cluttered it was. A real renovator's delight, he scoffed, while we gathered round the roaring fire and ate Soreen malt loaf with lashings of butter. My idea of total bliss, come to think of it. And anyway, beggars can't be choosers, so I try to keep a lid on my excitement and ask Audey whether she's started working for Wolfson's again. 'Don't be silly – I'm too old for all that estate agent nonsense. But the descriptive patter never leaves you, you know? Wonderful way with words, estate agents – even if they are all wankers. Anyway. For a small stipend, would you and those beautiful kids of yours want to stay here while I'm away? So you can dive into my bookshelves like you used to do, lick your wounds, get back on your feet, heal yourself and get back to being Annie again? My gorgeous, spirited, fun and feisty Annie. Ah,' she heaves a huge sigh, 'feisty Annie Beaton.'

Who? Oh yeah! I remember her… vaguely. Wasn't she the short one with somewhat of a sensual swell (as opposed to a hanging mummy-tummy)? The one with curly blonde hair that looked great air-dried with a ton of mousse in it, until she killed it with straightening irons so badly that she would end up looking like Garth out of *Wayne's World*? Wasn't she the one who had a half-decent sense of humour, a promising career in magazines and a lust for life that made her fun to be around (if not a little scary if she'd had one too many)?

Now you mention it, I *do* remember her. What the hell happened to her? The thought of revisiting the old me again (just, perhaps, without the scary-when-pissed bit) makes me break into a smile.

'How small is this stipend you speak of?' I ask, crossing my fingers. 'Four hundred pounds a month, just to keep the mortgage ticking over. Oh – and you'll need to pay for gas, leccy, and council tax, too. I don't have broadband, so if you want it, you'll need to sort it out. Is that okay?'

'Okay? If Joe gives us a decent amount of maintenance, it's perfect! How long are you likely to be away?'

'Hard to say. I'm embarking on a thrice-in-a-lifetime journey of self-discovery to the Amazon, here, so it's no small undertaking. I dunno – it depends. No less than

a year, no more than a decade – how's that grab you?'
'Sounds great! Consider it a done deal. Oh, I wish we could see you before you go. We'll miss you, Auntie Aud.'

'And I you, doll – but we're both starting new chapters in our lives and adventure won't wait!'

She sounds like an over-excited schoolgirl when she tells me she's going to the Amazon with a recently divorced man she met at her local AA meeting. Apparently he's a couple of years younger than her and quite the catch. He says his lazy ex-wife, having never been in paid work since she had their four kids about a hundred years ago, wanted to 'sponge off him' forever.

'Poor Keith,' Auntie Aud says, 'he had to divorce her because, as he said, he couldn't stand the thought of getting a shit ROI like that for the rest of his life.'

I spit my tea out.

'He said that?' I splutter. 'I mean, he *actually* said he was getting a *shit ROI*?'

'Yes,' says Aud. 'Those were his exact words. I remember because I didn't have a clue what he was on about! Maybe you know – what's an ROI when it's at home?'

I can't tell her what those letters really stand for, can I? She'd go off Keith in seconds flat. She hates that kind of yuppie, business, loadsamoney-speak. Which begs the question – what on earth is she doing with a twonk called *Keith* who comes out with that kind of crap?

'Er, I'm not sure. Something to do with RSI? Repetitive strain whatsit? Anyway. Back to your cosy cottage – I can't wait to tell the kids.'

'I'm so pleased, Annie, this place could really do with some youngies in it to brighten it up. Oh, I nearly forgot.

If you were, hypothetically speaking, of course, thinking of getting, say, a *pet* for the kids – a puppy, for example – to help them get over the split, I would be fine with it. Absolutely, one hundred per cent fine. Just saying...'

By the time Joe gets home, I'm buzzing. I sit him down in the kitchen and call the kids in for a family meeting. This is how it goes down:

ME: So... you know how Daddy and Mummy have been – just sit down and listen, Ben, this is important – arguing a lot lately and – seriously, I'll get cross if you don't – we think it's best if we don't live together anymore.

IZZY: Where are we going?

ME: Well, you and your bro— sit down! Oh, come and sit on my lap then, Ben – are coming with me and your dad will move somewhere close to us. Lightning McQueen can bloody wait, you've seen it a hundred times already!

BEN: *climbing onto Joe's lap* But I want to watch it with Daddy!

JOE: In a minute, Ben – can you speed it up a bit, Mummy?

ME: Right. So. We love you two very much and it's not because of anything either of you have done or said—

BEN: I didn't do anything!

IZZY: Well it's not my fault!

ME: Neither of you have done anything wrong and it's nobody's fault. We still love each other...

JOE: *Snorts, coughs and shuffles in his seat*

ME: ...we just want to be happy. So we may have to move away from here, which might mean you have to change schools...

IZZY: What? Noooo!

ME: … but if we go somewhere nice – like somewhere nice in the country – we'll be able to get a puppy!

BEN and JOE: Really?

ME: Yes!

BEN: Can I go now?

IZZY: A puppy? YAY!

JOE: The *country*? Since when…?

–

The kids leg it to the telly, bored by all this adult nonsense and I fill Joe in on my plans. And then, for reasons not immediately clear to me, I suddenly start acting all… sort of… *grown up*. Or something. For want of a better phrase.

Keeping it short, swift and to the point, I don't give him a chance to butt in and knock me off my perch. I'm all: 'I've decided', 'I've been advised' and 'I'm sure you'll agree it's best for the children if we move as soon as Christmas is over, so they can settle into their new home before school starts again. We'll have the car, you will pay £1200 per month for maintenance – by direct debit – and every second weekend you will have the kids stay over two nights at yours. Thank you and goodnight.'

Just like that! Talk about business woman of the year. He didn't have a clue what hit him – he just sat there looking gobsmacked, rubbing his slightly sweaty forehead, his thick eyebrows twitching and probably thinking: 'Wow – she's amazing. So smart, so sorted, so beautiful. Looks like she's lost weight, too'.

Not that I give a tinker's *toss* what he thinks. I'm just hoping this new can-do approach of mine continues. Because it sure beats the can't-be-arsed attitude I've been cursed with for, ooh – how long have I been with Joe? The last fifteen years or so?

I retire to my bedroom and for the first time in absolutely bloody ages, I start feeling a little less uncertain and incapable and a teensy bit more in control.

Which is a rare, but rather pleasant sensation – one I could get used to. My mobile bleeps twice in quick succession, signalling I have a text message. It's from Amelie:

> Atta girl! Welcome to my world – best thing that could ever happen to you. Soz took so long to reply – been, ah, busy with new man. In Florida! Will call on return. Congrats!!! xxx

Typical Amelie. She's got a lust for life (and men), that makes Katie Price look like a nun. Not that she was always like that – she did spend several years in the wilderness when she was married and her daughter was still very young. But as soon as she divorced her husband, a boring, miserable old scrote whose name I've actually forgotten, it was like she was born again – she went back to uni to get her law degree, met a whole slew of new and interesting people and now she's partner in some posh law firm in Bath, always full of fun, laughter and pinot grigio.

Maybe she's right and life truly begins when you get divorced. Hope so.

Just as I'm smiling at the screen, another message appears from her:

> BTW, thank GOD you kept your
> maiden name – always Beaton by
> name, never beaten by nature!
> Well done you!!! xxx

I like that – Beaton by name, not by nature. Maybe I should put it on a t-shirt.

My mobile jumps again with news that another text has come in. It's from Aisling this time. The lovely Aisling who I've known for what seems like forever, who has the perfect husband, the perfect kids, the perfect home and the most beautiful, translucent, perfect skin:

> Oh, hun – poor you. I'm so sorry
> to hear that. Your msg made me
> cry. You must be devastated! How
> are the little 'uns? Back from
> Dublin now – call me as soon as
> you can Axxx

Oh, bugger! I was feeling quite take-chargey a second ago, but now, with Aisling being so sympathetic, making out like it's the worst thing ever, I feel a ping of panic. What does she know that I don't? Are me and the kids doomed? Oh, shit, she's right, isn't she? Divorce *is* a horrendous thing. Everyone will be psychologically scarred to within an inch of their lives – and it's all my fault!

The opening bars of 'I Will Survive' strike up in my head and my bottom lip quivers ever so slightly.

I croak the lyrics quietly, hoping Ben doesn't hear and my singing makes his ears sad again.

Chapter Two

December

December 9 – 'Tis the Season...

... to be thoroughly hacked off. All those smiley, happy people bouncing around with their bobble hats and matching mittens and fake snow and ice-skating prowess and happy bloody families in tow? All that can bugger off! Hum and indeed, bug!

Haven't seen Joe for a while – he's moved out until we move out for good and then he'll tie up all the loose ends with the landlord etc. And you know what? I'm glad we're not a nuclear family anymore. No, really I am – it's just that I'm dreading the fallout when the kids start to really take it in.

–

December 25 – Worst Xmas Day, Like, EVER

Just imagine: the kids and I have been staying with Mum and Dad in their tiny basement flat for the past few days. We've heard neither hide nor hair from Joe, he won't answer his phone and Mum and Dad have banned him from coming within coo-ee of their place. So Happy Christmas, kids!

December 27 – And We're Off!

It takes over two hours to drive to Old Stoke via various A and B roads – but there's no way I'm venturing out onto the bloody M4.

I'm determinedly cheerful all the way, gee-ing the kids up – and myself – and really only have one or two mild panic attacks, usually following a quick glance at Izzy and Ben buggerising about on the back seat.

'Stop bickering – or I'll put you out by the side of the road,' I threaten.

'You always say that,' Izzy pipes up, 'but you never actually do it.'

'Just you try me,' I say, gritting my teeth as I feel the tiny pricks of panic piercing the tip of my nose.

This shuts the pair of them up quite nicely. For the next two and a half minutes, anyway.

Despite everything, we make it to Old Stoke in one piece and I feel a strange wave of fond familiarity wash over me as we enter the village from the posh end, making our way down to the not-so-posh bit, which is where Audrey's place is.

Old Stoke boasts two Indian restaurants – Minah's and RG Bhaji (see what they did there? Our postcode starts with RG, being near-ish to Reading as we are…), one fish and chip shop called Oh My Cod!, one enormous Chinese restaurant of no apparent name that's always completely empty, four pubs and about six Turkish barber shops.

One of the barber shops is a definite front for a drug operation – I mean, how many young men are there in this

33

village who need to get haircuts all the time and choose to hang out the front smoking fags and drinking Coke like they're at some trendy nightclub entrance? With their long hair and bushy beards?

On the other side of the roundabout is The Zebra, a hotel/pub done out in Shabby Colonial (I imagine that's the interior design term for it) and as we pass it, I tell the kids that this was where I met their daddy, at a country wedding and that after our own wedding reception, it was where we went to get well and truly wasted with a few friends.

'It was quite the celebration,' I smile, thinking that actually, it was a complete disaster.

Joe had got so hammered that when we went to bed in the hotel that night, there were no conjugals – instead, we had a massive row. I was annoyed that he'd got so trollied on our big night, and when I called him on it, he muttered something about it being his wedding night, so he deserved to get well and truly out of it.

I wasn't sure how to take that – did he have to drink to forget the horror of getting married? Not that it mattered in the end, though, because his mother (speaking of horrors), who was staying across the corridor, looking after two-year-old Izzy, banged on our bedroom door and yelled at us to shut up.

' "Memories",' I sing in my not-too-shabby, actually, Barbra Streisand imitation. Both kids groan in unison.

Anyway, we pass all these places, and the Co-op and a boarded-up bank, a florist, an estate agent, a wine market and then, after a particularly ropey-looking pub, a Ladbroke's and a Londis opposite, we turn right into the

34

driveway of Audrey's run-down mid-terrace. Sorry, that's what Joe would say – let's call it the cosy cottage.

'This is the family pile,' I say to the kids as they run up the stairs. 'You can do whatever you want – decorate your rooms however you want – and even sleep on your own. Won't that be great? No more sleeping with Mummy!'

I'm getting carried away, here, magnanimously thinking I'll give the bedrooms to the kids and I'll sleep on the sofa bed in the front room, my knickers in a bedside table in Ben's room and my clothes in his closet.

'Izzy? You can have the room with the carpet and the en suite,' I yell out, warming to my theme, 'and Ben? You can have the other room, with the floorboards so you can play cars, using the gaps between the boards as a makeshift Scalextric!'

Blissfully unaware that I've made the first big one in a long line of massive mistakes by giving the bedrooms to the kids, I smile to myself, picturing the satin sash they'll drape over my slim shoulders when I win that coveted Selfless Mother of the Year award.

As I'm congratulating myself and practising my 'well, you know, as a Single Mum, the kids always have to come first' speech, I notice several pieces of A4 paper Blu-tacked to the walls. In the centre of these pieces of paper are fake cheques with Auntie Audrey's spidery scrawl instructing the universe (yes, you read that right, the sodding *universe)* to pay Audrey Alford (that's Aud) one million pounds by this time next year.

I look closer at these cheques and see they've been printed from *The Secret* website and I chuckle to myself. Because this is typical. It's just like mad-as-cheese Auntie Audey to put her faith and future in the hands of some dodgy 'power of positive thinking' claptrap. I mean, really. Just in case, though, I make a mental note to check the bookshelves later for *The Secret* and see if I can pick up any tips. Just on the off-chance, you know, in case it's not all complete bollocks.

The kids take turns falling down the steep, dark, ridiculously narrow staircase, knocking the banister off and taking half the wall's plaster with it.

We all tumble, giggling, into the kitchen/dining room bit between the front room and the galley kitchen and I'm immediately struck by how at home I feel. The long oak kitchen table, complete with coffee-cup stains, newspapers piled high and books propping up the legs of just about every chair around it reminds me of the one my brother and I grew up with. Mum was always there, fag in one hand, coffee cup (or wine glass) in the other, reading her students' essays. Dad would often be there, too, having heated debates with Mum over some thorny philosophical issue while Olly and I would listen in, wolfing down Weetabix, Frosties or Marmite toast before school.

It was on a table just like this that we'd eat dinners made by Mum (when she could be arsed) that wouldn't look out of place on an episode of *The Galloping Gourmet* back in the seventies. When she wasn't bunging a can of baked beans on the hob (I mean literally – she didn't know how to use a can opener), she was all about terrines and jellies and prawns drowned in Marie Rose sauce.

Even the brightly coloured book with a British Gas envelope sticking out of it in the centre of the table looks oddly familiar. It sits there, safe and sure in its place and I can feel it practically winking at me, beckoning me closer, begging me to take a look inside.

I pick it up, squint and finally see it's called *A Year of Positive Thinking*.

'Tch,' I tut, thinking, *what an unspeakable load of utter shite*, and pull out the envelope. Auntie Aud's crazy writing is crammed onto the back of it, making it look like a doddery old witch's shopping list.

I expect to see 'tongue of toad' and 'eye of newt', but instead, she's written:

My Dearest Darling Annie,

    Now I know you're a committed cynic and probably thinking what a load of unutterable shite this positive thinking lark is, but I love you so much, I couldn't stand by any longer and watch you make a pig's ear out of your life. So here's one of my fave little books that just might make a huge difference to you. I often turn to it for both comfort and joy when I feel lost and alone and, as a bonus, it really works. Here's hoping it'll have the same effect on you. It's worth a look, my girl. Just give it a chance. You never know, you just might regain some confidence in yourself, rediscover your joie de vivre and maybe even begin to love yourself again. I very much hope so.

    But enough from me, I must away – don't want to get a rubbish ROI on my writing hand. Isn't it amazing how quickly one gets used to a keyboard – at the great expense of one's handwriting skills?!

    I'll be thinking of you, my sweet. Onward and upwards for both of us. And don't let the bastards grind you down!

    All my love as ever,
    Auntie Audey xxx

Silly old moo – what would some hippy-dippy, touchy-feely positive psychologist know about divorcing your booze-hound husband and bringing up two kids on your own? Bugger all, is my guess.

I inadvertently catch sight of myself in the stainless-steel kettle and see I'm all sunken of eye, red of bulbous nose, black of tooth and my hair looks like a partially peeled Cheese String. Oh, how the foxy have fallen. What an old hag!

There's no getting away from it now. I'm over the hill, past it – the kind of person whose ears prick up when she hears those 'over-fifties' life insurance ads they run during *Murder She Wrote*. So here I am, leaning on my imaginary zimmer frame, standing squarely in the middle of that most-feared demographic, the one referred to by youngsters, millennials and pensioners alike as *old farts*. Yup. It's official.

Izzy says I don't do myself any favours by often saying, in my doddery old goat voice, things like 'What the hell is an Instant Gram?' and 'Why do you have to go to school looking like Britney Bloody Spears?'. Still, that's what daughters are for, I suppose, to point out your horrific faults and horrendous foibles with alarming, acerbic regularity. It's just that I thought they did that in their teens – she's only bloody nine! And she's been doing it since she was four, for Christ's sake.

She might have a point, though. Better be vigilant and keep myself in check from now on – don't want to give the game away any more than I have to. Just because your hair makes you look over eighty doesn't mean you have to talk like an octogenarian, too.

Blimey – was that a load of old negative self-talk or what? Maybe Auntie Aud's right and it really is time to look on the bright side. Find the funny and accentuate the positive. Because getting old(er) *is* a positive, really, as opposed to a negative. Isn't it? Like, at least you're still alive. Which beats being dead. Mind you, if you're still kicking but your eyesight's failing, your hips are achingly sore and you've got a face like a rhino's scrote, what's the bloody point?

It's going to be quite the challenge to find the silver lining in every cloud after nearly fifty years of looking on, well, not the dark side of life, exactly – more the realistic side, I'd say. I mean, I don't think I've ever been described as a little ray of sunshine. Little *anything*, actually, given the rate I've been stacking it on lately. But I have been labelled 'negative' quite a few times recently. Mainly by Joe and his mum.

So perhaps, just for something different, positivity should become my new *modus operandi*. If only to avoid misery mouth, where the lines around your mouth turn so far down and are so deeply etched, you look like a ventriloquist's dummy (or like the mother-in-law, AKA the MILFH – the Mother-In-Law From Hell). Maybe I really should endeavour to banish my negativity, see Amelie and Aisling more often and put a smile on my dial, no matter what.

Can't hurt to give it a go at least. Because not looking on the bright side of life hasn't exactly worked out for me too well so far, has it?

And I've done it before, you know. I mean, I did used to be quite the inadvertent positive thinker, back in the day, when I was young and I hadn't had all the optimistic stuffing kicked out of me yet. So maybe after suffering the slings and arrows of life – rejections from boys, jobs, fall-outs with friends and family and diet failure after diet failure – I slowly but surely fell out of love with optimism and positivity. And, as a result, maybe that's when I fell out of love with myself, too.

So even though I really do think it's a load of old codswallop, I sneak a little peek inside the book and scan a page at the beginning. I'm immediately drawn to a bit that says the human brain naturally veers towards the negative and it takes three positive thoughts to neutralise one nasty negative one. Three?! Bit excessive…

Apparently, if you can find the positive, no matter how small, in any given situation, you'll be onto a winner. In fact, you should probably even call them 'wins'.

I close my eyes and concentrate hard, trying to think of just one. But all that comes to mind is the beginning of a lengthy to-do list. Does that count? I'm not sure. Probably not.

So… Here goes. Again.

Negative thought: My hair is a frizzy, frazzled mess.

Positive thoughts: 1) At least you still *have* hair, 2) And if you let it dry naturally, give the GHDs a swerve, your curls will come back, 3) and anyway, who's looking at your hair? It's your massive bum that's getting the stares!

Hmmm. This is going to be harder than I thought.

I'm furrowing my brow, wondering whether I'll ever be able to naturally err on the side of positivity, when Ben slams into my leg. We may be one man down, he reminds me, but we're also one beautiful boy up since we were last here. Which is a rather upbeat way of looking at a dead leg, isn't it?

'I'm starvating!' he giggles. 'Is it dinner time yet, Mummy?'

Izzy joins us and agrees:

'Yeah! What's for eats?'

'Right.' I put my hands on my hips in my newly adopted Mum In Charge stance. 'We've got bugger all in – let's go out for dinner!'

So we fall down the stairs, grab our coats and make for RG Bhaji, the closest of the two local Indian restaurants. And we're just about halfway there when I stop dead in my tracks, remember we're on a tight budget now, and head for the Co-op for chicken mayo sarnies instead.

Instead of feeling down that we can't afford a restaurant, I feel up that we're eating cheaply, saving money already. Positivity 1, negativity 0. Ha! This is going to be easy-peasy, squeeze the lemon, as they say in *Horrible Histories*.

–

Later

'How's this for the first night in our new house?' I break the ice – literally, as it turns out, as a stalactite forms at the end of my nose.

Since we got back from the Co-op and gobbled down our sandwiches, we've discovered we have no heating, no hot water (Izzy, clearly the brains of this outfit, suspects the two are related), one lightbulb is on its last flickering legs and a bit of an accidental ant farm is covering acreage at the back of the kitchen cupboards.

We can't be arsed to unpack properly yet, so I pull out the sofa bed, set our sleeping bags up on it and throw several duvets on top of them. I bundle the kids into their bags and hop over Ben a tad inelegantly to get into mine in the middle.

'Good,' mumbles Ben.

'It's going to be us three against the world! The Three Musketeers, The Three Amigos—'

'Three Blind Mice!' Ben offers.

'Yes!' I laugh. 'In a way, sort of… probably more like The Keystone Cops. Or The Three Stooges.'

'It's a disaster,' Izzy deadpans.

'Rubbish – it's an adventure! Now get to bloody sleep,' I rasp.

'I'm worried for Daddy,' Ben says.

I roll my eyes silently in the dark, hoping the kids can't feel the negative vibe I must be giving off.

'He might be lonely without us,' he goes on.

But before I can say any of the things I'm thinking, like, 'This was all his idea in the first bloody place! He wanted to be on his own – he's happier now than he's been for years!', I'm struck by how sweet and sensitive my boy sounds. Just like Joe used to. Maybe, I think to myself rather graciously, if I do say so myself, Joe wasn't always the selfish, computer games-obsessed, fond-of-a-pint-or-six husband he grew up to be.

But then I quickly remind myself that when it came to talking about his inner-most thoughts and feelings, he had about as much emotional depth as a petri dish.

'Mummy!' Izzy holds her head up.

Shit – did I just say that last bit out loud?

'I can hear something scratching! It sounds big – like it's got huge teeth.'

42

'Probably just a cute, friendly country mouse trying to bed down for the night. Now close your eyes, sweetheart and get some sleep,' I sigh, hoping she's wrong.

With the room now completely in darkness, a little traffic noise rattling the rickety old sash windows, it isn't long before the sound of two little people snuffling their way to Noddington fills the air.

And even though I'm exhausted, I'm also annoyingly awake, listening to the strange scratching sounds. I have no other choice but to stare into the abyss, wide-eyed and shell-shocked by not only the day that's been, but also the thought of the days ahead.

–

Three upbeat, positive things I might be able to call 'wins' so far:

- Um…
- God, give me a break! It's only been one day. And didn't I just say I was scared witless? *Concentrate and keep trying, Annie, keep on trying.* Yowch! I'll burst a blood vessel if I try any harder.
- Ooh, I know – Tunnock's Tea Cakes are only one pound in the Co-op. That's £1 for *six* of those little choc-coated marshmallowy mounds of yum. ONE POUND! Bargain of the century or what?!

–

December 28 – Wee Are Family

You know how when you think of the countryside, it's all heavy Victorian front doors with big knobs and

43

knockers done out in Farrow & Ball colours, roaring open fires, fabulous Elizabethan inns, cherries dotted about on Cath Kidston aprons, green rolling hills, endless blue skies, ruddy-cheeked children having picnics on red tartan blankets and everyone talking like they're stuck in an Enid Blyton book circa 1953?

'Well, wake up and smell the sewage, girlfriend,' I mutter to myself as I get a whiff of something unpleasant and try to extricate myself from the tangle of arms and legs pinning me to the sofa bed.

'Can... I... just... get... urgh! What's that? Have you...? Oh, Ben!'

He's only gone and wet himself. And the mattress. And the sleeping bags, the floor beneath the sofa bed, my jim jam bottoms...

'Wha—' he mumbles as he rolls over and inadvertently socks me in the eye with a lazy, but quite impressive left hook.

I mean, Jesus. We've only been here in this decrepit, decaying pit for a few hours and already I've been physically assaulted, we've nearly frozen our faces off and no doubt our Single Parent Family presence is sending local property prices crashing through the (original) oak floor boards.

Woah! That doesn't sound very grateful or upbeat! Come on, Annie – begin as you mean to go on...

Well, maybe I am making a mountain out of a molehill – the one crafty activity I have been known to indulge in on the odd occasion.

I clamber over Ben, muttering as I go about having to waste valuable integrating-into-the community time by being housebound, on my hands and knees, scrubbing wood floors, washing pyjamas, sheets and sleeping bags – if a sleeping bag will actually fit in the machine... and the washing machine even works.

An image of my chubby self in a sari, squatting on the banks of The Ganges, concentrating on a stubborn stain on a sheet no amount of Vanish could ever shift bursts into my brain and I let out a small whimper. Bet I didn't even pack any Febreze. Still, he's only five, of *course* he's going to have 'accidents' every so often. But then again, he is FIVE bloody years old – shouldn't he be past that kind of thing by now?

As the smell of urine momentarily overwhelms me, making the corners of my mouth turn down so far in disgust they nearly drop off my chin, Izzy moans quietly and unknowingly puts a protective arm over her baby brother. I can't help but soften at this, cocking my head to one side and letting a quiet 'aww' escape my lips.

But just as my heart's melting at this cosy scene, I misjudge where the edge of the bed ends and the floor begins, tumbling down to the floor with a most ungainly crash, my nose now mere millimetres away from the musty puddle of pee.

'Mu-um!' screeches Izzy. 'You woke me up! I was having the BEST dream – why do you always DO that?'

'Morning!' I trill, sneezing as I pick myself up – the dust on the floor of this old house is as thick as a brick. Dust bunnies? Dust grizzly *bears*, more like.

My hand instinctively moves to my unsupported right knee (you're not supposed to sleep with your elastic bandage support-thingy on, lest you cut off all circulation and have to have your leg amputated or something) which should, by all rights, be killing me right now, twisting as

45

it did when I tumbled off the sofa bed. But it's not. If anything, it feels slightly less swollen and a bit less hurty than usual. Which is weird.

Maybe the fact that it's absolutely freezing in here has something to do with it – like it's been packed in ice for the past few hours. I can not only *feel* the Siberian wind blowing through the cracks in the front door, I can hear it howling, too. Which is really saying something, considering how loudly the thin window panes are rattling in their loose beading.

And then I see something sliding under the whopping great chasm of a gap between the front door and the front door step. I take a step back and try to hold onto the wall. But my fingers find an old cobweb instead and I whip my hand away with a yelp, pulling at the fingers on my right hand as though I'm trying to take off a tight, invisible glove while I jog on the spot at the revoltingness of it all.

I bend down slowly and pick up the card that's just come in under the door.

'What have we got here, then?' I say, trying to sound light-hearted, despite my default setting of cynical old bag who's completely knackered.

'What is it, Mummy?' Ben's awake and beaming, not even remotely bothered by the sodden sleeping bags.

Unlike Izzy.

'Ben! You're DISGUSTING! You've wee'd all over us!'

'Did not!' comes his standard reply.

'Yeah, don't worry about it. I'll clean it up – but look! We've got mail!'

The kids couldn't be less interested as they slip and slosh about in the bed, hurling accusations of gross indecency while wrestling with each other.

Somehow I manage to block out their noise and concentrate on the note scrawled on the back of the postcard:

> *Hiya!*
>
> *We saw you moving in and wondered whether you'd like to pop over for a cup of tea sometime? It's not far – we're right next door at Number 72! We have one boy, Jack, 5 and our daughter, Jess, is 3. Then there's me – Jane – and my husband, John. No pets – thank God! So... welcome to the village. See you soon?*
>
> *Jane, John, Jack and Jess*
>
> *PS This card was brought to you by the letter 'J'!*

Ha!

'How nice is that?' I say out loud, a genuine smile spreading across my face, as I turn to confront the carnage.

'I HATE you!' shrieks Izzy.

'You don't really mean that. Repeat after me: you're my baby brother and I love you,' I say, calling for familial calm.

Ben bats his ludicrously long, black eyelashes at me. Izzy fixes me with her steely gaze and says:

'I was talking about YOU.'

'Charming,' I sigh, my gaze inexplicably drawn to Auntie Aud's heaving bookshelf. I pull down something called *Fathead*, about weight loss being all in the mind, and leaf through it. I stop when a sentence highlighted in fluoro pink grabs my eye and read it out loud:

'Chocolate will only make you put on weight if you *think* it will,' it says.

Ha! So maybe it isn't all those family blocks of Fruit 'n' Nut and packets of Tunnock's Tea Cakes I've scoffed – it's just my negative, chunky thoughts making me fat! As if. What a complete load of wishful thinking tosh!

–

Turns out the sleeping bags don't fit in the washing machine and it doesn't work, anyway. So I drag the soaking wet mattress out to the garden (dead patch of dirt out the back, more like), hang it on the line and hose it down so it's dripping a heady mix of urine and water onto the 'lawn'.

We – sorry, *I* – bundle all the bedding into bin bags, bung them in the car and head for the local launderette.

It's going to cost twenty pounds per sleeping bag to wash and dry. Which is outrageous, but they've got us by the short and curlies on this one, so we leave our loads with them and hit the high road for breakfast.

You'd think there'd be some lovely, rural homestyle bakery-stroke-coffee shop here in Old Stoke – but there isn't. Just one big Costa. We pass an empty, deserted shop, complete with those round blobs on the window squares, like the kind you'd find in Dickens' *The Old Curiosity Shop* and I briefly entertain thoughts of opening a bookshop café here myself one day. Which cheers me up. A smidge.

I'd have homemade bread, cakes and scones (made by someone else at their home, natch – not much of a baker, me), local jams and cheeses, great coffee, tea, soup and hot chocolate – and all sorts of books on dark mahogany shelves, available to buy or just browse, complete with cosy reading nooks and crannies as well as country Shaker-style kitchen chairs and tables, gingham tablecloths optional.

Local authors would be desperate to launch their books and do readings there – we'd get a licence to serve alcohol – and there'd be a children's books area where kids could lounge about on beanbags for hours on end while they discover the joys of reading, solitude and relative quiet. Pensioners would gather for afternoons of cribbage and it would become known as *the* place to hang out. We'd be local heroes for bringing something fab to the village as well as making loads of money and—

I come fer-lumping back to reality with a sigh when we join the longest queue in Christendom at Costa to order our breakfast.

No one smiles at us – no one even looks at us. And if someone did happen to steal a furtive glance, I bet they'd regard us with typical country-bumpkin suspicion. So much so that when the twelve-year-old behind the cash register asks for our order, I half expect her to look up, sneer and say something like 'you're not from round here, are you?'

Everyone knows country folk stick to their own and don't warm to outsiders. Wouldn't know kindness if it came up and bit them on the arse. But actually, she's nice and friendly and smiles warmly when Ben orders two packets of wafer biscuits and a hot choc-mint concoction while Izzy plumps for a chocolate muffin and a hot salted caramel milkshake. I see no point in starting my diet today, so end up devouring a brownie, a blueberry muffin and a very thin sliver of strawberry cheesecake, washing it all down with a large hot chocolate with extra whipped cream. No marshmallows, though – don't want to overdo it. And anyway, as long as I don't *think* I'll stack it on, I *won't*, according to *The Secret*!

We take in our surroundings while we scoff and discover that Old Stoke is simply *lousy* with nuclear families. Because even though it's a weekday morning (Thursday), there are plenty of dads doting on their kids while they look lovingly at their beautiful, slim, not-a-hair-out-of-place wives. I don't think Joe ever looked at me like that.

He'd never come with me and the kids to a café. Actually, that's a lie. Mere weeks after Izzy was born, we went to a Café Rouge. Tiny Izzy was in her pram and we sat outside because Joe wanted to smoke. It was cigarettes in those days – not vapes – and there was no way he'd come to a café if there was only coffee or tea on offer, so I must have lured him there with promises of Pernod – or more likely, pints of Stella.

Of course, back then I still wasn't smoking. I'd given up the whole sorry business for the duration of the pregnancy and was determined not to start again once Izzy was born, so you can imagine how down on Joe I was for continuing to do it – especially around our precious new papoose.

And now I think about it, I reckon it was right then and there, at that Café Rouge, that things changed irretrievably for us as a couple. Our paths were beginning to diverge and I started to change. It was that flagrant show of selfishness, not even feeling *bad* about smoking in front of Izzy or me that kicked it off. We practically *raced* downhill from that point on.

Obviously, it wasn't long before I was puffing away like a good 'un again – but never in front of Izzy, always making sure I washed my hands, doused myself in perfume and ate a packet of Extras before going anywhere near her after having had one. What a palaver!

Now, nine years on, remembering the bad old days like that, I'm suddenly overcome with cravings for a ciggie. But I don't see anyone else smoking here. It's far too arctic to nip outside for one – especially as the kids would be so cross with me and everyone would see and we'd instantly be the new feral family who've just moved here, trashing Auntie Aud's good name, bringing their vile big city drugs and attitudes with them. We'd be tarred and feathered and run out of town before you could say pitchforks at dawn! Or at least *I* would be – for being a sad, lonely, utterly hopeless single mum, incapable of looking after herself, let alone two great, innocent kids who need a good, safe, solid home and reliable, loving care – not a domestic disaster like me, a shambolic mess of a human being...

'Hoo-wee,' I shudder at the force of my negative, self-despising thoughts and try to calm my breathing.

'Shall we see whether the library's open? Or, indeed, whether there *is* a library here?'

Ben stares at his hot choc-mint in silence while Izzy fairly leaps off her seat with excitement.

'Of COURSE there's a library! It's next to the hardware shop. I'll meet you there!'

And with that, she shovels her muffin into her mouth, drains her milkshake, scrapes her chair across the hard-wearing lino and whizzes off out the door before I have a chance to yell at her to put her coat on, be careful on the road, try not to slip on the icy puddles, don't run etc etc etc.

By the time we get home, I'm gagging for some comfort (i.e. a giant bar of Cadbury's Dairy Milk or even just a couple of Creme Eggs) but settle for a nice cup of tea and some positive thinking instead.

Apparently, according to *A Year of Positive Thinking*, on January the first, I should be content in the knowledge that I am right where I should be.

'You are in exactly the right place,' my new bible states. 'That place may be scary, boring, exciting or heart-breaking. But whatever it is, sit tight. Instead of fighting your way out of it with everything you've got, sit still. Experience it. Let go. Rock on. You are exactly where you should be.'

I don't know why, but I feel like flinging the book across the room at this point. Maybe because it sounds so smug, so arrogant, so smirky and knowing, and I feel the exact opposite, floundering around in indecision and uncertainty.

I mean, we're *supposed* to be right here, in Old Stoke, languishing in Aud's crumbling cottage, are we? Well, who the hell says? And what would they know? And what if I was reading this in some fetid swamp in some Third World hellhole – would that be where I was supposed to be?

And what, pray tell, am I supposed to let go *of*? Hmm? My dreams, hopes and desires – or just the last shreds of my dignity and well-worn patience? And how the hell am I going to *rock on* when my back's killing me, I can't *see* my toes, let alone touch them and the only tunes I've got playing on a loop in my head are songs from kids' movies like *Cars, Tangled* and *Moana*? I mean, *experience* it? I already bloody well am!

And breathe.

All this positive thinking – it's just a load of empty, meaningless platitudes, pointless clichés and one-size-fits-all philosophy, really, isn't it? And who needs *that* when you're drowning in self-doubt? What kind of a deflated life vest is that?

I mean, *where I should be*? You might as well tell me what's done is done, it is what it is and I am what I am. Because it would still mean precisely the same thing to me – abso-bloody-lutely nothing.

I stop myself mid-rant and take stock. When did I get so angry? Why am I so resistant? How did I get so closed off? So mealy-mouthed, so po-faced? And when did I stop being able to see even the smallest sliver of the silver lining, focusing entirely on the big, black cloud?

I barely recognise myself. I mean, I've always thought of myself as naturally upbeat, cheerful and optimistic. But I suppose after life has a go at you and chucks a couple of decades of knock-backs, rejections, disasters and disappointments at you, you kind of lose that child-like positive outlook and become something of a bitter and twisted salt and vinegar version of your former self.

So. Not exactly a great start, I admit, but as I look up at Audrey's bookshelves, I think maybe it's high time I suspended my disbelief/disdain for long enough to give it a really good go.

I kind of owe it to Audrey and her bottomless pit of kindness and compassion to really make a concerted effort to adopt a positive mental attitude, now, because she's not only lent us her lovely house, she's provided all the how-to's a girl could ever want. And it seems to have worked for her, hasn't it?

Obviously it's going to take a bit of time to smooth down the sharp edges of my somewhat prickly exterior and it'll take more than a few tries to suppress my knee-jerk, default hostile reaction, but you'll never know until you give it a go, right?

So I throw down my own gauntlet (which I didn't even know I had – I mean, who wears gauntlets these days?) and take the plunge into the sparkling waters of personal empowerment and self-belief (read: Audrey's bookshelves).

And after an hour or so, not sweating the small stuff, getting to grips with *The Secret* and shutting my eyes tight to imagine what The Universe looks like so I can put my unquestioning trust in it, I find myself beaming my own face off.

Because now I think I'm ready to live my best life, be the best version of myself I can be and get healthier, fitter, richer, happier!

Despite inwardly groaning that I sound just like a fridge magnet, I continue my declaration: I will be the great mum I've always wanted to be *because* of my imperfections, not in spite of them. I will get out there again, maybe even go on some dates, make some new friends, show up, stand up, speak out and generally extend a lovely olive branch to The Universe.

Because you never know, all this positive thinking just might work. And even if it doesn't, it can't hurt. Can it? I mean, what's the worst that could happen?

–

Three good, upbeat positives so far:
- My knee's nowhere near as hurty as it was.

- We've been invited round to the neighbours. Get in!
- Despite my doubts, by gazing at my own navel for a little bit, I think I feel better already. Or maybe I'm just hungry?

Chapter Three

January

January 4 – Life Is Short And So Am I

There are approximately three million pencils dotted about the house already and I find myself wondering how the hell that's happened when we've only been here a few days and I've barely managed to put clean sheets on the beds, let alone erect an easel for a spot of light pointillism.

Mostly, though, they're the broken, coloured kind, only useful in those moments when you decide enough is enough and you can't possibly allow your progeny to grow up playing computer games and watching other kids play *Minecraft* on YouTube, so you turn the TV off, turn the radio on to Classic FM, get out the A4 and force them to draw something – *anything* – in a bid to kick start something vaguely resembling creativity, thinking for themselves and imagination.

'Let's do a panorama!' I clap my hands together with faux excitement. 'We can all do a part of the scene – like, we could draw our – er, Auntie Audrey's – house, here! You could draw the front of the house, Ben and Izzy, you could do the inside, like an open doll's house, no front façade!'

It's not a bad idea, but after ten or so minutes (max), the kids are bored stiff and I'm trying to remember how the hell you make an apple look 3D. Clearly, we need to try something else. Something family-ish, something simple, wholesome, full of country goodness and cosy cottageness.

So I suggest we mark our heights on the wall opposite the bottom of the stairs. I'd call it 'the hallway', but as the front door opens into the front room immediately, there is no hallway to speak of.

Grabbing a navy-blue pencil, I still a struggling Ben and put his back up against the wall, marking where the top of his head reaches.

'Not bad, babe – gosh you're getting tall,' I say, even though he just makes it nearly up to my boobs.

Next, it's Izzy's turn.

She stands on tiptoes, lowers her cute, helium voice, looks down at me and says: 'Fee fi fo fum, Mum!'

'Very funny – now put your feet flat on the floor. Let me just mark it there…'

'HA!' She whips herself away from the wall and studies the mark. 'Even without cheating I'm way taller than you!'

'That's not saying much, though, is it?' I can feel my lips getting thinner as I try to pretend that none of her jibes wound me in the slightest.

'S'pose not,' she grumbles, punching her little brother in the arm and tearing up the stairs, giggling while he lumbers after her, his little legs taking forever to scale each step.

Once they're out of sight, I sidle up to the wall and put the pencil flat on my head, being careful not to mark the wall, just see where the line might go. I untangle myself and see that Izzy is, in fact, still shorter than me. Just.

While I busy myself trying to open bank accounts over the phone (impossible), I hear the kids fighting, slamming doors and screaming at me to play hide and seek and I wonder whether I can sneak outside into the frost to have a quick fag.

I seem to really need one when I'm on the phone – especially if I'm dealing with such unpleasant things as money – must be a throwback to the days way before we had Izzy and Ben, when you could smoke inside pubs and your own house.

I can even remember smoking at work, yonks ago, sitting around a big sub-editors' table at the first magazine I ever worked at, chuffing away like the mature soph- isticate I dreamt of being but never actually grew into, surrounded by really funny, really clever men who were old hands at rewriting stories from *News of the World* and *The National Enquirer.*

It was a supermarket, bottom shelf men's 'news' magazine, complete with 'Home Girls' (like readers' wives, who, let's face it, were probably readers' sisters, mums and grans), crazy stories about UFOs, yetis, strip- pers and hero Aussies who invented Vegemite or could put away enough beer to make their bellies explode. You know, news.

So anyway, there I was, twenty-two years old, fresh(ish) out of uni, prancing about like I'm Anna Wintour, sitting around a desk with all the other blokes, looking at 'the norks on that one', laughing at the latest Elvis sighting in Milton Keynes and interviewing the Fat Slags from *Viz* by fax, all while smoking up a storm in the office on the seventh floor of a reputable and highly respectable publishing house.

Mum was so proud.

No, really, she was. Because I was off, making my way in the world, learning how to get along with all sorts of people from all sorts of backgrounds with all sorts of perspectives, while living the creative, independent life I'd yearned for. I felt like Mary Tyler Moore in the beginning credits of *The Mary Tyler Moore Show* when she throws her beret up into the air with the joy of it all – even though I never wore berets and I worked at a scuzzy soft-porn mag as opposed to the Minneapolis Nightly TV News or wherever Mary worked.

Still, working with all those hard-bitten, big-drinking guys taught me a huge amount (not, unfortunately, how to hold my booze) and it was such great fun.

I just hope somewhere deep down I still have some reserves of strength left over from those challenging days which will stand me in good stead for our new life at the frontier of the unknown.

Just as I'm bringing the fingers on my right hand to my lips, as though there's a much-missed cigarette between them, my reminiscing comes to an abrupt halt when I become aware of Ben watching me looking longingly out the kitchen window, salivating slightly at the thought of smoking with impunity.

'Mum!' he squeals. 'Can I eat something?'

'Erm,' I reply, succinctly.

'Tuna sandwich!'

'Hmm?'

'Tuna sandwich?'

'What do you say?'

'TU-NA SAND-*WICH*!'

'Don't shout! The neighbours and all… I didn't mean I couldn't *hear* you, I meant haven't you *forgotten* something?'

'No – but you have,' Izzy chimes in, barging into our exchange, squeezing through the galley kitchen to the fridge at the end, opening its door roughly. 'As always, there's NOTHING to eat!'

While I concede that such constant narkiness is rare in one so young, I also have to admit she's right. The thought of food and the eating thereof has completely slipped my mind. Which is definitely not like me. Nope, that's never happened before. Ever.

'You're right, Izz – but there's method in my madness,' I lie. 'I thought we could go to a country pub for lunch by an open, blazing fire. What do you reckon?'

'Yay!' shrieks Ben.

'Nyurgh,' tuts Izzy. 'Will they have Yorkshire puddings? I'm only going if they have Yorkshire puddings.'

And so, the acrid taste of my phantom fag still snaking about in my mouth, we hop in the car and take off in search of an inn where we might find some respite in a hearty repast.

–

Sod that for a game of soldiers – The Zebra, that quaint little country inn, saw us coming and cost a flaming fortune! It was eye-wateringly expensive: over seventy pounds for three lunches – one of which was just a plate with three giant Yorkshire puds on it.

Don't get me wrong, it was a gorgeous place, complete with roaring fire, the owner's lovely cocker spaniel monstering all the punters for food, yummy home-made sweet and savoury pies... It was rustic and warm and a real picture of life in the country, what with paintings of pheasants on the walls and the odd gent wearing a tweed flat cap and plus fours.

But blimey it was pricey.

Still, you never really know something until you've experienced it for yourself, now, do you?

Take being a single mum, for instance. Lots of women have uttered those immortal words, 'I feel like a single mum' when their husbands or boyfriends have only gone away for a few days and they have to handle everything on their own, but they couldn't *possibly* hope to have any clue as to what a single mum really feels like, could they? I mean, I thought the same stupid thing at the beginning – like, there'd be no change to the way I felt about anything or the way I did anything or, indeed, my outlook on life once Joe had buggered off, because me and the kids had always done everything without him anyway.

But right now, I'm really noticing his absence. And not just because it's bin day tomorrow and he needs to put the bin out tonight or because he'd know how to fix the heating or because he's an IT guy and he'd have computers, TVs and assorted other gadgets all up and running beautifully by now – it's also because it'd be nice to feel I had a safety net, someone there waiting to catch me should I fall. Which I inevitably will.

Oops! When/if I do end up falling and failing and generally effing things up right royally, I'll probably – no, I will definitely simply see the funny side, throw my beautiful head of lustrous hair back and laugh it off. I will pick myself up, dust myself off and carry on regardless, learning, growing and trusting in The

Universe. Ha! How's that for thinking positively? Not bad for an optimist on her 'L' plates.

The roar of the traffic thundering down the main road in front of our house suddenly drowns out not only my internal rumblings and grumblings, but also the kids bickering upstairs. So, you know, every cloud…

I even manage to sort out the school situation on the phone. It's not ideal, not by a long chalk – but it'll have to do.

Turns out the local school – a three-minute walk from our house – is chockers with kids and can't squeeze any more in, even if they're only little. I call up every school in a twenty-mile radius, and only one has a space in Year 1 for Ben and Year 4 for Izzy. And it's a thirty-minute *drive* from our house, in a little village called Thistlebend.

I even ordered the kids' school uniforms (a fetching navy blue and green combo) over the phone while the supercilious secretary took down all our details.

And because I'm not working at the mo' (apart from breaking my back trying to raise two honest, compassionate – LEAVE HER A-BLOODY-LONE! – sweet kids on my own), we qualify for free school dinners.

Talk about a major bonus! The kids will be over the moon – God knows they'd rather eat a burnt rubber tyre than one of my meals. Which, apparently, taste very much like burnt rubber, I've been told.

Just as I'm pulling the warring siblings apart and thinking of suggesting a bracing walk in the woods, the phone rings. It's Mum, checking everything's okay.

I wander into the upstairs en suite and inspect myself as I speak.

62

'The broadband's going to take about a million years to be installed because we're in the middle of bloody nowhere out here, the kids are going to have to go to school in the next bloody county, thirty long minutes away, I'm half-blind, my hearing's going, my teeth make Shane McGowan's look straight and—'

The line suddenly goes dead and I wonder whether it's the rubbish reception we've got out here, whether I need a hearing aid or whether I'm simply boring Mum to tears with my endless whingeing so much that she's hung up on me.

I hear the kids running down the stairs. I brush my thinning hair off my face and generally try to pull myself together, following them.

But as I near the bottom of the stairs, the tears start to flow, blurring my vision and stuffing up my perspective. Before I know it, a bloody pencil sitting there idly makes me slip on the loose shit-brown carpet on the second-to-last step. I hurtle forwards, let out a shriek, remembering in that instant that I really must re-attach that handrail soon and CRACK! My skull slams into the wall opposite the stairwell.

I slump to the floor, literally seeing stars and hearing birds tweet. Izzy takes this opportunity to humiliate me further, marking with a pencil where the top of my head is lolling about on the wall.

'Annie? Annie darling? Are you there?' I hear Mum's voice faintly calling out from the mobile that's still in my hand.

I bring the phone up to my ear.

'Yes,' I groan.

'Is everything all right? I heard a crack and a thump – are the kids okay? Annie?'

'Why am I so sodding *shor-hor-hort?*' I weep, the force of my sobs making a dust bear curl itself up in a big, fat ball and run for cover.

—

Three good, upbeat positives so far:
- The kids have now got a school to go to. Organisation, thy name is Annie!
- I found a silver lining in the cloud of traffic noise and embraced the idea of failure as part of my journey.
- I just said 'my journey'. With a straight face, no smirks or sneers in sight.

—

January 5 – Dingle, Dangle Dongle

'I'm sorry, darling,' says Mum, struggling to work out how the hell you turn the kettle on, 'there's nothing much we can do about the height issue, but your father's bought a dongle and a sat-nav for you.'

Mum and Dad arrived here shortly after nine this morning, while me and the kids were still in our PJs (i.e. every jumper we own over several pairs of trackie bottoms), bearing gifts that are going to change our lives.

'Now you kids can play on the computer – once we've set the dongle up—'

'Dingle, dangle dongle in the dirt – isn't there a song or a poem... no! It's a saying: as dry as a dead dingo's dongle!' Mum beams with pride.

64

'You can take the girl out of Sydney, but you can't take Sydney out of the girl,' Dad sighs. 'And it's donger, darl. Dead dingo's *donger*.'

'Ah, yes.' Mum looks off into the distance wistfully, as if she has fond memories of the phrase or, indeed, some poor actual dead dog's, um, member.

'What's a donger, Granddad?' asks Ben.

'It's this little machine that's going to connect us to the internet so we can play free online games like *Kizi* until we get broadband and the telly,' I explain.

'No it isn't,' Izzy pipes up, 'that's a dongle. A donger, as I understand it, bro, is a penis. A willy. A boy's bit.'

'Donger. *Donger*. Don…ger. That's a good new word, isn't it, Mummy?'

'Great,' I agree. 'Now shhhh while Granddad works it out. Once we've got that sorted, we can all jump in the car, plug in the sat-nav and figure out the quickest route to your new school.'

'Yeah,' whispers Izzy, 'shut up, you donger!'

'Izzy!' Both Mum and I wheel around and glare at our girl.

Not quite the edifying, intellectual family conversations I'd imagined us having around the big farmhouse kitchen table. But at least we're all here, present and accounted for.

'Thanks you guys, for all this,' I steer the subject away from willies, 'really, thank you.'

'We don't want your thanks,' Dad mutters.

Charming, I think to myself. No wonder my self-esteem's lower than a snake's belly, as Mum would say.

'What he means is,' Mum takes the baton from Dad, 'the best way you can thank us is by getting back on your feet again quick smart, going back to work,' and here she lowers her voice, 'and getting Joe out of your hair for good.'

She straightens up and smiles at Izzy, who has ears like a bat.

'And find yourself a new man,' Dad bellows. 'You're still young, not bad looking – you need to get out there and meet people.'

'But how can I when I have the kids? And I'm stuck out here in the boondocks. I can't nip down to the pub for a quick pint so I can get to know the locals. Anyway, I don't drink anymore.'

'You don't have to drink alcohol,' Dad slams the dongle's instruction pamphlet down on the table, 'for goodness damn sake! Have a Coke and a smile. *Diet* Coke, I mean.'

He coughs awkwardly and turns his attention back to the instructions.

'I don't know,' I try to look like I'm actually considering his suggestion (which I most certainly am not), 'I'd rather stay in, catch up on box sets, get stuff done. I don't think I'm ready. For *anyone* new, let alone a man.'

'You have a man,' Ben squeaks. 'Daddy!'

I flash him my best beatific smile and my heart breaks a little bit.

'Well, no, sweetheart,' I stroke Ben's thick, curly bowl-cut of a hairdo, 'he'll always be your daddy, nothing can ever change that. But Mummy and Daddy are no longer married. We've split up. He's free to have as many girl-friends as he wants now and he won't get in any trouble with me about it. And vice versa.'

'Nope,' says Izzy.

'You mean he isn't our daddy?' Ben looks confused.

'He'll always be your daddy, right Izzy?'

'Well, yeah,' she sniffs, 'but you can't ever have a boyfriend.'

Typical, I think. Why can't I see some action for once? When I feel a bit better about myself, I might even join an internet dating club, site, whatever. Because it's up to *me*, not these little schnippets. They can't dictate my life. Can they?

'Why the hell not?' Dad enters the fray. 'She's a good-looking woman, your mum.'

From 'not bad' to 'good' in about three seconds! At this rate, I'll be drop-dead gorgeous any minute now.

'But that's not all she has to offer,' Mum adds. 'She has… a lively mind and… ah…'

'She can't have a boyfriend, though, because she has to love us. There won't be any love left for me and Ben if she gets a boyfriend.'

Just when you think you have the narkiest, sarkiest little girl on the planet, with a mouth way older than her years, she comes out with something sweet and innocent like that, exposing her fragility and vulnerability for all to see.

I stare at her, astounded. She looks up from studying her nails and falls into me, headbutting my ribcage, wrapping her arms around me and cries, like the frightened little girl she is.

Directing her over to the couch in the front room, I rub her back and make soothing sounds and say, 'it's okay, everything's going to be just fine – Mummy's here'.

Out of the blue, I imagine myself in one of the local pubs as per Dad's suggestion and wince as an image of me clinking glasses, laughing uproariously and snogging some stranger's face off flashes past my mind's eye. I shake my head slowly, as if I'm telling myself I'm not angry about my appalling behaviour, just disappointed. Which, as we all know, is way worse.

'Done it!' Dad cries out. 'You are now, officially, connected to the web. Google something! Go on!'

'Elite Singles!' Mum yelps.

We all gasp and Izzy and I wander back into the kitchen.

'Amelie told me about her adventures with them, that's all,' Mum says, by way of explanation. 'It might be worth a try, Annie, you know, when you're feeling up to it.'

'How come you're having protracted dating convos with my best friend and I haven't even bloody *heard* from her for over a week?'

'How the hell should I know?' Mum raises her palms to the ceiling and shrugs her shoulders.

'*Kizi*!' Ben says. '*Kizi, Ki-zi, KIZI!*'

'Tell you what,' Dad puffs his chest out, visibly swelling with pride, 'why don't you and I give the sat-nav a test run while your mother stays here, playing computer games with the kids?'

'That's a good idea, you know,' I smile, fishing about in my coat pocket for the car keys.

'Great,' Mum says deadpan. 'No, I mean, really. Really great.'

–

Poor old Mum. She's not at her best with little kids – she finds them boring, but scary at the same time. Dull, but unpredictable – much like drunks.

'Poor Mum,' I say to Dad as we go over the toll bridge.

'Poor Mum nothing – she loves her grandkids,' he replies. 'And it gives us a chance to have a talk on our own, without interruption.'

Oh, God. What fresh hell is this? Which riot act is he going to read me now? What's today's lecture on? What an utterly hopeless, pathetic failure I am?

'I really do have to concentrate – these windy roads are a real bugger –'

'That's why you should go on the motorway. Why did you say to avoid motorways when the sat-nav asked which route you'd prefer?'

'Because they scare the bejesus out of me!'

As I'm explaining my decision to Dad, we go over a particularly deep pothole, which, when I try to correct the car, sends us veering towards the ten-foot-high hedge at the side of the road. The hedge barely touches the car before we're back on the road.

'Christ almighty – watch out! You're going to kill me and it's nowhere near my time, yet, I have far too much left to do!'

He shifts nervously in his seat and then loses his temper.

'Jesus – you MUST drive on the motorway – these tiny roads are too old and narrow – they're dangerous and you'll either end up killing me, your mother, yourself, your kids or someone else entirely. Really, Annie! It's time you grew up and took responsibility for yourself. And us – you owe us that at least.'

What was I saying about this little drive together being a good idea?

'Wow, Dad, look! A deer!'

I nod at the road ahead where a beautiful creature, looking exactly like Bambi, calmly meanders across the road, all huge of eye and gangly of leg.

'You keep your eyes on the road. For goodness damn sake!'

Never let it be said that my dad's easily distracted. But he does cool down relatively fast and before too long, we're discussing how lucky we are to be living in this official Area of Outstanding Natural Beauty, with its four distinct seasons, its stunning scenery, its beautiful animals...

'...and its treacherous fucking roads!' Dad grabs the steering wheel and jerks us to the left as a massive lorry judders by, hogging most of the tiny road.

'It's a bloody disgrace,' he goes on, as he runs his hands through his crazy head of fine, nutty professor-esque white hair.

'You're right, Dad – but I think we're nearly there. According to the sat-nav, it's just off to the right, into this car park here. Hang on – this can't be right, can it?'

Dad seems to instinctively know that this is, indeed, the exact right place. There's an old church in the car park, harbouring a fabulously tasteful home interiors shop (which stocks Farrow & Ball, surprise, surprise) and a divine-smelling café, full of home-made, hot cheese scones and delicious-looking lentil salads.

Just through the big gates is Thistlebend Community Primary School, a chocolate-box rural building that was probably once a barn or a manger, its roof beautifully thatched and its oak beams proudly exposed.

Dad and I lean on the gate and gaze at the school, unaware that we probably look like a couple of paedos, waiting for school to finish for the day.

'So how's that knee of yours?' Dad ventures.

I look down at the support.

'A bit better, actually – the pain's much less sharp than it was.'

'That's because Joe's not around. You don't have to see his miserable mug every day anymore.'

'You may well be right – I just felt a twinge then, when you said his name.'

'It's important you regain your sense of self amidst all this divorce kerfuffle, darling,' Dad says, his bright blue Paul Newman eyes twinkling with kindness. 'You're so much more than just a mother.'

'What's wrong with being *just a mother*?'

'We can't afford to pay for it! Joe will go to the Child Maintenance Service any day now, you mark my words. He'll cry unemployed, like all these rich IT contractors do – and then he won't have to give you anything for the kids' upkeep and we'll have to subsidise you. We can't do it now, not at our age.'

I suck on my lips, not having the faintest clue what to say. I needn't have worried – Dad fills in the uncomfortable silence with some stats.

'Did you know that nearly fifty per cent of all marriages end in divorce? And that ninety per cent of all single parents are women? Worst of all, the Tory, male-led CMS recommends that whatever the non-resident parent earns, they only need to give sixteen per cent of that to their kids. SIXTEEN PER CENT?! It's an outrage!'

'No, I didn't—'

'Well it's true. It's only a matter of time before Joe reneges on your divorce settlement. And when he gets another woman, if he hasn't already, you won't see him or any maintenance money for dust. So get on your bike!'

I ponder our grave situation.

'And now you've made me come over all Norman bloody Tebbit with worry! What are you doing to me, darling?'

'I'm sorry, Dad.'

'Don't give me sorry,' he snarls. 'Give me rest from the endless worry about you and the kids. Get moving. Don't let yourself descend into the quagmire of domestic drudgery. Get out there. Enjoy your life. And try to find a nice guy. There are plenty out there, you just have to be open to the unexpected.'

I nod and we both turn around to face the café at the same time, leaning back on the gate nonchalantly.

Suddenly I feel Dad's bony elbow in my ribs.

'Ow! What did you do that for?'

Dad doesn't say anything, but widens his eyes, stares at the ground like a mad man and jerks his head towards the man walking out of the café.

'Dad? Oh God… Dad! Are you having a str—'

'You donger,' Dad whispers, still staring at the ground. 'New husband material at twelve o'clock!'

Relieved he's not having a fit of some kind, but embarrassed that my old man has now taken it upon himself to act as matchmaker and hot guy talent scout, I groan. How did it come to this?

But then I check out the bloke heading over to his Range Rover. His cheeks are ruddy with fine wine and untold wealth. He's in his fifties, slim and tall and even though he's wearing a boring old brown waxed Barbour, he is devastatingly handsome. He looks like a Jilly Cooper hero, all lust-worthy swagger and sexy, chiselled features.

He smiles at us as he pulls the giant car's door shut and drives smoothly, almost noiselessly away.

'Now that's the kind of bloke you want – a gentleman farmer. Gentleman Farmer George. Yes. He'll do nicely.'

'Oh, Dad!' I roll my eyes and jump a bit when the school bell rings. 'Shit! We'd better get back – Joe's coming to pick the kids up for his first weekend with them at his new place at five this arvo. No wonder my knee's starting to throb. Come on, Dad – leg it!'

–

Mum and Dad leave pretty much as soon as we get back from Thistlebend. I know they're only an hour and a bit away in London, and always there for me at the end of the phone, but as soon as they've gone, I feel the heavy weight of something unnerving sitting at the base of my neck, just between my shoulder blades. Am I sad? Lonely? Absolutely starving?

That was unsettling enough, but it's nothing compared to how I feel when the kids drive off with their dad.

I'd packed their little suitcases for them: knickers (four pairs each, just in case), jumpers (three each – one can double up as a pyjama top), leggings (four pairs for Izzy), tracksuit bottoms (three pairs for Ben), vests (loads for both of them, long-sleeved and sleeveless), t-shirts (too many to count), toothbrushes, toothpaste, flannels (flannels? Who uses *flannels*?!) and their respective favourite cuddly toys.

When Joe knocks on the door, I leap up off the couch, jarring my unsuspecting, but already fragile knee, and yell out to the kids to come downstairs. My voice cracks halfway through and I curse myself for sounding like a nervous Theresa May.

I open the door and there he is, grinning like the cat who got the cream.

'Halloo!' he strides into the house, grabbing my arm and planting a dry kiss on my cheek.

What the—?

'Um, cup of tea?'

'Yeah, great. Where are the kids?'

He plonks himself down at the kitchen table, putting his feet up on the chair next to him.

'Jeez, I'm cream-crackered – so tired!' He rubs his eyes like a little boy and when the kids run into him, he pulls Ben onto his lap and puts his arm around Izzy's shoulders.

'Hey – here they are! You two crazies – I've missed you!'

The kids giggle and fuss over him and I feel several stabs of jealousy while I struggle with the stupid kettle and clatter cups about in the cupboard.

'Ooh – I need a quick Jimmy,' he says, gently sliding Ben off his lap and walking towards the loo. 'Meant to go before I left home, but I was in too much of a rush to see the kids!'

He's jollier than a green giant and he puts his hands on my hips as he squeezes past me, smelling of beer. Ah, so that's why he needs the loo – he's been boozing in the pub!

As soon as the flimsy louvre doors between the utility room and bathroom stop shuddering, I hear his trademark,

74

unfeasibly loud peeing and I can't help but roll my eyes to the ceiling, sighing heavily. I can hear it even over the rumble of the boiling kettle and through two sets of doors! Immediately I imagine I'm back in the Teddington house, pulling the duvet over my head to block out the unsavoury sounds of him weeing once again.

Except that here, now, it's louder than ever and even more loaded with symbolism. Christ! It's not even symbolic – I mean, he's *quite literally* marking his territory.

Finally he flushes and walks out of the loo, still doing up his fly.

'Actually forget the tea, babe,' he says 'I don't want to get stuck in traffic, so we'd better shoot. Have you got their bags? Great. Come on, kids, let's go!'

I walk out with them to see his brand spanking new Mini Cooper Clubman – perfect for fitting golf bags in, Joe smugly informs us.

The kids are delighted, bouncing about in the new car and barely notice I'm still there. I blow kisses to them till the massive Mini is out of sight, sniffing softly and murmuring 'Bye bye, my lovely loves!'

So... Now what?

I can do whatever I want, that's what! I can watch what I want to watch on YouTube, chat on the phone to Aisling or Amelie for hours, uninterrupted, and I can eat whatever I fancy, without having to worry about modelling good food choices or any of that gubbins.

So I do what any self-respecting woman in my position would do – I nearly get whiplash, I take off so fast, and bolt into the back yard for a cigarette. I call both Aisling and Amelie while I chuff away, standing on the slippery, mossy deck – but neither of them answers. My exhaled smoke mingles with the frosty air until I can't tell which is which and I wonder whether this is what freedom really looks like: standing outside, freezing your tits off while you choke yourself. It's never as good as you imagine it's going to be, is it? And sometimes, it's actually a lot worse.

There's nothing else for it – I put the fag out in an old tuna can full of water and cigarette butts, its hiss still sounding in my ears as I go inside, grab my purse and head for the Co-op, two doors down.

Stepping through the sliding doors, I'm suddenly gripped by glucose panic – which particular type of sugar shall I stuff into my face?

I debate with myself. Oreos? Nah, too American. A five-pack of Crunchies? I do have that Friday feeling, after all... nope. Too greedy. A four-pack of original Magnums? Too bloody cold.

Circling the sugar aisle like this for ages, I half-heartedly try to talk myself out of buying anything at all, while simultaneously egging myself on to indulge in a chocolate binge of such gargantuan proportions, it would shock Willy Wonka.

In the end, I'm rather proud of myself, actually, for showing restraint and not wholly succumbing to the lonely-old-single-mum-sans-kids-for-the-weekend-scoffing-her-face-off cliché.

I buy a Co-op plastic bag to hide my insulin-spiking Friday night food, lest anyone see me, even though I've only bought two boxes of Lindor Balls and one teensy-weensy family-sized block of Fruit & Nut – nothing to be ashamed of, really. And by the time I close and lock the front door behind me, I'm a little over-excited about the goodies I have in store for myself.

I set my laptop and the dongle up next to me as I sit on the couch, demolishing chocolate and Googling books on divorce and single mums.

There are serious, weighty tomes by American professors about single motherhood and other books on how to go about being a single mum by choice, with chapters on choosing a sperm donor and telling your parents.

There's also one book about how to survive single motherhood on Amazon that talks about forgiveness and neuro-linguistic programming and a load of other touchy-feely crap. I bite down hard on a Lindor ball.

I mean, really – I don't need to be re-programmed in order to survive! I'm not a robot, I am woman, remember – hear me roar and all that? What I need is a set of rules for me, a list of things I can do – or not do – that will help me enjoy life, not dwell on the hellness of it all, see the funny side and be my best self, as Oprah would say. I need a realistic design for life as a divorcée. A DIY guide, an instruction manual for women just like me...

Suddenly, energised by the glucose rush, I get a blank Word document up on my screen and before I know it, I'm typing:

THE TEN COMMANDMENTS OF THE NEWLY DIVORCED SINGLE MUM

Thou shalt not eat thy feelings – especially if thy feelings are made out of Lindor Balls. Try a small block of Fruit & Nut instead – 'tis way cheaper and even part of thy five a day.

I save the document for later and polish off the rest of the chocolate, while I look at weight loss success stories on YouTube. And somehow, disappearing down various holes of the veritable rabbit warren that is the internet, I stumble upon tips on visualisation.

Apparently athletes, pop stars, public speakers and slimmers alike all use visualisation as a technique to boost their chances of success. It's like if they can see it, they can be it.

I wonder whether it might be helpful for me, too, in my quest to banish negative self-talk, think positively, lose the lard and become once again the confident woman I used to be.

So I picture myself in a flowery, floaty summer dress (long-sleeved, of course – I can't for the life of me imagine my bingo wings will ever disappear) smiling and laughing with my guests as I flit about the summer lawn of my gorgeous country pile that looks a bit like Versailles. My face is over-exposed so I can make out neither spots nor wrinkles, my lips are plump and my hair is perfect with a nice, sleek, purposeful wave (as opposed to an accidental frizzy tangle).

I smile to myself when I see I've grown several inches so I'm no longer arm-pit level with my pals (which can be a real bummer on the Tube in a heatwave, let me tell you), but now on a level playing field, able to look people in the eye. Suddenly I look demure and sexy. I gasp and bite my bottom lip as a dashing man, who looks just like the guy Dad and I saw in the school car park, saunters towards me, smiling his long dimply smile, his riding boots shining in the sun as he fixes me with his intense eyes, obviously smitten by my cool, calm confidence and blissfully unaware that this beauty with the exceptionally good sartorial taste actually has upper arms like a Russian shotputter.

Arranging the cushions for maximum comfort, I lie back on the couch, put my feet up and, promising myself I'll start a new diet tomorrow, promptly fall into a sugar coma.

–

Three upbeat, positive things so far:
- The dongle is a life-saver – I am truly grateful to M&D for what we have received. Gratitude is fairly flowing out of me!
- And that sat-nav has already made me feel more confident, on the road at least. Farewell frightening panic attacks!
- I get to have a whole weekend to myself! How many married mums get that 'me-time' every two weeks?

–

January 6 – Everybody Needs Good Neighbours

My knee's killing me, I realise, when I wake up contorted and cranky on the couch.

Sitting up too quickly, I put a crick in my neck, as well as sending my laptop flying onto the floor.

Typical, I think, as I pick up the laptop and blink into the light of my mobile only to see, after the blurriness clears, that it's 02:13.

Urgh. I feel heavy, confused and slightly nauseous. My mouth's as dry as... something excessively dusty and dry – a dead dingo's donger? My heart's beating like crazy and as I'm trudging up those hideous stairs to get to Izzy's bed – I can't be arsed to pull out and set up the sofa bed – a familiar but completely unwelcome sense of shame washes over me.

It's almost like I'm hungover. But I haven't touched a drop for weeks! I fall into the double bed and snuggle into the brushed cotton duvet cover that smells of my little girl. And even though I'm cosy and warm and completely knackered, I can't sleep or shake the uneasy feeling my latest dream has left me with. Or was it a nightmare?

I was in a pub with Joe and although I didn't set out with the express intention to, I did end up drinking a shedload of wine. We were laughing and smoking up a storm until Joe just upped and left, putting his arms around a faceless woman with a fantastic body in a floral frock as he walked away. I could feel my flabby tummy jiggling as I laughed it up, until I realised, painfully and in slo-mo, that there's nothing remotely amusing about being left in a pub, pissed, alone and half-kippered by a gazillion Marlboro Lights.

It was one of those maddeningly vivid dreams that leaves you a little breathless upon waking, unsure whether you've actually lived your humiliation in real life or whether your subconscious is just being a bit of a bitch.

This time, I'm pretty sure – say, eighty-seven per cent – that it was my mean girl subconscious. As seems to be happening an awful lot these days.

What's my take-away from this bad dream? Not that it's just a dream, let it go – oh no. I take my fears and turn them into fact: I've let everybody down, Joe hates me, I'm the worst mother in the world, I've got a wobbly tummy and I keep making it worse by scoffing Cadbury's. I'm a filthy addict, smoking when I know it's a killer and I'm so selfish I'm prepared to do whatever I have to in order to get my fix, even if it renders the kids orphans (deep breath in). I can't give anyone what they need – hell, I can't even look after myself in my *sleep*, let alone on a responsible, sensible, wide-awake day to day basis...

And slowly exhale.

'Shhhh,' I hush myself out loud over and over in an attempt to silence the negative self-talk that I could do a PhD in. Strangely, my self-soothing must work because I fall asleep eventually, only to dream about enormous stone tablets and men in full-length white smocks.

I wake up smiling and, if not exactly *leaping* out of bed, at least managing a sort of slow commando roll onto the floor, coming face to face with broken loom bands and dried mud and God knows what else on the once-cream carpet. I dutifully ignore the little girl detritus, pick myself up, dust myself off and get downstairs to my laptop so I can make the most of my kid-free time, sorting out doctors and dentists and dicking about on weight loss websites for hours, gaining inspiration from other tubsters who've lost the lard.

But first, a quick cup of tea and a gasper.

Outside, it's bitter. But with my warm size eighteen parka on, that swamps me, making me look more Ewok than fashion icon, I laugh at the cold. The cold probably laughs straight back, but I don't care. Anything for my drug of choice.

As I watch the plumes of smoke leave my lips and hang heavy in the dank air, I tell myself how pathetic it is to be smoking again, at my age, in my situation etc. I go judge*mental* on my own self and in between drags, as I slide about on the moss, a limerick comes to mind and I say it out loud:

The woman stood on the slippery deck
Her lungs were full of smoke
She'd quit when she had had the kids
But she was just a joke.

'In so many ways,' I add, shaking my head and looking up into the calico-coloured sky as if asking for help or expecting a sign or something.

And then I see, over the fence, the top of next-door's back door opening. Through the slats on the fence I can just about make out someone hanging up washing – little kids' clothes, to be precise – and I practically swallow my cig in an effort to get rid of the blighter fast.

'Hello?' comes a friendly, female voice from behind the flimsy plywood divide. 'Are you reading poetry?'

And the embarrassment continues – she must've heard me! I flap my hands around furiously to chase the lingering smoke away, lest she find out I'm a disgraceful (gulp) smoker.

'Um, yes – hello! Jane? Is that you? It's Annie here. Your new next-door neighbour!'

'What are you doing out here, you silly moo? It's perishing!'

'I, ah… great day for line drying, huh?'

'You think so?' she sounds unconvinced. 'Bit heavy and moist, if you ask me. And not in a good way, if you know what I mean!'

'Ha! Yes,' I laugh, even though I can't remember the last time I thought something heavy and/or moist was a good thing. Obviously, she's making an oblique reference to sex, but I've forgotten what that feels like. And when it comes to weather, there's no such thing as 'good' heavy moisture – everyone knows that sort of thing freaks fine, curly hair out so much that mere seconds after you step outside, your perfectly straight, GHD'd do will frizz up fast and before you know it, you'll be a dead ringer for Miriam Margolyes.

'Listen, Annie...' Jane approaches the fence and drops her voice so instead of being all sing-song as she was a few seconds ago, she sounds conspiratorial and serious.

Oh, Christ. Here we go. She's going to tell me off about smoking and say she won't stand for old farts like me blowing their secondary smoke into her little ones' faces and onto their clothes etc. She's got a point and she has every right, obviously, but still. I brace myself.

'This might sound a bit previous and tell me if I'm being out of order,' she begins. My heart sinks and I'm instantly transported back to that poky, airless, empty office in Hammersmith, about to get the sack from Suzette again.

'Jack's taking the kids to his mother's for a sleepover tonight a little later on, and I know your darling two have gone away for the weekend—'

'You do? How?'

'We heard them squealing "Daddy! Daddy!" Not that I'm a curtain-twitcher or anything,' she snorts. 'No need – I can hear everything important without even trying, the walls between these old cottages are so thin!'

I have heard her little girl screaming and crying the place down – but that's toddlers for you – they're naturally loud. The walls can't be that flimsy, because I never hear Jane or Jack shouting – at each other or the kids – and that's just not normal. Is it?

'Oh, right.' I make a mental note: must try harder to keep the noise down.

'So anyway,' Jane continues, 'I thought I'd organise a little shindigette, a small get-together here, in your honour.'

Eh?

'Just you, me and a couple of the local mums. What do you think?'

'I think… that's a great idea!' I say, my relief audible.

'Oh, I'm so glad.' Jane moves away from the fence, takes down the clothes she's just hung up and as she's about to go inside she whispers in my general direction:

'Don't bring anything – we've got plenty of booze. See you at about eight?'

'I'm as good as there!' I say, even though on the inside, all-out war begins waging between me, myself and I.

You'd think, wouldn't you, that having just been invited to a friendly neighbour's house for a night of getting to know some of the locals, I'd be well chuffed, a warm glow emanating from my very soul. But no. As per usual these days, all I can see is a muddy, bloody battlefield in front of me – any social occasion a potential Somme-like situation.

Because if I drink, I'll want to smoke. And vice versa. But I can't – not in front of the *mums*! Then again, if I do neither, thinking I'm manoeuvring myself neatly away from the prospect of feeling mortified in the morning,

I'll only embarrass myself by the enormous amount of crisps and nuts I'm capable of eating, especially when I'm nervous. Or happy. Or sad. Bored, excited, majorly stressed, feeling frustrated, nice and relaxed – let's face it, pigging out for me has bugger all to do with being hungry. If it's there, I'll eat it. And if it isn't, I'll run out to the Co-op to get it.

Oh, what to do, what to do? I can't *not* go – that'd just be rude. And dumb – I mean, how am I going to integrate and settle in if I don't put myself out there a little bit, get out of my comfort-eating zone and mingle? And anyway, it's not like I have anything else planned, thanks to my best friends blanking me and the broadband and Freesat box taking their sweet time... But I don't want to trip myself up before I've barely begun in this town, village, whatever. And I don't want to scupper the kids' chances of making new friends just because their mother's a disgrace. Oh bugger. There's nothing else for it, I'm going to have to go, aren't I?

I wasn't always like this, you know. I was once quite the gregarious one before the kids came along and Joe all but disappeared. Don't get me wrong, I'm glad I had the kids – even though I did leave it a bit late – and I'm so lucky to have any at all, let alone two robust, obscenely healthy bambinos. It's just... I dunno. I'm lucky and grateful and blessed and over the moon and everything... I guess sometimes, though, I kind of feel like... where did I go? What happened to me? That good time girl, the fun one, the one who didn't care what anybody else thought, the one who was always up for a laugh and a great night out, sod the consequences?

Obviously, there's more to life than sharing a giggle over a few G&Ts, but it's hard to get excited about anything when you have about as much energy as a dead Duracell and all the joie de vivre of a burst balloon.

How did I end up like this? So socially awkward, almost hermit-like, preferring to stay in and catch up on missed YouTube videos of people actually getting their hair cut instead of going to a party? What the hell has happened to me?

Ooh, that's not very positive, is it? Up your game, Annie!

I reach up to one of Aud's higher shelves and pluck out *The 6 Pillars of Self-Esteem* by Nathaniel Branden. I start to flick through it, but I can't settle into it. It's all about conscious and purposeful living and integrity and a whole load of other completely confusing yet achingly Zen phrases. I try to remember the six pillars and ponder their meaning – but I get all mixed up and can't tell the difference between being a hundred per cent authentic and the practice of self-responsibility. And it's not immediate enough for me. I haven't got time for practice – I need results now!

One thing that does stick in my mind, though, is the idea that to build your own self-esteem, you have to learn how to accept those things about yourself that you have no control over and make an effort to work on those things about yourself that you can improve and change. According to Nathaniel, if you go around comparing yourself to others, and you keep coming off worst, you'll never accept yourself. And if you never accept yourself, you'll never improve yourself. So I think of my upper arms and tell myself I accept the fact that they're humongous. Which is a lie, but I'm a beginner, remember. I tell myself again and again that I accept my larger-than-I'd-like upper arms and before you can say Sumo wrestler, I brighten at the thought that now the way is clear for me to start doing weights and improving the appearance of my strong, capable arms.

And here's the weird thing – strangely, I think it works. Not the doing weights bit, but the idea that accepting something can move you further towards positive change. I feel better already – excited and energised!

I do some jumping jacks (two to be exact) and spy *Kick the Drink… Easily!* by Jason Vale at the top of the other bookshelf. Home gym session complete, I reach up, pull it down and dive straight in.

—

The first thing I see when I get to Jane's (apart from her beautiful, beaming face) is their wood-burning stove in the living room, flashing red and orange dancing flames, making me feel instantly warm and welcome.

'Annie!' she shrieks by way of greeting when she opens their sage-coloured country-style barn door. 'Come in, come in!'

She ushers me inside and I shove a box of Celebrations at her with one hand, a bunch of dreary, sad-looking garage forecourt flowers with the other and rush over to the stove, rubbing my hands together.

There's a wooden train set strewn all over the floor-boards, several green and pink plastic IKEA storage bins overflowing with Lego on the cream and navy Persian rug and the bookshelves are overflowing with books, magazines and more kids' toys.

'God, your place is gorgeous!' I can't help but blurt out.

'Thank you! It's exactly the same as Audrey's though, isn't it?'

'It's nothing like ours! Ours looks like Miss Havisham's front room compared to this – the cobwebs have been there for at least a hundred years… And it's so warm here – our heating's up the spout, God knows when we'll be able to get it fixed.'

I can't help it, words are simply tumbling from my mouth. I almost feel like my old self again – not shy and judgey, just open and interested. A bit negative, but not to the extent it's going to bring everybody down. And Rome wasn't built in a day etc. I feel good, though. Weird. Must be those pillars of self-esteem I read about earlier.

Jane gestures towards the kitchen and I'm suddenly aware that there are two other people here.

'I'll give you Paul's number – he's the local handyman and what he can't fix ain't worth having. Now come and meet the girls.'

There's Sue, an English teacher at the local secondary school, who has one boy Ben's age and one boy Izzy's age as well as the friendliest face I think I've ever seen – when she smiles at you, it's like she's giving you a big hug. Next, there's Elizabeth ('call me Liz!') who has four – yep, FOUR – boys. One is Ben's age, one's two years older than Ben and the twins are not yet two.

'Wow – twins, eh?' I'm aghast at the thought.

'Don't get me started,' Liz groans as she brings a glass of deep, dark red wine to her lips. 'Total accident. Didn't even want any more kids, let alone twins! Walked around the hospital bawling my eyes out after they told us. Nightmare. Red or white, Annie? I also brought some beer if you'd rather...'

Here we go. Crunch time. I can either have a drink or not – it's a simple decision to make, a choice between staying sober and in control or getting tipsy, running the risk of ruining our new lives before we've even finished unpacking and getting a rep as the lush divorcée at Number 74. *Just think of your poor, low self-esteem!* Mind you, I'm not feeling quite as nervous or disconnected as I was this morning, so I'd probably be able to pace myself. What harm could it do? There's nothing wrong with a drink every now and then and it'd be really nice to join in, bond over the booze, take the edge off...

'No, no – I'm fine, thanks,' I surprise myself by saying. 'I'd love a cup of tea, though, if one's going?'

'Of course!' Jane bustles about, banging cupboards and crashing the crockery. 'Think I'll join you, actually. I know while the fam's away, the mouse should play, but I'm simply gasping for an Earl Grey. Hey! That rhymes! You appreciate a good rhyme, don't you Annie? Heard you reading some poetry just this morning! Is an Earl Grey okay with you?'

'Oh yes,' I gush, sounding for all the world like one of The Famous Five, 'with lashings of skim milk please, Jane!'

Relieved she doesn't ask me to recite any poems, I sit down at the kitchen table and instantly feel at ease – like I've been sitting around this big hunk of oak, under the charcoal-coloured, low pendant lights for years, gabbing away with my girls, putting the world to rights, having a laugh and fitting in.

And from that moment on, my first foray out into Old Stoke society goes brilliantly. Jane, Sue and Liz are fantastic – ten years younger than me and big fans of five a.m. fitness boot camps, but differences aside, we get along famously.

I tell them all about how Joe and I met, got married here, had Izz, went to Sydney for five years, had Ben, went back to London and then back here, just me this time, with two kids in tow and a whole new life to sort out.

Jane and Sue are so wonderfully supportive, making all the right noises ('what a cock!' and 'he didn't deserve you!' and 'no, those years weren't wasted because you have two great kids!'), I feel safe and warm and maybe even liked. Which is quite the alien feeling.

The only weird thing is Liz. I mean, she's really nice and very funny, but there's something, I dunno... something of the religious fanatic about her, maybe? The way she goes on about the sanctity of marriage, family life and how kids need two parents living together and people change spouses like knickers these days, doing irreparable damage to children and life as we know it, blah blah blah.

'So, Annie...' Sue kicks Liz under the table. 'Are you seeing anyone?'

I nearly spit my tea out at the suggestion.

'God, no! I'm not in the right frame of body *or* mind for that sort of thing. Yet.'

'There are quite a few eligible bachelors around town,' Jane winks at me.

'Well, a bachelor's out of the question for a start. If I was ever interested in getting back into the dating game – which I won't be anytime soon – he'd have to have been married at least once before and have kids. He'd have to understand what family life's all about—'

'The sanctity of marriage, yes!' Liz charges her glass into the air.

'So who are these eligible men, just out of interest?' I ignore the increasingly pissed Liz.

Silence.

'Anyone?' I ask again.

'Umm,' Sue glances at Jane. 'James? The solicitor?'

Now it's Jane's turn to nearly spit her tea out.

'Don't be ridiculous!' she says. 'He's a screaming alcoholic! That's why his wife left him. Probably hit her, too – you know how alcoholics are.'

'Is he still?' Sue says. 'I mean, obviously he was before she left him, but does he still drink like a fish now?'

' 'Course he does,' Liz chimes in. 'And his law career's gone down the pan, thanks to his endless drunkenness, womanising and wanton—'

'So,' I cut her off, 'there are no eligible men around, after all? Not that I care...'

They go through a few more names, but no, seems like there aren't any even half-decent blokes in or around Old Stoke. Which is fine by me – I'm hardly in the market for a new man when I'm still trying to wash the old one out of my hair.

I leave just as Liz goes over the precipice, slurring her words and stumbling about, making even less sense than before and prompting Jane to put her to bed in her kids' room to sleep it off.

Awkwardly straddling the pointy picket fence between our houses and nearly giving myself a hysterectomy in the process, I shake my head as I think about Liz and mutter: 'there but for the grace of God or what?!'

Not the religious craziness, of course: the drunk in denial-ness.

And as soon as I walk in to our cold, dark cottage, my mobile bleeps. It's a message from Amelie:

> Sorry haven't been in touch – too busy shagging! Taking breather now. How was move? Settling in nicely? BTW, got a tip for you – do not ever, ever, EVER let Joe into the house when he comes to get the kids. Just saying. You must make clear the lines of demarcation. More later xxx

–

Three good things:
- Met some local mums and they're really nice – even Liz the lush.
- I didn't disgrace myself by either drinking or smoking at a stressful social event – I was even unapologetically authentic. Imagine!
- And I didn't eat the crisps on the table. Well, not all of them, anyway – I even managed to leave a few. Now *that's* progress.

–

'Come here, you gorgies! I've missed you so much! Get inside, get your shoes off and let's snuggle on the couch till dinner's ready,' I'm full of the joys of spring as I herd the kids into the house, blocking the doorway with my considerable frame when Joe starts to follow them in.

'Something smells yum!' Izzy tears off into the kitchen and I feel a sense of never-before experienced homemaker pride. Or at least, that's what I think it is.

'Great,' I call after her. 'It's roast chicken, sweetheart – with Yorkshire puddings!'

'Yay!' Ben hugs me, missing my cheek and kissing my hair instead as he runs after his sister.

I wanted the house to be all cosy and homey for the kids when they got home this afternoon – or at least the front room and the kitchen, those two rooms being the hearth of the home and all that – so I hot-footed it in to Henley this morning to buy stuff for a roast from Waitrose, an electric fan-heater that looks like a real wood-burning stove that positively *chucks* out the heat from Henley Hardware and a standard lamp from Biggie Best, an interiors shop. Fair broke the bank, in fact, just to create an ambience you might find somewhere like, ooh, I dunno... Jane's place?

Worth it, though, I think, as I turn to face Joe, my smile fading.

'Aren't I allowed in? It's technically my house, you know, if you're paying Audrey rent out of the mainten-ance I give you,' he smirks.

'Ah, well, probably best if—'

'Actually, speaking of maintenance, I need you to get a job so I can stop paying so damn much of it! I need that money to buy somewhere because I hate renting – it's like you're paying someone else's mortgage for them, out of the goodness of your heart.'

I feel the blood draining out of me, rushing to pool at my feet.

'Are you all right?' he frowns.

'But where will we go, what will we do? There are no jobs for someone like me who's too old for technology and whose kids are too young to fend for themselves! OH MY GOD – what will become of us all?'

I'm huffing and puffing and feel like flinging the door wide open and running away, leaving him, the kids, even the divine-smelling roast in my wake and never looking back, when suddenly Jane's door opens.

'Oh, hello there,' she grins, a tad menacingly if you ask me, 'you must be Joe – I've heard a lot about you. I'm Jane, Audrey and Annie's neighbour. There seems to be some sort of problem. Can I help?'

I'm gobsmacked and so is Joe – so much so, his face turns red and he starts stuttering.

'N-no, not really – we're just di-di-discussing—'

'May I suggest you discuss it via email? Annie's got enough to contend with without you coming here, shouting the odds and airing your dirty linen on the street.'

To be fair, it was me doing the linen-airing and odds-shouting – and we're not exactly on the street, we have a comparatively long driveway, so we're quite set back from the road. But far be it from me to split hairs when my knight in shining armour is coming to my rescue. Even though she's sporting a rather fetching fifties retro rose-patterned Cath Kidston pinny, as opposed to iron breast plates and chain mail. But, you know, potato, potarto.

94

'Well, I-I—' Joe hasn't got a clue what to say.

'That's a good idea, Jane,' I offer. 'The bit about the email, I mean.'

The three of us stand there, Jane and I with our arms folded across our chests, giving Joe the hairy eyeball, while Joe looks at one of us, then to the other, back and forth like this for what feels like ages.

'Right. Okay, then. If that's how you want to play it, fine. I'll send you an email. If you'll still accept emails from me – or have you blocked me?' Joe looks a little wounded, his top lip trembling at the corner.

That's not a bad idea, either, I think to myself – but I'm so technologically stupid, I wouldn't know how to do it.

And then, just like that (imagine I've just clicked my fingers), he switches. His lip stops twitching, his eyes go hard and his stutter disappears.

'No,' Joe sneers, 'of *course* you haven't blocked me! You struggle just to turn your laptop *on*, let alone sort out the settings. Well what are you going to do now, Annie Baby? Now that your own personal IT department is no longer at your beck and call? And what about money? Hmmm? How are you going to pay for diffusers and scented candles and all that other useless tat when your cash cow has officially left the building? Huh?'

'What are you burbling on about?' I inadvertently spit as he turns on his heel and swaggers away. 'I've never bought a scented candle in my life! Everyone knows they don't work!'

At this, I'm almost certain I can hear him mutter, 'Just like you, then'.

I stand on my tip toes on the front door step to yell a brilliant riposte, but my mind goes blank and I can't think of a single thing to say. Jane sighs next to me as we watch him go.

'Just goes to show how little he really knows you, doesn't it?'

'Gor – thanks for that! You're a star. Come in for a cuppa?'

'Ooh, don't mind if I do.' She steps over the falling down picket fence between our houses and closes the door behind her.

'What were you saying last night about cobwebs and haunted houses? This place looks amazing! Kind of reminds me of somewhere...'

I feel myself blush.

'I copied yours,' I confess. 'Or tried to at any rate. Couldn't afford a wood burner – or those fab low-hanging pendant lights, or the lovely rug, but I have got the toys and the general clutter that comes with kids...'

'How dare you?!' she smiles and wanders into the kitchen. 'Mmm, what's cooking?'

'Special Sunday roast.' I stand up a little straighter as I fiddle about trying to turn the stupid kettle on. 'I want to set up some nice, cosy traditions for us, as a solid family of three. Bet you guys have a roast every Sunday...'

'You must be joking!' Jane snorts. 'Waste all that good scran on children who refuse to eat decent food, anyway? Nah, fish fingers and peas will do us.'

Suddenly I feel a bit embarrassed by the extravagant meal I'm preparing – the lemon thyme cost a fortune and it took me hours to fully understand the Jamie Oliver recipe I Googled – even though he says it's the most basic, standard recipe he's ever written.

'Kids back safe and sound, then?' She looks up at the ceiling when we hear a loud thud.

'Yeah, thank God.'

'Why thank God?'

'Oh, nothing. I was just taken aback by how much I missed them, really. And how much I hated not seeing their little faces all day, nagging them to pick their clothes up off the floor and brush their teeth or whatever.'

'Flushing their poo away when they don't, clearing up their vomit after yet another food poisoning debacle, rushing them to A&E when they fall out of a tree...'

'Well, I didn't miss any of that, obviously. I dunno – I missed them just being around, basically, and not being the main influence over them, not being in control.'

'Ha! Who's ever in control?'

'You know what I mean.'

'I guess, when marriages break down—'

'Ooh, can we just call it "coming to its natural conclusion" or something?'

'When marriages *fail*,' she goes on with a wink, 'and there are kids involved, the one who ends up looking after the kids is really the lucky one. I almost felt a bit sorry for Joe then. He thinks he's hit the jackpot and can do whatever he wants without the burden of a family, but one day he'll regret not having been around them full-time.'

'I don't know about that,' I say. 'I'm not sure he's deep enough to think about things like that. He'll just be happy that he can go down the pub whenever he wants, and not have anyone to answer to, not get nagged into doing anything he doesn't want to do. Like, I used to say to him, "Do you want to take Ben to the park? Play a bit of football with him?" And he wouldn't even look up or take his eyes off his computer screen. He'd just say, "No." '

'Ooh,' Jane squints and screws up her nose as she takes a sip of tea. 'Cold.'

'Oh, sorry about that – I thought it had boiled. I still can't work out that sodding kettle!'

'The *tea* is hot – I meant Joe's *behaviour* was cold, you donut!'

At that, Izzy and Ben come tumbling down the stairs, keen to find out whether I'm talking to myself, as is my wont, or whether, indeed, we have a visitor.

'Hey, hey! Here they are, the loves of my life!'

My lively little chicks get all shy and snuggle under my (bingo) wings for safety.

'Ben, Izzy – this is Jane. She lives next door and has a five-year-old son called Jack and a little girl, Jess, who's two.'

'Hi Jane,' they say sweetly in unison. Butter wouldn't melt.

'Have you guys been at your daddy's this weekend?' Jane asks them.

'Yeah!' they say in unison again.

'Mummy, you should see Daddy's new house!' Izzy jumps up and down on the spot a bit while hanging onto the kitchen table. 'It's got a balcony and huge electronic iron gates to keep the riff-raff out and there are swans on the river and there are two bathrooms—'

'Gated development, huh?' Jane nods slowly, glancing at me.

'Yeah,' Izzy says. 'And did I say he has two bathrooms?'

'We have two bathrooms here!' My back's immediately up. 'And we've got swans, down by the river, just a few short blocks away—'

'And Daddy has his own bedroom,' Izzy goes on. 'And a walk-in closet and a dining room and chandeliers and—'

'TVs and computers in EVERY room, Mummy – and an XBOX in mine!' Ben's entranced.

I feel a sting of envy for a second – and then tell myself it's the screens they love most of all in this battle for the kids' affections.

'Can we play on the laptop, Mummy?' Izzy asks.

'Okay – as long as you're not playing *Halo* or whatever violent, bloody game you play on the Xbox at Daddy's.'

'*Halo*! Yesss!' Ben punches the air.

'*Halo*?' Jane nearly spits her tea out in shock. 'Isn't that a bit full-on for a five-year-old?'

'Well, *obviously*, it is – but Joe doesn't care what he plonks Ben in front of as long as it keeps him entertained and Joe can get on with whatever it is *he's* doing. Shirking responsibilities and looking at porn, mainly,' I say under my breath so the kids don't hear.

Jane shakes her head in resigned despair and Izzy shoots me daggers.

'We'll just get onto *Kizi* and play the free, family-friendly games, don't worry,' she sighs.

'Yep, fine. You can sort it out, can't you Izz? And when I say it's time for dinner, I want you two to come straight away. I don't want to hear any whining, okay?'

'Okaaaay,' they chorus and run into the front room, where the laptop is sitting on the couch.

'The good old square au pair,' Jane nods as she watches them go to rack up some serious screen time. 'You've got two lovely kids there – you're doing a great job, you know.'

'Really? You think so?' Clearly I'm fishing for compliments at this point.

'Yeah! They seem sweet and well-adjusted. All down to you, I don't doubt.'

'Not according to Joe.' I purse my lips. 'The way he tells it, I'm a crap parent, who sits around all day watching Jeremy Kyle, waiting to see if any of my deadbeat mates appear in the stage. He says I don't know what hard work is. Reckons I'm lazy.'

'Tosser,' Jane tuts, rolling her eyes.

'I think he really believes it, too. Which makes me even more determined to do well at this whole single mum lark.'

'You go, girlfriend!' Jane holds her cup aloft in cheers.

'So tell me – what gives you the balls to stand up to Joe like that? In a way I don't think I'll *ever* be able to.'

'You will,' she says, taking a sip of her tea. 'You just need to get your mojo back.'

She lets such a warm, comforting, reassuring smile spread across her face, that I don't doubt for a second that she's right.

'So why *did* you stand up to Joe like that?' I ask.

'I just can't stand to see men pushing women around, basically. My parents split up when I was Izzy's age and I swore that if I was ever married, I'd never let a man manipulate me or gaslight me like my dad did to my mum. He didn't push her around physically – that I ever saw – but emotionally. He convinced her she was mad and he really wasn't sleeping with half the women he met on his business trips, it was just her imagination.'

'So it wasn't? Her imagination, I mean?'

'Well, only if the herpes and chlamydia she suffered with were in her imagination, too.'

'That must've been hard for you – but I guess you didn't know it at the time, being only nine years old.'

'Oh, I knew,' she says. 'I knew he was a philanderer who had other girlfriends and had given Mum some nasty STDs.'

'How?'

'Because Mum told me.'

'Really?'

'Yeah,' she smiles as though she's recalling the memory as she runs her finger around the rim of her mug. 'I didn't really know what it all meant at that age, but Mum was always straight with us kids. When they divorced, Mum got tough, fast. She told us why she'd booted Dad out and we all just kind of got on with it.'

'Wow,' I sigh. 'I never know how to tell the kids tricky stuff – or even whether to say anything at all.'

'You must always tell them the truth. Okay, you don't have to go into the gory details, but you must always be honest with them. Don't try to sugar-coat things. Just give them the facts. They're not stupid and they'll know things are going on and if you don't tell them the truth, they'll make up all sorts of crazy stuff in their heads and that's when the real trauma begins.'

'Good advice,' I nod sagely, 'I suppose you're right.'

'Of course I'm right! Now I'd better run, Jack and the kids'll be back soon. And is something burning? I'll let myself out – thanks for the tea!'

Bunch of arse!

I leap up and run over to the cooker. It's one of those bulky, ad-in-the-back-of-*Country Living* magazine RangeMasters that, I have to admit, is extremely good-looking, but it's so bloody powerful, it's hard to get the timings and temperatures just right. Too efficient for its own good. *Our* own good, I mean.

Luckily, only the unwaxed-lemon half and sprigs of lemon thyme sitting on top of the chicken have burned – the rest looks just perfect.

'I'll just bung on the Aunt Bessie's and it'll be ready in ten!' I yell out to the kids.

I admire my handiwork. Doesn't look much like the pic on the recipe, but it's not a million miles away from it either. And it smells *gorgeous*.

Once the puds are ready and I've made a pretty good gravy (if I do say so myself), I dish it up, take it to the table and wait for the rapturous applause.

'Is that a real chicken?' Ben asks, peering at the carcass on the kitchen bench, prodding the meat on his plate with a fork.

'Der – *no,*' Izzy teases, 'it's plastic.'

'The poor chicken! I don't want to eat it, Mummy. Can I have chips?'

Jane's words about wasting good food on unappreciative children ring in my ears.

'No!' I'm surprisingly upset by this. 'I made this from scratch! I've been slaving over a hot stove all afternoon to create this… this… five-star feast for you! And all you can say is: "Can I have chips?"'

I don't sound like myself, but I do sound familiar… Mum! I sound just like my mum when I was a nipper!

'Well, can I?' Ben stares up at me with his big brown eyes while Izzy looks on, keen to see which way I'll go.

'I said no.' I thrust my nose in the air, proud of myself for sticking to my guns.

'Only because we don't *have* any chips,' Izzy points out. 'You shouldn't jump to his every request, Mummy. You'll just spoil him. He should have to eat whatever you make, like the rest of us. Tell him the kitchen's now closed.'

'I don't need parenting tips from you!' I pretend to be offended, even though she's obviously right and any parenting tips from *anyone* are always gratefully received. 'I know how to handle my own son, thank you very much. Now. How about… bread and gravy?'

'Ha! Highly nutritious for a growing boy,' Izzy says, shoving a whole Yorkshire pudding into her mouth.

Soon, however, it's bathtime and as I wash the smell of Joe's aftershave out of Ben's hair, we discuss the plan for tomorrow morning.

'So. We have to get up at six, get dressed in your lovely new uniform, have breakfast, brush teeth, pack lunch – oh, wait, you have school dinners now, don't you? Chips! Yay!'

'Yay!' Ben agrees.

'Now. We have to be in the car by five to eight so we can leave by eight. On the dot! We can't get caught up in traffic and be late on your first day at your new school, can we?'

Ben shakes his head from side to side as if he knows or, indeed, cares what I'm on about.

He's dried, in his PJs and scrunched down under his brushed cotton duvet. He's dog-tired, but never even closes his eyes until I'm reading to him.

I pick up *Schnitzel Von Krumm* (with the very low tum) and read it as though it's the first time we've come across this story and not, as it actually is, the trillionth. When I finish, I look next to me and see that Ben's flat out. I try to get up, but his hand shoots out from under the duvet and grabs my arm. It's like that bit at the end of the original *Carrie* movie, when Carrie's dead arm shoots up through the dirt on top of her grave.

I yelp. His eyes flip open.

'Stay with me, Mummy. Please?'

'Okay,' I say. 'But I have to go and do stuff soon, so get to sleep quick.'

I lie there, thinking about Joe and how he can bugger off. Mercifully, he's quickly replaced by Jane, Sue and Liz in my mind's eye and I smile, wondering whether I might actually have made some new friends.

The next thing I know, Izzy's pulling me out of Ben's bed.

'You've been up here for aaages! It's special time with me now – come downstairs!'

'Shhhh. I must've fallen asleep! Sorry sweetie,' I yawn.

'Not FAIR!' she yells and runs off into the en suite.

'Oh, come on, Izzy! There's still time. Tell you what, why don't we have a look at pictures of puppies, eh? We can see which ones we like the best and I shall make enquiries!'

'In a MINUTE!' she yells.

When I get downstairs and sit in front of the laptop, Messenger is open on the screen. Izzy's been having an online conversation with Joe. I know it's private and I really, really shouldn't, but I can't help reading what they've written:

Joe: What are you doing up so late, gorgeous?

Izzy: I'm bored.

Joe: Where's Mummy?

Izzy: With Ben of course.

Joe: Everyone's up so late!

Izzy: No, Ben's asleep. And so is Mummy. She's sleeping next to him. She is SOOOO lazy. I hate her.

Joe: Hmmm. Time for bed. Night night. Love you xxx

'What the—?' I pull my chin way back into my neck, probably making me look more like a fat buddha than usual, such is the force of my shock and disbelief.

'Isabelle Josephine Cartwright! Get down here this minute!'

I'm struck, for a second, by just how ridiculous it is that the kids don't have my last name anywhere in their names. It seems ludicrous, really. I did all the hard work, let's face it, but I don't even get name-checked.

'What is it? I'm really tired.' A sleepy Izzy slides onto my lap.

'What the *hell* are you saying about me to Daddy on Messenger?'

I don't give her a chance to answer.

'You're saying I'm lazy! Me! Your mother! The one who does everything for you, the one who loves you beyond all reason, no matter how much we argue – me!'

'I was joking?' she says, her voice raising at the end, so it sounds like a question.

'The hell you were. You were trying to bond with Daddy by bitching about me, playing us off against each other! Weren't you? You've heard him call me lazy before, you know that's what he mistakenly thinks. Well, I may be exhausted, I may be stressed, I may be frustrated as FUCK, but one thing I most certainly am not, young lady, is lazy!'

I don't know where on earth I manage to dredge these words up from, but I'm pretty damn impressed with myself, let me tell you. Apart from swearing, obviously.

Izzy's eyes hop back and forth between mine, searching for some sign of the old mum, the old pushover welcome mat mum she's used to wrapping around her little finger.

But I'm fuming and she can sense the futility of resistance, so her face crumples and she hangs her head, butting softly into my shoulder while she sobs.

'I'm sorry,' she wails. 'I heard you talking with Jane and… I'm sorry.'

I stay silent for a bit until I've fully calmed down. Then I tell her it's been an emotional few days, we're all knackered and it's high time she was asleep, too, getting some much-needed rest for the big day tomorrow.

Once upstairs, it doesn't take long before she's gone off to Noddington, cradled in my arms, holding her favourite cuddly toy puppy tight. And once I'm convinced she's not going to suddenly open her eyes or anything else scary, I go downstairs to get changed, brush my teeth and set up the sofa bed. But before I turn out the light, I open up the laptop, get into The Ten Commandments document and type:

2. **Thou shalt not badmouth thine ex in front of thy kids – even if thine Ex hast been a bit of a dick.**

–

Three upbeat, positive things so far:

- Wasn't Jane impressive? And what a great tip about being honest with the kids.
- I made a roast chicken. So nobody liked it and I ate the whole thing – who cares? I actually followed a recipe and did it, no matter how daunting it was.
- I stood up for myself and put Izzy straight on a few things. I also recognise that Izzy wasn't really bitching about me (although, technically, she was), she was merely expressing her jealousy of Ben and her distress over the divorce. Which, I believe, is the emotionally healthy thing to do, as opposed to harbouring grudges and internalising trauma. In other words, better out than in.

January 8 – Step We Gaily

Of course, the kids were nigh on *impossible* to raise out of their beds this morning. Mind you, I was none too happy about my phone alarm going off at sparrow's fart, either.

Needless to say, our collective mood was as dark as the pitch-black morning outside as I shouted at the kids to 'Bloody well move it and a-groove it, for fsssssss!' followed by the unmistakeable groans of intense displeasure bouncing off the walls.

It takes a while for us all to thaw out, but the icicles melt somewhat when I move the heater into the kitchen, turn it on full blast to the Mt Etna setting and present my brood with two big, steaming bowls of Ready Brek.

'MUM!' she wails. 'It's eight o'clock already! We're going to be SO LATE!'

She's practically in tears as we scatter to our various panic stations: me to the hooks on the back of the front door to grab our coats, Izzy to her new enormous Smiggle rucksack sitting on the kitchen floor and Ben up the stairs, Izzy's scream scaring the Ready Brek out of him. Not literally, though, thankfully.

'Ben!' I bellow. 'Get down here! Let's GO!'

'I knew it, I knew it!' Izzy gets hysterical. 'I knew we'd be late – we're ALWAYS late! For everything! And it's ALL YOUR FAULT!'

'Shhh for a second, Izz.'

She breathes heavily through her nose, like a dragon whose fire has just gone out, and in the distance we hear soft sniffs and quiet cries.

'Ben?' I say soothingly as I ascend the Stairs of Doom. 'Sweetie pie?'

I turn left at the top of the stairs and see a mound under his duvet rising and falling in time with its sobs.

'Oh, baby – what's the matter?'

He doesn't answer – and why the hell should he? He's only five, for Christ's sake! He hasn't got a clue what all this is about – why his daddy isn't here with him, why he has to go to a new school, why his mother's singing songs in an Indian accent...

I sit on the edge of the bed.

'Come here, beautiful boy,' I coo, 'come out from under there and give me a cuddle. Please? Mummy needs a cuddle.'

This is actually true, I realise in that moment.

'Mummy needs a cuddle – but not just from anyone – it *has* to be from Ben.'

Nothing. No change.

'Babe, I know this is really hard and nothing makes much sense right now, but things are going to get easier and better and loads more fun – I promise!'

I attack him à la Tickle Monster and he writhes about under the covers, laughing so much, I fear he'll asphyxiate.

When most of Ben's breakfast is plastered all over the table, floor and walls, I decide it's time to quickly get him upstairs and dressed for the day. But it's never quick enough for Izzy.

'WHEN YOU'RE READY!' she yells up at us from downstairs.

'Bugger!' I jeté off the bed. 'Come on darl, let's go!'

Buckling Ben into his car seat in the back, I can't even be arsed to argue with Izzy about plonking herself into the front passenger seat without so much as a by your leave. So when I've done it, I run around the back of the car and hop in to the driver's seat, turning the key in the ignition and the heating on to full.

And that's when I notice I can't see a bloody thing out of the windscreen. The layer of frost covering it is so deep, I think I'm going to need a pick axe, hiking boots and a sherpa to de-ice it.

'Wait here!' I say, unnecessarily, and run back into the house.

I wet a tea towel under the kitchen tap and carry it, dripping all over the floor, back to the car. As I hum 'Marie's Wedding', I throw the tea towel onto the windscreen with a flourish that would make any caber-tosser proud. In fact, I smile to myself, that's exactly what I must look like right now. Without the beard. And the kilt. Okay, okay… without the kilt.

Which reminds me. As soon as the kids are in school, I'm going to check out my hair removal options in Old Stoke. As well as sort out the dentist, doctor and getting the handyman around to fix whatever's wrong with the heating.

That is, if we ever get to school, I think, as we wait at least five minutes before someone lets us into the line of cars in front of our place that's moving slower than a snail on a tea break.

But once we're in that line and on the road for real, things calm down a bit.

'Keep your eyes peeled for foxes and squirrels—'

'And deer!' Ben adds. 'Granddad saw a Bambi, didn't he, Mummy?'

'Yes he did, darl,' I confirm. 'And take in the stunning scenery, too – we are so lucky to live here, aren't we? I mean, get a lungful of that air, why don'cha – it's fresher than a box of Persil!'

I put my window down and exaggerate taking a deep breath in.

'Mmmm! Now that's what I call—'

'CLOSE YOUR WINDOW,' the kids scream at me, 'IT'S FREEZING!'

I do as I'm told and concentrate on the road for the rest of the trip, marvelling (inwardly) at just how gorgeous the Chilterns are, despite not knowing what an actual 'chiltern' is. I mean, is it a type of hill? A particular kind of soil or grass? Maybe it's just someone's last name…?

'Who cares?' Izzy groans, turning the radio on and re-tuning to Radio 1 once she hears the serious, boring, droney voice of some poor old person on Radio 4.

So much for thinking inwardly! God knows what other things I've thought I was merely thinking, but have actually, inadvertently, said out loud.

'Only boring stuff,' she says.

Now this is getting creepy.

—

We get to the school car park just as most of the other cars are leaving – which means the bell's already gone. Bit of a bummer, that – but at least we get a parking space, right next to the big gates, so all is not lost.

'I can't believe you made us late,' Izzy says as she's getting out of the car, casually hoiking one strap of her backpack over her shoulder.

'Yeah, Mum,' Ben smiles and sticks his hand out for me to hold, as I stare at Izzy and point the key to the car, locking it with an unnecessarily fierce pinch of the key fob.

We go into the front office and the receptionist is as frosty in the flesh as she was over the phone. This sort of behaviour always makes me nervous – I buy into their assumption of superiority, like they know something I don't and they're a hundred times better than me. In every way.

'Can I help you?' she purses her whole face, looking the three of us up and down.

'I hope so!' I flash her what I think is a winning smile, but she simply stares me down for a few seconds, not even blinking once. 'Ah, my kids are starting today – Izzy is in year four and Ben is in year one. We're the Cartwrights? Well, actually, *these* two are the Cartwrights – I didn't change my name when we got married, so

I'm still Beaton. Once a Beaton, always a Beaton! Or, as one of my best friends always says, "Beaton by name, not by nature"! Yeah… It's good though, because, now we're divorced, I don't have to faff around with any of that legal palaver, changing my name back, re-naming my social media accounts etc. Not that I have any social media accounts – bit of a Luddite, me – although I do have Facebook, it's true. I rarely put anything up on it, of course, but I do admit to the odd bout of Facebook envy when I see what some of my old friends from school are up to—'

'MUM!' Izzy elbows me.

'You do know the bell's gone?' the ice queen says, sounding more like Maggie Smith in *Downton Abbey* every time she speaks.

'Yes, but—'

'Follow me,' she sighs, like it's the biggest inconvenience ever.

She leads us to Izzy's classroom first, and before I get a chance to kiss her goodbye and wish her luck, she sprints into the room and sits down at the back of the big rug next to some very friendly-looking girls.

I try to catch her eye and wave, but she refuses to look at me, instead staring straight ahead, looking at the whiteboard, hoping beyond all hope that I'll give up and leave her alone.

Which of course I do virtually immediately. I know when I'm not wanted. Sometimes.

When we get to Ben's class, the teacher stands up, introduces Ben to everyone and assigns him a 'buddy', a sweet-looking lad who'll show Ben where the loos are and where to hang his coat and bag.

I watch as his buddy puts a protective arm around Ben's shoulder and leads him to the spare seat next to him at his table, and my eyes fill to the brim with tears.

'Let them get on with it,' Maggie snaps, walking back to the front office. 'Now, normally this is a parent-free zone. The bell goes at eight fifty on the dot and pick up is at twenty past three precisely. Good day, Miss Beaton. Or is it Ms?'

I can tell she's not remotely interested in the answer, because she smirks and shuffles the paper about on her desk, letting me know I'm dismissed. She's clearly got important stuff to do and couldn't, quite frankly, give a toss whether I'm a miss, a ms, a missus or, indeed, a mister.

So I thrust my nose in the air and sniff, desperately trying to wrest back some dignity and stop my nose running like mad, as it always does when I cry.

Back in the car, I sit in silence for a minute, thinking. After all the chaos and clutter of the last few weeks, we've finally done it: we've moved house, got into a new school, driven down scary country roads, ditched the deadbeat dad—

And that's when I dissolve.

Hands on the steering wheel, chin pulled into my chest, I start blubbing for Britain, big tear drops falling onto my not-particularly-waterproof parka. Those poor, brave kids! Everyone says children are resilient little creatures and bounce back surprisingly well from things like divorce and/or crap parenting, but Izzy seems so angry and Ben's terrified all the time – what have I done to them?

The weather seems to match my mood and the sky turns almost black, a nanosecond before I hear rain pounding on the roof of the car.

Lightning flashes and thunder roars, making me forget myself for a moment and marvel at the forces of nature surrounding me.

My mobile rings and I see on the screen it's Aisling. Ha! Finally, a friend! But I'm sure I've heard somewhere that you can get electrocuted if you're on a mobile in a thunderstorm. And even though I'm in the car, isn't metal a conductor? So, like, if lightning struck the car, beams of electricity would leap to the phone, burning my hand and killing me stone dead on the spot, right? Actually, Aisling would know, having done a PhD in astrophysics – but I'm not going to take any chances and ask her now. In this weather? You must be crazy!

Buoyed by the fact that one of my best friends has remembered me and even tried to call me, I wipe my eyes and blow my nose. Weirdly enough, when I open my eyes after blowing my nose, I can see the rain's eased off, see the sky has brightened a bit and I notice a weak rainbow appearing in the distance.

I smile the kind of smile one does when one's looking at puppies.

Which is exactly what I'll do when I get home. Look at pictures of puppies, I mean. And call Aisling back. Full morning ahead of me, then!

I start the car up, put Radio 4 back on and manoeuvre past all the haphazardly parked Range Rovers, BMWs and Mercedes, out of the car park.

Passing through all the pretty chocolate-box villages on the way home cheers me no end. Speaking of chocolate boxes, as we so very often are, I remind myself to stop off for a box of Cadbury's Heroes from the Co-op. And before I know it, my inner Pollyanna resurfaces and I just know everything's going to be fine. In fact, it's going to be brilliant from now on, every day full of joy and laughter. I can practically feel it in my bones!

–

Three upbeat, positive things so far:
- The scenery around here is breathtakingly beautiful.
- I noticed a rainbow – and it made me smile.
- We were a bit late, but we made it to the school in one piece, without any panic attacks whatsoever.

–

January 27 – For the Love of Pete!

'Long time, no interest from you whatsoever,' I say to Aisling in mock umbrage when she answers her phone.

'I'm so sorry, Annie,' she says, sounding genuinely apologetic, 'but things have been so hectic—'

'Tell me about it!'

'I was just about to, if you'd let me—'

'Honestly, Ash, you should see the countryside up here – it's *stunning*. It's like we're living in an old episode of *All Creatures Great and Small* or something – without anyone's arm disappearing up a cow's backside at regular intervals, obvs, but you know – the views!'

'It sounds gor—'

'And the people!' I gush further. 'I mean, who'd have thought country bumpkins could be so nice and friendly and funny and just… just wonderful, really. Yesterday afternoon, in fact—'

'Can you take a breath for a second?'

'Sorry, yeah – whoo. Slow down, relax… it's all been so full-on! There's so much to tell you, so many things I need your advice on – when are you and the boys coming down to stay? Not that we have enough duvets and the heating's still up the spout, but—'

'Will you FECKIN' SHUT UP, Annie?'

'Alright, alright. Jeez, no need for—'

'Pete's having an affair,' she says, all matter-of-fact and monotone.

'What?'

'Or at least I think he is.'

'Who with?'

'Some woman at work.'

'Some young popsie who's not completely knackered from raising his beautiful but rambunctious children, eh?'

'No, but he is her boss. Jill's her name. I think she's actually older than me. Which is saying something…'

Aisling's a petite, auburn-haired beauty who's fifty, but looks thirty-five, thanks to her fair Gaelic genes, always keeping out of the sun, doing yoga four times a week, drinking more water than you'd think humanly possible and virtually being a breatharian, considering she won't eat salt, meat, eggs, dairy, wheat, gluten or anything else that might give her food some flavour.

'God, really? Are you sure? About him having an affair, I mean – not about her being older than you…'

'Not a hundred per cent, no – but there are some pretty unmistakeable signs there, I think. God, how could I have been so stupid?'

'You're not stupid! You've got a PhD in astrophysics!'

'Well, that was a long time ago – and anyway, I must be as thick as feckin' mince not to see what a lying, cheating prick Pete has become.'

I wince at this, because Pete hasn't just become a lying, cheating prick – he's always been one. Thing is, no one's ever had the heart to tell Aisling of his dalliances, for fear of bursting her perfect world view, sullying her sunny disposition and souring her sweet outlook on life. Well, *that* – and the fact that no one's ever been able to get any hard evidence on him.

Apart from, maybe, all those times he made blatant passes at Amelie – or was it sexual assault? Bit of both, probably. But in those days, at uni in the late eighties, that sort of behaviour was dismissed as merely misjudged lunges and harmless, though unwanted, arse-squeezes.

I remember one time in particular. We were all at the uni bar, getting bladdered on a 'Jazz 'n' Jug' night, as was one of our monthly rituals as an undergraduate gang, (the other rituals mainly involving copious quantities of alcohol – tequila slammer nights etc – and endless recrimination-filled next-day post mortems, spending hours trying to unravel the goings on of the night before – like trying to undo a Gordian knot of debauchery).

It was always a big laugh and a huge thrill, that feeling of collective risk, gambling on the unknown (i.e. who would make the bigger tit out of themselves and who would get off with who) and not having to think about the consequences until… well, if you didn't remember it, it didn't happen, so if you were lucky, you never had to think about the consequences.

When Pete made his play for Amelie, I was the only one who clocked it. And I was either too far gone to say anything at the time – or too shocked to believe it was really happening. But there he was, nuzzling into her neck, his hand running up her thigh, disappearing under the folds of her ra-ra skirt. At this point, Ash was dancing up a storm to the generic jazz with one of her many admirers, as she always did when she'd had a skinful.

Amelie slowly pushed his hand away and turned her back on Pete, trying to resume flirting with Tom, the BMOC (Big Man On Campus) of our year, all shoulders and biceps, his incessant rugby-playing giving him the physique someone lanky and bespectacled like Pete could only envy. Amelie had been smitten with Tom ever since she'd laid eyes on him in 'O' Week, Orientation week in our first year.

Tom was a nice enough guy and a big hit with the ladies, but he left me cold. Too perfect-looking, like he'd never had to try (apart from on the rugby field) at anything, never knowing what it felt like to be rejected, never getting anything lower than a 'B' and never, ever, facing the mortification of waking up and finding a painful blind pimple on his manly, dimpled chin.

He was a hero to men and a hunk to women – but he just didn't do it for me. Bet he was devastated.

So anyway, back at the bar in 1987, Amelie was batting Pete's hand away from her bum, while simultaneously flicking her hair and batting her eyelashes at Tom. She's always been a real multi-tasker, has our Amelie – with an eye for the lads and a lust for life (or is it the other way round?) that's still getting her into trouble to this day.

Anyway, Pete was hammered, and kept manhandling Amelie, unable to take no for an answer. Until Tom reached over Amelie's shoulder and put his hand up right in front of Pete's floppy face. Now, I'm no expert lip-reader or anything, and my memory is hazy at best, but I'm pretty sure Tom shouted something like, 'piss off will you, mate?'

Pete swerved away from Tom's hand and undeterred, kept going at Amelie. Tom, taller than average and, as I alluded to before, built like a brick shithouse, put his hand on top of Pete's head, so that they looked like Scooby-Doo holding back an overly enthusiastic Scrappy-Doo.

Amelie wisely scooted out of the way and Tom ended up carrying Pete out of the bar, setting him onto the grass in the beer garden and turning the hose on him. Pete was, quite literally, hosed out of the bar.

No one ever told Aisling about this and she never knew.

Pete was always causing a ruckus like that – if it wasn't Amelie, it was some other poor, unsuspecting girl. There were rumours he was constantly shagging, but he always came up smelling of roses in Aisling's eyes. She truly believed she'd found her Prince Charming and no one had the guts to disabuse her of that notion. Not even me. And certainly not Amelie, even though she hated finding herself the object of Pete's desire. I know, I know – we were her best friends, we should have known better, done the right thing and told her.

I guess we just couldn't bear to see her hurt. Pete has always been in the ascendancy of his and Ash's relationship, what with his wandering eye, wandering hands and firm knowledge that even if word *did* get back to Aisling about his infidelities, she would forgive him in a trice and before you could say 'genital warts' it'd be back to business as usual.

I've always thought that while Pete is an unreliable, sleazy waste of space to all of *us*, to Ash, he's *her* unreliable, sleazy waste of space. And he is very funny. Not that that's any kind of excuse or anything, it's just that she, adopted at birth, would be irreparably broken by his betrayal, even if she took him back.

So anyway, to cut a long story short, I'm perhaps not quite as surprised by Ash's suspicions as she expects me to be.

'I can't believe it!' she says again. 'I'm going to kill him!'

'Steady on, Ash – you don't even know he is playing away for sure yet. What makes you think he is?'

While I tuck into some Tunnock's Tea Cakes, she tells me how he closes his laptop and looks guilty every time she walks into the room and then, when she questions him, he says she's mad, where would he find the time to have an affair and the only reason he closes his laptop is because he knows that she thinks he spends too much time online and her presence reminds him of that and he's trying to do the right thing and anyway, why would he go out to eat a kebab when he could have steak at home?

Personally, I think to myself, I'd prefer the kebab, steak looking far too much like what it actually is, for my often verging-on-vegetarian tastes.

'It's nice he thinks of me as a classy steak as opposed to a cheap, nasty kebab, I suppose,' Aisling says, as if being likened to a hunk of meat is some kind of compliment or something, 'but if that really is the case, why do I get the feeling that things just aren't right? What can I do to fix them? Do you think I should have a boob job?'

This really is unlike the Aisling I know and love – so confident, so sure of herself, so real and earth-mothery.

Now's my chance. I gird my loins, picture Helen Reddy singing 'I Am Woman' in some fabulously hideous seventies outfit, think of the sisterhood, take a deep breath and launch into it.

'Firstly, Ash, it could be true about the laptop and stuff – but I don't like that he says you're acting crazy – that sounds a bit like gaslighting to me. Secondly, don't be ridiculous! A boob job, indeed! You look fab, just the way you are. And thirdly, if he *is* having an affair, that would be something I would imagine he's thought long and hard about doing, weighing up the pros and cons, calculating the risk and, ultimately deciding to go for it, irrespective of his wife and kids—'

'We're not married, remember?' she interrupts me.

'Wife, girlfriend, whatever. The point is, he's a fifty-two-year-old man, a grown up with two kids, a mortgage, a good job and responsibilities coming out of his kazoo.'

Aisling blows her nose loudly, the nasal equivalent of putting her hands over her ears and going 'la la la la' in a bid to not hear the truth, so I raise my voice.

'SO IF HE IS HAVING AN AFFAIR, IT'S PRE-MEDITATED, NOT A SILLY ONE-NIGHT STAND HE BITTERLY REGRETS...'

She lets out a wail.

'But he'd never do that to me – to us. We may not be married, but we have kids and that's a way bigger commitment than a piece of paper! Isn't it?'

'Well, to *you* maybe,' I shut my eyes tight in anticipation, 'but he's never wanted to get married, has he? I mean, *you* do, you've even been quite obsessed by the idea from time to time, every time you go on holiday, thinking this is the one he'll propose to you on, this is it. But it never has been, has it?'

'No, not so far, no.'

'He always says he doesn't want to get married because he couldn't bear it if it didn't work out and you ended up getting divorced, doesn't he?'

'He does, yes,' Ash says softly. 'But that's because his brother got divorced and he's seen how it can destroy a family, so, you know, I get that.'

'No you bloody well don't! Stop making excuses for him. Divorce doesn't ruin families – people do! And if he's having an affair, that's exactly what he's doing. With his eyes wide open.'

She considers this briefly.

'And speaking as someone who *is* divorced, I can tell you it doesn't even have to ruin a family – Joe and I will one day be better friends than we ever were, once our decree absolute arrives and I've got a high-paying job and—'

'We're not talking about you two, though, are we? We're talking about Pete and I!'

'Pete and *me*,' I correct her.

'Still a grammar nazi, then?'

She doesn't wait for my reply.

'But I don't want to be a single mum! Even if he is having an affair, I couldn't bear to break up our happy home!'

'Happy, is it?' I hear the sneer in my own voice.

'Mostly,' she says. 'When he's there with us.'

'Which is how often?'

'He has a lot of pressure at work, you know – he hates it, but he has to go on business trips to New York a lot. It's been Paris and Berlin a bit lately, too. But he doesn't want to go, he hates being away from us.'

'Really?' I probe. 'How do you know?'

'Well, he's always texting me, saying how much he misses us...'

'Does he ever actually call? Does he say he loves you?'

'Sometimes. Sort of...' her voice trails off. 'No, not really. But he's never been a big one for saying soppy stuff like that, he's more of a do-er than a say-er. And I'd hate to interrupt him in a meeting or something, so we've agreed I should never call.'

'I see,' I say, my heart sinking for her, 'and what's he like when he comes back from these business trips that he hates so much?'

'Oh, he's absolutely shattered. They make him go out and drink till the wee small hours, just to keep the suppliers happy, you know. He has to go on a yacht next month, with the big boss, sailing around Positano. He's dreading it.'

'I bet he is,' I can't help but snark, going outside to smoke myself stupid.

'But even though he's knackered, he can't seem to get enough of me. In bed, I mean. That's how I know he's really missed me. And he's just the perfect dad, too, spending loads of time with the boys, going to the park, riding bikes...'

'When was the last time you two went out? On your own, just the pair of you? To dinner or even a caff for a cuppa?'

She's silent for a bit.

'Not for ages,' she says.

'Why not?'

'It's more me than him, I think. I'm just so tired looking after the boys all day, trying to keep the house clean and tidy, make delicious, nutritious meals for them – I don't really feel like going out much anymore.'

'Know what you mean – I'd rather demolish a packet of Fondant Fancies and sleep. Even the thought of getting all dolled up and changing out of my leggings leaves me in a cold sweat.'

'Ha! Also, Annie,' she says in a whisper, 'I looked on his laptop last night when he went swimming with the kids and I found a Facebook page dedicated to their company, a closed group thing. He'd only just left, so he was still logged on. There's no one else on this page, there are only two members, Jill and Pete. I read the messages that had been flying between them, only minutes before and… oh God! He's definitely having it off with her!'

'What do they say? The messages?'

'Like he can't wait to see her and she makes him so hot – you know, the usual. But the last message is a selfie of her. She sent him a picture of herself, pouting with her huge lips and squeezing her massive boobs together, so she looks like Katie Price out on a bender. She'd drawn an arrow to her cleavage and written, "Insert your lovely cock here".'

I can't speak. Ash can't speak. For about thirty seconds, before she starts crying.

'Oh, Annie,' she sobs, 'I don't want to be a single mu-hu-hum!'

'Why not? It's great!' I pick my jaw off the floor. 'You don't have to worry about what some stupid bloke's up to, you just get on with it. And hey! If worse comes to worst, you can always move down here and live with us – we could be single mums in the country together. Just like the old days! It'd be a right laugh!'

'Yeah, hilarious,' she says, deadpan.

'Jeez, Ash – you really saved the best for last, didn't you? I mean, talk about incriminating evidence—'

'Look, I've got to go – I've got to clean myself up and get to a school concert in fifteen minutes. The kids need to see at least one of their parents there, supporting them. Pete's got back-to-back meetings on today, so he won't be home till late...'

'Right, well. Don't do anything rash and don't, whatever you do, let on to Pete that you know what he's up to. And call me whenever you want to talk – or even if you don't want to talk, give me a call anyway. Hang on in there, Ash, lots of love.'

As I take the phone away from my ear, milliseconds before I press the red end call button, I hear her saying:

'So do *you* think he's having an affair then?'

I feel a bolt of sadness shoot through me as my fingers fail to react in time and I cut her off.

'Well of *course* he bloody well is,' I say to myself and light another cigarette, pondering my next move.

–

Once I'm back inside, feeling no difference in air temperature whatsoever, I call the local handyman, Paul.

He's at our place in seconds flat, which is totally unexpected, being used, as I am, to London tradies requiring three weeks' notice for an emergency call out.

And while he's busy checking the boiler and running up and down the stairs, twiddling knobs on the radiators, I Google solicitors in the area, determined to a) support local business and b) get rid of my London solicitor who did sod all for me, apart from sending me the Form E to fill out and sign at the same time as his whopping great invoice.

As luck would have it, there's an actual solicitor, specialising in divorce and family law, practising right here in little Old Stoke. So I give him a quick ring, see if he can make sense of all this financial remedy/maintenance debacle.

'Hello?' a surprised voice says.

'Oh, hello there,' I begin, 'I was wondering whether I could speak to James Raphael, please.'

'Certainly.' I hear glass smashing in the background. 'Who shall I say is calling?'

'My name's Annie. Annie Beaton.'

'And can I tell him what your call is about?'

'I'm new to the village and I'm getting divorced and I wonder whether I could just ask for a bit of advice, a bit of clarification on a financial remedy, just so I can be sure I'm not in breach of anything and to check that—'

'Sorry to stop you, madam,' he croaks, 'but let me get this straight. You want to instruct me as your solicitor?'

'You're James Raphael?'

'Ah, please hold the line,' he says, putting what sounds like his hand over the receiver so that the connection goes all muffled in my ear.

'Ahem,' the same voice clears its throat, 'how can I help you, Mrs Beaton?'

'It's Ms, actually.'

'As you wish,' he says, sounding like Westley in *The Princess Bride*.

'Well, yes, I suppose I do want to instruct you. At some time in the future, that is, depending on the advice you give me now. And whether that advice is free?' I chance my arm and wince at the audacity.

'Of course, of course!' he sounds delighted. 'So tell me – what's the problem?'

I tell him all about the *contretemps* Joe and I had the other day and ask him whether Joe is being a dick, or whether it's perfectly okay, in the eyes of the law, for him to virtually threaten his ex-wife and kids with homelessness. I tell him about my lack of job, not having a brass razoo to my name and having bugger all clue what to do about it.

'Why don't you go back to London and get a job? Get the ex off your back?' he offers.

'Because the kids have been moved around enough! All this being shunted around is no good for my and the kids' mental health—'

'The kids' and *my* mental health,' he butts in. 'Never forget the correct order of pronouns, my dear.'

Don't you just hate it when people do that? Pedants. Grammar nazis. Sign of raging insecurity, if you ask me. It's as though their own false sense of superiority gets a boost by pulling others up on minor technical mistakes, putting them down to bolster their own selves up or something. Pathetic.

'So the kids' and *my* mental health have taken enough of a battering lately and we're depending on favours from family and friends as it is and he only pays twelve hundred a month, for maintenance and—'

'It's not much these days, is it?' he says.

I can't tell whether he's being sarcastic or whether he actually means it.

'Sounds like he's trying to force you to get a job,' he goes on. 'A lot of men take this approach after a divorce, as though they want to really attack the woman, regardless of what it does to the kids.'

'I know!' My bum lifts off the chair a bit. 'But I will get a job! Just as soon as I've got us settled in here.'

'It won't be easy, though, if your little ones are still young, needing you before, after and sometimes even during school…'

He seems to know a lot about it. And he sounds like he's on my side – which makes for a nice change.

Probably pissed, that's why. Sue and Jane and Liz told me he was a raging alcoholic, didn't they?

'That's exactly right,' I say, smiling at the thought of a man who might understand what it's like to be a mum.

What a rare specimen, I think, as we ring off after agreeing he'll call me to arrange a meeting at his office above the butcher's on the high street, when he's had a chance to check his 'packed-to-capacity' schedule.

'Annie?' Paul calls from upstairs. 'Can you put your hand on one of the rads downstairs, please? See if you can feel anything?'

I do as I'm told and nearly faint with relief when I whip my hand away from the ancient-looking contraption. It's boiling!

'It's boiling!' I shout up the stairs.

'Fan-dabby-dozy,' he yells back. 'I'll be down in half a mo'.'

True to his word, he's downstairs in thirty seconds, tops, standing by the front door, tools all packed up, smiling his face off as he hands me an invoice.

'One hundred and seventy-five pounds?' I shriek when I read the bill. 'Are you having a Turkish Bath, mate?'

I'm momentarily stunned by my own outburst until I remember Joe always told me to barter and negotiate with tradies – never take their word for it, always be suspicious, let them know you're onto them and pretend you know loads about whatever it is they're doing. He said tradesmen were rip-off merchants. Actually, come to think of it, Joe thought *most* people were rip-off merchants, out to get him, use him and make a fool of him somehow. Particularly me, in the end. Fleecing him, bleeding him dry, never lifting a finger to do any work yet reaping the considerable benefits of his blood, sweat and tears.

I, on the other hand, have always been far too quick to believe what anyone tells me – call me gullible, too trusting, a bit bloody dim if you must – but I can't see the point of expecting the worst before you even begin. I mean, where's the fun in that? Ooh, get me – all positive and thinking the best and bright side of life-ing like a pro.

'Well, there's your call-out fee, my time, my expertise...'

'All you did was twiddle a few knobs!' I continue, channelling my inner Joe.

He stops smiling.

'I can twiddle them back and all, if you want. All the way back to brass monkeys. It'll only take a tick. *Mate*.'

'No, no – what I meant to say was thank you. Kind sir. Is it all right if I put the money in your account? I don't have that kind of cash on me.'

I don't have that kind of cash at all. But he doesn't need to know that.

He gives me his account details and leaves, whistling a jaunty tune as he walks down our driveway and out of sight.

–

Three upbeat, positive things so far:
- The heating now works – Hallelujah!
- I've organised a meeting with a solicitor who sounds like he might be on my side.
- And he didn't sound remotely drunk.

Chapter Four

February

February 12 – Ms Beaton's Book of Household Mis-Management

I get a call from the old bag in the front office of Thistlebend Primary School just after lunch (a chicken and mayo sandwich, Diet Coke and another packet of those Tunnock's Tea Cakes from the Co-op – I know! Just too yum!), telling me, first of all, not to worry, nothing bad has happened to either Izzy or Ben, really, everything's okay, and to please stop screaming.

My heart's pounding – she hasn't exactly got the warmest bedside manner – but I manage to bring it back to a more or less normal rate (i.e. not threatening to jump out of my chest any second), by going outside for some fresh air (read: fags).

'There's no need to worry, Mrs Cartwright,' she says, knowing full well that my last name's not Cartwright. 'The children are fine. But Ben's teachers do want a word with you. Would you be able to come in at ten to three?'

'Yes, yes.' My mind's reeling. 'Of course.'

I do the mental arithmetic – it really is mental when I do it – and after a few goes, involving coming inside and actually writing times down on the back of a Thames Water envelope, I manage to work out that I'll need to leave at a quarter past two at the latest in order to get to Thistlebend by a quarter to three, thus giving me a minute or two to compose myself, before I go in to face the music.

I make myself a cup of tea and put on some make-up. Which is not as easy as it sounds when your liquid foundation has separated into oil and chalk and it never was the right shade for your complexion anyway.

It's been aeons since I've worn any make-up and it's no doubt all gone off. Still, I carry on regardless, rubbing the too-pale emulsion into my face like it's moisturiser and trying to create Claudia Winkleman eyes. Within ten minutes, max, I'm in the car, listening to Radio Chilterns (turn on, tune in, chill out with Radio Chilterns!) and barrelling through the countryside, wondering what the hell Ben's done to warrant a summons from his teachers.

Or am I being negative? Maybe it's nothing bad, after all. Maybe it's something good – like they've discovered he's a child genius and they want my permission for him to sit university exams!

Even though I know I'm getting carried away here, I rather like the idea of Ben being a scarily brainy child prodigy. But then I remember I've read somewhere that positive thinking isn't just a one-way ticket to Fantasy Island, and such flights of fancy can be detrimental to your self-esteem. It's all about setting realistic goals and setting yourself up for realistic success, managing your expectations and all that, isn't it? And I should leave poor little Ben out of it.

I get a parking space easily when I get to Thistlebend – there are only a few 'prestige' cars lolling about, and I realise that getting here early is the key to parking success. Obviously not this early – pick up's not till twenty past three – but if we can get here ten minutes before everyone else joins the scrum, both in the morning and the afternoon, we'll never be late again.

I congratulate myself on having made it with minutes to spare and toy with the idea of stealing behind the bike sheds for a quick ciggie before my meeting.

But I don't want to sacrifice the heady concoction of all that good perfume, toothpaste, chewing gum and a few extra spritzes of Nivea deodorant under the arms for good measure just for a few guilty puffs, so I take the cigarette packet out of my parka pocket and carefully put it in the front pouch of my black leather John Lewis backpack.

The woman in the front office barely looks up from her paperwork when I present myself at the door.

'Take a seat,' she says, pointing her pencil at the wooden bench lining the wall to the staff room.

Something inside me stirs, and the spirit of the old rebellious schoolgirl I thought I'd left far behind rises up and steadfastly refuses to do as she's told. Maybe the worm is turning, maybe I'm asserting myself – or maybe I just don't want to take any chances while my tummy's feeling decidedly dodgy, desperately trying to digest those six tea cakes I wolfed down earlier.

Either way, I ignore the battleaxe's order and, instead, turn to take a look at some really rather wonderful art work on the walls. I've got my hands behind my back, inspecting the gallery and cupping the bottom of my ruck sack in my hands, when the staff room door opens.

'Ah, Mrs Cartwright?' A young woman with enormous brown eyes and thick, chestnut-brown, straight hair extends her hand to me.

'Yes!' I wheel around and clumsily offer my hand for shaking, too. 'But it's not Cartwright, actually, it's—'

'Mrs Beeton,' my new best friend in the front office smirks. 'As in *Mrs Beeton's Book of Household Management*. Rather ironic, don't you think? Considering the circumstances...'

Momentarily, I'm reminded of that Alanis Morissette song, 'Ironic', where she goes through all sorts of mildly irritating things – none of which are ironic, really, just a bit of a pisser.

But what is the Goddess of Hellfire, the Gatekeeper of Doom trying to say? Is she alluding to the fact that I'm a single mum? That I'm a divorcée and therefore incapable of managing a household – or at least keeping one together with a mother, a father and two-point-four children, a nuclear family, all happy together, living under one roof?

Maybe I'm suffering my first real bout of Single Mum Paranoia – but seriously! Why has she got such a bug up her arse about me?

'Actually,' I sigh, standing up as straight as possible, looking the teacher in the eyes, 'it's Beaton with an "a". And ms, as in "mrs" without the "r".'

'Nice to meet you,' the nice one says, 'I'm Mrs Xavier, with an "x" not a "z"! I'm one of Ben's teachers. I job-share with Mrs Danbeigh, but she was called away on a family emergency. The children are doing PE with Mr Stewart now, so shall we go into the classroom? There's no one in there and we can have a private little chat.'

I swear she ever-so-briefly gives the cow in the front office a dirty look as we walk past and head to the Year One and Reception classroom.

She offers me a tiny kid's chair and I take my backpack off, followed by my parka. It may be as warm as toast when I've got it on outside, but when I'm wearing it inside, I melt like hot butter.

'So,' Mrs Xavier begins, 'I just wanted to get a little bit of background on Ben so I can help him settle in. Like, for starters, why is he coming to school in Thistlebend, when he lives so far away in Old Stoke?'

I fill her in on the divorce.

'Oh, I'm sorry to hear that,' she says, looking concerned.

'Don't be.' I lift up out of my seat a little bit, such is the force of my enthusiasm. 'It's the best thing that ever happened to us! We're all so much happier and sorted now. Honestly.'

She's sucking on her lips and frowning, as though she doesn't believe me or something.

'Or at least we will be when we're properly settled in,' I say. 'Won't be long, now that we've found Thistlebend!'

I regale her with the story of how we relocated to Old Stoke, but after a while, I notice her beautiful, big brown eyes are sort of glazing over, so I fast-forward to the debacle surrounding getting school places close to home.

'So actually, we had little choice in the matter. And here we are!'

She sighs and shifts about in the smallest seat known to man.

'Mmhmm,' she hums. 'So how do you think Ben's coping with everything? All the upheaval, the new house, having to go to a new school...'

'Oh, the house isn't new – it's a poky Victorian mid-terrace disaster area – it's as old as the hills, and twice as crumbly!'

'And Ben?'

'I think he's fine. A few tantrums here and there – but show me a five-year-old who doesn't lose his sh— *temper* every now and again!'

'And how do these temper tantrums manifest themselves at home?'

'The usual, I imagine – a bit of door slamming, a raspberry or two dotted about the place...'

'Any biting?'

'No!' I'm incensed.

'Kicking?'

'No?' I can't quite believe these ludicrous questions.

'What about spitting?'

'No! Look, I don't know what's happened with Ben here today, but if there's been any physical violence, I bet he was just protecting himself. One of the other kids must have started it.'

'Well, I'm sorry Ms Beaton, but he wasn't reacting to anything, he simply lashed out, *à propos* of nothing at all. I know it's hard to hear, but I saw it happen with my own eyes.' Mrs Xavier reaches across the table to touch my forearm in what I can only imagine is a gesture of reassurance and support. 'It's not the first time I've seen this happen – and I'm pretty sure it won't be the last, either.'

'So what exactly *did* happen?' I feel my bottom lip tremble and my chin start to dimple.

'A lovely little boy approached Ben to offer him a home-made, gluten-free, nut-free biscuit and with a grin, Ben bit the boy's hand.'

'Bit the boy's hand? He's never done that before. Ever!'

Knowing Ben is as fond of baked goods as I am, I'm amazed by this – he must have missed his target.

'He wasn't aiming for the biscuit, was he? Kind of like a joke? You know, Cookie monster-style, nom, nom, nom?'

Mrs Xavier shakes her head slowly.

'Right. Okay.'

'And then, at morning break, he was playing with a football and when some other children tried to join in, he spat at them.'

'What?' I'm incredulous. 'Ben? Really? That's totally unlike him – he's never, ever done that! Spitting's just not his thing. Why—?'

'And *then*,' Mrs Xavier goes on, looking as uncomfortable as I feel, cataloguing Ben's disastrous day, 'he kicked a little girl on the bottom when they were lining up for their lunch in the dinner hall.'

'That's just – God! I don't get it – I mean, he's a sweet little guy most of the time. Apart from when he's having a tantrum, of course, then he can be a real little terror. I keep saying, "I don't negotiate with terrorists," to him, and that tends to lift him out of his black mood reasonably swiftly... but aggressive and violent? No, that's not our Ben.'

'I'm not suggesting for one second that he's a troublesome child, I think it might take a little time for him to settle in, that's all. He's had an awful lot of change to deal with, and when five-year-olds who don't understand what's going on and can't fully express themselves come up against difficult emotional situations, it's extremely common for them to act out in uncharacteristic ways.'

Just like his dad. Although *his* inability to express himself or understand difficult emotional situations has always been dealt with in ways that are now completely characteristic – i.e. running to the pub and downing his body weight in lager.

'Hmm – his dad's not the best at talking about his feelings – maybe Ben's inherited this anti-social behaviour from him…'

'And you? How do you cope with tricky emotions?'

'Are you kidding me?' I cross my legs on the minuscule seat, inadvertently kicking my bag. 'I love nothing more than banging on at great length about how I'm feeling, what I'm thinking and how recent events are shaping our future.'

Mrs Xavier smiles at me as though she doesn't believe me.

'Seriously! I can chat about that sort of stuff till the cows come home! That's why I loved couples counselling when Ben's dad and I did it – finally there was a chance to get all this important stuff off my chest – and the ex was forced to listen! He hated it, of course, but it got to the stage where it felt like a release for me. A healthy release. Like talking to a good friend – a trouble shared is a trouble halved and all that!'

'Don't take this the wrong way, Ms Beaton,' Mrs Xavier studies the floor next to my feet, 'but I can't help wondering whether Ben has, sort of, absorbed your anxieties and pain about your imploding marriage.'

Steady on, Xavier – *imploding*?

'It's obvious the two of you are very close and there's a somewhat symbiotic relationship between you – is it not possible that he has been literally feeling your distress? And if you really do love to talk as much as you say, isn't it likely that he's overheard you running his dad down at some time or another? To a friend over the phone or even in the house?'

What the hell is she saying? That it's me who's the villain in the piece? That I'm stressing Ben out? That Ben's behaviour is all *my* fault?

'No! Well, maybe… I mean, we are exceptionally close and there have been times when I've been so consumed by what's going on in my life, I've almost let my mouth run away with itself, no filters. But never in front of the kids, no. When they've been asleep, maybe or…'

I think back to when Jane was at ours.

Bugger.

'I'm not saying Ben's behaviour is your fault.' She pats the air down in the space between us with her palms and gives a nervous little laugh. 'No, no, no. All I'm saying is that as resilient and tough as children can seem on the outside, they really are as fragile and soft as marshmallow on the inside.'

Hmm. Marshmallow. Tunnock's Tea Cakes.

'But I'm so careful! I know little kids have big ears like bats, so I bite my tongue and restrain myself all the time! Not that I'm constantly angry or raging against their dad…'

I break off and decide to leave it there. I could be digging myself into a whopping great chasm full of fodder for Social Services here, doing more damage than good trying to explain myself to Mrs X.

'Don't worry, I'm not interested in judging you or blaming you – or your ex-husband – I just want Ben to settle in here and be happy.'

'Me too,' I nod, my annoyance subsiding into sadness. 'The poor little mite.'

Mrs Xavier gets up and walks over to me, putting her arm around my shoulders.

'Everything's going to be fine, I'm sure of it. But I'm going to have to ask you to wait outside with the other mums, now. The children have to come back in, pack up and get ready to go home, because the bell's about to go. Ms Beaton? Are you okay?'

'Yep, yep,' I sniff, bending down to pick up my parka, swinging my bag over my shoulder and moving slowly towards the door out into the playground. 'What a day, eh? Thanks for your concern, Mrs Xavier.'

'Anytime,' she says, smiling sweetly as she ushers me out.

It's total brass monkeys, as the handyman would say, so I get my parka on quick smart once I'm outside. I'm trying not to look too conspicuous among the tall, blonde, straight-haired, perfect-complexioned mums milling about, but honestly, it's like a Celtic & Co catalogue out here, with all those lambswool sweaters, ribbed beanies and sheepskin mittens. I must look like the cleaner's daggy cousin, I think to myself, and shove my hands in my parka pockets.

Just as I'm admiring someone's Ugg boots, Ben and his new class run past us, crashing into their classroom.

They look so sweet and innocent – particularly Ben with his enormous doe eyes and charming smile. When he's not spitting at or biting you, obviously, that is.

'We're not allowed to go inside,' one of the other mums informs me, as I stand on my tiptoes trying to see inside the classroom.

'Oh!' I gasp, relieved someone has spoken to me. 'I wasn't sure… we're new, you see. And today's been the most—'

'Ms Beaton?' Mrs Xavier pops her head out the door and proffers me a packet of Marlboro Lights. 'You left these.'

I can feel my cheeks burning as my eyes dart about, searching for the right thing to say. Tiny pricks of embarrassment dance around my hairline and I glance around at the crowd of mums closing in on me, suddenly silent, large and looming, like a moral lynch mob.

'What? Who?' I stall for time.

'They were on the floor next to where you were sitting just now.' She looks slightly bemused and sort of shakes the packet at me.

What should I do? Own up and face the wrath of the beautiful, addiction-free gang of model mums surrounding me, thus scuppering Ben's chances of ever being invited for playdates or any of the mums letting their kids come to ours? Or should I deny any knowledge of the offending fags. It's going to be tough getting away with that – Mrs X is smiling at me, urging me to take the cigarettes from her and everyone else is waiting in breathless anticipation for my answer.

Nothing ventured, nothing gained, as they say.

'Nope, not mine, never seen 'em before,' I finally blurt out. 'I mean, they're not mine because I don't smoke – not because they're not my brand or anything. Urgh. Cigarettes. Yukky poo!'

I screw up my face, trying not to blink as I stare Mrs X down.

Which is no walk in the park, let me tell you. She has this glare that makes you feel both small and as guilty as sin simultaneously. I feel like I'm shrinking and the mums are growing, all distorted like they're funhouse mirror versions of themselves, still skinny, but their scary faces slowly melting into dead ringers for Edvard Munch's *The Scream* face. It's getting darker and colder by the second and Mrs Xavier refuses to let it go.

'Really? Are you sure? No one else has been—' and she stops abruptly, remembering she hasn't got time for game-playing adults or addicts in denial. 'I'll put them in the front office with Miss King in case you change your mind.'

She quickly slips back inside, probably wondering what on earth just happened.

A collective sigh can be heard as the mums who were corralling me mere seconds ago disperse somewhat and recommence chit-chatting with their pals.

I shrug my shoulders and raise my eyebrows at the friendly-looking mum, as if to say, 'what was that all about?' and Izzy taps me on the arm.

'Oh, Izzy! My lovely love! How was it?'

I grab her head and kiss her face all over. She pushes me away and scowls, looking round to see whether any kids saw this flagrant display of motherly love.

'Get OFF me, you loser,' she says under her breath.

'Missed you too,' I smile, feeling the sting of embarrassment again, what with being spoken to like that and having my advances spurned so publicly by my darling daughter.

'Why are you here? Why aren't you out the front of my classroom?'

'Um, I—'

'Ah, forget it,' she tuts. 'Where is Ben, anyway? Why is he taking so long?'

'I don't know.'

Just then, Ben comes hurtling out of the classroom, his book bag flying behind him.

'Mummy!' he squeals and leaps into my arms, wrapping his legs around my waist and throwing his arms around my neck.

'Typical.' Izzy rolls her eyes.

Bereft of any other ideas and wanting to look like a good, warm, happy mum, I clap my hands together twice and make my eyes go so wide, I can practically feel another deep crevasse forming in my forehead.

'I know! Let's go to the café for a cup of tea and a cake!' I scan the kids for a show of excitement.

Izzy? Barely a flicker. Ben? An all-out explosion.

And as we ascend the hill to the school gates, I shake the thought of popping into the front office to pick up my cigarettes out of my head and wonder what glucosey delights the café will have lying in wait for us.

—

'So, how was your day?' I address them both, once we're settled in to the empty café at a high table with equally lofty stools, which prove dashed difficult to clamber up onto with any semblance of dignity.

'Fine,' says Izzy, not looking up from prodding her slice of carrot cake with her fork.

'Good,' nods Ben, the brown icing from his Chocolate Mudge Cake (a cross between mud and fudge, I guess) already smeared across his forehead, chin and cheeks.

'Was it really?'

'The girls seem nice,' Izzy says.

'What about the boys?'

'Urgh.'

'And how about you, Ben?'

'Good,' he says again.

'I mean the kids in your class – not the cake!'

'I know!' he grins. 'They're good.'

I haven't the faintest clue how to play this. I don't want to tell him off, make a big song and dance about it, have him develop a complex about being 'naughty' and end up being tarred with that brush for the rest of his school life. Equally, I can't ignore it and say nothing, just because I feel sorry for him. He simply can't be left to think it's perfectly okay to go around biting, hitting and spitting.

Also, on top of all *that*, I don't want him or Izzy to not like me. I don't want to always have to be the bad cop, doing all the discipline and telling off all the time while Joe gets to have all the fun of being the Disney Dad every two weeks for two sodding nights. Why can't I be the fun one?

'So the heating's fixed at home.' I swerve my parental disciplining duties for the time being and open with perhaps the most un-fun thing I possibly ever could. 'We're going to be all snuggly tonight, then!'

Ben nods enthusiastically.

'Big whoop,' Izzy snarks.

'Christ, Izz – could you at least *try* to not to be so relentlessly downbeat? It's getting a little wearing, to be honest. Or TBH, as you'd probably say.'

'Well, TBTH, I don't really care!'

This is going well.

After a few moments of silence (awkward for me – no doubt a blessed relief for the kids), an impossibly tall woman, reminiscent of Cate Blanchett, strides purposefully in, her red Hunter wellington boots perfectly unscuffed, her long legs going on forever. She's cradling a puppy in her long, sheepskin-wrapped arms, her two kids looking for all the world like Topsy and Tim jumping for joy around her hips.

The three of us gasp. Me more than the little ones, probably, but still.

'Awww,' Izzy virtually melts, 'isn't she *adorable*?'

'Mummy! She's soooooo cuuuuute!' Ben's face crumples up as though he might just burst into tears any second.

'And how does she get her hair so straight, so completely bereft of frizz?' I join in, shaking my head in disbelief. 'Mind you, look how tall and slim she is – obviously one of the lucky winners in life's genetic lottery...'

'The puppy!' the kids shout.

'Oh, yeah,' I grin, feeling caught out, thanks to those pesky inner thoughts of mine escaping at inopportune moments again. 'Wonder what it is...'

'A Hungarian vizsla,' the Cate Blanchett lookalike says, with that heady, posh mix of nonchalance, authority and condescension. 'I can't put her on the floor – she hasn't had all her shots yet.'

'She's ten weeks old,' the little boy says.

'Her name's Willow,' the little girl adds.

'She's divine.' I struggle getting off the stool while the kids fairly fly off theirs and we descend upon the frightened little pup.

Vizslas, Cate tells us – when prompted, of course, rich people never volunteer info about themselves or their pets to the likes of us, the hoi polloi, without having consulted our family lineage and looked our father up in *Who's Who* first – are apparently the *dog du jour* in the country these days, having overtaken the labrador and golden retriever in the desirability stakes.

'She's absolutely gorgeous,' I say. 'And she has the same green eyes as you!'

'It's a vizsla thing,' Cate half-smiles, looking a tiny bit confused – half because she can't fathom how on earth someone so short can see high enough to be able to tell what colour her eyes are and half because she can't quite place me in the local social hierarchy. I mean, here I am, short and dumpy in a TK Maxx parka with ridiculous hair that badly needs highlights and a good going over with the GHDs – here, in the eye-wateringly expensive, not remotely ostentatiously named café, "The Pantry" at Thistlebend, scarfing cake on a Monday afternoon – I can't be a total oik. Can I?

Maybe she thinks we're a bit creepy, swarming around her like a pack of hungry hyenas. Then again, maybe she's flattered by all the attention.

'Would you mind stepping back a bit,' she says, 'giving Willow some room to breathe?'

Not flattered, then.

'My name's Annie,' I venture. 'We're new to the school.'

Her mouth turns down and she nods reluctantly, as one might if one had just been offered roadkill for canapes.

'This is Izzy, she's in year four at the school and this is Ben. He's in year one.'

The little boy hides behind his mother's leg and grips her thigh.

'That's him, Mummy,' he says.

'Oh, I've heard all about you, Ben.' She looks down her long nose at my boy. I instinctively pull an oblivious Ben to me and put my hands on his shoulders.

'He's a bit unsettled at the mo',' I say, 'what with all the moving and the divorce and everything. Sorry if he's been a little bit, um, rambunctious?'

'You're divorced?' she asks, brightening ever so slightly.

'Yes. Well, the decree absolute hasn't come through yet, but for all intents and purposes, yep, I'm divorced.'

'I'm sorry to hear that...'

'Why? It's not *your* fault!' I laugh.

'No, it's yours, Mummy.' Izzy looks up momentarily from patting the puppy.

'Everything is Mummy's fault, Mummy's fault, Mummy's fault – everything is Mummy's fault, Mu-mmy's fault!' Ben tra-las this lovely little ditty the kids made up with Joe.

'My name's Charlotte,' the Amazon softens. 'Tough job, bringing kids up on your own – my mother was a single mum, too. Respect.'

'Really?'

I'm surprised by this and somewhat slapped in the face by my own prejudices here. I mean, she doesn't *look* like the child of a single mum. But what exactly *does* that look like, I ask myself. Little kids in sepia tones, wearing rags for clothes, soot-smeared faces holding empty bowls of gruel up and looking pleadingly at you while saying, 'More, please'?

'Yes,' she leans down conspiratorially, 'and just between you and me, I might be joining your ranks soon, too. That's why I got Willow now, in preparation. It's so good for children to grow up with dogs, don't you think?'

'I couldn't agree more,' I beam back at her.

'She's gifted and talented, I've been told,' she smiles.

I look down at the little girl and try not to sound too creepy when I say:

'Brains and beauty, eh? Lucky old you!'

'Not her,' Charlotte barks, 'Willow!'

The little girl looks crestfallen and I feel embarrassed for all of us. Well, all of us except Willow.

'Sorry,' Charlotte coughs. 'I'm not really feeling myself. Think I'm coming down with something.'

'If you couldn't agree more, Mummy,' Izzy rounds on me, 'where's our puppy?'

'Yeah, *Mum*,' her little brother does the same.

'You promised!' they chorus.

Charlotte winks at me, snuggles her face into the puppy's fur and leads her charges into the loo at the back of the café.

And all the way home (that's thirty minutes non-stop, remember), Izzy and Ben bang on about how much they'd love a puppy and how I'm the Worst Mother in the World for reneging on iron-clad promises.

—

'Of course you've got to get a puppy!' Amelie cries when I tell her of our encounter with posh mum Charlotte. 'Real man magnets they are, too – you'll be beating them off with a stick before you know it!'

'But I'm not interested in men at the mo' – beating them off with a stick or anything else for that matter!'

'Yeah, yeah.' I hear her smirking as she exhales smoke over the phone.

'Oh! And I got sprung badly with cigarettes on me at school!'

'How old are you again?' she laughs.

I tell her all about Mrs Xavier and the gang of mums. She thinks it's funny.

'Why are you laughing, Am? It's horrendous! I'm still utterly mortified – I'm fast turning into a crappy cliché!'

'No you're not,' she says, almost sounding reassuring, 'you've always been one! And anyway, what kind of a crappy cliché are you talking about?'

'You know – short, tubby, badly dressed single mum with unruly hair and feral kids who spends her time chuffing away on fags, bitching about benefits. Not that there's anything wrong with that, I mean, we've all had our moments—'

'You've been reading the *Daily Mail* again, haven't you?' she sniffs. 'Look, just because you're a single mum doesn't mean Jack about you personally – except you're a real hero, working twice as hard as married mums with a fraction of the money. So your marriage didn't work out – so what? It's not a character flaw or a life sentence. I've told you before; it's the best thing that's ever happened to you. Get over yourself, wrap up this personal pity party and get on with your life. And you can keep your

149

outdated, offensive stereotypes to yourself, too – jump off your judgey high horse.'

That's me told, then.

'You're right, you're right,' I take the hit.

'But you do have to stop smoking,' she says, as she takes an enormous drag, 'I do, too – I just can't seem to find the time.'

'What do you need time for?'

'To listen to the two-hour lecture.'

'What two-hour lecture?'

'The one Jason Vale does.'

'Who?'

'Gor – you really are out of the loop, aren't you?'

I don't answer her because I'm thinking about how familiar that name sounds. Jay-something whatshisface… isn't that the name of the man who wrote that book about stopping drinking I was reading the other night?

'You know the juicing guy? He did this huge juice experiment with all these poor people with diabetes and asthma and stuff and cured them with kale and beetroot and avocado juices. Didn't you hear about it?'

I haven't got the faintest clue what she's burbling on about.

'Never mind.' She pauses to take another drag. 'He does this free app. Called *Stop Smoking in Two Hours*. You get it on your phone. But you have to have two hours straight to listen to him telling you about the evils of tobacco or whatever. And then you have to play the meditation thing every night in bed before you go to sleep. My brother did it three years ago and hasn't smoked since. Hasn't even wanted to. And you know how keen he was for a pint and a gasper.'

'I don't drink anymore,' I say. And all of a sudden it's as if I've sounded a klaxon down the phone.

'*What?*' she splutters.

'I just don't see the point. Maybe it's in answer to Joe's excessive drinking, I dunno. All I know is I haven't fancied it and I just can't see myself getting stuck into the wine again. Until the kids have left home at least.'

'But… but…'

People really do find the whole notion of not drinking very hard to take. It's as if you're saying you just got off the first rocket back from Neptune or something – it's virtually impossible to understand. As Jason Thingy says, alcohol really is the only drug you get grief for *not* taking.

'I just can't handle the hangovers anymore. And it was making me fat. Ter.'

'Yeah, right – nothing to do with crates of Mr Kipling's Fondant Fancies and truckloads of Tunnock's Tea Cakes…'

'Now you're talking!' My mouth starts to water. 'So listen, when are you going to come down and see us?'

'When you've got the puppy and you've started drinking again. Couple of weeks?'

Oh, she of little – nay, *no* – faith.

–

Unable as I am to do anything off my own bat without first checking with Mum and Dad (decisions by committee lately, that's me), I call them once the kids are in bed to get their take on the puppy situation and whether they think it might settle Ben a bit.

'Brilliant!' Dad's encouraging.

'Don't be ridiculous!' Mum a little less so.

'I did promise the kids, though, and—'

'No! You can't possibly bring a dog into that tiny house. You can barely manage the kids, let alone a puppy! And it'll cost a fortune, what with food and vet's bills – and we've got our eye on a lovely cream fake-Persian rug from IKEA for you to say thanks to Audrey for letting you stay – but it'll shit and puke all over *that* and—'

'What breed were you thinking of?' Dad grabs the phone from Mum and I can hear him smiling.

'Um… a Hungarian vizsla, maybe? Or a working cocker spaniel – those ears! Those eyelashes!'

'Those carpet-cleaning bills!' Mum bellows in the distance.

'Ah, don't listen to your mother – no romance in her soul,' Dad dismisses her. 'What about an Irish setter?'

'Well, I wouldn't want Ruby—'

'RIP,' we all say in unison.

'… to think I was trying to replace her or anything…'

'Oh, for Christ's sake!' I can practically hear Mum throwing her hands up in frustration.

'No, there's no way anyone could ever replace her.' Dad goes all solemn.

'Having said that, we could get a *boy* Irish setter… that way there'd be no danger in comparing them, because they'd be so different! And it's probably what Ruby—'

'RIP,' Dad and I say again – Mum must have left the room in disgust.

'… would have wanted. And she was just what we needed, me and Orlando, when we were growing up…'

'She was a real member of the family, wasn't she?' Dad sounds misty. 'Remember how she'd steal the whole leg of lamb on a Sunday while we were in the other room eating? And how we did the doggy intelligence test on her, wrapping the biscuit in layers of Kleenex?'

'And she ate all the Kleenex, completely ignoring the biscuit!' I grin at the memory. 'Mind you, it *was* just a plain digestive – can't say I blame her – I'd probably have left that, too. But if it was, say, a Rich Tea biscuit, that'd be a different story. Then, obviously, I'd be forced to—'

'He must be pedigree, from a good line. None of these puppy farms you hear about – poor little sods. The puppies, not the farmers. Those people are absolute ar—'

'Yeah, I know. But a pedigree puppy will cost a bomb, won't it?'

'Maybe. First things first, though, find out which breeders are expecting puppies – locally if possible. Then get your name down on their lists and make sure they're reputable breeders – members of the Kennel Club and all that. I'll send you some possibilities when I get a mo' – you concentrate on getting a job. Those kids'll be leaving home any minute now and then what'll you have?'

'A dog?'

'Don't do it, sweetheart.' Mum's obviously calmed down, come back into the room and is now trying the cool, rational approach. 'The last thing you need in your life right now is another child. And don't think for a minute the kids will be any help looking after it. Remember I didn't even want Ruby.'

'RI—'

'Oh, *do* give over!' I can picture Mum batting Dad away as he tries to take the phone from her. 'And I was the one who fed her, took her to the vet, drove all around the place looking for her when she ran away that time. Oh, you do know I'm right, don't you, darling?'

'Ah, yes, look here – there's an Irish setter rescue centre in Lambourn… not a million miles away from where you are!' Dad snatches the phone back.

'Send me the link thingy on the email and I'll call them in the morning!' I nearly jump with excitement.

I search my bag and parka pockets for my cigarettes, so I can go outside in the freezing cold of the dark and stormy night to have a celebratory ciggie and, after a few minutes scrabbling about, remember the debacle at the school earlier.

'Bollocks,' I mutter.

There's nothing else for it, I think to myself – I might as well make hay while the sun shines and do that app thingy, and rid myself of this foul addiction while I haven't got any cigarettes on me.

Somehow I manage to find and download the app onto my phone and settle down on the couch to listen, interruption-free, to what Mr Vale has to say.

The lecture goes on for bloody ages. But it does throw up some very good points and I do a lot of nodding in agreement, a lot of eye-widening in surprise and a lot of lip pursing and head shaking in self-loathing.

But once Jason's finished wittering on, I pull out the sofa bed, settle myself down and press play on the hypnosis part of day one.

The swirly, soft music starts up, merging seamlessly with JV's voice.

In his soothing, not-as-creepy-as-you-might-expect hypnotising tones, he burbles on about lying down and making sure you can concentrate on what he's saying by locking the doors.

My eyes flip open at this point and I say a silent prayer to the Goddess of Struggling Mothers – 'please make the kids stay asleep long enough for me to do this'.

He continues talking softly about already being a non-smoker and the most important decisions in life and going deep into the sub-conscious and...

Zzzzzzzzzzzzzzzzzzzzzzzzzzzzzzzzzzzzzzzzzzzzzzzzzzz.

—

Three upbeat, positive things that I might be able to call 'wins':

- A fellow mum at the school gates has actually introduced herself to me, like, properly told me her name and everything. And even though she's scarily composed, decidedly unharried and uber-capable-looking, we might even become friends.
- We might be getting a puppy soon – even better, *rescuing* one.
- I've got a really good feeling this stopping smoking thing's going to work.

Chapter Five

March

March 5 – The Menopausal Mum v The Narky Nine-Year-Old

Just when you think it's safe to go back into Boots and totally ignore the feminine hygiene aisle, swanning past the Tampax, chuffed you no longer have to pay a fortune for them (with or without the 'luxury' tax)... Just when you think you're probably post-menopause by now, considering it's been approximately a million years since your last period... And just when you think it's time you stocked up on the Tena Lady discreet pants, given that your pelvic floor was demolished irreparably years ago and no amount of Kegels are ever going to fix that, you go to the loo after an inconvenient 'oops moment' and realise you're actually mid-blood bath at the house of death.

It's not an uncommon scenario for those of us sandwiched in between not looking young enough to be asked for ID at a pub, but not looking old enough to be asked for your Freedom pass on the train, either. Yet.

And there goes yet another comfy pair of knickers that didn't cut into your bum cheeks or ride up your arse – unless you don't give a toss about crime-scene-style dark red stains on your smalls, that is.

So anyway, even though the period itself – not to mention its force and vim – comes as a bit of a shock, its appearance does, at least, go some way to explaining my snappy mood and lust for all things chocolatey lately. As if I needed a reason or a hoary old biological excuse.

I suppose, what I'm trying to say is, getting your period at *un certain âge* can be a bit of a sur-bloody-prise. Literally.

In fact, come to think of it, it's a lot like your ex-husband bowling up on your doorstep when you've forgotten it's his turn to have the kids at his place for the weekend.

There you are, patting yourself on the back for the fantastic job you're doing, bringing up two recalcitrant kids single-handedly, thinking how brilliant you are for not even poisoning them yet with those ever-so-slightly out of date chicken Kievs the Co-op was going to throw out… There you are, about to tuck into some Tunnock's, while you enjoy Friday Family Fun Night watching *Wreck It Ralph*, promising the kids you'll stop swearing – or at least say 'Fix It Felix' instead of the 'F' word – when all of a sudden, out of the blue, your ex shows up, standing in front of you with a cheesy grin that would make a Domino's delivery boy proud.

And even though your heart sinks when you realise the knock on the door had nothing to do with pizza, you still have to put a brave face on it and sometimes go so far as to pretend you're delighted.

'Oh,' I say when I answer the door. 'It's you.'

I sound like the woman Rupert Holmes sings about in 'The Pina Colada Song' when she realises that her hot new date is actually the same old boring guy she's been shagging for the past God knows how many years.

My disappointment ricochets off Joe's shiny forehead, hits me in the face and bounces back onto his cheek with a nearly audible splat, then slowly slumps down the front of his jumper. His new Ralph Lauren jumper.

Joe looks a bit disheartened by my decidedly under-whelmed reaction, which I don't really care about, but thinking of the kids, as always, putting them first etc etc etc, I change tack.

'I mean, hey! *You*! How've you been? I hear your new place is fantastic! A gated community, no less! Anything to keep the riff-raff out, eh?'

I try to laugh as though I don't care that he's now living in a brand, spanking new apartment that isn't falling down around his ears and it's cool that he's got loads of money to spend on himself and his ace new bachelor pad and aren't they new trainers? Snazzy, red Kanye West ones? That don't in any way whatsoever look anything remotely like mutton dressed as lamb? As I say, I *try* to laugh, but don't quite pull it off and I end up emitting a strangely high-pitched squeak instead of the couldn't-care-less chortle I was aiming for.

'Great, thanks,' he says. 'Your neighbour not here to evict me off the premises this time?'

'Oh.' I feel the pores on the end of my nose snapping shut – a sure sign the tension's ratcheting up a notch or twelve and if I don't do something quick to quell the rising tide of panic, I could lose it any second now. 'No, no, sorry about that.'

'Can I come in, then?' he nods in the general direction of the kitchen, just beyond me.

I deflect this seemingly innocent request by simply pulling the door closer to my side, thereby blocking his path.

'You're not serious, are you?' his inner John McEnroe comes out to play.

Feeling silly, hating this confrontation and not having a clue how to answer him, I do what any self-respecting woman in my situation would do: I shout at the kids over my shoulder.

'Guys? Daddy's here! Yay!' I bellow, the last bit a little weakly, to be honest.

'Urgh,' Joe grunts, 'guess we'll be on our way, then. Have you packed their bags?'

Fix It Fucking Felix – I forgot!

'DADDY!' the kids yell, elbowing me aside in their haste to get to Joe.

While Ben and Izzy kiss and hug their dad as though he's just returned from several years on a desert island, I stand there, frozen onto The Spot of Indecision.

Shall I run upstairs and sort their bags out? But everything's dirty – knickers, socks, jumpers, vests – argh! The sodding washing machine's still not bloody working and I was going to make a day of it at the launderette tomorrow...

Or should I casually and oh-so-breezily suggest Joe splash some of his cash on some new gear for the kids, so he can have their stuff at his place and we don't have to faff about with time-consuming bag-packing and bemoaning broken down old white goods?

Maybe I should give Mum, Dad, Jane next door, Amelie or Aisling a quick ring so I can consult them and they can help me decide. Or just ask Izzy – she always knows what to do... But just as I'm wondering about all that, berating myself for being oh so scared and unsure, like poor old Sandra Dee, Joe puts his arms round both kids' shoulders turns them about face and marches them down the driveway.

'Hang on!' I squeal. 'What about their clothes?'

'We'll go into Reading and get some for my gaff. It'll be fun, won't it, kids?'

What? More fun than the village launderette on a wet Saturday afternoon?

'YAY!' the traitors reply in the affirmative.

'Well how about a kiss goodbye?' I jog after them.

'Nah, you're all right,' Joe screws up his nose as he slides into the driver's seat. 'Kids might want one, though!'

Well ha bloody ha.

–

Back inside, I go through the obligatory ten minutes of feeling bereft, now the kids have gone. I marvel at the silence (the comparative silence, that is – *Wreck It Ralph*'s still chuntering on) and wonder how the hell we got here. It's like we're no longer a couple, but we're still together in some way, still married somehow. Forever bound by the kids, I suppose. Which is good – for them. And we'll be a great ex-couple, better friends than ever before and always there for our lovely little lot.

Although that might take a bit longer than I'd previously thought. Because he's a bit Jekyll and Hyde sometimes, isn't he? I mean, last time he was here, he was all 'loads less maintenance' serious and business-like – and this time, he's cracking jokes about not wanting a kiss from me. Which isn't at all funny, considering the circs.

It's like I can't get him straight in my mind – is he an arsehole or a nice guy? Arsehole or nice guy? Arsehole or – you get the idea.

But what if I was the real piece of work, chipping away at his niceness day after day, year after year, until he couldn't take it anymore and he was forced to flee the bitch his beautiful bride has become? Bitch or beautiful bride? Bitch or beautiful bride? Bitch or – sorry. Can't help myself sometimes.

It's important for my mental health, self-esteem and ability to move on, I believe, to get a consistent – if not wholly accurate – picture of his personality in my head. As any half-decent manual on how to handle a break-up would say, I need to construct a new narrative and stick to it. Think whatever it takes to get you through these tempestuous times, I tell myself – preferably a story about how he couldn't possibly meet my emotional needs, being the stranger to self-awareness that he is.

I ponder this for a minute or two and then, as though I've said my prayers, I throw my head back and laugh. No, really. It's like I'm possessed by a demon and I can feel my eyes going all fiery on me, and I imagine flames licking at my eyebrows (which is quite good, really – they could do with a bit of a trim).

I'm practically off my head with indecision now – I mean, what should I do first with all this kid-free time spreading out before me? Go out for a fag? Ooh, that's weird. First time I've thought about smoking since – well, since the hypnotism thing. Which is insane! I know Jason says there's no need to count the days you've been a non-smoker for, but I've been listening to the hypnosis every night for the past at least seven days, so… wow. Get me! I never in a million years thought I would ever axe the fags. Or find it so ridiculously easy. I know it's early days, but still – this is a really big deal for me.

So what then?

Healthy, hearty country pursuits, that's what. I rub my hands together and build a fire. Even though I still haven't got round to getting the chimney checked and the weather's almost turning a little bit warm lately (ever since we got the heating fixed, funnily enough) – hell, even *my* thoughts are starting to turn to t-shirts and flip flops. Which reminds me – I really must stop eating entirely soon, if I ever want to wear anything but kaftans with boxer shorts underneath them (you know, to minimise painful chafing). Monday. I'll start stopping eating on Monday.

Now where was I? Oh yes, country fun. Unfortunately I've missed *The Archers* on BBC Radio 4 (when will I remember it's on every night just after the seven o'clock news?) again, but maybe that food show's on – what's it called? I quite fancy that Jay Rayner, with his sharp wit and love of scoffery… maybe it's *Gardeners' Question Time*. Speaking of gardening, perhaps I should trim my herbaceous borders. Sounds like a euphemism for getting a bikini wax, doesn't it? I nearly giggle to myself and then suddenly, like a bolt out of the blue, I remember that we're in the twenty-first century.

So I jump on the internet. Google. YouTube. Of course!

One hour later, I cut a YouTube video off half-way through, disgusted and a little surprised with myself for wasting time watching someone actually getting a manicure. Not exactly the same as watching paint dry, but close.

I then trawl through Google images of Irish setter puppies for a while, spurring me on to contact that Irish setter rescue centre. Which seems awfully productive to me – like, just by putting my name down for the pup, I've done a good day's work, now truly deserving of that silk Mother of the Year sash.

It's kind of the same as when I was at uni and after several hours spent in sepulchral silence in the library, searching for, finding and photocopying various texts I'd probably never read, I'd call it a solid day's study and hit the uni bar, thirsty and exhausted.

Except that now I don't even drink anymore!

I shake my head from side to side as though if I do it fast enough, all ghosts of good times past will be jettisoned, scattered to the four corners of the kitchen, pebbledashed onto the already pretty grubby walls. Metaphorically speaking.

Thinking of the more shabby than chic look of our place, I jump onto the Wayfair site (well, if it's good enough for Lorraine Kelly...) and then Dunelm, putting chandeliers and Baroque-style wall mirrors into my 'shopping baskets' with absolutely no intention whatsoever of 'proceeding to checkout'. Because it's strictly fantasy interiors time for me and it doesn't take long before I'm ordering catalogues from The Dormy House, The Cotswold Furniture Co. and the prohibitively expensive but lust-worthy Celtic & Co. Well, I've got to fit in with the yummy mummies like Charlotte, somehow, haven't I? Once I've lost three stone, that is.

So now what? I know – I'll finish my Ten Command-ments, because that sort of thing counts for fun these days. And you never know, I might even actually get round to actually selling it to a magazine and making some money out of it or something.

But I don't get very far with it – I can't shake the nostalgia trip I'm on, thinking back to the good old days when I worked on teen magazines, making up silly quizzes and writing scripts for shockingly stupid photo love stories. Which gives me an idea and quick as a flash, I start writing on a Word document:

QUIZ

What Kind Of Single Mum Are You?

1. **It's 5:15 p.m., you've forgotten the kids need feeding and there's nothing without furr on it in the fridge. You:**
   a) Tell the kids it's time to play *Junior MasterChef* and get *them* to rustle up dinner with a can of tuna, some frozen peas and a mushy cucumber
   b) Take them to Maccy Ds
   c) What's wrong with furry food?
2. **What is your favourite time of year?**
   a) Christmas
   b) The summer holidays
   c) 9 a.m. to 3 p.m. weekdays during school term time
3. **You think of iPads and TV for kids as:**
   a) Detrimental to young minds
   b) OK in controlled, small doses
   c) Free babysitting

4. **Your latest TV crush is:**
   a) All the guys in *Horrible Histories* – even the chubby one
   b) Jeremy Kyle
   c) That bucket of chicken in the latest KFC ad
5. **Which TV Single Mum is most like you?**
   a) Stella in, um, *Stella*
   b) No-nonsense Northerner Lizzie in *Motherland*
   c) Dilys Price in *Fireman Sam*
6. **Upon waking the kids up for school in the morning, their usual response is:**
   a) A hug, a smile and an enthusiastic 'Morning Mummy – I love you!'
   b) To continue sleeping and ignoring you
   c) A text from your eldest of an emoji giving you the finger
7. **You're in the car off to school and once again, in the chaotic rush to get out the door, you've forgotten to nag the kids to brush their teeth. So you:**
   a) Get them to use the sleeves of their school jumpers as makeshift toothbrushes as per
   b) Pop an Extra (sugar-free!) into their mouths after you've kissed them goodbye
   c) Suffer a rare burst of selflessness and share your secret stash of peppermint Aero with them while you drive

And the verdict?

Tot up how many times you've answered with As, Bs or Cs and then refer to the highly scientific data analysis table below to see just exactly what kind of Single Mum you are:

Mostly As – a great one!
Mostly Bs – a great one!
Mostly Cs – a great one!

I don't know where it's all coming from, but it's just spewing out of me. And once again I'm startled by how much TV I watch – I mean, *Dilys Price*?

There must be a way to make money out of this, surely.

What if I started a blog? Everyone seems to be doing it these days – everyone under forty, that is. And it's nigh-on a million years since I was the right side of forty. Even though, quite frankly, I'm starting to think fifty *is* the right side of forty... But either way, why should I let my age dictate what I do? I shouldn't, that's why!

And I know that I have special needs when it comes to technology – but Izzy did Coding For Kids back in Teddington and she's pretty much glued to her phone these days, so she'll know what to do, how to set up a blog.

Normally I'd ask Joe – but now I'd rather drink nuclear waste. There's just no way I'd ask him for help now, adding fuel to his fire. He already thinks I'm overly dependent upon him; that I'm stupid, lazy and incompetent... before you know it, he'd be taking the kids away from me, amid accusations of being an unfit mother...

...And breathe.

I text Izzy:

> Hello sweet pea! Mummy here – missing you like crazy! Hope you're having fun with Daddy

(My fingers press extra hard on the screen keyboard and my lips thin, harden and practically disappear into the abyss when I write that last bit)

> Just wondering... Will you help me
> set up a blog when you get back?
> I've already written some stuff,
> just need you to put it up and
> out! xxx

She texts back in seconds:

> K.

It takes me probably three whole minutes to reply:

> Which one should I go for?
> Blogger or Wordpress? Both free,
> right? Or is there something else I
> should be looking at??? Xxx

A nano-second passes:

> DOH! You're such a dufus!
> Everyone knows you do Blogger –
> it's by far the best for Google
> Chrome

What the Fix It Felix is she on about? I resist the temptation to take this line of enquiry any further – particularly now she's sending abuse down the line – and plump for:

OK. Fab! Thanks Honey Bunny.
Give your baby bro a big kiss from
me. Be good – see you on
Sunday! xxxxxxxxxxxxxxxxxxxxx

She can't be arsed to send anything more. Not even a couple of 'X's.

–

March 7 – On a Blog Roll

By the time the kids came back today, I'd managed to sort of find my way around Blogger and call my site 'How to be a Divorced Single Mum – Because a Good Man(ual) Is Hard To Find'.

Which is met with outright derision from the kids.

Ben (still not really getting it): But you're married to Daddy!

Izzy (not looking up from her phone): Lame.

But, well, you know. Yeah.

As Izzy's fingers fly over the keyboard, setting up my site so that millions of women floundering in the aftermath of divorce will easily be able to access my words of wisdom, helping them get back in the saddle on that horse we call life, she begrudgingly answers the questions I throw at her about her weekend at Daddy's.

'So...' I say in the best off-hand way I can. 'What did you guys get up to this weekend? Anything interesting?'

'I played *Halo*! I love *Halo*! Can we get an Xbox here at your house, Mummy? You could play it with me!'

'It's not *my* house – it's *your* house. *Our* house,' I smile.

'An Xbox is about four hundred pounds, Ben,' Izzy sneers, 'and we're *poor*.'

She literally spits that last word out and I, in a fit of over-zealous house-keeping, wipe the spittle from the keys of the laptop.

'Just… clear that up… a bit,' I say as I flick a tea towel lightly over the keys. 'Anything else, guys? What about you, Iz? Did you play *Halo* too?'

'NO!' she snaps.

'Okay, okay – jeez! Only asking! And we're not poor – we just have to be a bit more careful now.'

'Why? Daddy gives you loads of money,' Ben says, like he's stating a well-known fact.

'Um, actually, Ben,' I feel my heart start to race, 'Daddy doesn't *give me* money – he puts a small amount in *our* account so you can have a roof over your head, a nice warm bed to sleep in, yummy food to eat and decent clothes to wear.'

'That's what I said.' Ben's fascinated by what Izzy's doing, staring at the laptop screen all the while. 'He gives you loads of money.'

Close your eyes, take a deep breath in through your nose, hold it for a sec, let your shoulders relax and slowly exhale through your mouth.

'Don't blow on me, Mum, you weirdo – yuk!' Izzy leans away from me and I get that familiar feeling – they've only been back for five minutes and already I feel under attack, under siege and, quite frankly, over it.

Calm, I tell myself, calm down. There's no point arguing the toss with a five-year-old boy who so far seems to take after his father in the emotional intelligence stakes. And Izzy's doing you a big favour, which is nice, so just steer the convo back into a safe harbour. Think the twinkling lights of Hong Kong at night. That old Boz Scaggs song 'Harbour Lights'. Cosy nights in with the family. Ahhhhh.

'So, Iz? What did you get up to?'

'Oh, I don't know! If you'd asked me at the time I would have remembered, but—'

'It was only an hour ago! Bloody hell – excuse me for living, but the graveyard was closed!' My inner three-year-old surfaces and I feel like chucking a tantrum myself. 'I don't know what goes on over at Daddy's – apart from playing highly inappropriate computer games for hours on end – but when you come back snapping and sniping and banging on about what a fu-uh-uh-uh-ix It Felixing hero Daddy is, well I—'

'We met Daddy's new girlfriend,' Izzy cuts me off.

I go to speak, but no sound comes out. I swallow hard and try again. But only manage a small squeak. I clear my throat. You *what*?

'Yay!' Ben squeals in delight. 'Fitnanny!'

'Wait a minute,' I have to close my eyes to think straight. 'Daddy has a new girlfriend or he's got you a fit nanny? What's the story?'

'Idiot,' Izzy shoots daggers at Ben. 'We met his girlfriend. She's called Tiffani.'

'I said that! She played *Halo* with me!' Ben punches the air like a mini US marine.

'Wowsers,' I say softly, trying to focus on the laptop screen, while all the letters and numbers start swimming in front of me.

'You should be nicer to him,' Ben adds helpfully.

'What do you mean?' I pull my chin in to my chest and stare the little boy down.

'If you weren't so mean to Daddy, you could be his girlfriend too.'

'But I *am* nice to him! And I've already been his girlfriend – tried it once, didn't like it. But we're friends, now. We have a laugh together, don't we? I make an extra-special effort to be nice to him, actually.'

I physically put my fingers in my mouth and actually hold my tongue at this point, afraid I'll come out with some horrible home truths that could potentially scar the kids for life.

'But you're so fake with each other!' Izzy looks me in the eye. 'You're not really being friends, no one believes that, Mum – it's always so awkward and awful between you!'

'Is it?'

'Yes,' both Izzy and Ben look at me, wide-eyed and wounded.

'Well, not anymore.' I puff my chest out and brush myself down. 'I solemnly do swear that from here on in, all you guys will see is reality in the raw and all you will hear is straight-up honesty: no sugar-coating, no messing. All right?'

'All right,' they chorus.

And even though I'm desperate to ask them all about Tiffany, I decide to let it lie, not make them feel any more weird about the sitch than they absolutely have to.

We hug, albeit briefly, and Izzy shows me how to log on and publish blogs on the site. She's right, you know – it is a piece of pee. Even for me.

I transfer the quiz onto the site, and while the kids curl their lips at my handiwork and crush any burgeoning confidence I may have been experiencing, I can't help feeling it needs something. More questions, perhaps. But that'll have to wait till tomorrow – it's bath and bed time any minute now.

'Upstairs for baths!' I yell at the kids, even though they're standing right behind me. 'Oh! I thought you were in the front room! Sorry about your lugholes, my lovely loves!'

'I had a bath at Daddy's,' Izzy says.

'Me too,' Ben tries it on.

'Good for you,' I smile back. 'Now you can have one here, too. Both of you need hair-washing and you've got school tomorrow. Up those stairs now – HUT two, three, four, HUT two, three, four...'

No one moves.

'Guys?' I feel my strength draining. 'Come on...'

They sit stock still, staring at the screen, faces blank.

'Bath? Anyone? Step we gaily?'

Nothing.

I'm too old for this – my patience ran out years ago. Took off like a shot, it did, trying its best to catch up to my dignity – which, in turn was chasing my self-esteem and confidence, never to be seen again.

I'm tired, annoyed, frustrated and feeling really fat, so with nary a thought for my actions, I close the lid of the laptop and force a smile.

'WHAT?' Izzy looks up at me in disbelief.

'MU-UM!' shrieks Ben, launching himself at me with such force, I nearly topple over.

'Ow! Look, it's getting late and you've got school tomorrow and we need some good, calm wind-down time after your bath—'

'We've *had* our baths!' he says through clenched teeth.

All of a sudden, I feel the seriousness of this situation. Ben's not playing, he's as mad as hell. His face is red, his eyebrows are furrowed into the 'fierce' setting and I'm almost certain I just saw some steam coming out of his ears.

'Let me play on your computer,' he says, with barely controlled rage.

'No,' I half-laugh, in a desperate attempt to lighten things up.

'Let. Me. Play.'

'Oh, this is crazy,' I brush his hair off his face. 'Let's go upstairs and we can—'

'Let. Me. Play.' He sounds even more menacing now. And that stare of his is actually quite scary.

An image of him as an eighteen-year-old prop forward springs into my mind's eye and I realise it won't be all that long before he'll be able to floor me with the back of his hand. I'd better sort this out fast.

'Ben. I'm your mother, I'm the boss. You do as I say!'

'Ha!' Izzy pipes up, reopening the laptop and logging in again.

'NO!' Ben's eyes fill up. 'It's YOUR fault Daddy doesn't live with us. You're such a monster! I bet if he lived here, we'd have the Xbox all the time!'

'So that's what this is about, is it?' I'm a bit relieved, to be honest. 'The bloody Xbox?'

'No,' Ben starts to smile, his body relaxing into mine and I hug him hard.

173

Poor little bugger. Left to sit in front of a giant screen playing wholly inappropriate games for hours on end while his Daddy does God knows what; neglected and ignored to within an inch of his life. I know just how he feels.

From somewhere deep, down among all the parenting books I've read through the years, I manage to dredge up a half-decent line:

'You know, Ben, that no matter how cross and angry you get with me, I will always love you. You can't stop me. Even if you feel like you hate me, always remember that I love you.'

'Me too,' he dissolves into tears.

'Well, what about me?' Izzy looks wounded.

'Same goes for you, sweetheart. Of course! Now where's that tickle monster I saw here earlier? Must be around here somewhere...'

I tickle Ben gently and as he giggles, he stands on my feet so I can walk him over to the stairs.

'Yay! Bath, bed, book and then sleep, perchance to dream sweet dreams. You too, gorgeous,' I direct to Izzy.

'NO!'

'Christ Almi—'

'NO WAY! I'll have it later. Ben has to go to bed first.'

'Do you need some special time alone with me?' I ask, ever-hopeful.

'No,' she answers, 'actually, yes. Yes, that's exactly what I want!'

'If I let you stay up till nine—'

'Ten!'

'Nine.'

'Nine-thirty, then. It's a deal. Night, night Ben. Love you, Mummy!'

'I don't know why I bother sometimes, I really don't,' I say, as I place Ben's feet onto the stairs. And Izzy's quick reply gives me the last answer for another question in the Single Mum quiz:

1. **When you've asked the kids five million times (approx.) to do something and you finally get exasperated, shouting, 'I don't know why I bother!', your kids will usually say:**

   a) 'I'm so sorry Mummy! I hate to see you sad – I'll do it straight away!'

   b) 'I said in a *MINUTE*!'

   c) 'Samesies.'

   –

Three upbeat, positive things I could count as 'wins' so far:

- I'm online! Not that I have any idea how I got there... (thanks Izz).
- I haven't had any cigarettes for days – haven't even thought about them.
- I managed to quell Ben's quite frankly frightening tantrum without losing my own temper. And my creative juices are flowing. Not sure where they're flowing *to*, but it feels good regardless.

   –

Well that didn't take him long. Unless he was already been seeing her before he dumped me, of course. But Tiffany? *Tiffany?* I mean, come on! Seriously?

'What's wrong with Tiffany?' Izzy sniffs from the passenger seat.

Damn that gobby inner voice.

'Oh! Nothing, nothing.' I keep my eyes on the road, lest I look at her and she detects some hurt in my countenance. 'It's just a... I dunno... it's a very *young* name. Don't you think?'

'No. She spells it with an "i" at the end instead of a "y",' she says, straight-faced, as though this is a good thing and the alternative spelling makes it sound more grown up or something.

'Tih-fah-neeee!' Ben beams at himself and stares out the window.

'All right, all right,' I almost snap when I check the rear-view mirror and see him looking so happy at the sound of her name. 'I think we've established the who. Now all we have to do is figure out the *why*.'

'What do you mean?' Izzy looks up from her phone, but I stare dead ahead.

'Well, I... how old is she, do you know?'

'Really old,' Ben says.

'Yeah,' Izzy agrees. 'About twenty—'

I narrowly miss a squirrel bounding across the road as I swerve in shock.

'*Twenty*? She's twenty? That practically makes him a bloody paedo—'

'*Five* – about twenty-five, I was going to say, if you'd just let me finish,' Izzy tuts.

'Hmph,' I scoff. 'Still…'

'Tih-fah-neee is so pre-tty,' Ben sings, as if he's trying to get me all riled up on purpose.

'Daddy only ever goes out with pretty women,' I say, shifting in my seat as I thrust my nose in the air, desperately trying to wrest back some long-lost pride.

'So why did he go out with you? Was it a dare?' Izzy can barely get the words out, she's so pleased with herself.

Ben laughs – possibly only because Izzy's nearly doubled over with delight, and he's copying her, but nevertheless, he's really roaring at this, while I'm busy being mock-offended, gasping at the sheer audacity of my little girl, my mouth in an open oval.

'Outrageous behaviour!' I say, in my best Victorian school mistress tones.

'Well,' Izzy straightens up, wiping a tear of mirth from her eye, 'you were going to say, *what would a young, pretty girl like Tiffani be doing with an old man like Daddy*? weren't you?'

'No I wasn't!'

Which is sort of true – I would never have referred to Tiffani as 'pretty', even if she was. And I would never openly say Joe was an old man even if, comparatively speaking, he clearly is.

But really, what could they possibly see in each other? Obviously there's the sex. For him. But what's in it for her? He was never what you might call a 'master swordsman' even at the height of his powers. And I suppose he wasn't bad-looking, when he had hair, but he was never going to give George Clooney anything to worry about.

And anyway, that's hardly the point. The point is, I remind myself, that he's introduced his kids – his two impressionable, vulnerable and fragile kids, who are in the middle of the biggest emotional maelstrom of their lives so far – to some one-night stand who probably smokes like a chimney, looks like Bet Lynch and wears leopard-print head-to-peep toe. Not that there's anything wrong with that, per se…

I read something in a magazine once that said divorced men thought it was acceptable to introduce the kids to their new squeeze after they'd been split up for two months. Divorced women, on the other hand, said *two years* would be okay.

Which only goes to show how differently the sexes view important relationships – both sexual and familial. Oh – and that men can be such stupid, insensitive, selfish prats.

Contrary to what it sounds like, though, I'm actually fine with it. My feelings are most definitely not hurt, I don't feel anything remotely resembling jealousy and I… well, I don't feel anything much at all. Apart from a bit sorry for the kids. You know, for having such a fickle, unthinking, leopard-print-loving guy for a father.

'Leopard-print is cool – it doesn't mean what it did in your day, like you're all slutty,' Izzy says absent-mindedly, squinting at her phone.

This is getting crazy. Can she read my mind? Is she psychic? Maybe she's got ESP! Must get her to try to bend some spoons when we get home tonight.

'How do you know words like "slutty"? And how did you know I was thinking about leopard-print?' I'm vexed by just about everything that comes out of her mouth these days, let's face it.

'You were muttering about someone called Bet Lynch who wears leopard-print. You're always talking to yourself like that – it's weird.'

Am I? I mean, I know I have a rich inner life and I'm often giving myself a good talking to about something or other – but it's all in my head, isn't it? It's not like I say any of this stuff out loud or anything. Is it?

'YES IT IS!' both Izzy and Ben shout in the affirmative.

–

At the school gates, I'm struck by how many dads are here to see their little cherubs off with a kiss and a cuddle and a hey-nonny-no. Now, I realise some of these guys must work from home – possibly making more millions for their own companies, run by themselves at their kitchen tables, take-away lattes from The Pantry in hand. But some of them must have jobs they have to get to in Henley, Reading or London – and maybe some don't have jobs at all, lounging about all day in trakkie daks and Uggs, living off endowment funds and inheritances and the like.

But whatever their financial circs, I find it really touching that a load of the Thistlebend dads are there saying goodbye for the day. It's almost as if they know it's important to be there for your kids whenever and wherever you can. Even if – or maybe even *especially* if – you're their dad. Imagine!

At once impressed and saddened, I watch the kids navigating their way around the other new children in their new lives. And then, while I'm admiring their courage and bravery, as if out of nowhere, I feel that familiar micro-needling effect on the tip of my nose and my eyes fill with tears.

The bell goes and I wave at the kids. Izzy rolls her eyes and turns her back on me (*quelle surprise*) and Ben waves back, smiling like an emoji on Ecstasy.

Wearily, I trudge up the hill, thinking how nice it would be to have a pal to meet in The Pantry for a swift hot choc or three (extra whipped cream on mine, three marshmallows, too, thanks). I glance around furtively and see everyone else in clusters of two or three, all chattering and guffawing like a pack of hyenas and wonder why no one has been particularly friendly to me.

Maybe I'm giving off too much of a Single Mum vibe and none of the yummies want to catch the divorce lurgy. Perhaps they've seen me staring at their menfolk and while I'm thinking how lucky their wives are to have them as the fathers of their children, they think I'm lusting after their property, ever-watchful for that moment when the wife's back's turned and I can pounce on them, seducing them with my feminine wiles. Which would be a majorly tall order for me, considering I've never had the faintest clue what 'wiles' were. 'Whales' in a really bad Australian accent? They deserted me years ago, whatever they were, anyway.

I'm muttering to myself, 'Just seen a pod of wiles, mate, round the coast of New South Wiles,' with that aforementioned dodgy Aussie accent, when all of a sudden, I feel something snuffling around and prodding at my bum.

'Oh!' I wheel around and discover it's Willow, the Hungarian vizsla. 'Hello you!'

'Sorry about that,' I hear someone say — someone in the distance, far away, almost above the clouds. 'She's just being friendly. In her way.'

I look up, feeling the crick in my neck and see it's Charlotte – the ridiculously tall potential new friend I met in The Pantry the other day.

'Oh, hello,' I wipe the tears away and try not to draw too much attention to the glaring height difference between us as the other mums and dads make their way to the car park. Although I realise, of course, that it's utterly futile.

'Pardon?' she cups a long, elegant-fingered hand around her ear and bends down towards me. 'I didn't quite catch that – could you say it again?'

'Very droll,' I sniff and smile.

'So how are the kids settling in?' she asks, straightening up and shouting down to me, so I can hear.

'They're goo—' I pause for effect, cupping my hands around my mouth to amplify the sound of my shouting. 'I SAID, THEY'RE GOOOOOD!'

Charlotte giggles and points to The Pantry with her index finger.

'Got time for a coffee?'

I'm so excited, I nearly pee in my pants at this point. Which reminds me – I must try to remember to actually put those Tena Lady pads in my knickers before I leave the house, otherwise there's little or no point, really.

Managing to restrain myself, I nod enthusiastically and try to act nonchalant as we go in.

I needn't have bothered, though, because it's packed and no one notices me at all. I come over all super-self-conscious anyway, as is my wont lately, as Charlotte leads the way through the crowd, Willow and I tripping over each other's feet/paws in our haste behind her.

She makes a beeline for the only empty seat in the house – a small, cosy corner nook by the wood-burning fire, fairly festooned with cushions of varying designs in shades of pink, red and orange that gives it a distinctly Moroccan hookah-bar feel (not that I've ever been to Morocco – or, indeed a hookah bar. But I have been to a caff on Edgware Road where everyone was smoking the Hubbly Bubbly out on the street, so…). It's opulent and gorgeous and totally out of step with the rest of the Farrow & Ball-drenched wood everywhere else in here.

I briefly wonder why no one else has nabbed it yet, until I see the RESERVED card in the middle of the table.

'I don't think we can sit here,' I say, my heart sinking at the thought of not having a coffee and chat in The Pantry with my New Friend.

Charlotte totally ignores me, takes off her expensive-looking camel-coloured coat and hangs it on a black velvet hanger on the hat stand nearby. When she glides down onto the bench, all impossibly long limbs, pearls and cashmere, Willow sits on the floor in front of her, like a guard dog, keeping watch.

It's as though Cleopatra's come to the café. Without her Pharoah goatee, natch. From what I've seen, Charlotte is completely untroubled by unwanted facial hair.

So the table is reserved for her! Blimey, who is she? Minor royalty? Major royalty? A celebrity of some sort? She does have a certain *Made In Chelsea* look about her, now I think about it…

'Are you going to sit down?' Charlotte looks up at me, standing there like a lemon. 'We'll be on a more even playing field that way.'

She's right, I think, and I slide in next to her, taking my coat off as I go and sitting on it in an attempt to give myself a little extra height.

'So...' I say. Mainly because I can't think of anything else.

'I own this place,' she says, looking around, discreetly nodding at a barista who comes rushing over to take our order. 'As well as a couple of others. What about you, Kiki?'

Kiki? Who's Kiki?

'Sorry – what did you say your name was the other day?'

'I can't remember – but it wasn't Kiki! It's Annie, actually. Annie Beaton. With an "ea" not a double "e" like Mrs Beeton who, you know, did the *Book of Household Management.*'

I have a small tendency to babble a bit when I'm nervous. Although what I have to be nervous about is beyond me. There's something about Charlotte – her demeanour or scent (First by Van Cleef and Arpels – I'd know it anywhere – Mum used to wear it in the winter, too) or maybe it's just her translucent, flawless skin. Whatever it is, it puts me a teensy bit on edge, that's for sure.

I shake my head as if trying to erase the past few seconds and ask the barista, an eager young man who looks like a model, whether I could have an extra-large hot chocolate. With extra whipped cream.

Charlotte plumps for an espresso.

'So what do you do, Annie?' she smiles.

'Bugger all,' I answer.

'Really?'

'No, not really – I don't know why I said that – it's more something my ex-husband would say about me. Silly moo. Oops – there's another one! Funny how those things seep into your own consciousness, isn't it?'

Charlotte looks right through me.

'Go on,' she says.

'Well, I used to write for magazines a million years ago and even a website… until they sacked me for being crap at technology. Which I was. I mean, I still am, obviously, but Izzy, my daughter – she was here with me the other day – she's a whizz at all that sort of stuff so she's helping me start up my blog.'

I take a breath and wait for Charlotte to jump in, but she doesn't. Even though the café is rammed and noisy, I still feel the awkwardness of the silence at our table. So what do I do? Do my best to fill it in, of course, just as our beverages arrive.

'Yeah – I never thought I'd be online, banging on about stuff, but my aunt's obsessed with self-help, you see, so when I realised there was nothing out there for divorced single mums – a very exacting breed – I decided to take matters into my own hands and if not offer advice, at least have a laugh about our situation. Because as we all know, if you don't laugh—'

'You cry,' Charlotte finishes my sentence.

'Precisely my point! So anyway, the blog's called *How To Be A Divorced Single Mum*. And the line under that is: *Because A Good Man* – and then in brackets, "u, a, l", so it looks like "manual"– *Is Hard To Find.*'

I wait for a flicker of recognition or acknowledgement or *something* to cross Charlotte's face. And wait. And wait some more. Then I give up.

'Yeah, so I'm working on The Ten Commandments of The Divorced Single Mum – like, you know, thou shalt not eat thy feelings – unless thy feelings art made out of Lindor Balls or Tunnock's Tea Cakes, in which case, thou hast our blessing. Or something – can't quite remember now... But what I've actually put up online is a quiz. It's inspired by all the quizzes we used to write when I worked on teen magazines way back in the day. It's called *What Kind Of A Single Mum Are You?* and it goes through all these scenarios, like forgetting that kids need feeding and there only being furr in the fridge—'

'What's wrong with furry food?' Charlotte grins at me.

'That's one of the possible answers!'

'It is?'

'Yeah – hey! You haven't seen it online, have you?'

Charlotte drains her espresso and makes to leave.

'Listen, Ki... *Annie,*' she says, 'I have a proposition for you. Apart from owning several high-end cafés and bistros in the area, I'm also the editor-in-chief of the local glossy magazine, *Chilterns Today (Forever in your heart)*. We're having a bit of a re-vamp at the minute and we could really do with a sort of agony aunt advice column from someone new – someone who can inject a bit of sass into it, let us into a different world – or at least different from the yummy mummy, hunky hubby, two-point-four-children, labradoodle kind of world that can be so tedious. You know?'

'I'd give my right arm for some of that tediousness,' I sigh.

'Tedium,' Charlotte corrects me. 'Everyone needs an editor, don't worry.'

I stand up and put my crumpled, over-sized parka on, following her lead. And Willow's.

'I won't lie to you,' she says over her shoulder as we weave our way out of the café, 'I'm building up a bank of tips that I may find useful one day if I ever, you know...' she looks around, 'and you're my bank manager, so to speak. No one around here ever talks of such things as divorce or single mums.' She says the words 'divorce' and 'single mums' in a loud whisper. 'In fact, I think you're the first one I've ever seen. I mean, *met*. Anyway, I have a feeling that more women than just little ol' me are weighing up the pros and cons of binning the boy... So as our resident agony aunt who's been around the block a bit, I think you'll be providing an essential local service.'

'Wowsers,' I say, a bit stuck for proper words.

'I'm afraid I won't be able to pay you anything for the time being...'

'That's fine!' I lie. 'Doesn't matter – times are tough everywhere, I know...'

'I'll need a profile pic, of course – put some make-up on, would you? Bit of eyeliner, mascara, lipstick – and take a selfie. No need for faffing around. I'll send you a question and you can dispense the advice. And start work on a list of the pros and cons of being a divorced single mum, with the pros far outweighing the cons, obvs – 750 words? Inbox me with the Q&A by... this time next week?'

And with that, she lets Willow hop over the driver's seat of her diabolically expensive-looking Mercedes-Benz SUV, with her following suit seconds later. Except Charlotte doesn't hop – she steps in gracefully and seamlessly, becoming one with the plush, all-leather cream interior.

She noiselessly reverses and takes off, waving goodbye in her rear-view mirror. Or maybe that was Willow. Ah, who cares?! I've got a job!

Three positive things:
- I've got a job!
- I've got a job!
- I've got a job!

Chapter Six

April

April 17 – Cock of the Talk

We're in the car on the way to school singing 'Good Morning (How Are You?)' – an ancient song by an Australian group called The Moir Sisters which, for some inexplicable reason, I've had bouncing around in my brain ever since I rediscovered Helen Reddy and The Raspberries. I often wonder about what else is lurking about in there, in the dim, dark recesses of my mind – but why I've developed a thing about early seventies hits in particular is puzzling me. Maybe it's because I'm fifty.

I sing faux-operatically about having a good morning and asking how they are. And when I get to the bit about it being nice to see their faces, Ben pipes up and says: 'It's nice to see your FARTS!'

He's in stitches and I'm impressed with his creativity, so I tell him so.

'Ha! Well done, sweetie, very good!'

'You can't *see* a fart,' Izzy informs us.

'Yes you can,' I disagree. 'You can see Ben's anyway – they're sort of khaki green...'

'God, Mum, you sound so proud of him,' she sneers.

'Well, I am!'

Izzy harrumphs, crosses her arms over her chest and looks out the side window. I can feel the annoyance radiating from her.

'I'm proud of both of you!' And I leave it there, so as not to add fuel to the sibling rivalry fires that are constantly breaking out all over the shop these days.

And while it's true, I am proud of both of them, I'm particularly chuffed when Ben starts mucking about with sounds and words, because he's had so much trouble with his ears and, consequently, his speech over the years. Izzy's been able to talk under wet cement ever since she was about one, but poor old Ben has always struggled and now I guess I grab anything I can to reassure myself that progress is being made and getting grommets fitted when we were in Sydney was worth it.

I remember when he'd had them put in, the surgeon said they'd had to suck out 'about a ton of gunk' that had been wedged deep within both of his ears.

I took him to speech therapy soon after the operation and the therapist said at his age (two and a half), he should have been babbling like a madman, mimicking me and everyone else around him all the time – especially in the car.

She said that the first words of lots of kids with hearing/speech problems were often swear words, because they copied their mums, shouting obscenities at other drivers.

So you can imagine me fairly bursting with pride when one day, about four months afterwards, I forgot my 'no swearing – well, no really bad, advanced swearing in front of the kids' rule and, indignant at being cut off by some young guy, mufflers roaring and going at least sixty in a thirty zone, I yelled: 'What a COCK!' to his fast-disappearing tail fins.

My road rage quickly turned to unbridled joy, though, when I heard the cutest little voice coming from the Maxi Cosi car seat in the back:

'COCK!' it said.

It was Ben! He could speak! Clear as a bell! He was copying me in fine style, just like the speech therapist said he would.

'Good BOY!' I trilled.

'COCK!' he said again, basking in the glow of my approval.

'Yes! Who's a clever boy, then?' I remember saying, as if I was talking to a parrot.

We both must have said 'cock' about a million more times before we got home, practising this latest addition to his vocab. When we walked through the front door, Ben ran straight over to Joe, leapt into his arms and, calling it as he saw it, said right to Daddy's face:

'COCK!'

'Charming,' Joe said.

In retrospect, of course, Ben was right. And I couldn't've said it better myself.

'Ah, happy days,' I sigh.

And then this weird, electronic bubbly sort of sound fills up the car. It turns into tinny music and I haven't got a Scooby where it's coming from or what it wants with us.

'What the fa-aa-aa—?' I manage, despite being scared witless.

'Fix It Felix!' says Izzy. 'No need to panic – it's just your phone.'

'That's not my phone – mine's got a different ringtone! And anyway, no one I know would be calling me at this ungodly hour!'

'Only because you don't know anyone, Mummy-no-mates,' she says.

'I do too,' I take offence at this accusation.

'Do not,' she counters.

'Do too – oh, just shut it up, will you? I can't concentrate on these bloody roads with that cacophony.'

Izzy leans over to the steering wheel and pushes a button with a green phone receiver on it.

'Hello? Annie?' Her voice is crackly and a bit muffled, but I think it's Aisling.

'Ash?' I say, grinning expectantly at the road ahead while I simultaneously marvel at modern technology and curse myself for not having the faintest clue what to do with it. 'Is that you?'

'Of course it feckin' is,' she barks back at me. 'What are you doing tonight?'

'Good thanks! You?' I wink at Izzy.

'Stop messing,' says Aisling, sounding cross. 'I haven't got time for games. You in or out tonight?'

'Um, now let me see...' I say slowly. 'It's a toss-up between *Miss Marple* and *Poirot*. Or the umpteenth repeat of a *Midsomer Murders*, if we're lucky...'

'Ah, sure, well as soon as school's finished, I'm grabbing the boys and tearing down the M4 to see you. We'll be staying the night, if that's okay – if it doesn't interfere too much with your hectic TV detective-watching schedule?'

Izzy sniggers. I shoot her a sharp look.

'You sure you're not going out with friends?' Aisling goes on. 'Ach! What am I saying? Of course you're not!'

'I know, right?' Izzy pipes up. 'Like, what friends?!'

'I thought you didn't have time for stupid games?' I say, sounding a little more thin-lipped than I'd intended.

'Ha! Looking forward to seeing you, Izzy,' says Ash.

'What about me?' Ben squeaks from the back.

'Is that you, Ben?'

'YES!'

'I'm sorry, young man – I didn't know you were there! It's Auntie Aisling here – the boys can't wait to see you. You do have an Xbox, don't you, Annie?'

'No I do bloody not!' I say.

'Daddy does!' Ben shouts out.

And you play all sorts of shite with him when you're at his place, I think to myself.

'No, I don't,' says Ben, 'Daddy doesn't play it with me – I play *Halo* by my own.'

'Ah, for fuck's sake,' I say under my breath, my mood lowering so far, I swear I can hear it smashing through the footwell.

'Can it, Fix It!' Ben delights in saying.

'Well, we do finally have a Freesat Box and the broadband's on, so we've got Netflix and Amazon and… BBC iPlayer? If anyone wants to watch, I dunno – *Horrible Histories*?' I say hopefully.

'We'll bring what we can. See you at about four thirty? Maybe a bit later if we get stuck in traffic. And Annie?'

'Hmmm?' I hum, still thinking about poor neglected Ben playing wildly inappropriate, violent, bloodthirsty, stupid bloody computer games by himself. Now if that

doesn't sound like the standard serial killer's perfect child-
hood, I don't know what does.

'Have you got any gin?'

-

While the kids are at school, I high-tail it over to Dunelm,
which is in some horrible trading estate off the A33,
housing a massive Sainsbury's, a McDonald's, a Boots, a
NEXT, a Sports Direct warehouse and best of all, an
absolutely giant IKEA, where I'll go when I'm done with
Dunelm.

Which may take some time, I think to myself, as I walk
through the double doors into a veritable magic kingdom
of expensive interior design brands and their cheaper,
more me-friendly, own-brand knock-offs.

There are curtains and duvet covers, towels and bean
bags, mirrors and rugs, lamps and sun-loungers, throws
and cushions, storage units and furniture and... a café! But
I'm too interested in the enormous mirrors that would
look nice hanging on the wall opposite the window in
our front room, thus making it look a bit larger as well as
a bit more chic, and a whole lot less shabby.

I mean, it's incredible! I've never been to a Dunelm
before – but there are some really nice things here. And
if I were to, say, buy a couple of brushed cotton, tartan
duvet sets, so Aisling and the boys can be extra cosy in
Ben's triple-sleeper, while the kids and I get super-snug
in Izzy's bed, well, the kids' rooms would start looking a
bit more like the kind of bedrooms kids might have in the
country and...

Before I can say, 'But you're a single mum on a tiny
budget – are you crazy?' to myself, I've grabbed three

lightweight summer duvets, two tartan duvet sets (one red, the other bluey-green), one grey and white duvet set, for me, called 'Chantilly', four medium-firm Dunelm own-brand pillows, a standard lamp painted in what they're calling 'honeystone', complete with a matching linen-look lamp-shade for the front room, a mirror for the landing at the top of the stairwell and wouldn't you know, in less than fifteen Fix It Felixing minutes, I've spent a fucking fortune! Still, I console myself as I make my way over to IKEA, I will be earning soon, what with my brand spanking new advice column at *Chilterns Today (Forever in your heart)* and all. And even if it only pays peanuts in the end, who knows where it might lead?

Also, I think, as I clock the (free) creche near the entrance of IKEA and make a mental note to lug the kids over here one of these days so they can have a play in the plastic balls while I mooch about the kitchens and stuff, since I've stopped smoking and drinking, I must be saving stacks!

I've found myself on various furniture shop websites lately, lusting after a blanket box here, a radiator table there – and I figure that's okay. I mean, if I'm going to be swapping one addiction for another, thank God it's only going to cost me my life savings, as opposed to my life.

I meander around, blissfully unaware that I'm blindly obeying my stylish, Swedish masters, being shepherded to exactly where they want me to go – even staying within the yellow lines at all times – until eventually, I find myself in the rug department.

And there it is. The exact same rug that Jane has. It's only fifty quid – bargainous – and super soft, almost velvety to the touch. It's the same colours as hers – cream and navy-blue. It *is* Jane's fake Persian rug (a Version rug?) and it'd look fab on Aud's front room floor, beautifully covering the worn-out, chipped original oak floor boards.

I um: I ah. I um: I ah. I um and ah some more.

Me: We can't afford that!

Myself: But we need a rug for the front room! Carpet would cost way more…

I: Still, it is a bit extravagant – especially after the Dunelm disaster just now.

Me: I say no. Sorry.

I: It's a no from me, too. I mean I.

Myself: What? Now I'm all confused! Ah, sod it – let's get down to the warehousey bit quick and grab one before they run out of stock and there you are, later on this evening, banging on about how lovely life is in the country to Aisling, while she's sitting on a crappy old oak floor, getting piles thinking you must have gone mad!

'Are you all right, madam?' an impossibly young-looking lady in a yellow and blue polo shirt asks me, looking quite concerned as she does so.

'Mmm? Oh, fine, yes, sorry, we're all fine,' I say, slowly coming out of my *Three Faces of Eve* moment. 'I think we'd – sorry, *I'd* like to buy this rug, actually.'

Well, what's another fifty quid when I've already forked out over three hundred pounds in Dunelm? And it *is* an investment piece, after all.

—

Back at home, before I set off to collect the kids, I call Amelie to a) tell her off for never calling me and b) gloat that Aisling is coming down to see us tonight.

Of course, my call goes straight to voicemail.

'So then,' I sigh, 'it appears that in your dogged pursuit of no-doubt unsavoury shagging shenanigans, you are dumping your mates. I suppose this is to be expected, what with your daughter having flown the coop, freeing you up for... well, whatever you fancy, I suppose. Just wanted to let you know that Ash – remember her? Our really good friend? She's coming down to stay the night here with the boys and you will be missed. We'll probably bitch about you madly, though, so it's probably for the best, really, that you're *otherwise engaged* and all. Your loss, though. Call soon, you old bag. Love you!'

Only a couple of minutes pass before my phone bleeps, telling me I've got a text message. It's from Amelie:

> Ooh, I wish I could be there! Still,
> at least I've got Rodrigo to
> provide me with the solace I need
> while I weep into my lace hankie,
> bereft at the thought of not
> drinking tea and scoffing scones
> with my two old muckers.
> Hopefully I'll make it through the
> night. XXX PS Got another top
> tip for you – make sure you're
> getting all the benefits you're
> entitled to – school dinners?
> Working tax credits? Call the
> relevant govt. dept. and find out.
> You can thank me later. Big love
> to you and Ash. MWAH!

God she's fast! That would have taken me at least ten minutes to write, given the state of my fat fingers and all.

And who the hell's Rodrigo when he's at home? Good call about the scones, though – maybe I should stop in at the Co-op on the way back from school to see if they've got any in stock. I'm nothing if not auto-suggestive and I think my mouth may have started to water a little when Amelie mentioned scones in her text. Better get some jam and some of that yumsters whipped cream in a can, too. Not to mention a couple of extra packets of Tunnock's Tea Cakes. They're only a pound a pack, so they're not going to exactly break the bank, are they?

Must grab some gin, too. Sounds like Ash's need for booze is almost as great as my need for sugar. Almost.

–

Wins so far:
- Ben's speech is getting better and more nimble every day – and I take full credit for it.
- Aisling is coming to stay. A friend! To stay! I can hardly believe it.
- One word, two syllables: Dunelm. What a fantastic find.

–

Still April 17 – It's Getting Hot in Here

Even though it's really getting quite warm outside, I insist on showing off the country cosiness of our place by having a roaring fire in the front room, hot chocolates at the ready and my biggest, snuggliest, most hygge-ish cardigan on for when Ash and the boys arrive, which they do about an hour after the kids and I get home from Thistlebend.

'Come in, come in!' I stand on the doorstep, wrapping my cardi around me and shivering in an exaggerated manner. 'You must be exhausted and near-frozen after your perilous journey. Do come inside, weary travellers – warm your toes by the fire for a while. There's hot chocolate and marshmallows ready to go and—'

'Just pour me a fag and light me a G&T, will you?' Aisling rasps as she brushes past me, dumping a big leather holdall in the 'hallway'. 'And can someone open a window in here? It's stifling!'

'Auntie Ash!' the kids leap up from the fab new rug they've been lying on and nearly knock her over in their excitement.

'You poor wretches,' she hugs them back extra-hard and smooths their hair over their foreheads. 'It can't have been easy, these past few months... what with a mother like that... so! How's your new school?'

'Good,' says Ben. 'Where's Jimmy and Joshie?'

'Nyurgh,' Izzy grunts. Whether this guttural sound is a reply to Aisling's question about school or simply a response to Ben's mentioning the twin boys is unclear. But whatever the source, her displeasure is duly noted.

'Still watching *Shrek* in the back of the car,' Ash jerks her head towards the driveway. 'Now what's up with you, Missy? Let's get comfy and you can tell Auntie Ash all about it.'

Aisling focuses her attention on Izzy as she simultaneously struggles with trying to open the broken sash window and take off her long, charcoal-coloured, gorgeously soft-looking cardigan, no doubt bought from The White Company in Kingston. Ben rushes out the front door to join the boys in the state of the art family

SUV in the driveway and Ash gives up on the window, holding Izzy's hands as they sit down on the couch together.

'Right, well,' I begin, feeling surplus to requirements – like a shag on a rock, as Mum would say. Although I can't remember the last time I felt like a shag. And wouldn't doing it on a rock just be bloody uncomfortable and practically impossible? Suppose it depends on the rock. And the shag. I make a mental note to quiz Mum about this, next time we talk. 'I'll get both of you a hot choc while you catch up, then.'

'Water for me,' Izzy's adoring gaze barely strays from Auntie Ash. 'With ice if we've got any.'

'Screw the feckin' hot chocolate,' Aisling growls. 'Gin's in my bag there. So's the tonic. Couple of limes, too. Chop chop! Now. Where were we, darling girl?'

I brush a trickle of sweat away from my temple, wondering whether it's a hot flush or whether it is, as everyone else seems to suggest, like a Swedish sauna in here.

'And don't be stingy with the gin!' Ash calls out.

Now it's my turn to roll my eyes skywards. I mutter to myself as I root around in the cupboards only to discover we have no long, tall glasses – in fact, we have no glasses at all. The only drinking receptacles we have are mugs and cups (either melamine or Lightning McQueen-adorned plastic) and how the hell do you make a G&T? Beer or wine was always my drink of choice, when I was in a boozy mood – buggered if I know how to do cocktails, for Christ's sake!

'It's not like I asked for a Flaming Lamborghini or anything,' Ash grumbles, coming into the kitchen. 'What's taking you so long?'

'Nice to see you too, long-lost best friend,' I sark. '*So how is it being a divorced single mum, Annie?* Well, Ash, good question, I'm glad you asked me that—'

'All right, all right,' Ash smiles as she slices up a lime and sloshes the Bombay Sapphire into a Minnie Mouse mug. 'Of course I was going to feckin' ask you all about that. I just wanted to get my story in first.'

'*Your* story?'

'Yeah. *My* story. About me and Pete,' Ash takes a glug. 'You're not the only one going through it, you know.'

Oh yeah! Amid all the hoohah and melee of my own frenetic life, I'd completely forgotten about Ash's drama. Which is unlike me. I mean, I'm usually such a good friend, always asking how things are going, always remembering quandaries and conundrums and never forgetting to show due diligence at all times.

I guess the older we all get, the more we get mired down in the minutiae of our own personal problems and that once tight-knit friendship circle starts to unravel a bit with neglect. This is possibly even more marked when it comes to older mothers like myself and Aisling, come to think of it – where we did our own thing for so long, continuing to live our twenties and thirties long past our Best Before dates, only having ourselves to look after, the only downer being a thrice-weekly hangover from Hades to contend with…

'You not having one?' Ash raises her mug and takes a slug.

'Nah.' I turn the cooker on and put the saucepan with the tepid chocolate on to warm up. 'I'm off the booze.'

'Why?'

'I just can't handle everything – *anything* – if I'm recovering from a big night. And now I'm solely responsible for the bairns, I can't bear the thought of—'

'Oh, go on,' Ash grins at me and nudges the air with her elbow, bent in her standard, two-handed drinking stance. 'It's not every day we get to see each other in such bucolic bliss, is it?'

'Do you like it? It is pretty special, I must admit. It's the cosiness, all this country living, out here gettin' hygge with it—'

'Hoo-gah,' she says. 'It's pronounced hoogah, not *higgy.*'

Oh.

'Just have the one! Maybe two? Three max. Oh go on, I hate to drink alone and I am definitely drinking tonight… We lined our stomachs with a few Happy Meals on the way down, so I'm good to go.'

Surprisingly, I stay strong and decline her kind offer with thanks. Which isn't actually all that difficult. Especially when you consider the last time I was knocking them back with Aisling, about three years ago, she was so knackered, she drained half a bottle of Valpolicella in seconds flat, threw her head back to laugh at something and promptly flopped forwards onto her kitchen table, instantly falling fast asleep and snoring like a drunken sailor.

Well, it's understandable. Saturday nights just aren't the same after you've had kids. Particularly when you're over forty-five.

'Nope. Not for me. You go ahead though. Now tell me – what the hell is going on?'

'Aren't we going to wait for the kids to be in bed?' she asks, wide-eyed.

'Up to you,' I shrug. 'I just thought you were desperate to talk – and I must warn you, I'm so cream-crackered these days, I'm lucky if I can manage to stay awake for a full ten minutes after I've put the kids to sleep—'

Izzy wanders into the kitchen just as I'm saying this and throws *her* head back in that scoffing way she has.

'Ha! You fall asleep *waaaay* before we do! Before I do, anyway, you lazy old moo—'

'Hey! That's no way to speak to your mother,' Ash comes to my rescue. 'Besides, she only understands swear words.'

'Is l-a-z-y a swear?' Izzy grins at Ash. 'It *is* a four-letter word…'

'Let's not get bogged down in all that bollocks again.' I put my hands on Izzy's shoulders, trying to turn her around and gently shoo her out of the kitchen.

'See what I mean?' Ash grins back at Izzy. 'Although "bollocks" is a big, long word, to be honest. If, you know, we're getting technical, here…'

'Are you directing me somewhere?' Izzy asks, mock-offended.

'Go into the front room, watch some TV,' I say, 'make sure the boys are all right, go up to your room, I dunno – can you just let Auntie Ash and I talk?'

'Don't mind me,' she smiles innocently. 'Just pretend I'm not here.'

'Annie,' Ash lowers her voice, indicating the serious-ness of what she's about to say. 'Let her stay. Won't do her any harm to hear all this. Might help her a bit, too. She's not having a great time herself at the mo'.'

'What do you mean?'

'Tell you later – let her stay?'

I nod in dumb agreement just as we hear three heavy-footed boys come tumbling through the front door, laughing and screaming and tearing up the stairs.

'Shut the door!' I yell out.

Of course, no one moves a muscle.

'I see your voice of authority is still feared and revered,' Ash chuckles.

Izzy loves this, her head practically falling off with all that nodding as she agrees with Ash.

Izzy's sort of the daughter Ash never had, I suppose, and they share a close bond. Sometimes I feel they might even be closer than myself and Izzy, even though they rarely see each other. If I'm feeling vulnerable and insecure, that can really make me feel quite anxious. Like, I'm deficient in everything – height, love, Vitamin D... And why are my mothering 'skills' so crap?

I know, it's great that Izzy has someone she can talk to honestly and openly and freely and stuff – I just wish that someone was *me*.

As I walk into the front room to close the door, muttering about catching our death in this bitter cold, I see Ash's car doors in the driveway are wide open. Bloody kids. So I wrap my cardi around me and cross my arms over my chest, stepping out, expecting freezing Siberian winds to hit me in the face, only to feel a massive wave of humid heat wash over me.

Bloody hot flushes, I think to myself as I re-enter the house, simultaneously wiping my sweaty brow and closing the door behind me. And as I do, I catch the tail end of the conversation happening in the kitchen:

'It'll get better, I can guarantee you that,' Ash says in soothing tones.

'But she's so mean!' Izzy stamps her foot.

'She'll get her comeuppance, don't you worry – bullies never win. If anything, you should feel sorry for her, rather than angry. She deserves your pity because obviously she's not a happy bunny, or else she wouldn't behave like that. Something in her life's making her miserable, I bet. Hey! Maybe she's jealous of you...'

'Am *not*!' I burst into the kitchen. 'Well, maybe a little envious of your effortlessly slim figure, Izz, even though you eat more junk than I bloody well do, which is really saying something—'

'We weren't talking about you,' Ash tuts. 'It's not all about you, you know.'

Well, of course I know it isn't! I was simply trying to make a joke out of my clearly-rubbish mothering skills, not having picked up on the fact that Izzy's being bullied! Also, the fact that she's confiding in Ash not me cuts to the absolute quick – but I can't let either of them know that, can I? I mean, can I?

'Right, right,' I acquiesce. 'So go on, Ash, spill 'em – give us all the goss on your latest trauma while you can still speak without slurring.'

Ash is at the kitchen table, the bottle of Bombay Sapphire in front of her (the tonic and limes have already gone by the wayside) and Izzy's sitting *on* the table, swinging her long legs in time to Wagner's *The Ride of the Valkyries*, playing on Classic FM.

I've planned all this, of course – well, the Classic FM bit, not the actual tune, which is a bit dark and scary for my tastes, I was hoping more for Vivaldi's *Four Seasons* on a loop or something. But at seven p.m., if Ash is still standing – which, given the rapid rate she is knocking the gins back is looking doubtful – I'm going to switch the radio over to *The Archers* on BBC Radio 4, just so there can be absolutely no doubt that we're here in the country, warm and cosy and having good, wholesome family fun that beats city debauchery hands down. It's all part of my cunning ruse to convince Ash that she should chuck Pete and come and live out here in the sticks with us. It'd be great – two single mums against the world, sisters doing it for themselves, etc, etc. Not all together in this tiny house, of course – Ash is loaded and could afford to buy one of the mammoth mansions in Upper Old Stoke. But if we were both in the same vicinity, life would be so much sweeter.

Ash takes a deep breath in and lets us have it.

'So he's been getting up to all sorts of feckin' stuff. I tell you, I'm up to high doh with it all,' she begins. 'Excuse my French, Izz.'

'Who's *he*?' asks Izzy.

'And where the hell's this "high doh" you speak of?' I chip in.

'He is Pete and *high doh* is, like, off the scale with nervous excitement. My Ma always says it – I think it's like the top, last, highest note, as in; doh re mi fa so la ti doh. Make sense? You both sitting comfortably? Good. Now, let us proceed.'

She goes on – pretty much without pausing for breath – to tell us how she confronted Pete with the Facebook business group page and that photo of his mistress's chest giving directions to Pete about where to put his 'lovely' willy. He was stuck like a deer in the headlights at this, apparently, and didn't say a word.

Just as well he didn't even try to get a word in, Ash says, because she was on a roll. And if he *had* interrupted her, she might have lost the thread or some of her anger. Although that was unlikely. Because the worm had officially turned: she was sick of playing the good little woman at home while he gallivanted around the world, staying in posh hotels, sipping vintage champagne with *her* (the chesty one) while Ash sat at home hoping he was getting some rest as she stayed up all night worrying about how she could make their sex life more interesting, soothing the night terrors of one sleepless twin, then washing the sheets, duvets and PJs of the other bed-wetting one.

'Ooh, which reminds me,' I sit bolt upright, 'I've put fab new brushed cotton sheets and tartan duvet covers on the beds – the twins can sleep in the bottom half of Ben's bed and he can sleep on the top bunk. You're going to be so cosy! Best remind Joshie to go to the loo before he goes to sleep, though, just to be on the safe si—'

'Shush!' Izzy puts her index finger up to her puckering mouth. 'Let Auntie Ash tell the story!'

I hang my head in shame and gesture to Ash that she take the floor.

'He just stood there, with a dumb look on his face. Didn't try to deny anything or say sorry or tell me I'd got the wrong end of the stick – he's been having an affair with Booby for ten months. TEN MONTHS!!! That's nearly a year!'

I close my eyes and picture an old-school printed calendar – one I had as a child, actually, with pictures of baskets of adorable puppies on each month – so I can count, starting from January…

'So what did you do?' Izzy asks.

'Yeah!' I open my eyes, now safe in the knowledge that ten months is, indeed, nearly a whole year (which is twelve months). 'What happened next?'

'I know!' Izzy leaps off the table, clearly up to high doh. 'You threw all his clothes out of the bedroom window!'

Ash shakes her head.

'Sewed prawn shells into the hems of his suit trousers?' Izzy continues.

'Nope,' Ash says.

'Kicked him in the peanuts!' Ben puts his head round the door jamb.

'Argh, Ben! What are you doing down here? You're supposed to be playing in your room, aren't you? We'll have dinner soon – what's up, little man?' I say.

'Joshie says you brought up an Xbox,' he says to Ash. 'Can we play on it?'

'Oh, later, darling,' I wave him away. 'After dinner. Now you go back upstairs and entertain your guests with those millions of marvellous toys you have up there.'

He turns tail and goes upstairs. Which is amazing in itself, really, Ben rarely does what he's told and never takes just the one 'no' for an answer.

'So…' Ash pours herself another gargantuan gin. 'Where was I again?'

'You weren't sewing prawn shells into his hems,' I help her out.

'Right, right. So what did I do? I did what any right-thinking woman in my position would do,' she picks up where she left off. 'I grabbed his hand, marched him up to the bedroom and f——'

'Fix It Felix!' I jump in, sensing sweariness approaching.

Ash looks taken aback.

'Oh, Mu-um!' Izzy cries, looking apologetically at Aisling. 'She wants us to say "Fix It Felix" instead of the "F" word. As if Ben and I don't hear *her* saying it all the time...'

'Okay, then, just to keep this PG, I grabbed his hand, dragged him upstairs and Fix It Felixed his feckin' brains out.'

I'm aghast.

Izzy's disappointed.

Ash is so pleased with herself, she pours herself another one and hiccups.

'But——' I begin.

'Why did you do that?' Izzy studies her nails. 'You've already got the twins – you don't actually want to get pregnant, do you?'

She's just started PSHE at school, you see, and they've been told the only reason anyone would actually ever *have* sex is because they want to make a baby. Just this week, in fact, the class was shown a film of two naked people having a pillow fight which, Izzy told me, was supposed to show the kids what having sex was like.

'Messy,' I muttered at the time. 'And a whopping great waste of perfectly decent feathers.'

'I know, right? Then they told us that the man puts his penis into the woman's vagina,' she'd said, not flinching

208

or whispering or showing any embarrassment about using such words in the slightest. 'So they can make a baby.'

God, I think to myself, when I was her age and those words were uttered in the classroom, the teachers wouldn't be able to get a word in while we all giggled and guffawed our way through the rest of the lesson. Guess we were hopelessly immature by comparison. Perhaps because we didn't have the internet and Kim Kardashian in those days.

'It just looks so yuk!' Izzy went on. 'There's just got to be a better way to get a baby. If you want one. Which I don't.'

'I'm relieved to hear you say that, my love,' I smiled back at her. 'Can you keep thinking that way for, ooh, I dunno... the next twenty years?'

She looked at me quizzically and I wondered how the hell she got to be so sensible and mature.

But anyway, back to Ash and her bizarre behaviour.

'I know it sounds strange,' she says, 'but I've read about it and it's a thing. It's sort of the fight or flight of the relationship world. People respond to trauma in different ways, and a common response to sexual infidelity is to jump the bones of your partner and demand physical intimacy. Like you're reclaiming your property, what is rightfully yours.'

She does away with the Minnie Mouse mug now and swigs straight from the bottle.

'Wow,' I say – more about her drinking from the bottle than her weird sexual reaction. Although that, too, is well worthy of a wow, let's face it.

'I know, I know,' she smiles wickedly, 'it is a little bit peculiar, I suppose. But we've been at it with each other ever since. I've never felt so alive!'

209

'So when's he going to move out?' I steer the convo away from sex, feeling more awkward than usual, considering Izzy's here and it's been so long since I've had a shag.

'He isn't,' she says.

'Well you shouldn't be the one to move! You're the mother; the kids need to stay with you and you all need a safe, secure home. Unless you're thinking of moving out here... Are you?'

'God! This is so bor-ring!' Izzy flounces off into the front room.

'Watch *Mean Girls* on Netflix, then, hun – that'll cheer you up,' Ash calls out.

'Ooh! That sounds good,' Izzy says. 'Mu-um! Can I turn this fire off now? I'm boiling!'

'Okay, okay,' I yell. 'Just let it die down. And open the window if you can.'

'So no, neither of us is moving out. We're staying together. I love him and actually have no other choice than to fight for our relationship with every fibre of my being.' She looks like she needs a scarf on her head, a muscly arm and a man's shirt sleeves rolled up, like those old World War II posters showing women fighting battles on the home front.

'Blimey,' is all I can manage.

'Well, things haven't been right between us for ages – it's time we put in some of that work everyone says you need to do in order to have a successful marriage.'

'Yeah, yeah – but has he confessed to the affair at least?'

'Yep,' she says, pointing her nose to the ceiling as though this is some valiant victory.

'And has he ended it?'

'Yep,' she says, lowering her nose a bit. 'Or at least he's going to. On Monday morning. First thing.'

Hmm.

'Have you asked him point blank whether he loves you?'

'Yes, I have, as a matter of fact,' she says, sounding a little bit snippy in amongst all the slurring. 'And he said he did. Which is why we're going to go to counselling every Tuesday night for as long as it takes to get us back on track. I don't want to end up... you know... like you.'

Eh?

'Look,' she says quickly, 'I know you say it's great and everything, being on your own with the kids but I dunno – I just don't think I could do it. And don't you get lonely?'

'I haven't got time to be lonely!' I snap.

'Well, what's so good about it, then? Being a divorced single mum?'

'Interesting question – I'm glad you asked me that,' I grin. 'I'm supposed to have written an agony column for *Chilterns Today (Forever in your heart)* about the pros and cons of being in my situation in the country. Might as well do it now!'

I search for an unbroken, sharp(ish) pencil and grab a Chilterns Council Tax envelope.

'Now let's see...' I put the pencil's eraser to my mouth and tap it on my bottom lip, the universally recognised sign for being deep in thought.

'How about... when you're divorced, you don't have to stay awake all night wondering where the feck he is and who the feck he's doing because he's now officially none of your feckin' business?' Ash suggests.

'Yes, yes,' I agree. 'That's defo one big pro right there…'

'And what about,' Ash warms to her theme, 'you no longer have to worry that you're too feckin' fat or too feckin' thin or too crap a cook or too boring a shag or too dull to talk to… because the kids love you just the way you are.'

'Like it, like it,' I say.

'… And you no longer have to feel like the biggest feckin' fool in the whole world because you've been turning a blind feckin' eye to his dalliances and misdemeanours and the clumsy feckin' piss-poor, pathetic passes he's been making *at your friends* for the past fifty feckin' years…'

'Erm,' I don't know what to say to this. 'Yeah… Maybe without all the swearing?'

Ash is pretty hammered by now, obviously not as cool about Pete as she seemed earlier and, quite frankly, starting to scare me a little bit.

This is a whole new side to drunken Ash I've never seen before. Or maybe I've never been sober enough to notice. Usually she's silly and dancey and not remotely nasty. Normally, after several hours dancing, she curls up in a corner and passes out. But tonight, it's like watching Elizabeth Taylor go from happy-go-lucky young starlet in *National Velvet* to bitter, twisted old drunk in *Who's Afraid of Virginia Woolf?* in the space of an hour and a half.

'Oh, you all thought I was so stupid and sweet and innocent, didn't you?' she spits. 'And you never said a word to me. Did you think I didn't know what he was up to? Did you think I didn't *know* he fancied the pants off Amelie?'

I don't know how to answer this, so I don't say anything. But I feel pretty rotten, because I had no idea she knew all about Pete's extra-curricular activities at uni. No idea at all. In my defence, I didn't think he'd ever been successful in any of his sexual pursuits then – I mean, everyone knew he was Ash's man, so no one took him seriously on that front. I imagined it was the same now, all these years later. I'm almost more surprised that he managed to find some unsuspecting, gullible woman to be his mistress for ten whole months than by the fact that Ash is going to stay with him. Almost.

It sounds cruel, but he really is no oil painting. He's got teeth like elephant's toenails and a persistent dandruff problem. He's loud, too – possibly because in his extended adolescence, he stood too close to the speakers in his tie-dyed rainbow shirt, waving glow sticks around, off his face on E or ketamine or whatever at some random rave – and now he's half-deaf. He is, however, really funny.

'Poor, silly little Aisling – such a doormat, such a sucker, such a pitiful excuse for a modern woman,' she goes on, 'so blinkered, so clueless… Well, not anymore. I will wage war on anyone who threatens my relationship. I shall fight them in the hills and in the streets, I shall fight them on the beaches, I shall fight them on the feckin'—'

'Ash? Are you okay?'

Ash turns, well, ashen-faced, actually, and shoots out of the chair, holding her hand over her mouth. She stumbles to the loo and I hear her throwing up violently into the bowl.

I race after her and manage to scoop her hair up into a hand-held ponytail, out of the line of fire, just in time.

'Urgh,' she straightens up after a few minutes, thinking she's finished. 'Someone must've spiked my – oh. Oh God. Did you spike my *druurrrrghhh*...'

'No need,' I smile. 'Knocking back nearly a whole bottle of Bombay Sapphire on your own will have the same effect. If that's what you're going for.'

Once she's jettisoned all the liquid from her body – as well as most of her internal organs, by the sound of it, I guide her into the front room, while she burbles on about McFood poisoning and terrorism by takeaway.

When we eventually shuffle in there, we're greeted by four little bodies all lying on the Version Rug, watching Lindsay Lohan in *Mean Girls*, the embers of the once-roaring fire glowing in the grate.

'Did you say takeaway, Mum?' Izzy doesn't look up from the telly. 'I'm starving!'

'Me too!' scream the three boys.

Oh, shit! I forgot all about dinner!

As I gently let Ash fall onto the chair, I decide there's nothing else for it, it's got to be pizza again.

'What does "butter my muffin" mean?' Ben asks, eyes out on stalks.

'Um...' I stall for time while I set up the sofa bed. 'Exactly what it sounds like – "would you please put some butter on my muffin and perhaps a dollop of strawberry jam, too?" you know, just like you say to me sometimes at breakfast. Just not as polite, a bit more brusque.'

'What's wrong with Mummy?' Joshie's up and poking Ash on the shoulder.

'She's just very tired,' I say.

'Urgh!' Jimmy joins Joshie in the prodding. 'She stinks!'

'Leave her alone, boys,' I say in my best voice of authority. Which has exactly no effect whatsoever.

Thankfully, the pizza arrives a mere forty minutes later, when Ash is sleeping like a log in the sofa bed, oblivious to the three boys jumping on it.

We eat straight from the box on the new rug, resulting in a few minor stains, which I very magnanimously ignore, even though inside I'm panicking and, sadly, really looking forward to watching it come up a treat after I pour Vanish all over it tomorrow morning.

But for now, all is good (ish) with the world and once I've arranged Ash into the recovery position and optimistically put our big Mason mixing bowl on the floor, just in case she hurls in the middle of the night, I manage to get the boys into bed in Ben's room (if not actually asleep) and crawl into Izzy's double bed, marvelling at the warmth and almost unbearable cosiness of the brushed cotton sheets and duvet cover combo.

As Izzy sleeps the sleep of the just, snoring softly next to me, something like inspiration hits and I fumble around for a piece of paper or a journal or something to write on. Finally, I find a notebook in the shape of a unicorn tucked under her bed, turn on the desk lamp on her bedside table and start writing:

PROS OF BEING A DIVORCED SINGLE MUM
1. You don't have to argue about who's the most tired or whose turn it is to perform some deeply unpleasant task – you just get on with it, like you always did, only now without the aggro and seething resentment.

2. You don't have to worry about him having affairs – and you can go for it with anyone you fancy now, too. If you're into that sort of thing.

3. Once you've checked YouTube to find out where the feck your fusebox might be and what a blown fuse looks like, you'll sense that long-lost feeling of competence returning.

4. You get to have the remote control. When the kids aren't there.

5. Speaking of, every two weeks, when you're just about to have a nervous breakdown, if your ex is half-decent, he should take your little cherubs off your hands to spend some time with them and inadvertently give you a bit of a break.

6. You don't have to listen to ear cartilage-shaking snoring throughout the night and revoltingly loud peeing in the morning.

7. You realise you're the main influence over the kids. And once you get past the overwhelming, crushing weight of that particular burden, you start to feel like the lucky one – privileged, proud and maybe even a little bit powerful.

CONS OF BEING A DIVORCED SINGLE MUM

1. Money is tight. Almost as tight as your ex.

2. There's still a stigma attached to being a DSM – people think you're going to race off their husbands, live in squalor and raise feral children. As if that's the preserve of the DSM.

3. You can't blame your ex when things go wrong. Actually, yes you can – everything is his fault, let's face it, even if only indirectly.

And then I run out of ideas.

I can't resist sneaking a peek at some of the things Izzy's written in the notebook and think how adorable she is when she describes a visit to the British Museum with Grannie and Granddad and how taken she was by both the Egyptian mummies and the gluten-free brownies in the café.

Just as I'm about to chuck the notebook on the floor and turn out the light, something scribbled on the back page, under a cute picture of a unicorn flying over a rainbow, catches my eye. And on closer inspection, I see my darling little girl has written in her very best calligraphy:

LIST OF BITCHES
1. Victoria
2. Ava
3. Mum

-

Three upbeat, positive things:
- I've done some work. On a Friday night?!
- I'm not going to wake up with a hangover tomorrow.
- At least I'm not #1 on Izzy's Bitch List.

-

April 18 – Hung Waaay the Hell Over

The next day, once Ash surfaces, bleary-eyed and still a little unsteady on her pins, that 'there but for the grace of God' sensation that's getting to be quite familiar these days starts swimming about in my veins.

She walks – staggers, really – into the kitchen where the kids and I are making (burning) lumpy pancakes and groans.

'I know, I know,' she croaks, 'I brought it on myself, yada yada yada.'

'Oh, you poor bugger, Ash,' I sympathise. 'Anything to eat? Or just coffee? Instant, mind – I'm sure we've got some Nescafé in the cupboard somewhere...'

I don't subscribe to that old 'you brought your hangover on yourself and therefore deserve absolutely zero sympathy from your nearest and dearest'. Having suffered from some major stinkers over the years, I know that this is *exactly* the time for empathy, reassurances and a well-earned day on the couch. With tons of water to drink on the floor. And maybe an Indian takeaway later if you're up to it. A medium heat Rogan Josh with Basmati rice and garlic naan will soak up the booze nicely. Although takeaways don't usually open till six p.m. Better make do with cake in the interim, then.

'I've got some Tunnock's Tea Cakes somewhere in here... Well, I thought I did. Ben! Izzy? Disappointing behaviour, really!'

I shake two empty boxes of tea cakes, only for several scrunched-up foil wrappers to fall out onto the kitchen floor.

'Urgh!' Ash sits in a chair and puts her head in her hands. 'Why'd you let me drink all that gin? I don't even like the stuff – bitter and sour and—'

I skip over to her and give her a big hug, tell her everything's going to be okay, tell her she wasn't that bad last night and at least no one saw her. And that I think she's doing the right thing *vis-à-vis* Pete. Well, that it's worth a shot, anyway. And then I carry on popping the bubbles in the pancake with the egg slice.

'Was I rambling?' Ash asks, looking small and shivering.

'Are you cold? I can light a fire if—'

'NOOOOOOO!' everyone yells.

'All right, all right – keep your hair on,' I mutter. 'And no, Ash, you weren't rambling. Much. At all. More ranting. But in a good way! In a rousing, Churchillian way.'

'Jesus, Mary and Joseph,' she sighs and puts her head on the table, cheek-side down. 'Feckin' eejit.'

And just as Ben and Jimmy and Joshie are pointing accusingly at Aisling, nyah-nyah-nyah-nyah-nyahing that she used the F-word, the smoke alarm goes off, drowning the boys out with its own ear-splitting, insistent cry.

'Time's up! Bakers, stop baking now,' Aisling shouts, holding her hands over her ears and running back into the front room.

I throw the hissing frying pan in the sink, turn off the gas, jog over to the table, grab a chair, place it under the smoke alarm on the ceiling at that bit of hallway space between the kitchen and the front room and stand on it. On tippy-toes.

'It's... times like... these,' I grimace as I try to reach the alarm, 'you really need a ma—' I stop myself. What am I saying? '...a tall person with long fingers who... can... easily just... turn this bloody thing off!'

Eventually, after poking every button I can see on the alarm with a wooden spoon (which isn't as easy as it sounds, given my eyesight's rubbish, the spoon's drenched in batter and the air is covered in an acrid blanket of smoke), it stops screeching at us and everything returns to normal.

If watching the boys punching each other, Izzy rolling her eyes as she reads *Murder Most Unladylike* and Aisling rocking gently on the sofa bed, hugging her knees to her chest is normal.

'Ah, honey pie...' My heart goes out to Ash. 'Everything's going to be okay. You know what you want, you know how to get it and I admire you enormously.'

I scramble onto the bed and put my arm around her bony frame.

'You do?' she sniffs. 'Why?'

'Because against all odds, against what everyone else says, against probably even your own better judgement, you're wresting back some control over your life – with you sitting up straight in the driver's seat, calling the shots, directing your own life.'

'You don't half talk some utter garbage sometimes, you know?' she smiles weakly. 'I just can't believe I've been so shite, letting him take advantage of my good nature for so long.'

'Well, all that's set to change with the new regime.' I tuck some strands of ridiculously thick, ginger hair back behind her ear.

'I feel so stupid,' she pouts.

'Well you're not – you're amazing!'

'But what if he doesn't really love me and even after all the therapy, we can't make it work and he runs off with Miss Chesticles?'

'Who's Miss Chesticles?'

'His fancy woman. The one with the big tits.'

'Oh, right.' The image of her boobs with *insert cock here* written over them with lipstick flashes into my brain. 'Well, if that happens, she's welcome to him. You'll have done everything you possibly could, but if he's too blind to see what a fantastic person he has in you, then fuck him. Not literally, obviously – got to be careful with you. No, I mean chuck him and move on. You deserve so much better, Ash. Like a nice, handsome gentleman who'll treat you with the respect you command – the kind you might find, ooh, I dunno – somewhere out here in the country perhaps?'

'Ha!' I can tell the thought of this cheers her up a bit. Or maybe it was the shagging reference. Whatever it was, she rolls over out of the sofa bed and stands up effortlessly. Like a commando.

'Nice rug, by the way,' she says as she pads over it, going back into the kitchen. 'IKEA?'

'How'd you know?'

'Everyone's got one in Twickenham, too. It's the *rug du jour*. I fancy stopping off on the way home to get one for us, actually.'

'I thought maybe we could go to The Pantry, the great café in the car park of Thistlebend Primary School. They do scrummy cakes and fab hot chocs. Only takes thirty minutes to get there and—'

'Thirty feckin' minutes? Just to get to school?'

'Yup,' I say proudly.

'What a nightmare!' She shakes her head and wanders over to the kettle. 'I don't know how you do it – four times a day? You must be crazy. Can't you get the kids into a closer school?'

'No places,' I shrug. 'But it's lovely, Thistlebend – and that's where I met the editor of *Chilterns Today (Forever in your heart)*! So, you know, it's all working out… in one way or another…'

'Yeah, I suppose it is,' she says. 'Think I'll just have a quick kipper tie and then we'll be on our way. If that's okay? I'd like to have the rug down before Pete gets back.'

'From where?'

'Football. His work's playing a match against some other, rival company,' she says, as though it's no big deal that her marriage is in major crisis and he's swanned off to kick a ball around a field with a bunch of other blokes while his mistress watches on, cheering from the side-lines. 'Last match of the season before the summer break. They're all staying up in Scotland somewhere.'

I'm speechless.

'Don't say a word,' she says, avoiding my open-mouthed gaze. 'I know what you're thinking. But this is the last time he'll be doing anything like this – after today, he says he'll be concentrating solely on me and the boys.'

Still speechless.

'Actually, sod the tea…' She wheels around, marching over to the twins who are still punching Ben and each other. 'Let's get our stuff together and go, guys!'

Twenty minutes later, as they're leaving, Ash stands on the doorstep, looks me up and down and says to Izzy, who's standing by my side:

'Can you help your mother, by the way? Help the aged, as Jarvis Cocker would say? I mean, look at the state of her!'

I look down at the pyjamas from Sainsbury's that I'm still wearing.

'They're pyjamas,' I point out. 'What's wrong with them?'

'When did you buy them? 1975?' Ash grins.

'They're just bloody pyjamas!' The heels of my bare feet lift off the floor a bit in indignation when I say this, as if for added emphasis.

'Life is a catwalk,' Izzy joins in. 'But you look like you've been in a cat *fight*!'

'Christ on a bike!' I sigh, feeling a little bit under attack. 'Is it pick-on-Mummy day again? So soon after the last one? That was only, like, yesterday?'

'You just need a little help, that's all,' Ash says.

'I've never been interested in being trendy or on trend...'

'Clearly,' Izzy giggles.

'... or on fleek or fashion-forward or whatever it is they call it—'

'Fashion-backward, in your case,' Aisling winks at Izzy, who's nodding furiously in agreement.

'Ha bloody ha – feeling better now, are you?' I purse my lips, pretending to be offended.

Ash leaves laughing, and we both know that she's lying unashamedly when she says that she and the boys will be down again really, really soon.

God! She is nothing if not a mistress of self-deception, denial and der-inking, I think to myself as I close the door and sort out the sofa bed.

And you know what? Even after two rounds of that Vanish powder stuff, the tomato pizza stain still doesn't come out of the Version Rug. But what the hell – we're a real family with real mess, not a pristine show home somewhere in Tediousville. Or do I mean Tediumville?

I say to the kids, who are both watching *Mean Girls* again, that eating on the rug or anywhere else other than the kitchen table is now forbidden. Against the rules. Not allowed. Strictly verboten.

No one is to bring any food or drink into the front room again because even though we rarely have visitors and I'm not at all interested in pathetically trying to keep up with the Joneses, it would be good if we could at least try to keep the house looking nice, just for us. And Auntie Audrey. Parts of it, anyway.

Proud of my laying-down-the-law disciplinary efforts, even if they come to nought, I make myself a cup of tea and put it on the side table next to the couch, curling up to watch the movie. Of course, within seconds I've spilled some on the rug.

I keep quiet about it, though, lest the kids turn around, see the stain and promptly realise they have a raging hypocrite for a mother.

As if they didn't already know.

–

Three upbeat, positive things I might be able to call 'wins':
- I got to sit and talk with one of my oldest, bestest friends.
- The kids ate all the Tunnock's Tea Cakes, thus saving me from myself.
- The house didn't burn down as a result of extreme hygge or pancake-making.

Chapter Seven

May

May 16 – Dog Day Barf-ternoon

'Just put him on me and stop fussing,' Dad says as I ever-so-gently lower the wriggling puppy onto his lap.

'I don't want to drop him,' I wince. 'Careful, careful!'

We've driven up to the Irish setter rescue centre to collect our new pup. Mum and Dad have come with me, so a) Dad could cuddle the cute little guy in the back seat while I drive us home and b) they could see their grandkids' darling faces when they get home from school and walk through the front door – only to be greeted by this mewling, dishevelled, absolutely lovely fella. And the gorgeous little puppy he's holding.

'Fark! He's just pissed all over me!' Dad informs us once we've left the rescue centre.

'Lucky you've got that seat protector—'

'That's on the bloody seat though, isn't it?' he whines. Or maybe that was the puppy. 'Argh! Now I look like some poor old coot with a prostate problem!'

Mum's sitting in the passenger seat next to me and laughs as she looks over her shoulder at poor Dad.

'Comes to us all in the end, I'm afraid, darl,' she sniggers.

By the time we get home, an hour and a half later, the puppy's been sick all over Dad's shirt, his trousers and his right hand.

'Oh, isn't he simply adorable?' I say, picking the puppy off Dad.

'Yeah,' says Dad. 'Totes adorbs.'

I ignore Dad's attempt at sounding 'with it' or cool or whatever weird thing he's trying to do and gingerly walk up the driveway, careful not to trigger any more bodily eruptions from the shivering animal.

When I get in, I put the little one on the floor and he promptly wees, stepping in the puddle of pee and traipsing it all over the floor and, of course, the rug, as he bounds about, familiarising himself with his new surroundings.

'Awww,' I coo, 'who's a little cutie, eh? Who's a little cutie? That's right, you are. Yes! Even though you're weeing over everyone and everything, you can't help it, can you? You're just a widdle bubba – ha! Widdle, get it? You're just a widdle bubba, aren't you? Yes you are – yes you *are*!'

'Bloody hell, Annie,' I hear Mum say, 'clean up that urine – someone could slip on that – probably me – and stop talking like a half-wit. It's a dog, for Christ's sake.'

Sometimes Mum's lack of sentimentality can really hit you for six. I mean, I know she's totally anti us getting a dog – but look at him! He's *unbearably* cute, with his legs too long for his body, and his little black nose with loose light mahogany – more caramel, really, now that I think about it – fur wrinkling about on his snout. His tiny paw pads are soft and black and his chunky little eyebrows (think Noel Gallagher as a baby) are already so expressive, I swear I can tell when he's laughing or curious or getting annoyed at being manhandled. Shame those eyebrows can't signal to me that he needs to go to the toilet. You can tell he's clever, too, because he'll fix you for a nanosecond with his big brown eyes and tilt his head to the side as if to say: 'I can't be one hundred per cent certain, but I suspect you might be a bit of a prat'.

It's a look I know well – Izzy has regarded me in the same manner ever since she was six months old. And Aisling and Amelie always give me this look, just without the head tilt – we know each other too well for that and we're all too old to take the risk of putting more cricks in our delicate turkey necks now, anyway.

Mum must have a heart like a fridge, though, because he's quite simply divine, capable of turning even the most hardened cynic into a blancmange of wibbly, wobbly silliness.

'Ah, there he is, the scoundrel,' Dad beams when he walks in and the pup skids on the wee in his haste to get to him. 'Who's a cad and a bounder, eh? Who's a cad and a bounder?! Who was too much for the family of four who couldn't handle your bounciness, eh? Who's a cad and a bounder?'

Mum rolls her eyes skywards so hard and slow, you can see only the whites for about a minute and I fear the coloured bits will never come down.

'Makes you sick,' she says, her mouth turning down. 'Time for a quick coffee, then we'd better go and the get the kids, okay?'

I want to answer Mum – I mean, I can hear her and everything, but I just can't take my eyes off the puppy being gently bounced around by Dad. My adoring gaze cannot be averted. And I'm rooted to the spot, watching

Dad play rough and tumble on his knees, like he's ten years old again, as opposed to seventy. My heart's melting at this scene until old fridge-face interrupts:

'Okay?'

'Yes, yes, sorry, Mum.' I drag myself away. 'It's just he's sooooo gorgeous.'

'Give me strength,' she groans. 'What are you going to call this... this... *creature*, anyway?'

'Raoul!' Dad calls out from the front room. 'Or Rufus!'

'Rua?' I suggest. 'Or Fergus or Seamus – something Irish. Rafferty? Actually, I thought I'd let the kids decide.'

'Don't do that!' Dad whines. 'They'll only want to call him Cutie Pie or Waggy or something. He'll grow to be a big, regal beast soon – he deserves a strong, commanding name that reflects his majesty. Don't you, little Rufus. Yes you do, little Roofie, widdle woofie, yes you do! A widdle woofie woo, who's a widdle woofie Wooster?'

—

When we walk through the front door, having been up to Thistlebend and back, Mum and I lag behind Izzy and Ben and wait for the explosion of glee. But there are no whoops of surprise or squeals of delight – instead, the kids look over their shoulders at us with what can only be described as faintly frightened faces.

'What?' I say, puzzled by their complete lack of enthusiasm.

As I peer through the door jamb, I see Dad lying on the couch, eyes shut, with the puppy lying on his chest, both front and back legs splayed, as though he just went SPLAT! with exhaustion and hasn't moved since. That's the puppy, not Dad.

It's the kind of pose proud new mums take endless aaaah-inspiring photos of, when they find their partners flat out on their backs on the sofa, their tiny baby fast asleep on their torsos. But in our case, instead of a baby, Dad's cradling the snoozing puppy.

'Is Granddad okay?' Izzy asks tentatively.

'Of course he is.' I creep up to him to check, relieved to see his stomach's moving up and down, the puppy and his gigantic ears moving in time to his respiratory rhythm. 'Yes, he is, he's just sleeping.'

'What's that smell?' Mum brings up the rear with a pressing question.

'Why has Granddad got a puppy on him?' Izzy asks.

'Wake up, Granddad!' Ben runs over to the couch and jumps on his Granddad's knees.

'What? Hmmm? Just dozing… Oof! Ben! Shhh! You'll wake Rufus!'

'Something smells disgusting in here…' Mum won't let it go.

'Oh. My God!' says Izzy, her voice lowering a few octaves. 'Is that an Irish setter puppy?'

'Sure is,' I say. 'Go on, pat him. Gently, be careful with him…'

The puppy opens his sleepy eyes and yawns, exposing a curling, pink, extraordinarily long tongue and his baby teeth that look almost plastic in their obvious harmlessness.

The pup rolls off Dad's torso and Ben catches him mid-drop to the floor. Rufus – or whatshisname, as Mum prefers to call him – licks Ben's face off with gratitude. Or, I wonder, maybe he's a bit peckish? God knows Ben's bound to have some food smooshed onto his skin somewhere on his face. Just hope it's not chocolate. Chocolate is poisonous for dogs, isn't it? Not that there's much actual chocolate, real cacao in Freddo Frogs – I mean, it's all sugar and milk solids right?

'Nothing solid about that,' Mum deadpans, pointing to what looks like a pile of egg whites whipped into a meringue in the middle of the rug. Except it's mustard-yellow and more liquid than stiff peaks. And you can virtually *see* the foul fumes rising from the puppy poo.

'Did I say all that stuff about Freddo Frogs out loud?'

'Christ!' Mum holds her nose. 'What the hell have they been feeding it?'

'Pedigree for puppies, I think,' I say, 'or at least that's what they gave us to feed him tonight.'

'I warned you about that rug.' Mum shakes her head. 'That ill-advised, fake Persian, cream-coloured rug. He'll tear it to shreds and shit all over it before you can say—'

'Oh, bite your bum.' Dad sits up. 'He's only a puppy. He needs to learn. And it's up to you to teach him, Annie. You too, kids.'

'You mean we can keep him?' Izzy picks up the pup who simultaneously licks her nose and wees all over her uniform.

'Oh, can we, Mummy?' Ben looks pleadingly at me with those brown eyes that are possibly even bigger than the puppy's.

'If you promise you'll help me train him,' I smile. 'And take him for walks and love him and look after him and—'

'WE PROMISE!' the pair of them shout. Probably with their fingers crossed behind their backs.

'Seriously, you must train him otherwise he'll be a nightmare,' Dad warns. 'Annie never properly trained Ruby—'

'RIP,' I hang my head to say.

'And she used to escape over the back fence all the time,' Dad goes on. 'She'd take off for days, coming back when she was too exhausted to carry on. But at least she knew where she lived. That was in the suburbs, though – out here, a dog like Roofie wouldn't stand a chance, what with all the foxes and tractors and deer – not to mention farmers who have every right to shoot a dog straying onto their land in order to protect their sheep or cows. And don't forget, if he scares horses, they'll trample him to death. You've got to be careful in the country – red in tooth and claw, it is. Red in tooth and claw.'

We're all silent for a reverent three seconds until Mum breaks the seriousness and solemnity of the moment by declaring: 'I think I'm going to be sick,' as she darts out of the front room, making a beeline for the loo. Or 'dunny' as she still sometimes, most embarrassingly, calls it.

As I clean up the mess, which, surprisingly enough, doesn't make me gag, we talk about where indeed we will walk Sir Poo-A-Lot and what we might end up calling him. (Clue: no one likes Sir Poo-A-Lot).

There are the fields behind the Co-op, where he can run free, of course, then there's the meadow by the river (not the Thames, mind, a little offshoot of it called Little Chalky, for some unknown reason, which is more of a stream than a river – actually, more of a puddle, now I think about it), which is lousy with dog-walkers. Then there are the woods just up the road which are not only beautiful, but they'll keep us cool in summer and sheltered in winter – we're absolutely spoiled for choice!

I spread newspaper out by the back door, just as Mum's coming out of the loo.

'Really, darling,' she checks her lipstick in the laundry mirror, 'I hate to say I told you so, but—'

'Then don't say it,' I cut her off. 'Anyway, it's going to be great! He's such a cutie, he's going to transform the kids' lives, cheer us all up – you just wait and see!'

'All right, Pollyanna,' she says, walking back into the front room. 'Don't say I didn't warn you, though.'

I'm just about to go back in there myself when I hear my whole family groaning, saying 'Yuk!' (Ben), 'Gross!' (Izzy) and 'For Christ's sake!' (Dad and Mum in unison).

I take a deep breath as I walk past the stairwell and then it hits me: that unmistakeable, biley, cheesy-but-at-the-same-time-a-bit-pooey smell of sick.

'Here we go,' I think to myself, girding my loins for the inevitable olfactory and haberdashery disaster that awaits me.

And there, sitting in the middle of the rug is Rufus, gobbling up his own vomit (well, I'm assuming it's his) while the rest of the family back away from him, all turning a rather unsettling shade of green.

–

'Hellooo!' says Jane when I answer the front door later on. 'We hear there's a new member of the Beaton family to welcome into the fold – can we come in?'

'As long as you've got pegs for your noses.' I half-open the door so the neighbours can slip in without Rufus making a break for it. 'He's a bit of a stinky mutt at the moment.'

Jane, Jess, Jack and John pile into the house and pretty much dissolve at the sight of Rufus – who bounds over to them, biting their bodies and clothes while wagging his tail like a lunatic.

'Oh, what a bundle of cute!' Jane laughs.

'A bundle of cute terror,' I sigh, sitting on the arm of the couch that's already been chewed a bit at the base. 'He seems all sweet and fluffy, but actually, his bodily functions are way out of control and if it moves, he'll try to chomp on it. Actually, it doesn't even have to move – like the couch – and he'll start trying to tear it to pieces.'

'Must be teething, the poor little guy. Are those teeth sore, puppy, eh? Gums giving you grief, you poor widdle puppy wuppy wongle?'

We all turn to stare at John – this big, strong, six-foot-two strapping brick shithouse of a man going all gooey in front of us.

'What?' he says. 'He's just too cute!'

At that, Izzy and Ben come screaming down the stairs, the excitement of a new puppy and visitors being nearly too much for them.

Jane and I leave them to roughhouse together on The Rug of Questionable Cleanliness and head towards the kettle for a brew.

'Like your new rug by the way,' Jane smirks.

'Yeah,' I reply. 'I hear it's all the rage in Twickenham, too. Not that it's going to stay cream for very much longer, what with Roofie exploding all over it every five seconds.'

'Is that his name? Roofie?' She looks disapproving. 'Like the date rape drug?'

I'm shocked that Jane not only knows about drugs like Rohypnol – she also knows the American slang term for them, too.

'No,' I snort, 'Roofie as in short for Rufus! Actually we haven't had a chance to decide on his forever name yet, but Roofie'll do for the interim.'

'What are you going to do with him when you're taking Izzy and Ben to school?' she asks.

'He'll come with us,' I say. 'Bet the other kids will go berserk when they see him!'

'If he makes it that far – thirty minutes is a long time for a baby like Rufus. How long did it take you to get back from the rescue centre?'

'Not that long,' I lie. 'About thirty minutes... Or so.'

It was actually about two hours, but it *should* have been only thirty minutes. I'm not sure why I'm so cagey about the truth – maybe the fear of being judged by the neighbours about my dog-parenting prowess? Or lack thereof? I can't quite believe it, but I'm already feeling guilty for carting him so far around the countryside, putting him in a car for the first time, jerking and jolting him about while we careened over country roads – and he's still so tiny. Although I swear he's grown about two inches in height and about an inch in width since we got him home, in the space of just a few hours.

It's weird, but it's true what everyone says – getting a puppy *is* like having a baby. I feel guilty about everything, he's pooing, weeing and spewing everywhere with not so much as a by your leave, he's breaking hearts left, right and centre – and already I wouldn't be without him.

'EEEEEEEEEEEEEEEKKKKKK!' Jess cries from the front room.

Jane and I race in to see what's happened. A lightning-fast scan of the room reveals four kids all present, accounted for and apparently unharmed, one outrageously cute puppy looking a bit frightened – and one adult, Big John, clutching his cheek, his eyes watery with fat blobs of blood trickling out from between his fingers.

'What the f—' Jane begins.

'—Fix It Felix happened?' I finish the sentence for her in our favourite family-friendly way.

'Bloody dog – took a swipe at me with his paw, didn't he?' John sniffs, shooting daggers at Rufus. 'It all happened in slo-mo – one minute he was all soft and sweet, mewling like a kitten, the next he was coming at me like Cujo! With nails like Freddy Bloody Krueger!'

'Daddy did a swear!' Jess and Jack sing. 'Daddy did a swear!'

'It's not a swear if it's a medical emergency,' John says.

Rufus tilts his little head to the side, as though he's trying hard to make sense of what John's saying. The rest of us do the same, making us look like a synchronised swimming team with our heads just above water.

'Has he got any Alsatian in him?' John wonders aloud.

'Nope – one hundred per cent pure breed, show-stopping, prize-winning pedigree.' I puff up a little with pride. Either that or the Kit Kat Chunkies I scarfed on the way back from the rescue centre are already bloating me out, making me look like a pufferfish that's swallowed a spacehopper.

'Pitt bull?' John carries on, unconvinced. 'Rottweiler!'

'You scared him,' Ben says, picking Rufus up. 'Come on, Roofie, let's go to my room.'

'NOOOOOOOOOOO!' I scream, backing up to the foot of the stairs, hands outstretched in an effort to stop them in their tracks. 'Not until he's fully toilet trained, sweetheart. Until the both of you are.'

I don't know why I said that, it just slipped out. I'm so thoughtless sometimes.

Ben looks at me, wide-eyed and wounded while Jack clutches his tummy, doubles up with laughter and points accusingly at Ben:

'Ha ha – Ben wets the bed! Ben wets the bed! Ben the bed-wetter! Ha ha!'

Ben drops Roofie, glares at me so hard I can almost see the steam coming out of his ears and stomps up the stairs.

The room falls silent. Well, except for the sound of Rufus gnawing at the leg of the side table and some rather disconcerting whimpering coming from upstairs.

'Ah, maybe we should go now,' Jane says, ever the one to pour oil over troubled waters when it's needed most. 'I think I can smell our dinner burning. Come on, you lot, wagons roll.'

'God, I'm so sorry about the dog, John, really I am,' I grovel as they make their way out the door. 'I hope it doesn't get infected. If there's anything we can do...'

John sniffs, Jack's still laughing like a horrible little hyena, Jess pulls Rufus to her chest for one last hug and Jane says:

'Don't be silly, Annie – it's nothing. I'm only sorry Jack's displaying his nastier side that seems to be emerging an awful lot, lately.' She clips the boy around the ear when she says this and gives him a really dirty, wait-till-I-get-you-home look.

236

I wave my hand in dismissal, Jess reluctantly hands Rufus back to Izzy and they step over the broken-down picket fence between our properties.

'Drama,' says Izzy. 'Brilliant!'

I turn around and narrow my eyes, looking straight at Rufus. '*You* are going to get us in to big trouble if you keep acting like that, you little monster!'

'Mum! He's an innocent widdle pup! Yes he is! Yes you are, aren't you? Hmmm? Who's a sweet, innocent, widdle puppy?'

'Let's take him up to Ben – take the risk,' I say, feeling bad about what I said before. 'God knows, things can't get much worse. Can they?'

–

So there I am, an hour later, leaving Ben's duvet, duvet cover and fitted sheet with the ladies at the laundrette with special instructions to use non-bio detergent as opposed to ordinary bio, because, according to one of the millions of websites I've been trawling lately about how to look after a puppy, only non-bio can really get rid of the smell of dog urine. No one really knows what the difference between bio and non-bio is, but it's important to really get the whiff out so the dog won't be able to smell it again and think that's where they ought to wee on a regular basis.

Not that Roofie's ever going to be allowed anywhere near duvets or, indeed, upstairs again. Still, he did the trick, cheering Ben up and making me look like the good guy. Just as well he doesn't go to the same school as Jack from next door – word of Ben's penchant for bed-wetting would be all over the playground by Monday lunchtime if he did. He seems like quite the unpleasant piece of work to me now. Which is strange, because when we first met him, butter wouldn't melt. He's reminiscent of Aled Jones as a youngster – all sweetness, light and high of voice. Maybe five-year-old boys are prone to the mysteries of hormones, too, and testosterone's making its presence known now in all sorts of weird and wonderful ways. But mainly bloody awful ways if you're talking about Jack from next door.

Mind you, Ben's no saint, either, it's true – but I don't think he'd laugh at and taunt someone else if they had dry night issues. Then again, maybe he would, what do I know? I was shocked to hear of him hitting and kicking, before. And the spitting! God knows where that came from. And that tantrum he had when he came home from Joe's that night a while ago – it just didn't seem like him.

I guess none of us really know our kids, do we? I mean, we're all so busy worrying about whether they're obese or not, whether they'll need tutoring to pass the eleven-plus, whether they've got the right brand of trainers and whether you're a Crocs-loving Mum or whether you think they're ugly, plastic abominations, we've all lost sight of the basics. Like, are our offspring nice? Do they know how to be kind to others? Have they got a shred of decency in their souls? Or are they out pulling the wings off butterflies when summer comes, congregating around fires made out of tyres, warming their hands in winter?

The thought of burnt rubber makes me wonder what on earth we're going to have for dinner tonight. I can't stop off at the Co-op, leaving the kids on their own for too long with Jaws, the tiny puppy, so I'll just have to see whether we've got any baked beans in the cupboard.

I come through the front door to the strains of my mobile letting me know that Amelie's calling.

'About bloody time,' I answer the phone, 'where the hell have you been?'

'Ha!' she half-laughs, half-exhales a staccato stream of smoke. 'Soz 'bout the radio silence, Annie Banannie – just been run off my feet. Well, *somethinged* off my feet anyway, if you know what I mean?!'

'I don't,' I say, putting an aural full stop to the sex convo she's no doubt trying to start up and engage me in. 'And I don't want to know, either. Hey! Guess what?'

'Erm...' she plays for time – or maybe she's just distracted by some guy – you never can tell with Amelie. 'Gimme a clue.'

'Okay,' I bend down to stroke Roofie's beautiful soft head, while he responds by nipping at my fingers. 'Yow! It's got sharp teeth...'

'You're back with Joe?' she sounds shocked.

'... it's a gorgeous, light caramel colour, but will turn redder the older it gets...'

'Aisling? Ash is there! God it's been yonks since I've seen—'

'No, it's not Ash,' I say. 'But I do have news on that front. Guess what I've got here first, then I'll tell you all about it...'

'Oh, just tell me, Annie, will you?' she cries.

'Okay, okay – we just got an Irish setter puppy. Today!'

'Aww!' she squeals down the phone.

'I know!' I squeal back.

Rufus tries to join in, making some sort of squeaky, mewling noises – almost like a baby bark, but too high and sweet.

'Oh, he's just divine, Am – you've *got* to come down…
up… whatever it is from Bath, you've *got* to come and see
him.'

'Well, now I have a reason, I will!'

'What? One of your oldest mates getting divorced and
moving with her kids from the smoke to the sticks wasn't
a good enough reason to come and see us before?'

'Well, you know,' I think I can hear her filing her nails,
'busy, busy busy!'

As if that's some sort of valid reason. I let it slide.

'Tell you what,' she goes on, 'why don't I come down
in, let me… see…'

I can hear her flicking through pages. Probably the
latest issue of *Good Housekeeping* or something, but she
tries to pretend it's a Filofax.

'… just checking the old Filofax…'

Told you.

'… God, Annie – I'm totally booked up! I won't
be able to come and see the little schnooks till, erm…
November! I'm away for most of the summer, then back
for conferences, partners' jollies – it's mental!'

'*You're* mental,' I reply, sounding for all the world like
Izzy when she's getting all snippy. 'Not to worry, though –
that might be a good thing. You know, give us the summer
to train him and prepare him for meeting you.'

'It's a date, then,' she says. 'Now gimme the goss on
Ash.'

I dutifully pass on all the info I managed to glean from
Ash's gin-soaked sojourn here – including the fact that
she always knew that Pete was making passes at Amelie
and anything else that moved, and that since she found
out, they've been at it like rabbits.

Amelie's duly speechless with confusion.

'I know,' I agree. 'She says she just grabbed his hand, dragged him upstairs, threw him on the bed, like in some housewife-gets-saucy Channel Five afternoon movie and went for it!'

'Well of course she did!' Amelie recovers her lost powers of speech. 'And so would any other red-blooded woman in her right mind—'

'Well—'

'Not you, of course – we're talking red-blooded, not ice in your veins!'

'Steady on! Are you having a dig at me? Like, just because I haven't had sex for God knows how many years, it means I'm some sort of cold fish who's never enjoyed a bit of rumpy-pumpy—'

'Urgh – there you go, twee names for adult things… you're fifty, for fuck's sake! It's like you see the world and all its delights through a pre-watershed, Teletubbies, C-bloody-Beebies lens all the time, it's no wonder—'

She cuts herself off at this point, shocked by what she's about to say.

'No wonder what?' I feel my hackles rising. 'No wonder Joe wanted a divorce? No wonder I'm alone, with only two kids to talk to? No wonder I got a puppy – a man-substitute to keep me company in my fast-approaching dotage? My old age? The winter of my discon-bloody-tent? Like when you come down, you'll find me covered in cobwebs, rocking back and forth, like a wrinkled old Miss Havisham? Hmm? No wonder *what, Am*?'

She hesitates for a moment, unsure how to answer me.

'What I find amazing,' she says calmly, 'is not that Ash wants to shag Pete's brains out – totally normal behaviour, by the way – but that she wants to *stay* with him. After ten months of tarting about town? While she stays at home and raises the kids? Uh-uh. No deal.'

'It's all a mystery to me,' I sigh.

'Annie, darling,' she starts carefully, 'you know I love you, you know I think you're wonderful, you know I think any half-decent man would be *lucky* to have you – but how will any of the millions of great guys out there know you exist, if you don't get yourself out and about? I bet you haven't even joined Elite Singles yet, have you? You know, the online dating thingy? I've met loads of fabulous men through that. You really should do it, Annie. We'll set your profile up when I come down.'

'But that's not for aaaages!'

'It'll give you time to sort yourself out, then, won't it? And once we've done that, we'll hit the town, scope the talent in Old Stoke. It won't know what's hit it!'

'Couldn't we just stay in and watch telly? You know, cosy up on the couch and take it easy? I'm not sure I'm ready to, you know, get back out there again…'

'It's time, Annie,' she says ominously. 'It's time.'

—

Three upbeat, positive things I might be able to call 'wins':
- We've got a puppy!
- We've got a puppy!
- We've got a puppy!

242

Chapter Eight

June

Chilterns Today (Forever in your Heart) – June Issue

Q: Dear Auntie Annie,

I'm in my early forties and I'm thinking very seriously about leaving my husband. We have two wonderful children together (twins, both five years old) and a lovely house, but the thought of breathing the same air as him for the next fifty-odd years makes me feel strangled. And sick. We hardly speak to each other anymore, communicating via a complex system of screaming and yelling most of the time and he's practically living in one of the outbuildings on our estate. I have my own flourishing businesses, so I'm not worried about money – I'm just scared the kids will suffer if we split.

What should I do?

Name and Address Withheld

PS He's not getting the dog, either. She's mine, I tell you, all mine!

A: Dear Name and Address,

It sounds to me like you've already left him. In your head, anyway.

It's funny, you know, because when my ex asked me for a divorce, it came as a bit of a bolt out of the blue. I mean, obviously we'd been having problems (no sex, no speaks, no interest) for ages, but I kind of sank myself into the quagmire of motherhood and forgot about it, hoping somehow it would work itself out, all come out in the wash, as it were. I thought maybe when the kids were in secondary school, we'd be able to get our lives together back, a bit older, a lot wiser and madly in love like we were before.

Little did I know, though, that the writing was on the wall for the ex when, two days after giving birth to my youngest, I gently rebuffed his amorous advances, citing a distinct lack of energy and up for it-ness.

I don't think he ever recovered from that rejection. Which might have something to do with the fact that five years later, on my birthday, he most unceremoniously gave me my marching orders.

My point is, while you're busy umming and aahing about the pros and cons of leaving your man and the psychological damage it may inflict on your children, he probably made his peace with your split yonks ago and now he's just waiting for you to drive the final nail into your marital coffin. So to speak.

Because, really, if I'm honest, my ex giving me the boot like that wasn't wholly unexpected – nor was it entirely negative. It was a bit of a shock, sure, but not really surprising. And in retrospect, he did the best thing for us all – the brave thing. I suppose I should thank him for it. Maybe one day I will.

But back to you and your dilemma. If the kids only hear you and your man rowing, never seeing any kindnesses or loving embraces exchanged between the pair of you, then you're probably doing the best thing by taking them out of such an aggressive, hostile environment.

And what kind of an example of a loving relationship are you showing those little cherubs if you stay? Not a healthy one, that's for sure.

It seems to me you have no other option *but* to leave him. Your marriage is moribund, your relationship as dead as a dodo. There's no going back now, you've already come too far. So kick him to the kerb. And welcome to the club!

Best of luck with it all, Annie xxx

Chapter Nine

July

July 24 – These Hols, Too, Shall Pass

The summer holidays lumber on in a horrendous haze of tears, tantrums and thigh-chafing. And that's just me. It was bad enough with two kids in tow, but two kids and a dog? Are you quite mad?

Actually, speaking of the kids, they've been having a bit of a rubbish time of it, too, to be honest. Once the novelty of the new puppy wore off and the real business of training and looking after a dog came into play, they no longer cared or wanted to know, really – and the resulting constant whining about it does everyone's head in. That's me again, by the way, doing the whining.

Most of their rich friends from school have gone to India, the Maldives or Cornwall for six weeks and the few who're having a staycation at home in Thistlebend can't be arsed to come to Old Stoke for playdates. Which is a relief for me, who's getting rather sick of spending hours apologising profusely for Rufus' boisterous behaviour, scaring children, eating grown-ups' sunglasses and generally being a right royal pain in the ane. And quite frankly, I can't be arsed to go to Thistlebend, either.

Not that Izzy's showing much interest in her friends, lately. I noticed her becoming slightly withdrawn and even more sullen not long after Auntie Aisling's visit.

So one bright, sunny day, once we've completed our usual morning routine of Izzy yelling at me till she's in tears and hoarse and I've done the same back at her while the bloody dog jumps up and bites my boobs, Ben cracking up laughing until the dog turns on *him*, I decide the time is right for me to take swift and definitive action. So as soon as the house stops shaking – thanks to Izzy's bedroom door being slammed with such frightening brute force I worry about the damp course coming loose – I take it as my cue. And call Ash for advice.

'So what's the story with Izzy?' I bypass all the usual social niceties and get straight to the meat of the matter. 'Hmm? You had a good chat with her when you were down here, didn't you?'

'Grand, thanks,' she says, 'and how's yourself?'

Sometimes I forget that some of my nearest and dearest aren't privy to my train of thought and inner dialogue – even though Izzy and Ben seem to have taken up permanent residence inside my head.

'Good, good,' I reply, more out of habit than anything else. But then I remember who I'm speaking to – and how you don't have to spout lie after casual, polite lie when you're talking to your mates. 'Actually, it's all pretty *shite*, if you want to know the truth.'

I can hear her closing a door, the creak of a comfy couch and the loud slurp of someone taking a huge slug of tea. Or, you know, vodka. It's Ash I'm talking to, after all.

'You just take a deep breath and tell Auntie Aisling all about it.'

It's her favourite phrase – or at least, it's her favourite phrase when she's talking to my family. She's thinking of going to medical school and studying psychiatry when the kids are old enough. She's got the brains for it, got the degree for it and even has the caring, compassionate bedside manner for it. But since the twins came along and turned her world upside down, I'm not sure she has the time or, indeed, the energy for it.

'Remember when you came down?'

She coughs and says softly: 'Vaguely.'

'Get OFF me! Bloody Roof—' I can't help myself.

'Who's that?'

'Roofie. Rufus. We couldn't come up with a better name and it's kind of stuck now.'

'What?'

'The pup… oh, God! Have I not told you? We got a puppy!'

'Blimey O'Reilly,' she says. 'Do you think that's wise? What with all the upheaval and everything?'

'You said it was a good idea!'

'A good *idea*, yes…'

'Well, it's too late now.' I kick a tennis ball along the floor, hoping Roofie will lunge at it, all cute like a kitten playing with a ball of string, but he completely ignores it and continues pawing me. 'And anyway, he's lovely, really.'

'Is he trained yet?'

'In subterfuge and terrorism, yes. Oh, and he'll sit when you ask him to. Sometimes. If you bribe him with food.'

'You don't *ask* a dog to sit,' she tuts, 'you *tell* it to sit.'

'Well, you try telling twenty kilos of rambunctious red fur to sit and see how you get on. He's so strong, he'd probably knock you down with a single swipe from his powerful paw.'

'Don't be ridic—'

'I'm serious! He's scraped his claws across my arms so many times, I have scars. I look like a self-harmer!'

'Self-harm is nothing to joke about,' she says solemnly.

'No, no,' I hang my head, 'of course it isn't.'

'A boy, right?' she says. 'I mean, the dog is a boy, is he not?'

'Oh yeah, he's a boy all right. Humps anything that moves. Or anything that's still. He'll hump air if he has to!'

'Get his knackers lopped off, then he'll calm down,' she says.

'Sorry, who are you? The Dog Whisperer? The Supervet?'

'I know a thing or two about dogs,' she says, a little bit like she's talking about the Mafia. 'Just like men. Hostages to their little fellas.'

I look down at Rufus and for a second I'm hypnotised by those huge brown eyes and those enormous floppy ears. I come back into the room pretty bloody quickly, though, when I see he's just turned my best blue and white striped, long-sleeved, White sodding Company t-shirt into a string vest. Honestly, there's more holes than fabric left! Those claws, those teeth...

'Ah, fuck,' is all I can say.

'Fix It Felix, you mean,' I can hear Ash smile. 'How are those little beauties of yours?'

'Well, actually, Ash,' I put my hand over the receiver so that Izzy won't hear, even though she's probably bursting her ear drums, playing disaffected youth music through those big headphones Joe bought her. 'That's what I'm calling about.'

'Oh,' she sarks, 'so you didn't call to see how I was going with the therapy, the straying man, the unstoppable twins...?'

'Well, yes, of course I did,' I defend myself, 'I was just going to ask you all about that *after*...'

'S'all right,' she sniffs. 'It's all under control here, anyway. Therapy's throwing up a lot of surprising stuff for the both of us, but in a good way, I think. Pete's got his second interview for a new job next week and the boys are settling down a bit, now their daddy's back in the fold. He's doing well, you know – so much more present with us all now than he was. Than he's ever been, come to think of it.'

I resist the urge to say: 'Oh yeah? I'll believe *that* when I see it!' and just say something beige like: 'Oh, that's good.' Because, really – what else are you going to say?

'It's the best it's been in a long time, to be honest – despite the fact that our social lives have been replaced by therapy... So what's your problem?' Ash asks.

'Argh,' I reply, pushing Rufus off my leg while he humps the hell out of it. 'Apart from this bloody – sorry, yes, I didn't mean to swear, you're not a bloody anything, are you? You're a handsome hound, yes you are, aren't you? You're a vewwy handsome—'

'GET ON WITH IT!' Ash shouts down the line, breaking the spell.

'Right, yeah,' I shake my head and re-focus. 'It's the kids! Ben's a nightmare, chucking tantrums every five minutes about not having an Xbox or an ice cream or whatever he wants... The dog, as you can hear, is a total and utter menace, under my feet, pooing and weeing in the house – on the not-so-new-anymore and not so cream-coloured anymore, either, rug – it's more a light khaki in some places, alarming uranium yellow in others...'

I take a breath and watch as Rufus rolls onto his back on said rug.

'It stinks. I'm going to have to chuck it out – it's practically stiff with chemicals that are useless at getting the smell out. I've spent most of the summer on my hands and knees, scrubbing away at various stains and whiffs. And the minute my head's down and my bum's up, who comes over to have a go, mounting me like I'm asking for it?'

'George Clooney,' Ash deadpans.

'Roofie!' I giggle. 'I'm up and down all night—'

'That George – such stamina!'

'... to let him outside so he can *be clever* – that's what you're supposed to call it – but he just wants cuddles, really, so he sniffs outside, looks up at you adoringly, whimpers a bit and then wees all over your foot!'

It's just all flowing out of me. Like Rufus with a full bladder. Talk about therapy.

'And if it's not Roofie, it's Ben – I'm putting out mini fires all the time, it's doing my bloody head in! So our country hideaway, our small, but once beautifully formed country pile has been reduced to merely a pit of excrement and dried up bodily fluids. All it took was two kids and a puppy! And, obviously, me – but I can't keep up with the cleaning this place demands. And now I think we're getting a rep around town as the kind of people who ask their visitors to keep their shoes *on* when they enter the house, in case our rugs and floors make their feet filthy!'

She laughs that kind of half-hearted laugh you do when you don't really find it funny, but you've remembered your manners.

'Where's Joe? Isn't he supposed to have the kids every two weeks?'

'Yes, he is.' I feel my lips tighten – which for me is not a good look. They're thin enough as it is. 'But he's gone away for six weeks, hasn't he? The whole sodding school holidays!'

I can tell she thinks this is really dodgy, bad dad behaviour (because I do and, let's be honest, here, who wouldn't?), but she skips over it.

'Have you made any friends yet?'

'No, not really. Except for Jane next door – but they're away for the summer – and a couple of other friends of hers, but I never see them or get to know them, because usually we're either in bloody Thistlebend or in the car, travelling to and from the sodding place.'

I look out the window in the front room that no one's ever been able to open and give it another try, sandwiching the phone between my ear and my shoulder, so I can still talk. Or grunt, as the case may be.

'How's Izzy?'

'Well, that's what I'm really worried about,' I lower my voice. 'You had a bit of a heart to heart with her when you came down, didn't you?'

'Yeah, before I got that... *food poisoning*.' I can practically hear Ash shaking her head in dismay.

'What were you talking about? Is she okay? I mean, it's me, isn't it? There's a problem with me. I knew it! She hates me. Hates me for divorcing her dad. I knew it!'

'Calm down, Annie,' Ash says in her best spa retreat soothing tones. 'It's not you. Well... it's not *all* you.'

'Who else is it?'

'Some girls at her school. There are only about eight girls in her whole class, anyway, but the thing is, they've all known each other since they were babies. About five of them live in the same street, for God's sake – they've grown up together and they're just not that open to outsiders. Small-minded villagers who aren't used to difference, with their pitchforks at the ready. They see her as a threat, I reckon. She's cleverer and nicer and prettier than the lot of them put together.'

'What did she say to that?'

'She said: "How would you know? You've never even met them?"'

'She's got a point,' I nod to myself. 'What did you say to that?'

'I said I didn't need to meet them to know that she's a cut above. Because she is. Always has been.'

It's true, actually. Then again, we would say that, wouldn't we? But she is much more mature than kids her age, though. Maybe because she's had to be, what with her mum and dad and everything. I've probably said it before, but I'll say it again; she's been running rings around me ever since she was four and a half.

And articulate! Not quite Russell Brand's level of verbosity, yet, but by God, she's getting there. With a sting in the tail, too, because she's got a tongue like an asp. Which she unleashes on me a lot, unfortunately, hurting my feelings with alarming regularity.

'So how did you suggest she handle the girls at her new school in Thistlebend, then?' I ask Ash.

'I didn't really offer her any advice,' Ash says, 'because I know she can handle herself in just about any situation life throws at her.'

'That's my girl,' I beam.

'Except the one she finds herself in at the moment with you and Joe.'

Bugger.

'I knew it was me, I just knew it!' I cry. 'But what can I do?'

'Stop doing Joe down every chance you get.'

'I don't!'

'Well, she says you do. And it's pissing her off, almost making her take sides.'

Suddenly the temperature drops inside and the clouds roll in to obscure the bright, warm sun.

'Take sides?' I repeat as the swirls of colour on the rug start swimming in front of my face. 'She doesn't. Does she?'

'And I don't think you're going to like whose side she's on.'

It's my worst nightmare come true. Well one of them, anyway. But she can't prefer Joe to me, she just can't! What's that saying? Something like:

A son is a son till he takes him a wife
But a daughter's a daughter for the rest of her life

'Yeah,' says Ash. 'It's an old Irish proverb.'

I didn't say that out loud, did I?

'Yes you did,' she says. 'But look, you can fix this, Felix. You really can.'

'How?' I say softly. I'm close to tears at this point – how could I have been so blind?

'Just talk to her. Be there for her. Listen to her. She's been through a lot lately and she needs to know that you're on *her* side, whatever happens.'

'Did she actually say she likes Joe more than me?'

'No,' Ash sighs. 'But she says he never speaks badly of you. Which is good, she said, because it would make her not want to be with him if he did.'

'Hmmm,' I hum.

'But I was quite surprised by that, Annie,' Ash continues. 'I mean, you know you're not supposed to badmouth your ex to the kids, don't you? It's basic stuff, that, Annie. Divorce 101!'

'I'm surprised, too,' I manage to speak through my confusion. 'I wasn't aware I was doing it. I may have said nasty things about Joe to myself, in my head, but...'

'One of the first signs of madness,' Ash says authoritatively. 'Talking to yourself and not even being aware of it. Tell me, Annie, my love – is it always your voice you hear in your head, or is it other people's?'

'What are you saying? That I'm insane?'

'No, I—'

'Or schizophrenic?'

'No, if you'd just let me—'

'I may have many issues, but as far as we're aware, I do *not* have multiple personalities!'

'Who's "we"?'

'I don't know!'

'You said: "as far as we're aware".'

'No I didn't!'

'Yes you did!'

'Did not!'

'Did too!'

'Did not!'

'Did – look! This is ridiculous! I was joking about the first sign of madness thing. I'm not saying you have multiple personality disorder. What I *am* saying, though, is that you need to get out there a bit more, Annie. Talking to yourself, or thinking out loud or whatever you want to call it, is a sign of loneliness. That's all. Annie?'

I'm quiet for the first time in yonks – both in and outside of my head.

'Annie, sweetheart? Are you okay?' she sounds worried now.

'Fine, fine,' I reassure her. 'I guess it's just come as a bit of a shock.' I flump onto the couch, as though someone's just pushed me down. 'But I don't *feel* particularly lonely, I'm always running around like a blue-arsed fly and—'

'When was the last time you talked to an adult?'

'A couple of weeks ago, I suppose. Amelie. She sends her love by the way.'

'Send mine back if you ever manage to speak to her again – honestly, this International Woman of Mystery stuff she goes in for, shagging Rico in Acapulco one minute, jetting off to Marbella for an orgy with D'Angelo the next... there's something going on there, I reckon. I just don't buy any of that Life Begins At Fifty rubbish she's always spouting.'

'You don't? I do. Anyway, why would she lie?'

'Make herself feel better, I suppose. We all tell ourselves little lies all the time, put on a front of some sort or another. Build a nice, tidy narrative for ourselves that suits whatever image we're trying to project, just to cope with life. Hey! Maybe she's got Munchausen's by proxy!'

Now it's my turn to roll my eyes and sigh. Bloody armchair analysts, amateur shrinks. No wonder we're all paranoid – they *are* out to get us…

'So how did the pros and cons go with the local newsletter?' she changes the subject swiftly.

'Local newsletter?' I'm offended. 'It's a monthly glossy, is *Chilterns Today (Forever in your heart)*! And anyway, I don't know, haven't heard anything back from the ed, yet, so I assume it's all okay. I'm working on my next one, now.'

She doesn't ask what the question for my next advice column is, just gives me a bit of a pep talk.

'You know I think you're amazing,' she says wistfully, like she's looking off into the middle distance, through her fabulous Georgian windows.

'Really?' I need to hear something nice – a compliment would be just fab and I defo sense one's in the offing. 'You do? Um… why, exactly?'

'Well,' she takes a deep breath in. 'You get sacked on your birthday, asked for a divorce on the same day, but you don't cry and howl like I've seen you do a thousand times before, you pick yourself up, dust yourself off, sort out a new life for you and your kids in the country, become an agony aunt at the local newsl… sorry, *magazine*, buy a beautiful Irish setter – who you should have called CuCullain, by the way, Irish mythological hero, red hair, strong, brave etc etc – Hero of the Hounds, in fact. But anyway, you integrate into your new community, nearly make some friends and maybe even lose some weight!'

She gasps for air, nearly hyperventilating, while I nearly choke on her last words.

'What?' I splutter. 'Do you think I *have* lost weight or are you saying it's time I *did* lose some weight?'

'Oh, hey hun, mwah!' she makes kissy noises slightly away from the phone's mouthpiece. 'Look, Annie, Pete's home early – gotta go!'

'Oh, okay, I—'

'No, you come here – ooh, the things I'm gonna do to you…' she hangs up, giggling and I imagine her chasing Pete up the stairs, like a female Benny Hill, ravaging him and rolling about on their emperor-sized, humungous bed.

Urgh. As Izzy says, there must be a better way.

—

Three Great Things

- Now I know a bit about how she's feeling, I can fix it for poor old Izzy.
- Now I know where I've stuffed up, I can stop making mistakes.
- Having made so many 'mistakes', I'm learning and growing every day. Or at least that's my story now – and I'm sticking to it.

Chapter Ten

August

August 28 – Outclassed and Outcast

Rufus has already been expelled from a couple of village hall puppy classes in the area surrounding Old Stoke and I'm at my wits' end. Sure, he's cute – but at twenty-five kilos and wilder than a blackberry patch, he's a nuisance, wanting to 'play' with every dog and person he meets, literally bowling them over and often drawing blood.

So there I am, being pulled in all sorts of impossible directions by Roofie down by the river, when I meet a couple of guys who suggest I take him to gun dog training. He is a gun dog, after all – and while I have no intention of taking him hunting, Roofie could definitely do with some serious whipping into shape.

So I call Chilterns Gun Dogs and book us in for a big group session. Training is the first step towards a happy pup and its happy owners, they say – and we could do with all the help we can get.

Of course, it takes about forty-five minutes to get Ben away from the computer. In fact, it probably takes longer, considering he ping-pongs back and forth between the computer and the telly, making me more and more furious as I feel any authority I may once have had slipping further and further away from me, laughing in my face as it disappears entirely.

And then there's Izzy. I have about as much luck getting her out of her sulky room as I do winning the lottery (i.e. none), so I'm forced to resort to guerrilla tactics.

Desperate times, desperate measures and all that.

'Izzy!' I bellow from the bottom of the stairwell. 'If you don't come down here THIS INSTANT and get in the car IMMEDIATELY, I will not only take that stupid bloody phone away from you, I'll throw it in the fu-uh-uh-loody river!'

Ben looks up from the computer with mouth and eyes wide open.

'Is there a flood?' he asks, all cute, innocent and blinky, as if he hasn't played a starring role in this farce.

'And as for *you*, young man!' I can feel the fire in my belly rage as my vision goes wonky. Is it from abject fury or is my eyesight fast failing, I wonder. Bit of both, I hazard a guess, and make a mental note to go to SpecSavers as soon as the kids go back to school.

I walk over to the front door and shout up in Izzy's general direction.

'I'm going to count to te—no, *twenty* – and if you're not here...'

She comes stomping down the stairs so hard, I fear her feet are going to go through the (probably rotten) steps. But they don't. Instead, she shoves them into the expensive Adidas rose-gold trainers that Daddy bought for her and shoots me daggers.

'Good girl,' I venture, risking her wrath by commenting.

She checks her phone, taps something on its screen and strides towards me. I actually feel a teensy bit scared when I see her narrowed eyes and thunderous expression. But I hold my ground. I mean, who's the adult in this situation?

I don't answer my own question, just try to hold my tongue as she ever-so-slightly bashes her shoulder into mine when she marches past me onto the driveway.

'KEY?' she shouts without turning to face me. 'Have you unlocked the CAR?'

Ooh, that's a point – where on earth *is* the car key?

I look absolutely everywhere and just when I start thinking I might have to buy some puppy laxative to, er, force the issue, Ben produces the one and only car key from one of the pocket pouches in his commando-style shorts. ('Commando' as in army, not as in without undies.)

I'm a little bit excited by the prospect of gun dog training. And not just because it might sort Roofie out, either. I mean, what if I meet some nice, dog-loving man there? Someone who'll help me civilise The Roofster and maybe sort me out, too? I wince at the thought. I sound like Amelie, seeing a shagging opportunity in everything! So I text her to tell her we're going to gun dog training and quick as a flash, she texts back:

Wear lipstick!

Incorrigible. But God – what if she's right? What if my dream man is there? What if it *is* time? What if I *am* ready? The man who runs the training sounded quite lovely on the phone, come to think of it – slight Yorkshire accent, deep voice, easy laugh – what if I'm about to meet The One?

Once we get there, the fields are positively heaving with dogs, dog owners, whistles, flat caps, Barbours and walking boots. It's quite hot, but some of these die-hard country folk still insist on wearing the right gear. I spot a group of tall, horsey-looking women haw-hawing together in tight cream jodhpurs, riding boots and tweedy hacking jackets casually slung over their shoulders, and not for the first time, I wish I was at least five inches taller and three stone lighter, so I wouldn't look quite so a Thelwell Angel on Horseback.

I feel so conspicuous and self-conscious, that when Izzy refuses to get out of the car, I don't lose my rag as I normally would, I let her stay there, cool, calm and in control. I'm fast losing the will to live lately and I just don't have the energy to argue anymore. And besides, if Mr Wonderful is watching, I can't have him see me in my true light. Not yet, anyway.

Ben and I try to steer Roofie towards a big tent where loads of people are milling around, gabbling on about shoots and hounds and guns and whatnot. Roofie needs no encouragement and drags us straight through the centre of the biggest cluster of people there and leaps onto a man in a tweed waistcoat, licking his face like a lunatic, nearly knocking him down.

'Roofie!' I gasp. 'I'm so sorry, ROOFIE! Get OFF... DOWN!'

Ben tries to wrestle Roofie off the man, but it must be like a fly on a hippo's back to Roofie and he completely ignores him.

'Hey, hey,' says the man, his eyes twinkling as he smiles and looks fondly at Roofie, ruffling his big floppy ears. 'What's the rush, eh? Why the big hurry?'

The man's lovely Yorkshire accent calms Rufus somewhat and he drops to the ground, leaning on the man and panting.

'Wow,' I say. 'I've never seen him do that before – stop crashing around, I mean.'

'You must be Annie,' he says. 'And this, I'm guessing, is Rufus.'

He pats Roofie's side so hard it makes a reassuring thudding sound. Rufus looks up at him adoringly.

'Are you Stanley?' I ask, as the crowd around us slowly dissipates.

'That I am, lass,' he winks, and somewhere in the distance, choral music plays while the sun's rays single us out, shining brightly on just us two.

My heart starts beating a little bit faster and even though he has a silver beard and must be at least sixty-five, romantic images flash through my brain: the pair of us laughing over a pint of real ale in a cosy pub, complete with roaring fire and faithful hounds at our feet; having snowball fights, laughing our heads off and doing snow angels in a blizzard; the steam of a shared hot chocolate rising to meet our faces, mere centimetres from each other, just about to connect in a deep, sensuous ki—

'And over there's the good lady wife who runs t'business with us,' he grins, pointing to a dumpy blonde woman in a man's short-sleeved checked shirt who's leaning on a tent pole, surveying the scene. I can't quite put my finger on who, but she definitely reminds me of someone.

The sky clouds over once more, the music stops and we get sorted out into groups. Ben, Roofie and I are obviously in the beginners group – but all the other dogs and owners in our set appear to have done this before.

The dogs have to pick up a small, brick-sized solid sausage-type thing covered in canvas called a 'dummy', stay still and then bring the dummy back to you, dropping it at your feet.

Well.

Just before it's our turn and I feel us all getting nervous, Ben tells me he has to do a poo, so I direct him to the bushes over yonder. I can't possibly go with him – it's nearly Roofie's time to shine and all this training's costing us a fortune.

'Can it wait?' I ask him.

'Nooooooo!' he answers.

'You'll just have to go without me, then. Don't worry, Vikings and cavemen have always done it in the woods – be brave, Ben, you can do it!'

And off he goes, crossing his legs as he walks so he sort of bunny hops to the bushes.

Of course, when Roofie gleefully picks up the dummy in his mouth, he runs for the hills. I imagine I can hear him chuckling as he bolts, like Muttley off *Wacky Races,* and I take off after him, only to give up, totally out of puff within seconds.

Roofie senses I've stopped, so he slows down and even looks like he's heading for my Dream Man's missus, when he artfully dodges her outstretched hand, cackling wheezily as he dives through the tent, knocking down the table of merch and pulling the tent down behind him.

He's heading for the bushes where Ben's 'being clever', leaving a line of dog-owners on the ground, falling as they try to pounce on Rufus flying by.

Suddenly, what sounds like sixty shrill whistles blow and the trainer's wife looks super-cross as she marches over and waits expectantly just outside the bushes.

But who emerges? Poor little Ben, that's who. He's got his shorts round his ankles, his hands over his ears and he's bawling his eyes out.

'That sound hurt my ears,' he wails. 'It scared me so much I didn't get to finish my poo-hoo-hoo...'

I run to him, remarkably full of puff all of a sudden, bend down, bat the half-in, half-out poo from his bum with a handy nearby stick and help him on with his pants.

'You're going to be fine, sweetie, everything's—'

I'm cut short, though, when Roofie rams into us, sending both of us splatting to the ground, splayed in the middle of the training field. I feel one of his paws using my forehead as a launch pad, the final humiliation as he springs off us and sprints towards the trainer.

The trainer laughs and grabs Roofie's collar masterfully. Roofie lets the dummy fall, searches the trainer's face for approval and looks so pleased with himself, you'd think he *meant* to cause this carnage.

I, on the other hand, bury my face further into the dirt, in the vain hope that the ground might swallow me up.

—

Three upbeat, positive things I could call 'wins':

- My visualisation may be misplaced, fantasising about a sixty-five-year-old, married dog trainer, but

I didn't put myself down while I was doing it did I? So I'm definitely getting better at that.

- I'm out and about, meeting and talking to other adults, as Ash suggested.
- School's nearly about to start again. Thank God.

Chapter Eleven

September

September 3 – But Didn't He Have a Vasectomy?

'Tiffani's pregnant,' Izzy announces with no fanfare whatsoever as she follows Ben through the front door after being at Joe's for the weekend.

It's the last Sunday afternoon of the school holidays and I was hoping to get a few mountains of washing done while they were at their dad's, but the siren song of the couch was simply too strong for me to resist, so I've been napping most of the weekend – save for getting pawed to death when an insistent Roofie won't take no for an answer and I have to take him out for a walk.

Which is really starting to grind me down, to be honest. I mean, I know dogs are great, they get you out and about when you'd rather doze in front of the telly, they love you unconditionally and there's nothing quite like the sight of an Irish setter in full flight to really lift the spirits, but— wait, what? What did Izzy just say?

'Yep.' Izzy flops on the still-warm couch and looks up at me with wet eyes. 'She showed us the latest scan.'

She did *what*?!

'There's an alien in Fit Nanny's tummy,' Ben chirrups, looking for the remote.

'Is there, now?' I cross my arms over my chest. 'And I suppose Daddy's the, um, father? Of this alien?'

Izzy nods, looking at me like she's about to melt into a sea of tears and Ben rolls a sleeping Rufus off the remote.

'Oh, babe.' I sit down next to Izzy and she buries her head in my arm pit. 'That's a bit of a shocker, isn't it, eh? How does that news make you feel, darling?'

'Blurphhhnyurgh.' Whatever she's saying, it's all muffled and I can't understand a word.

'I can't wait to have a baby alien brother,' Ben says, putting the TV onto YouTube and flicking through videos of young men playing *Minecraft*. 'It will be here for Christmas. Daddy said.'

At this, Izzy shoots up off the couch and storms upstairs. I'm not sure what to do, but when her wailing and gnashing of teeth threatens to drown out the asinine ramblings of American teenagers playing computer games, I go upstairs to see her.

'Sweetheart...' I open her bedroom door gingerly, wary of what I might find on the other side.

I needn't have worried, though, because she's assumed the standard adolescent-in-distress position, lying on her stomach on her bed, her face pressed into her pillow.

'Blurphhhnyurgh,' she says again.

'Take your head out of the pillow and talk to me properly,' I say in my best soothing tones while I park my bum on the side of the bed.

She raises her head off the pillow and sniffs.

'I can tell you're upset, sweetie—'

'Congratulations, Sherlock.' She's all red of cheek and small of eye.

I ignore that snippy remark.

'Do you want to talk about it?' I plough on.

She doesn't say anything this time, just looks at me and swivels her legs around so that her feet are next to me, her back resting up against the wall.

We sit like that for a short time, as I desperately try to figure out how to handle this weird situation. Like, what's the good parent protocol? What should I say? What should I do? And what, if anything, should I feel?

If truth be told, I actually feel sorry for Tiffani. Because if Joe's past performance as a dad is anything to go by, she'll be bringing that little bundle up all on her ownsome, whether he's physically there or not.

Ben and Izzy, though, are a different story. Ben's possibly too young to really understand what this all means – particularly when it comes to his relationship with his dad – but underneath his *Minecraft* boy bravado, I'm sure he's been deeply affected by all this. And as for Izzy...

'Silly Daddy! He's just like Zeus and Poseidon!' she spits.

'Go easy,' I nearly choke. 'I know you love your dad, and in your eyes he's a bit of a hero, but he's hardly god-like, is he?'

'I mean like in the Percy Jackson books.' She shakes her head. 'They always say that when the gods came down and got the mortal women pregnant, it was because the gods *couldn't help themselves*. So obviously, Daddy *couldn't help himself* with Tiffani. Probably because she's so pretty...'

I feel slightly queasy at the thought.

'But he should have more self-control! He's OUR dad.'

'Damn straight he is – and nothing and no one can ever change that.' I pull her close to me. 'He loves you very much, you know. Always has, always will.'

'Yeah, yeah,' she says.

'So what did you say to Daddy? When he told you about the, ah, baby?'

'He didn't tell us,' she says. 'Tiffani was so excited, she showed us the scan over breakfast. I was so surprised, I didn't say anything to either of them.'

'Would you like to talk to Daddy about it?'

'No!' she looks affronted. 'He's no good at talking about emotions and feelings and stuff.'

Tell me something I don't know, I think to myself.

I hug her hard and for the first time in I don't know how long, she hugs me back. I try hard to hide my joy and we stay like that for a good minute and a half before she starts to pull away.

'Oh, don't go,' I say, sounding a lot more needy and whiney than I'd intended.

'Mu-um,' she protests, 'lemme go! Give me some space!'

'Okay, okay.' I put my hands up, like someone's pointing a gun at me. 'I just want you to know that I'm always here for you and you can talk to me. About anything. Anytime. Here. Always here. Just... whenever you need me, I'll be here.'

'I know,' she says, all grown up and serious. 'But you know, maybe you should find someone your own age to hang out with.'

Eh?

'I'll be ten soon and things are bound to change,' she goes on, the slings and arrows piercing my heart. 'I just want you to be happy and I think maybe you could do with getting a boyfriend. Or at least some more friends. What about the mums in Thistlebend?'

Things have come to a pretty pass when your precocious daughter tells you you've got a shit social life.

'They're all busy with their own lives,' I say, sounding sadder than I feel. 'But I've got so much to keep me occupied – there's you, Ben, bloody Roofie—'

'Mum,' she turns to face me, 'you need to go on some dates. Get online, set up a profile. Do you want me to help?'

'No!' I mean, it's one thing being told you're on the shelf by your kid, but quite another for her to fix you up online. 'I can do it myself.'

'Can you?' She obviously doubts this. 'So how's the blog going?'

'Good, good,' I nod slowly and stare at a stain on the carpet.

'Hmph,' she sighs. 'Any comments yet?'

'No, not that I'm aware of.'

'Have you checked?'

'No.'

'Mu-uu-um!'

'Well, I've got a million other things on my plate. Like you, for starters.'

Plates, starters – I'm getting hungry, now.

'What about me?' She looks so sweet, grabbing hold of the light blue stuffed donkey I bought her when she was three months old and sucking on its ear, just as she's always done.

'School. I know things aren't great at school at the mo' – do you want to tell me about it?'

She shakes her head.

'Well, if you do, you know where I am.'

'On the side of my bed?'

I get up off the bed and give her what I hope is a withering look.

'You could stay in my room tonight,' she murmurs, 'you know, if you wanted to.'

If I *wanted* to? That sofa bed's killing my back – I'd LOVE to sleep on her double bed with the mattress topper and the flannelette sheets and the brushed cotton tartan duvet cover... bloody LOVE to!

'Would you sleep on the top bunk?' I ask, getting rather excited about the prospect of having her fantastic bed all to myself.

'Couldn't I sleep on the bottom bunk with you?' She looks up at me with those sapphire eyes that have always had the power to totally disarm me. 'Promise I won't wriggle about or snore...'

'What about me?' Ben peers round Izzy's bedroom door. 'Can I sleep with you too?'

'Oh, come here, gorgey boy – of course you can!' I stretch out my arms and bring him into the fold.

After we've had dinner and cuddled Roofie to within an inch of his life, we all come upstairs to Izzy's room and play Top Trumps Marvel Super Heroes, a British Museum card memory game and finally, my favourite, Snap!

Then we all tumble into the bottom bunk, me in the middle, and proceed to have arguably the worst night's sleep of our lives.

–

September 5 – Getting Over the Hump

I'm driving back from Thistlebend in floods of tears as Heart radio plays 'Slipping Through My Fingers' by Abba.

It's the first day of a new school year and while Ben was fine with it, Izzy didn't want to go in at all and I can't say I blame her.

She still hasn't told me exactly what's gone on with her and those little bitches in her class, but it must be bad, because she gives me a tight hug when she says goodbye – and even says 'love you' before she turns away to face her fellow class mates. I vow to read *How To Talk So Kids Will Listen & How To Listen So Kids Will Talk* when I get home – even though I've never read it all the way through before – I see it more as a dip in, dip out sort of thing.

Speaking of dips, these country lanes don't make driving easy at the best of times, but when you're prone to panic attacks and your eyes are full of tears, what hope have you got?

I tell myself to slow down, take it easy and turn the radio off.

But I can't seem to bring myself to turn it off – it's like I want to sink into and completely submerge myself in sadness. Which is not like me, really – particularly since the split. I'm so much more 'jolly hockey sticks' and 'pull yourself together' and 'just bloody well get on with it' than I ever used to be. And it's precisely that attitude that's got us through so far, I think.

But today I just want to wallow in it.

As I come off the toll bridge and turn into our road, I see Jane skipping along with little Jess. I slow down and beep.

'What are you looking so happy about?' I lower the window and shout out.

'School's back! Why do you look so glum?' She tilts her head to the side.

'School's back...' I sniff.

'What are you? Nuts? School's great – now someone else can look after them all day!'

'I suppose so.'

'Go home, park the car and meet us at Costa in ten minutes – the girls'll be there, we can all weep into our skinny soy lattes together!'

A car behind beeps at me, so I wave, put the window up and only screech a tiny bit when I take off for home.

When I come through the front door, Roofie nearly knocks me down, leaping up on me, licking my face, whimpering and weeing on the floor. I clean that up, spit-spot and get back to saying hello to our little puppy who's now the size of a Shetland pony.

God – there's nothing like an excited Irish setter greeting. Makes you feel a bit special, like you really light up someone's life and mean the world to them. No wonder people leave fortunes to their dogs in their wills. It reminds me of the way Izzy used to react when Daddy would come home when she was two. We'd be sitting there, her on the floor with assorted toys surrounding her, me on the couch with a cup of tea, desperately hoping Joe would be back in time so he could put Izzy to bed and I could catch up with *Coronation Street*.

You could really get a complex after one too many of those greetings, let me tell you. I mean, she'd go *mental* when he came through the door – beaming and laughing, running over to him and grabbing hold of him as though he had come to save her from... well, me.

Picturing her as a two-year-old toddler, pushing herself up off the floor, from seated to standing, makes my face crease up again and I howl, really letting the tears flow.

I slump down into the couch and Roofie jumps on me, tries to sit on my lap, like a baby elephant and licks my cheeks so they're even wetter than before.

'Okay, okay!' I turn my head left and right to avoid his rough, stinking-of-Pedigree tongue. 'You can come with me – but only if you behave!'

So we're walking down the road towards Costa and roadworks have sprung up at the roundabout, causing traffic to pile up all the way to the Co-op on the other side of our house.

Roofie's dragging me along, passers-by are saying, 'Who's taking who for a walk?!' and I smile, even though it feels like my arm might pop out of its socket any minute.

When we walk into Costa, Jane, Sue and Liz are deep in chat, nursing their lattes, while Jess plays on the banquette with some Lego.

'Hey,' Sue says softly. 'How was the kids' first drop-off after the hols?' Her face is tear-stained, but her eyes are still welcoming and friendly.

'Good, good...' I collapse on the chair next to Jess and dissolve into tears.

Even though I've only met Sue once before and barely know her, she leaps up to put her arms around me, treating me like a dear, long-lost friend.

'I'll get you a tea,' says Jane, getting up, making for the counter. 'Better make it a grande.'

'It's a nightmare,' says Liz who is, I note, even in the depths of my distress, unfeasibly tall. 'You spend six weeks shouting at the little buggers and then when they go back to school, you curse yourself for being such a cow!'

I nod in agreement.

'They're just growing up so fast,' Sue says, welling up herself again. 'It's like the good bits are on fast-forward and the bad bits are in slo-mo.'

'I know,' I sniff, brushing off the hair that's stuck to my face. 'And Izzy's having a really shit time there, too. I feel like I'm leading a lamb to the slaughter, sending her into her classroom.'

I tell them about the girls in Izzy's class being horrible – and why my kids are at a school so far away.

Liz mutters something about role models and absent fathers and Sue, who's on an INSET day (the local secondary school, where she teaches English, isn't going back until Wednesday), says the whole situation's prepos- terous and grills me as to why I haven't spoken to Izzy's teacher about it.

'I only found out about it over the holidays,' I say. 'I'll request a meeting with her teacher tomorrow.'

'Annie's got an awful lot on her plate,' Jane calms Sue down. 'As a single mum with a delinquent dog and an ex who's just got his new girlfriend up the duff—'

What?

'How do you know?' I ask, wondering if I've been thinking out loud again.

'Oops, sorry,' Jane smiles. 'Thin walls.'

'Oh, right,' I say, reminding myself to Google some sort of noise-cancelling plaster or paint you can put on interior walls. 'It's just so hard, juggling everything – as it is for everyone, I mean, I don't think I'm special or anything, it's just...'

Rufus jumps up onto the arm of the chair and gives my cheek one solitary lick.

'He must be a handful,' Liz nods in Roofie's direction. 'The only man of the house.'

'That's putting it mildly.' Jane's eyes go big as she takes a sip of her latte.

'How do you know?' I ask.

'Thin walls!' Sue, Jane and Liz say in unison.

'Look, why don't you give the council a call, see if they've got any places at Chips?' says Sue.

'Chips?' I don't know what she's on about.

'Chilterns Primary School,' she sighs. 'In fact, don't you worry about it, I'll give Kate, the headteacher, a call – old friend, wicked laugh, filthy sense of humour – and see if she can't pull a few strings, get the kids into school here.'

'You'd do that?' I feel like Oliver, asking for more. 'For me?'

' 'Course!' she slaps me on the back. 'Cake!'

'Ooh, yes, please,' I grin.

'No, you muppet,' Jane steps in. 'She means it's a *piece of cake,* as in it'll be easy for her to get your kids into the local school.'

I feel my shoulders relax and the corners of my mouth lift as I imagine a three-minute walk to school instead of a thirty-minute drive; not spending a fortune on petrol and toll charges; getting up at seven thirty a.m. instead of six a.m.; the kids making friends with other children who could, quite possibly, live in *their* street…

'Leave it to me,' says Sue. 'And mine's a chocolate tiffin, if you're buying.'

–

Three upbeat, positive things I might be able to call 'wins':

277

- I haven't thought about smoking once – even in these upsetting times. And I haven't had chocolate for ages, either. Weird, but great.
- Roofie and I are providing roadside entertainment, a sort of community service for those stuck in traffic, so good deeds a-plenty. The Universe would definitely approve.
- We might soon be saying farewell to Thistlebend. Which is a good thing. Isn't it?

–

September 6 – A Hit With the Octogenarians

Despite Sue's promise of an easier life, I still can't help blubbing for Britain. I don't know what the hell's up with me, but every five minutes, *à propos* of absolutely nothing, I feel a tickle at the tip of my nose, my face crumples in on itself, the tears pour out of my eyes and when I catch sight of myself in a reflective surface (the toaster, usually), all I see staring back at me is an old man without his teeth, gurning.

Why…? Menopause? Probably…

'Ah!' I slap my thigh when I catch sight of my anti-depressants lurking behind the toaster. I've forgotten to take them for God knows how long – hence the tears! When you're on those things, it's like they completely dry your tear ducts up, you never really cry anymore. But when you forget to take them and you start reverting to type, you can't turn the sodding things off even if you try.

So it is with wet face and red eyes that I meet with Izzy's teacher, Mrs Plint, five minutes before the bell goes this morning.

We sit in those ridiculously small seats and within seconds it becomes clear that Mrs Plint is not only a local Thistlebend girl herself, but she also doesn't believe Izzy's being ostracised and bullied by the girls in her class.

'I'm sorry, Ms Beaton,' she emphasises the 'z' sound in Ms for so long, I start to wonder whether a bee's trapped somewhere in the room. 'But that sort of thing just doesn't happen in my classroom.'

'Well, maybe it happens more in the playground,' I suggest.

'Not on my watch.' She straightens her back and shifts in her seat.

'Perhaps you haven't been on duty when—'

'Look, I'll keep an eye out for anything untoward, but I very much doubt there's any unseemly behaviour… coming from *my* girls, anyway.'

Now, normally, I'd let this marked comment slide – I'd put on my best benign smile, stand up, shake her hand, thank her for her help and turn to leave, cussing silently as I walk away. But today I don't feel like rolling over and letting it go.

'What are you saying, Mrs Plint?' I cock my head to the side, like Roofie does when he can't figure out what we're on about.

'Nothing. Just that *my* girls are all well-brought up, well-behaved young ladies.' She thrusts her nose in the air, like she's Miss Jean Brodie and she's in her prime or something. 'They would never harass, cajole, ignore or in any other way conspire to make an outsider feel uncomfortable.'

'I see.' I feel like Poirot. 'And these girls you speak of – sorry, *your girls* – does this little group of children include Izzy? Or is she perhaps *the outsider* in this lovely little scenario?'

BBBRRRRRIIIIIIIIINNNNGGGG!

'I'm glad we understand each other, Mizzzzzzzzzzzzz Beaton.' She leaps up off the chair at the sound of the bell, bounds over to her desk, grabs a clipboard and stands at the classroom entrance to 'welcome' the kids coming in. 'But now you must excuse me. The school day is ready to begin!'

I linger long enough to see Izzy walking in, but decide at the last minute not to wave and woo-hoo to get her attention — she'd be beyond mortified if I did.

Without so much as a by-your-leave, then, I get out of there, keeping my head down, careful not to catch anybody's eye, and scuttle up to The Pantry. Poor Izzy, I mutter as I walk inside, no wonder she's so unhappy with an icicle like that for a teacher. The sooner I can get her into Chips the better.

'We don't do chips.' The barista behind the counter purses his lips and looks me up and down.

'What? Oh, sorry, no,' I backtrack. 'Of course you don't!'

Who said anything about chips? God, I wish I could have a cigarette.

A hot chocolate will have to do, though — better grab a take-away one, so I can try to drink as I drive, thus ensuring I spill scalding brown stuff over my lap and burn my lips off all before ten a.m.

Just as I'm imagining this scene, wincing as I think of my poor lips, I feel a light, perfumed tap on my shoulder.

I look around and get a face full of camel cashmere sweater.

Slowly I look up and there, looking down at me is the beauty in beige, Charlotte.

'I'll get this,' she says to the barista, pointing a beautifully manicured finger at me. 'Bring it over when it's ready, please. And a two-shot espresso. Thanks.'

She heads for her little table at the back and I nearly trip over Willow in my haste to follow her.

'So,' she says instead of hi, how are you, etc. 'You're a hit with the octogenarians.'

'I'm what?' I splutter.

'The over-eighties,' she smiles. 'They love your advice column. Like your style. Recognise you as one of their own.'

'They do?' I'm quite chuffed by this. Surprised but chuffed. 'I wonder why?'

'I expect you're on their wavelength – you know, over forty, over the hill, past it…'

'All right, all right,' I murmur, wondering whether she's trying to be funny. It's hard to tell with those chiselled cheekbones and skin so smooth, it wouldn't know a laughter line if it came up and bit it. 'Ha ha… ha?'

'So well done on that front,' she says, looking up to the barista who's bringing over our beverages and mouthing 'thankyou' at him.

'Ooh, thanks,' I say and greedily take a gulp as soon as he puts it on the table.

For all that's gracious and holy, that's HOT!

'Calm down,' Charlotte says coolly. 'You look like a bulldog chewing a wasp.'

'Charming,' I reply, once I get some feeling back in my lips.

'What *is* wrong with your face today, Annie?' she asks.

'Bit rude,' I say, unsure how to take this unnecessary barrage of abuse.

'I mean, usually you're so smiley and fresh with a youthful exuberance that belies your advanced years...'

Is she for real?

'... but today you look all washed out. Pale and... decidedly *uninteresting*.'

On the spot I decide to be the bigger (metaphorically speaking), better woman and gloss over the insulting nature of what she's said and imagine this is her way of saying she's concerned about me.

'I just feel...' I stop myself before my tear ducts erupt again. 'It's almost like...'

'Take your time.' Charlotte lets out a dainty little cough. 'It's not like we've got lives to lead or anything.'

She smirks a bit and even though she's obviously got a million better things to do, I feel an uncontrollable urge to unburden myself to her. So I do just that.

Twenty minutes later, Charlotte's standing up, signalling that this particular meeting is over.

'Delayed reaction,' she says, as though she's stating a fact.

'Hmmm?' I'm still blowing on my chocolate.

'You had all this trauma at the beginning of the year, you kept putting one foot in front of the other, kept it together for the kids and now you're having a mini breakdown. The breakdown you should have had months ago. But you had to be strong for everyone else. Now that *is* interesting,' she says. 'Another thing for us DSMs-in-waiting to consider. Why don't you make trauma delay a question topic for your next advice column?'

'I could, I suppose – if I can fit it in around the dog training, walking, kids—'

'Sounds tough,' she says, clearly not giving a stuff. 'Which reminds me. There's a do on in a few weeks, early October, I think – Small Country Business Awards. Insufferable. But as champions of the Chilterns, we need to be there and be in all the photographs. Our presence needs to be noted. Would you mind awfully going in my place? Ghastly things – but you need stay only long enough for the photos to be taken and then you can go home.'

'But surely you'll be nominated? I mean, you might even win an award for, ooh, I dunno – coolest café in a school car park?'

'You're right.' She looks around proudly, queen of all she surveys. 'But I don't believe in awards – just hard graft. Put in an appearance, accept my awards for me and give me five hundred words on the whole thing the following week. I'll ping you the deets. And if you do me proud on this, I'll make you editor-at-large – even though I know you're slimming… Ha! Get it? Large? Never mind.'

She's so pleased with her little joke, I worry her taut skin might split over her cheekbones as she manoeuvres her mouth into something like a smile.

'Thanks, Annie,' she says. 'You're a treasure. Ciao for now.'

And off she wafts, Willow panting at her white patent loafer heel.

–

Later, that afternoon...

When we get home, Roofie doesn't mow us down at the door, there's no obvious smell of poo or wee (even though if I ever get my hands on a surplus of money, the rug is out and a plastic outdoor mat is defo in) and the big red dog is nowhere to be seen.

'Roofie?' I wander through the house calling his name.

'ROOOOO-FEEEEEEE!' Ben joins in, looking under the cushions on the couch.

Izzy goes straight upstairs to lock herself in her bedroom, as per.

'Oh, Mum,' she calls out. 'You have to see this – it's *adorable*!'

Ben and I race to the bottom of the stairwell and begin our ascent when we see it. There's Rufus, all twenty-five kilos of him, sitting on the tiny landing at the top of the stairs, ears back, eyes smiling, pawing at the top step.

'What's he doing, Mum?' Ben asks.

'Trying to get the courage up to go downstairs,' Izzy tuts.

'Oh, Roofie, you big silly!' I say.

'You'll have to carry him down,' says Izzy. 'Just pick him up and go down, like you used to.'

'When he wasn't sixteen tonnes of gut-wrenching terror!' I laugh. 'There's no way I can pick him up now – and those stairs are a death trap as it is, let alone when you're carrying a wriggling, frightened hound!'

'I'll do it!' announces Ben.

'Don't be ridiculous.' Izzy brushes him aside and pushes her sleeves up. 'I'll sort this out.'

She bends down, sliding her hands in under his bulk and whipping them out again as he jumps up, personally affronted.

'Can't say I blame him,' I smile at her.

'Aww! I nearly had him there.' She puts her hands on her hips and stands with her feet apart, like she's Calamity Jane, about to belt out 'Whip Crack Away' on top of the Deadwood stage or something.

'None of us can carry him and he's too big and scared and unwieldy to manoeuvre himself down these narrow, steep steps,' I murmur.

'He can sleep in my bed!' shouts Ben.

'No! He can sleep in *my* bed,' Izzy yells louder.

'I wonder if John next door's home. Maybe he could help...' I ignore their ludicrous suggestions.

'But Mum!' Izzy looks accusingly at me. 'We don't need a man to do things for us! What happened to "we can do anything and we are women, hear us roar"?'

'Raaahr!' Ben comes at me with his pretend claws.

I'm not sure how to answer Izzy and the good points she's raised – so I don't. Instead, I take the stairs two by two and, leaning over the falling-down picket fence demarcating our two properties, knock on next door's door.

Jane answers.

'I hate to ask, Jane – but I'm a damsel in distress. Is John in?'

'Yeah,' she says. 'He's in the study. What's the problem?'

'Poor little Roofie—'

'Poor *humungous* Roofie, you mean.'

'Yeah! Well, he's only got himself stuck at the top of the stairs. He can't get himself down and I can't lift him, so I was wondering...'

'JO-O-O-O-OHN!' she calls up the stairs.

'How can I be of assistance?' he answers Jane immediately and is already coming down their stairs when he says this. Husband of the year or what?

'Rufus is stuck at the top of their stairs,' Jane fills him in. 'Could you go and carry him down for Annie?'

'I thought I heard some noise earlier,' he says as he puts his shoes on. 'But I just thought it was Izzy crying as usual.'

'Really?' I say.

'Told you they were thin walls...' Jane looks apologetic.

'Izzy's usually crying?' I ask.

'Ready! As long as he doesn't take a chunk out of my *other* cheek,' John smiles as he leaps over the fence, like a triumphant tennis player.

'I'm sorry to ask,' I say, following him, 'but he's too heavy for us and... well... that gash seems to have healed up nicely?'

'Not a problem,' he says, loping to the top of the stairs, scooping Rufus up in his arms, carefully carrying him down and gently depositing him on the floor.

'You're a legend!' I shake John's hand.

'Nothing to it.' He puffs his chest out a bit. 'Happy to help.'

'MU-UU-UM!' Ben squeaks when he lands next to us downstairs. 'Roofie's gone!'

I nearly snap my neck frantically looking hither and thither.

Hither and thither? Seriously? Maybe Charlotte's right and the octogenarians like me because I talk like them – like someone born in the 1940s.

'There he is!' John points to the front door just in time for us to see Roofie's feathery mahogany tail disappear through it.

'After him!' Ben screams, jumping up and down on the spot.

John runs off first and he's halfway down the front path when he lunges at Roofie's tail – only for him to misjudge things slightly, trip on a loose paving stone and fall face-first into the driveway.

'Ah! John! You okay?' I pat his back as I run past, putting on some speed in case Roofie crosses the main road.

But I'm nowhere near fast enough to catch up with this crazy dog and I can only look on ineffectually as he practically *throws* himself into the road, weaving between a Range Rover and an Audi, making it to the other side of the road in seconds flat, without (miraculousy) getting hit or causing a crash.

I wait for the cars to pass, then quickly and carefully walk to the other side, only to see Liz, she of the extraordinary height, dressed in shorts and a tank top holding onto Roofie's collar while he sits patiently at her feet.

'Oh my God!' I'm out of breath already. 'Thank you so much, Liz He's a total menace! Poor old John's face-down in our garden path back there – he got Roofie down from the stairs.'

'Did he now?' she says, eyeing me suspiciously. 'How very handy of him.'

I'm not one hundred per cent sure, but I think I detect a sarky note from Liz. Buggered if I know what that's about. And I'm not about to question her on it – I've had enough drama for one day.

'Yeah.' I grab a hold of Roofie's collar. 'Off to boot camp?'

'Just a quick 5K in the afternoon,' she says flatly.

I'm not sure where to go from here.

'Well, anyway, thanks again,' I say, and cross the road.

John's still brushing himself down when Roofie and I come back down the path.

'I'm so sorry, John,' I say. 'It's like Roofie saw his chance and made his bid for freedom!'

'Who?' John looks confused.

'Roofie!'

'Oh, yeah,' he nods. 'Now what did I say about the other cheek?'

Strange question.

'Turn it? If you're Christian?' I answer, a bit bewildered myself, now.

'No! I mean, look!' John juts his jaw out, turns his head to the side and there, on his previously uninjured cheek, is a long cut. It's bleeding.

'Bloody hell!' I gasp. 'I am so sorry! Come inside and I'll put some Dettol on it. Or maybe Savlon. We've got some great Lightning McQueen plasters...'

I walk in front of him towards our house, but he declines my kind offer.

And so does Jane.

'Come here, you big lummox.' Jane stretches her arms out to John. 'Let's clean you up and get all that dirt out.'

She goes up on her tiptoes to kiss him and ushers him back into their house once he's gingerly stepped over the fence.

'Thanks again!' I call out as their door closes.

Later on, I buy a box of Cadbury's Roses and take them round to next door, just to say thanks and sorry etc.

But when I knock on the door, no one answers, despite the fact that I see their front net curtain twitching and I hear thuds and whispers.

I stand there like a lemon for a few minutes wondering what on earth's going on. I think about taking the chocolates back home with me, but then I remember how the fence creaked and groaned under my weight when I climbed over it just now, so I think better of it, and leave the box on their doorstep instead.

—

Three upbeat, positive things I might be able to call 'wins':

- I'm off the meds and I didn't even know!
- I'm going to a country shindig!
- I gave away a full, completely unopened box of chocs! Hang on – who's the winner here?

Chapter Twelve

October

October 12 – And the Rest, As They Say, is a Mystery

Amelie's come down for our scheduled big night out in Old Stoke.

Except we're not going out in Old Stoke, as previously planned, we're heading to nearby village Ufson Downs, where the Small Country Business Awards (or Scubas, as they're known locally) are being held in some rich person's converted barn.

'This is going to be epic!' Amelie brushes past me when I open the front door. The big bags she's carrying prove too much of a temptation for Roofie and he launches himself at them, tearing them to shreds while wagging his tail furiously and alternately jumping on Amelie.

'Jesus Christ!' she laughs. 'You didn't tell me he was *this* fucking enormous!'

'I did tell you he was a major menace though, didn't I?'

'Oh, so who's a big boy, then, hmmm? Who's a big boysie-woysie? You are! Yes you are! It's you, yes it is, yes I know! You're a big—'

RRROARF!

Roofie barks and it's clear his voice has already broken – it's so deep and guttural. If I didn't know he was a giant teddy bear of a dog, I'd swear he was a vicious Doberman or something. Good for keeping burglars away, I suppose.

'Oh, ho!' Amelie's entranced. 'Who's a noisy boysie, eh? Who's a noisy-woisy boy—'

'What's in the bags?' I cut her off as all this baby talk is making me nauseous. 'You're only here for one night, aren't you?'

'One night only, that's me!' She gently pushes Roofie down and brushes his hair and slobber from her trousers. 'And yes, I do say that to all the boys.'

She puts one bag down and holds the other one aloft, shaking it.

It clinks excitedly.

'Now, what are we drinking – red, white, beer or prosecco?'

'Earl Grey with almond milk.' I draw myself to my full height and prepare for the inevitable torrent of abuse. Because resisting alcohol on a night out with Amelie takes true grit – I mean, she always seems to take my abstinence as a personal affront.

'Prosecco it is, then.' She barges past me and starts opening kitchen cupboards.

'Really, Am,' I say softly, 'I'm just not interested in drinking – especially not tonight – it is a work do for me, after all.'

'Ha! Yeah!' She continues her search, but settles on a Lightning McQueen cup and one chipped mug I took from Teddington that has a cartoon picture of a balloon next to a pair of boobs on it, saying BUST LOOSE ON YOUR BIRTHDAY!

Obviously, it's an old one of Joe's.

Amelie pours the prosecco into the cup and mug while I do my best to ignore her and turn on the kettle instead.

'A couple of heart-starters before we go won't hurt,' she says, offering me the cup.

I put my hand up and turn my face away, as though I can't bear the hideous sight of either Lightning McQueen or the booze the cup contains.

'God, when did you get so boring?' She settles down at the kitchen table.

I don't dignify the question with an answer.

'So, Amelie,' I skilfully avoid her prying eyes by staring at the kettle, 'tell me of your latest conquests.'

'How long have you got?' she giggles. 'Honestly, it's a jungle out there – and I'm swinging from vine to vine like the cheekiest monkey around! It's incredible, it really is – young guys are crazy about older women. Especially online.'

I couldn't be less interested, of course, but I indulge her, steering the convo away from me.

'Really?' I feign surprise.

'Oh, yeah! It's a smorgasbord of sex just waiting for you to tuck in. They're so energetic and athletic and hot! The six-packs I've come across lately – ha! And I do mean that literally – are *insane.*'

I don't know whether it's me, the menopause or the particularly yummy Lady Grey with a soupcon of orange in it that Twinings have just brought out, but I'd so much prefer a hot, sweet cup of tea to swinging from vines or chandeliers, feeling like I have to go to all that *effort.*

'Sex is overrated,' I mutter.

'Bollocks,' Amelie snorts. 'You've just got sexual amnesia – you can't remember what it's like and how good for you it is. Keeping you slim and all.'

Maybe she has a point. Maybe if I saw more action, I wouldn't be quite so weighty. Maybe I wouldn't be so keen to raid the chocolate aisle in the Co-op of an evening if I had some hot young stud with a six-pack waiting for me on the sofa bed once the kids had gone to bed.

I wince at the thought. Imagine getting naked in front of someone young, trying to suck your stomach in, but watching, powerless, as it flubbers towards the floor. And when you catch sight of your bum, you see so many lumps and bumps, it looks like a big batch of home-made guacamole, just without the green tinge. Hopefully.

Nope, I refuse to even entertain the thought of going out with anyone under forty-five. Better make that fifty. Because really, apart from all the physical problems, what on *earth* would you have to talk about?

'Who cares?' Amelie says, pouring herself another mugful of prosecco. 'You're not with them for their conversation, let's face it.'

'I dunno,' I sigh. 'It just seems so weird to me – all this fancying and shagging. I mean, I know I was into it when I was younger – but now, I can barely keep my eye on who's having what in their lunchbox, what we're having for dinner and whether I've remembered to feed Roofie or not.'

'You said "lunchbox",' Amelie sniggers.

'Honestly, it's like talking to Beavis and Butthead with you sometimes. Anyway, what happened to your dream man being someone with whom you could walk hand in hand around a garden centre on Sundays?'

'That is an idea *with which* I fell out of love,' she mocks me, 'once I turned fifty-two. Life's too short for acting like a pensioner on day release from the nursing home. And once my decree absolute came through, well, I figured I'd go for it.'

I nod and wrap my fingers around the melamine Mister Men cup I found at the back of the kitchen cupboard (Miss Naughty), warming my hands.

'But why does *going for it* or *not acting like a pensioner* mean you go around shagging twenty-five-year-old boys? Like, why don't you conquer Masada in Israel? Or go bungee-jumping in New Zealand?'

'Get real, Annie.' She drains the mug again. 'I'm not in an ad for Tena Lady!'

'Or do something with a social conscience, some pro bono work at your law firm – legal aid for divorced single mums, for example, you know, just off the top of my head?'

'Speaking of—' Amelie opens up the second bottle of prosecco. 'How are you finding being a divorced single mum – besides living in a sexual desert, I mean? Is it the best thing to have happened to you, like I said it would be?'

I take a sip of Lady Grey and savour the orangey sweetness while I consider her question.

'Of course it is!' she beats me to it. 'You don't have him pissing and moaning about his dinner not being on the table for him when he gets home from work, you don't have to constantly chew my ear off about how he never does anything with the kids, he no longer has to get all huffy and puffy because you don't know how to operate a Hoover...'

Seems she knew us as a couple pretty well.

'And now the way is clear for you to meet some hand-some young—'

'Handsome, yes – young, no. What is it with you and youth? It can bugger off as far as I'm concerned!'

'Already has,' she mutters, 'where you're concerned.'

'That's harsh, Am.' I summon my inner strength. 'Just because I'm not putting it about and having it away—'

'You sound like my mother,' she smirks.

I sound like my mother, too – but I don't tell her that.

'… it doesn't mean that I'm sad and miserable, sitting at home every night watching *Homes Under the Hammer* on catch-up. Not that there would be anything wrong with that if I was!'

Amelie sculls my Lightning McQueen cupful of prosecco (down in one), pushes the prosecco bottles aside, unscrews the lid of the white wine and pours us both a generous amount.

'Actually, things are going really well for me at the mo'.' I eye the wines suspiciously. Or should that be *hungrily*? 'And yes, I do think getting divorced is the best thing to have happened to me. I've got a job I love – even though it doesn't pay anything yet; the time I spend with the kids is now not filled with resentment and anger – most of the time; I feel more in charge of my own fate and more in control of our lives than…well, ever before! So, yeah. In answer to your question, yes! You *were* right.'

'Of course I was right!' She slams a perfectly manicured hand down on the kitchen table. 'Now stop being a killjoy and have something to drink so we can celebrate your good fortune!'

I shake my head and suck on my lips.

'God,' Amelie sighs in response. 'You've *got* to learn how to be normal – just have a few drinks. Put a cap on it and stop when you feel yourself getting a bit squiffy. Easy! I do it all the time. It's really no biggie!'

'And my blog's doing reasonably well...' I continue.

'I've never even seen it!'

I drag out the laptop, fire it up and show Amelie the blog. If she's impressed, she hides it well.

'What's your next post about, hmm? What've you got in the chamber?'

'I've been working on The Ten Commandments of The Divorced Single Mum,' I say proudly. 'But as you can see, I haven't got very far.'

Amelie roots around in her handbag for her glasses and when she finally finds them and puts them on, she looks like the librarian I remember from my primary school – eighty years old, cat's-eye glasses and permanently pissed off by everyone's lack of understanding of the Dewey Decimal System.

'Where'd you park your zimmer frame, Am?' I chortle. 'Those glasses make you look positively Jurassic!'

'Fifties glamour is so in these days.' She pouts her red lips. 'Especially when you're *in* your fifties. Old is the new young, doncha know?'

I didn't know that, as a matter of fact. But Amelie's always been a dedicated follower of fashion, so I take her word for it. I've always lagged way behind fashion, often going off in a different direction entirely, preferring big, baggy jumpers in any colour as long as it's black, regardless of what's in.

'Totally blind without them.' She peers at the laptop screen. 'Now let's see...'

There are only two commandments there and I brace myself for Amelie's inevitable harsh criticism.

'*Thou shalt not eat thy feelings,*' Amelie reads. '*Unless thy feelings are made out of Lindor Balls*... mumble, murmur... Yes! Very good.'

You could have knocked me down with a feather – to use an ancient expression, one that's familiar to us old biddies. Amelie's usually such a tough audience. But suddenly, she's getting into the spirit of the thing and even smiling.

'*Thou shalt not badmouth thine ex. Or at least not in front of thy kids,*' she says out loud as she types: '*Yay, verily, even if thine ex hast been a bit of a dick. Fear thee not, ye olde truth will out when thy kids art older.*'

'Love it,' I nod, basking in the warmth of Amelie's approval.

It feels just like old times, when Amelie and I used to make up silly stories, writing for the uni newspaper. We were more interested in having a laugh than getting our facts straight and it was such fun. Until we both got fired for not taking campus life seriously enough. Happy days, full of giggles and promise – I mean, we were going to conquer the world!

'I've got one!' I nudge Amelie in the ribs and write:

Thou shalt give it thy best shot at being friends with thine ex – even if thou canst not stand the guy. Bite thy tongue and think of thy kids. And thy maintenance payments.

'Yeah!' Amelie agrees.

And then it happens. As Amelie grabs the laptop to write her next commandment, I reach out for the cup of wine, as though it's the most natural thing in the world. And when I take a tentative sip, my tongue laps it up greedily, my tastebuds thank me and my throat and stomach sigh a humungous sigh. Instantly my emotional muscle memory kicks in and that old familiar relaxed, confident feeling syrups its way through my veins. Mama's coming home.

What are you doing? You don't drink anymore, remember? What if something happens to the kids and you can't drive to the hospital because you're inebriated? So what if they're at Joe's? It's the principle of the thing! And I don't care if it is just the one glass — you know how you get. You're a total lightweight, remember? One leads to two, two to three — and before you know it, you're off your face, lunging at any male who happens to be passing by and saying the most horrendous, heinous, humiliating things...

'Outside for a quick fag?' Amelie says, standing up.

'Nah.' I stare at the packet of Marlboro Lights she's holding in her hand. 'I'll come with you, though.'

As soon as we're outside and I've taken a few more sips of wine, I silently steal one of Amelie's cigarettes. She doesn't say a word, a small smirk spreading across her lips. I spark it up with her lighter.

And guess what? It doesn't make me choke, it doesn't hurt my throat — okay, it tastes a bit weird and is, let's face it, a *really weird* thing to do, but it's just like breathing in air. So innocuous!

Rufus follows us out and is about to jump up on me, but senses something strange is afoot, so he merely whimpers and scratches at the back door, giving me the message he needs to be let in.

He's totally trashing our back door and every other door in the house, come to think of it — deep rivulets carved out of the wood thanks to Roofie's massive claws.

But hey, whatever. It's no biggie – in fact, I can't think of a single big deal in my life at this point. The kids are all right, my job's going well, I'm in line for a promotion, even, we've got the most handsome hound ever as a part of the family now and – yeah. It's all good. And that's not even positive thinking – it's *fact*.

I take stock for a moment and realise my shoulders aren't tensed up by my ears, I'm having a laugh for the first time in… forever – and so what if I still believe, deep down somewhere in the dark depths of my soul, that the key to a good night out is plenty of ciggies, loads of booze and at least one really good old friend who knows you like the back of their wrinkly, thin-skinned, liver-spotted hand? It's only for one night. What harm could it possibly do?

I ask the cab to stop off at the Londis so I can buy a packet of Marlboro Lights and when I pay by the contactless thingy, I'm rocked to my very foundations to find that a pack of gaspers now costs a whopping eleven pounds fifty. My God! That's eleven packets of Tunnock's Tea Cakes from the Co-op.

But what the hell – you only live once, right? Or, as Amelie says when I get back in the cab and tell her of my surprise at the price, YOLO. It stands for You Only Live Once, she tells me. I suppose the acronym is perfect for young people today who can't be arsed to speak properly.

Young people today? What an old fart! I swear I'm getting older and fartier by the minute.

When we arrive at the converted barn, we're both bowled over by its beauty. It's done out so tastefully – drenched in country shades of Farrow & Ball, with cream lampshades on the floor lamps and loads of light green, sage-coloured pendant lights hanging from the ceiling way up high.

There are round tables, complete with table cloths and candelabras, a stage at one end and a bar at the other. A string quartet plays in the top righthand corner of the barn and the air is thick with expensive perfume and alcohol.

It's a much more formal do than I'd expected – my city v country prejudices rearing their ugly heads again. I mean, what *did* I expect? A couple of hay bales to sit on while we watch a couple of in-bred boys play 'Duelling Banjos'?

Well, um, yes, I suppose I did, I'm ashamed to admit.

The barn is adorning the cover of the next issue of *Country Living*, we're told by one of the waiters, and both Am and I wonder aloud who could ever possibly afford to live in a house like this, as we wend our way to the bar.

'Tom!' Amelie shrieks, stops dead in her tracks and grabs my arm.

'Ow! Tom who?' I yank my arm back.

'Tom Dashwood! From uni! Remember?! Oh, God, I used to absolutely *adore* him.'

I follow the end of Amelie's finger pointing towards the bar. And sure enough, there's the BMOC himself, Tom, leaning on the bar and holding court with a few female admirers.

'So it is,' I say. 'Wonder what he's doing here?'

'Gor – just look at him, Annie,' she practically swoons. 'He hasn't aged a bit. Soooo divine.'

Of course, I wouldn't go that far, always being the more refined and restrained one between the two of us, but she's right, to an extent – he is still a very good-looking guy.

'Maybe he's a Chilterns business magnate. Hey! Maybe I can set up an interview with him or something – and you can do it!'

I look into the distance and think of the possibilities when I feel my arm being tugged at again.

'Don't look now,' Amelie says, staring in the opposite direction. 'But there's a total silver *fox* over there who hasn't been able to take his eyes off you ever since we walked in.'

My head swivels around frantically in search of said fox.

'I told you not to look!' Amelie whispers loudly. 'Be calm, chill.'

I hold my head still and stare straight ahead, at Tom.

'How do you know he's looking at me? You're not wearing your glasses – he could be checking you out.'

'I'm short-sighted, not long-sighted,' she says out of the side of her mouth.

'So go on, then – tell me what he looks like.'

'Married.'

I drop my 'Cagney and Lacey on a stake-out' pose and purse my lips.

'Well, of course he is!' I cock my head. 'All the good ones are taken. Everyone knows that.'

I turn to face Amelie just in time to see her throwing herself at Tom, howling hello at him and squealing: 'Oh my God you haven't changed a bit!!'

She's so loud, everyone turns to look at her and in all the kerfuffle, I lose sight of the silver fox she was talking about, even when I stand on my tippy toes in my black pixie boots. I can't see anyone even remotely fitting that description, so I meander over to Amelie and poor old accosted, positively manhandled Tom.

'What the hell are you two doing here?' he asks, looking Amelie up and down while completely ignoring me. 'You are, quite literally, the last person I expected to see tonight!'

'Ditto.' Amelie bats her eyelashes at him. 'Oh – do you remember Annie? Annie Beaton?'

Tom looks at me blankly for a few seconds, then re-focuses on Amelie.

'Yeah, yeah – course I do!' he lies. 'Let me get you two a drink – this little reunion deserves champagne!'

It's actually quite exciting being here in this gorgeous barn conversion and it feels like the seriously good vibes shooting between Tom and Amelie are contagious, because gone are my nerves about coming to an event in Charlotte's stead. I feel warm, a bit buzzed – all of a flutter, actually.

As a result of all these feel-good endorphins zapping around my brain, I down the first glass of champagne in three large, possibly a tad unladylike, glugs.

I hold my glass out for Tom to top me up, and he obliges with the biggest bottle of Veuve Clicquot I've ever seen.

I feel compelled to tell him about the time Amelie and I went on the 'French Girls Don't Get Fat' diet for three months, basically eating Veuve Clicquot for breakfast, lunch and dinner. Amelie lost tons of weight, looking more and more chic and French with every passing day, while I put on a stone and a half and got a written warning from work. I spent the whole three months pissed, poor and getting even more portly.

I'm not even halfway through regaling him with my hilarious tale, when I sense I'm losing him. His eyes glaze over and someone taps me on the shoulder.

'Excuse me,' a tall man with a rather luxuriant full head of salt and pepper hair says. 'But are you here from *Chilterns Today*?'

'Forever in your heart? Why yes, kind sir,' I reply, trying to bat my eyelashes like Amelie.

'Have you got something in your eye?' he says.

I stop the batting.

'Yep, it's me, Annie,' I sigh. 'Annie Beaton. Beaton by name, not by nature!'

Amelie kicks my ankle and when I look at her, she widens her eyes and mouths something at me. I frown and narrow my eyes in concentration.

'What?' I ask, slightly irritated.

'The – *ahem* – silver fox I was telling you about...'

'What?' I'm still flummoxed.

'Yes, she's Annie,' Amelie fills the dead air between us.

'Yes, I'm here in a professional capacity. Because Charlotte, my editor, had a previous engagement.'

Tom snorts.

'Previous engagement my fat, hairy arse,' he says.

'Hope not,' Amelie says under her breath.

We all look at Tom.

'Well, *shit*, George,' he says, slamming his champagne flute down on the bar. 'We all know where she is – and with who.'

'Whom,' I correct him.

'Shh,' Amelie elbows me.

'You don't know for sure, Tom,' says the tall man next to me. 'And anyway, let's forget about all that for tonight, shall we? Just enjoy ourselves with our new friends here. So sorry, Annie. You were saying?'

'Um, nothing much, really,' I stutter. 'Sorry, what? Is your name George?'

'Yes,' he says, with a voice that sounds like cream. 'I've organised tonight – the Scubas – with Tom's help, of course, this is his house, after all. *One* of his houses...'

He sings 'Country House' by Blur like a drunken sailor and Amelie laughs like a drain. 'No, seriously – this is my house.'

Amelie visibly brightens – if that's at all possible. I mean, she was looking like a 1950s film star a second ago, all ample cleavage and well-lit close-ups, but now she's radiating goddess-like light.

I feel hot in her rays and a little faint, to be honest, so I head for the nearest table and go to pull out one of the gold chairs to sit on.

But before I can really get a good grip, George pops up from nowhere and grabs hold of the back of the chair, pulling it out for me.

And they say chivalry is dead, I think to myself. You know, I don't think I've *ever* had a chair pulled out for me like that in my whole life.

'Allow me, Miss,' he smiles at me and all of a sudden, the crowd around us turns into a fuzz of background noise. Maybe I've had too much champers. Maybe I haven't had enough. But one thing's for sure, this George is one handsome hound.

And, I note, it's truly astonishing at how quickly your taste for, say, alcohol or men can come back to you. Your whole body, mind and soul swiftly recalibrate and before you can say 'I prefer a nice cup of tea', you're, well, *home* –

even though you haven't had any for yonks and tell anyone who'll listen you haven't even missed it.

'It's mizz, actually – like Miss but said as though there's two zeds instead of "s"es.'

'Pardon?'

'Ah, forget it.' I wave his query away with my hand and sit down in the chair while he struggles to push it in for me.

'So what're you doing here, George? I mean, what made you organise such an event?' I say, once he's given up trying to push my chair in and he's sitting on his own next to me.

'Country enterprises need a bit of a boost, a bit of recognition and acknowledgement and I think it's important that we foster a real sense of community amongst ourselves. And as I'm into a bit of e-commerce myself...' he smiles. He's got these long dimples like ripples in a pond around his mouth and light, sparkling blue eyes, which, when he's looking at you, make you feel all funny – sort of warm and safe, but hopelessly exposed at the same time.

'Eek-*what*?' my lack of tech knowledge betrays me once again.

'E-commerce. Online shops,' he twinkles at me.

'Oh.' I don't even try to stifle a yawn. 'Sounds interesting.'

A waiter proffers a plate of hors d'oeuvres at us and I pick out a creamy-looking vol au vent.

'The food was terrible,' I say in possibly the worst New York accent ever heard. 'And such small portions!'

'Ah,' George nods sagely. 'Woody Allen fan, are we? I believe that's from *Annie Hall*.'

I nearly fall off my seat with surprise.

'You know it?'

'It's only my favourite movie!' He grins at me and I wonder whether he notices I've kind of gone for the Diane Keaton look tonight – albeit on a shorter, ever-so-slightly chubbier scale.

'One of mine, too! And I love how Diane Keaton dresses in it – all tall, willowy and effortlessly, almost unknowingly sexy.'

George looks a bit taken aback by my divulgence, so I rein it in. I look around for Amelie and Tom, but I can't see them anywhere.

'So how do you know Tom?' I ask.

'He's married to my sister. He's a good egg, really, just a bit... well, how do you know him?'

'I don't, really – we went to uni with him about a hundred years ago and Amelie always had a bit of a thing for him.' As soon as I've said this, I feel that small stab of regret – like, have I betrayed her? Is her adoration of Tom supposed to be a secret?

'He's quite the charmer,' George nods, 'when he wants to be.'

'So he's married to your sister, is he? She might want to be here and protect her man from Amelie, if you know what I mean.' God, I just can't seem to help wedging my foot further and further into my mouth with every word I utter.

'Oh, I think she knows how to handle herself. You must know that about her, too – she's your editor, Charlotte.'

'Oh!' I gasp. 'Really? The cashmere, the camel coat, the vizsla...'

'The one and the same,' he laughs.

'Wowsers,' is just about all I can manage at this stage. 'Talk about a small world. So what about you, Gee – where's *your* wife tonight?'

'I have no idea,' he says, 'and I have no interest, either. Quite frankly, my dear, I don't give a damn, as Rhett Butler would say.'

Oops. Touchy subject. Better steer clear…

'Oh really, why? What's happened? Had a big row or something?'

Good steering clear, you donut.

'Something like that, yes.' He looks around at people taking their seats, summoning a passing waiter. 'But it was all a long time ago and since the divorce, I haven't given it much thought. Just concentrated on the kids and building up the business again, working on the farm.'

'The farm? Does that mean you're, like, a farmer?'

'What insight you have!' he teases me. 'Yes, I'm a farmer – but more inside the farm working out the business side of it, rather than getting my hands dirty growing turnips.'

In that moment, I begin to see him in a whole new light: devastatingly handsome, divorced, a gentleman farmer whose name is actually George – Mum and Dad would give me their permission to marry him on the spot. Am I dreaming?

'Ah, just what the doctor ordered,' he says, as a waiter puts down a normal-sized bottle of Veuve Clicquot and two flutes. 'May I?'

I nod slowly, transfixed by the dazzling blue of George's eyes. They're like Paul Hollywood's – piercing and penetrating and… ooh. Is it just me or is it getting hot in here?

He pours the champagne and I wish I'd worn something a bit sexier, like one of those bombshell dresses you see advertised at the back of *Woman & Home* magazine, the wrap-around ones that Nigella Lawson wore when she was a little lardier.

'Why are you looking at me like that?' he says. 'You're making me nervous!'

'I'm sorry, I… I've just got this weird feeling – like I know you or we've met before or something.' I'm mightily confused now and babbling like a fool. 'God, that sounds like some crappy pick-up line, but I don't mean it to – you just seem, sort of, familiar…'

'I think I saw you at dog training with your Irish setter. I've got a bonkers wire-haired vizsla – very sweet, lovely to look at, brain of a bird. Maybe you saw me there?'

I shake my head no.

'You do look a lot like Charlotte, now I know you're related…'

'We're twins,' he says, nodding at someone in the distance and making to get up. 'But look, I've got to go and MC the awards now – stay there and wait for me, will you?'

I take a sip of champers and try to look demure as I agree to stay put.

As I'm watching George walk away, greeting people as he goes, women falling at his feet (not literally, but you can see the lusty looks in their eyes when they stare up at him, even from this distance), I tell myself to snap out of it. He must have squillions of girlfriends who all went to the right private schools – there's no *way* he'd ever be interested in me. For God's sake, woman, grow up. Stop living this ridiculous fantasy, day-dream life and get real!

'I am!' Amelie crashes down next to me, puffing and panting like Roofie. 'Getting about as real as one woman can possibly get! Now come outside for a fag with me and let me fill you in.'

On the way out, I spy Jane, Liz and Sue all sitting at a table with the wonderful John and two other nice-looking blokes.

I wave frantically and whoop a little bit, stumbling in my boots as I cross the floor to get to them.

'Good turnout, eh?' I say, by way of greeting.

Jane and Sue nod in agreement – but Liz looks at me like I'm something she might find on the bottom of her expensive trainers after running through a field full of cows.

'God – what *is* your problem, Liz? Why do you always look at me like you hate my guts? You don't even know me!'

Everyone sitting at the table turns to look at me at this point, but I don't care, I'm on a roll.

'Oh, it's all right for you, isn't it? You with your husband who's genuinely interested in you and the kids, your nanny who does all the hard work, your cleaner who you pay peanuts, your mum just up the road, your LinkedIn account bulging with top, six-figure job offers, your belly pinging back into place five minutes after you've given birth—'

'Annie, shhhh!' Amelie grabs my arms and pulls me backwards.

'You know,' I call out as I make my exit, 'some of us don't have that kind of support, Liz – and we could really do without your pompous, jumped-up, full-on judginess rubbing our noses in your good fortune all the time. Because that's all you've got, you know – luck. Dumb luck!'

At least I think that's what I said. Words to that effect, anyway.

'Take it easy,' Amelie says when we get outside. 'What have you got against her?'

'Oh, she just rubs me up the wrong way,' I say. 'Always so bloody super... super-silly... super... silly...'

'You mean supercilious?'

'That's what I just said, isn't it?'

Amelie leans coquettishly on the barn wall and tells me she's had a snog with Tom and would it be okay if he came back to mine to stay the night with her on the sofa bed?

'But he's married!' I yelp. 'To my boss!'

'Not for very much longer,' Amelie says, a wicked cloud of smoke curling out from the side of her mouth.

And that's the last thing I remember.

–

Three upbeat, positive things I might be able to call 'wins':
- Um...
- Let's see...
- Nope, nothing. I got nothing.

–

October 13 – And the Award For Biggest Bozo Goes To...

Urgh.

Must… Find… *Water.*

When I come downstairs on Sunday morning, the sofa bed's up, the front room looks more immaculate than it ever has and Amelie and Tom have disappeared. It almost looks as though they were never here. But of course they were. Weren't they?

Wandering into the kitchen, I blink furiously, trying to stop seeing double. And I have to bend down, hands on my knees, to really get in close and focus on the digital clock on the oven, while I try to stop swaying and not throw up. When finally the too-bright LED numbers stop dancing and calm down so I can read them properly, I realise it's not morning after all – it's three twenty-three in the sodding afternoon.

What am I going to do? What the HELL am I going to do? The kids'll be back in an hour, Roofie's probably starving, un-walked, neglected and tearing chunks out of the sofa, Sainsbury's shuts in forty minutes and what the *fark* was last night all about?

My heart starts racing. Oh God, oh God, OH GOD. I can't remember leaving the barn, getting home – I can't remember anything after going out for that ciga… urgh. The inside of my mouth feels like it's been sandpapered by mischievous elves all night and when I stand up – slowly, obviously – I even have to lean on the kitchen bench for support, lest I fall down, throw up or pass out. Or all three.

What a feckin' eejit, as Aisling would no doubt say.

I shuffle at snail's pace over to the kitchen table and squint. It's like those pesky elves have moved up into my brain now and they're blowing up a balloon, laughing hysterically as they go, making my head feel like it's going to explode. Or do I mean implode, considering it's the inside of my brain we're talking about? Ow, who cares? All I know is it hurts and the pressure's killing me.

Jesus – maybe this is it, the stroke I've been dreading.

Slumping onto the kitchen chair, I shut up and attempt to calm myself down. Breathe in, two, three, four… hold for a sec… and out, two, three, four…

But the ghosts of big nights past keep bouncing about in my brain, ricocheting off that bloody balloon and making me feel more emotionally nauseous than I've felt for… well, ever since I gave up drinking.

I didn't make a tit out of myself, did I? Odds are that I did – but how exactly this time? There was no one there that I fancied, so I wouldn't have lunged at anyone… I harbour no secret grudges against anyone there, so I wouldn't have said anything untoward to anyone, confronting some poor, unsuspecting country business person – I didn't even *know* anyone there for Christ's sake!

I've got no bruises – that can be seen by the naked eye, at any rate, nothing particularly hurts (except my head), so I probably didn't fall over…

Everything's fine. Sure it is.

Momentarily buoyed by the idea that I couldn't have been *too* much of a disgrace, I look up from the kitchen floor that's swimming disconcertingly in front of me, steady myself by holding onto the kitchen table and see a plastic gold statuette of a non-gender-specific figure in a business suit and a cowboy hat, chewing on a piece of straw on the table.

What the fa-ah-ahh-*ow*! My head thumps me from the inside even harder and slowly, I remember The Award.

Charlotte won an award for *Chilterns Today (Forever in your heart)* and I accepted it for her. Buggered if I can remember what it was for exactly, but I can picture myself smiling and waving at my devoted fans as I walked up to the lectern on stage, as though I'm perfectly made-up in a Dior evening gown at the Oscars (instead of a black pair of Primark trews and way too much bronzer). As I shut my eyes tight, I see some tall, dark, handsome stranger handing me the statuette, offering me the microphone and clapping as he backs away to the side of the stage.

A sea of faces gazes up at me adoringly, falling about laughing as I deliver brilliantly timed joke after brilliantly timed joke – and then… my mind goes blank.

Probably just accepted the award on Charlotte's behalf, said thanks and went back to my seat – nothing more dramatic than that. You know how the brain blacks out boring stuff sometimes? Probably that.

Well, either that or what went down is far too traumatic and painful for me to handle right now, so the brain's doing me a favour, saving me from myself and putting off the inevitable until a time when I can cope with the horrendousness.

I groan and open my eyes. And then I notice the statuette is acting as some sort of a paperweight to a handwritten note:

Thou shalt not get horribly pissed at work functions thus alienating friends, colleagues and potential lovers in the process. And thou must callst thy bessie mate when thou dost surface – we needst to discuss thy behaviour.

Am & Tom (Tam) XXX

-

October 14 – TMI

It's now Monday morning and I'm up with the lark, desperate to return to some semblance of teetotal normality – even though it's now too cold for even the bloody lark to be up and all I want to do is go back to bed and hide under the duvet. For a year.

I haven't called Amelie, despite the deluge of texts and calls I've received from her – because, well, why would I? I don't want to hear about Saturday night and my obviously atrocious behaviour. I don't want a lecture from her on how to be normal when I so obviously can't handle any amount of drink or fags and I *defo* don't want to hear about how gorgeous Tom is and how they're madly in love, consummating their union on our sofa bed. In front of Roofie!

Speaking of the hound, I let him out so he can 'be clever' and while we're outside, I take some deep breaths, watch the clouds of steam escape my lips and get into some positive self-talk. Now let's see. What would Aisling say to me if she were here?

'You can do this, you got this. You are in control and very competent. Even if you do sometimes take things too far and make a gigantic arse of yourself—'

'Talking to yourself again, eh?' comes a voice out of the darkness.

'Janie MAC!' I shriek and wheel around to face the fence.

'Just Jane'll do,' the voice says, sounding very much like Jane next door. 'What are you doing and who the hell is Janie Mac?'

'I haven't got the foggiest who Janie Mac is – but I was just thinking about my Irish friend, Aisling, and it's something she often says when she's taken by surprise.'

Jane grunts. 'What are you doing out here at this ungodly hour?' I ask.

'I thought I heard something and figured it was you, talking to yourself as per,' Jane sniffs.

'I was? I must stop that.' I shake my head at myself.

'Hmm – that and about a million other things, yes,' says Jane.

'What do you mean?'

'You're so in the shit with everyone, it's a wonder you still have the audacity to show your face. Even if it is only in your own back garden and it's still dark,' she mutters.

What?

'You heard,' she sniffs.

I feel my hairline tingle, the tiny hairs on my nose tickle and my unsightly, unwanted and still un-lasered hag hairs bristle when the penny drops.

I take a deep breath, close my eyes and on the exhale, tell her I'm a total lightweight, I've had a complete blackout, could she please tell me everything I did, get it out of the way and then I can begin to make amends.

Told you it was a deep breath.

'You really don't remember?' she says.

'Nope,' I say. 'I don't drink anymore, so—'

'Could've fooled me!' I can hear her lips pursing.

'Honestly, Jane – it wasn't me, it was an impostor! Someone masquerading as me. It's true! I have absolutely no idea what I've done – please help me!'

'You really want to know?'

'Erm…' I'm not sure, actually. 'Yes, yes I do. I'm a big girl now, I can take it.'

'Okay,' says Jane. 'Here goes.'

Now it's her turn to take a deep breath before she rattles off my misdemeanours.

'You made Liz leave in floods of tears. You do know her husband has left her, don't you? He took off with the nanny last week. Now she has to look after four boys all on her own – no parents to help, no cleaner, no husband, no job offers and, obviously, no nanny.'

'Oh my God. Poor Liz.' I hang my head and kick at the frozen ground.

'You got so pissed, and you were so thankful to John for rescuing your enormous, ridiculous dog, you tried to snog him. John, not your dog. I don't wanna know what you get up to behind closed doors… Anyway, when John put his hand up to say no, you batted it away and slobbered all over him anyway while he tried to push you off. Right in front of me.'

She takes a breath in, I gasp in horror.

'You then tried it on with Sue's husband, Alan. Just after Sue told you she'd managed to pull some strings and there are some places for Ben and Izzy at Old Stoke Primary.'

'Was I trying, in a roundabout way, to say thanks for that, too?' I say in a tiny voice.

'Shush! You told Sue she looked like Miss Piggy, actually. She'd had her hair highlighted and curled specially for the big night and you hurled insults at her!'

'But she doesn't look anything like— Hang on, maybe I meant her hairdo was reminiscent of—?'

'Shut up!'

In the interests of brevity and warm toes, she then proceeds to list my crimes against humanity, insisting on no further interruptions, in verbal bullet points.

Apparently, I:

- Thought it was hilarious to call Liz the Jolly Lean Giant because she's very tall, very funny and does all that boot camp.
- Did all this very loudly while people were trying to make speeches and accept their awards with no respect for restraint or propriety.
- Rugby-tackled George, Charlotte's brother, when he was on stage accepting his sister's award for *Chilterns Today (Forever in your heart)*.
- Wrestled the microphone out of George's hands, stood up (shakily) and addressed the audience by slurring: 'Well, helloooo hayseeds!'
- Ranted and raved on the mic about how people in the country aren't what I expected – they're actually nice and friendly, don't shoot on sight, saying things like, 'get off my land, you bugger!' and some of them even have a bit more than half a brain.
- Broke down in tears when telling my divorce story and then snogged the face off the permanently sozzled village solicitor who pulled me off the stage, no doubt recognising a fellow alkie and someone who will probably need some sound legal advice soon.

Jane stops and an eerie silence settles over our back gardens as the sun rises, the usually rickety fence between us ominously still.

'So,' Jane eventually says. 'What have you got to say for yourself?'

317

'I... I...'

'Thought as much.' Her disappointment seeps through the knotholes in the fence. 'Not so mouthy now, are you?'

'God, Jane, I'm so sorry,' I whimper. 'I don't know what got into me.'

'Hopefully not James,' she says.

'What?'

'Are you saying you *didn't* sleep with James?'

'Who?'

'James Raphael, the sozzled solicitor whose face you sucked off,' she says. 'Probably trying to get at any vodka that might still have been in his throat. I know he has beautiful, violet eyes like Elizabeth Taylor and he's a brilliant painter – but he's a loser, Annie! Ever since his wife and kids left him, he's gone to hell in a handcart, boozing too much and moonlighting as God-knows-what because his one-man law firm's going down the tubes... But that's not the point! You're a woman on her own, he could've been any random serial killer and you wouldn't have had a clue! You left with him shortly after your stage dive...'

Oh God, oh God, OH GOD.

I hang my head in shame.

'You really don't remember any of this, do you?' Jane softens a smidge. 'Nope...' I shake my head slowly.

'You bloody idiot,' she says, with just a slight edge of genuine concern to her voice. 'Just when you're making friends in the village – although Liz was always suspicious of you being so upbeat after the divorce... Look, you're getting some work, the kids are going to be able to settle in properly when they start their new school in January, people are helping you, showing you kindness—'

'I know,' I groan. 'Thanks for the recap. Although I didn't know Liz was suspicious of me – why?'

'For a start, divorced,' Jane says. 'And for seconds, too jolly and sorted *after* the divorce.'

'Jolly? SORTED?!'

'Don't take too long at your own private pity party, Annie – you'll be late for Thistlebend if you don't get a shift on.'

I hear her go back inside her house and close her back door, leaving me, my misery and piles of dog poo melting in the morning sun all by ourselves outside.

What an unutterable tool. Me, I mean – not Jane. There I was, thinking I was living the dream, but all the while I was sowing the seeds, laying the groundwork to turn our fab, shiny, new lives into one dark, endless nightmare. Talk about the Midas touch in reverse. No amount of positive thinking or Fro It Away will fix that.

Still, at least Jane's brutal litany of disaster has jogged my memory somewhat: now I remember why I don't drink anymore.

Mortified beyond the realms of what I would have thought possible for a non-drinker, I move like a zombie about the house getting the kids ready for school, a giant cloud of deep shame and regret hanging over my head. I don't even notice when Izzy jumps into the front passenger seat.

'Are you okay, Mum?' she uncharacteristically asks as we drive over the toll bridge in silence. 'Want me to turn the radio on?'

'Okay,' I say.

'I'm going to put it on Radio 1!' she taunts. 'I am, I swear it! I will if you don't give me two pounds! Mum? Are you all right?'

'Fine,' I lie.

Izzy stares at me.

Then she pokes my arm.

'Mum? Mum, stop it,' she says, her voice shaking a bit. 'You're scaring me. Mu-um! Tell us what's wrong!'

'Nothing, darling.' I stare straight ahead at the road. 'Just a bit contemplative this morning, that's all.'

'Mum?' Izzy sounds so sweet and caring all of a sudden. 'Your mobile's buzzing – want me to answer it?'

I nod as she scrabbles about in my bag.

'Oh. My. GOD!' Izzy slams her hand down onto her leg by way of exclamation. 'Listen to this:

Hiya Annie
    Just a quick note to let you know Tiffani and I are moving to Magaluf soon. We're going to set up a mani-pedi shop for ex-pats. Tiff says biz will boom. And she wants Junior to have an EU passport. She's the boss! Give kids my love, I'll send for them when we're settled in.
    Joe XXX

'What the fff—?' I manage.

'Fix It Felix!' Ben yelps.

'What on *earth* is he jabbering about?' I'm immediately livid.

Izzy starts to read the text again.

'No, no, sweetie,' I say. 'I know what it said. Put my phone away. Please. Put it back in my bag!'

I've come alive now, albeit in a weird way – a bit shocked and a whole lot pissed off – and put my foot down on the accelerator.

'Are we in a race? I'm Lightning McQueeeeeen!' Ben laughs.

'Mu-um!' Izzy clasps hold of the inside door handle.

'Don't want to be late for school, now, do we?' I grimace, taking a tight corner a little bit too fast.

I say goodbye to the kids in a most perfunctory manner when we get to school, telling them I'll answer all of their questions about Daddy and Fitnanny and Mag-a-bloody-luf when I've had a chance to talk to their father and find out myself.

I see Charlotte and Willow in the car park out of the corner of my eye and wave, just as I'm jumping into our car.

'Congrats for Saturday night!' she calls out to me. Charlotte, that is – not Willow. Although it wouldn't surprise me, that dog being so talented and all.

But what's *she* on about? Congratulations to *me*?

'I was going to say the same to you,' I yell back. 'For winning the award.'

'I'll email you,' she mouths and I beep the horn by way of farewell as I turn left out of the car park and head for home, going hell for leather.

I'm shaking my head, saying 'COCK!' repeatedly as I go maybe a tad over the speed limit through chocolate-box village after chocolate-box village. Finally, I remember to slow down along the stretch of road that has bunches of flowers laid on the verge for loved ones lost on these treacherously sharp bends.

My phone rings. I press the green phone icon on the steering wheel.

'Hello?' I say.

'Ah, Annie,' Joe says, sounding a bit smug and, at the same time, disappointed his call didn't go to voicemail.

'Ah yourself, you fu—'

'I take it you got my text?' I can hear him sneering, even on this bad, crackly line.

'No, I didn't, as it goes – Izzy did though. She read it out loud to me and Ben,' I spit, hoping he'll feel bad about this and apologise for being a crap, insensitive, selfish, hopeless Disney dad.

'Oh, good,' he says. 'I don't have to send her a separate text, then.'

'You—'

'Can't talk for long,' he interrupts me. 'I'm meeting Tiff in a mo'. Look, I'm no longer employed, strictly speaking, so I've sought advice and I'm told I don't have to pay any maintenance now. Also, the Child Maintenance Service can't do anything if I'm in Spain, so...'

'WHAT?' I can feel my blood start to boil.

'Well, I just won't be able to afford it, what with start-up costs and another little one on the way...'

I'm speechless. Apart from muttering 'cock' under my breath once or twice.

'Sorry? What was that?'

'I said—'

'Ooh – the line's breaking up, Annie! Gotta go! I'll be in—'

And he's gone.

I'm practically ablaze with rage. I can fairly *feel* the fury firing out of my pores. I grip the steering wheel tight, grit my teeth till I can almost taste old fillings, slam my foot down on the accelerator and take the upcoming bend way too fast.

In the few moments of consciousness that follow, the roadside flowers left for loved ones on the verge come up to greet me in slow motion. I can make out the individual yellow, orange and deep pink petals of the fresh gerberas, their bolshy beauty, their simple strength reaching out for me, drawing me in closer, ever closer...

—

Still Sodding October 14

'Annie? Annie!' A man's voice coming from far off in the distance gets closer, louder. 'Annie are you okay? Annie? Are you okay? Are you okay? Annie! Are you okay?'

I come to, groggily, imagining Michael Jackson's singing 'Smooth Criminal' to me in a weird dream.

'You *are* okay! Here, let me help you,' the voice (obvs not Michael Jackson) says, one arm reaching around me, gently pulling my shoulder back from the steering wheel I'm currently slumped over.

All I can see are those green and purple hypnotic swirls in front of me, like you see in *Scooby-Doo* and I feel woozy. My body lurches forward, involuntarily, just in time for me to be sick all over the man's trainers.

'Nice to see you again, too,' he says, stepping away from my vomit waterfall.

When I think I have nothing left inside me to throw up, I wipe my mouth with my aching right arm and fall back against the driver's seat.

Those pesky hangover elves are at it again, this time attacking the inside of my skull with an ice pick. Eventually the water drains from my eyes, though, and I'm able to focus on the figure standing next to the car door.

'Bet you'll have one humdinger of a headache in a minute…'

'Ow-wow-*wow*!' I scrunch my eyes up and put my palm up to my pounding forehead.

'Come on, Annie,' says the voice. 'Let's get you out of that seat.'

'Why? Is the car on fire? It's going to explode, isn't it? Jesus *Christ*, why didn't you say something? RUN!' I nearly add whiplash to my list of injuries as I feel the panic rising, looking round for tell-tale smoke and/or flames and trying to run up the bank at the side of the road.

'Calm down, Annie,' the guy says, holding onto my elbow, so now I look like Scrappy-Doo, my little legs working like mad but going absolutely nowhere. 'It's not *The Fast and the Furious*, you know! There's a tiny dent in your bumper – nothing that a bit of expert hammering and a lick of paint won't fix – you just need to calm the hell down and let me drive you home.'

'But I don't even know who you are!' I protest, my windmilling legs slowing down to a more manageable, albeit still wobbly, blancmange.

'It's me!' he says, rather unhelpfully. 'James? James Raphael? From the other night?'

I shake my head slowly, carefully – and he looks a little bit wounded that I don't immediately recognise him.

'No, sorry, can't place—'

'You remember! We had a little snogette at the awards – well, you kind of attacked me, to be more accurate, and I

324

drove you and your friends home. Remember? Your dog nearly took my bloody arm off when he saw me at the door!'

I still draw a blank.

'Never mind,' he says. 'You were pretty smashed, I suppose.'

'Just like now,' I sigh. 'Hey, hang on a minute! You're James? The alcoholic solicitor?'

'Solicitor yes, alcoholic no,' he corrects me, straightening up and puffing his chest out a bit.

'Didn't your wife and kids leave you, so you hit the bottle, hit the skids and now you have to moonlight as God-knows-what just to keep you in cheap wine?'

'Where *do* you get your information?'

'Over the garden fence, mostly.'

'Well, it's a load of old cobblers. The bit about the drinking, anyway,' he says. 'I'm teetotal, have been since my wife left me. And yes I do work two jobs – when the law business is slow, I work on my painting and panel-beating. I specialise in painting 1950s pin-ups on motor-cycles and hub caps, if you haven't already heard, and it's not urgent or anything, but when you decide you want it done, I'll be able to fix your car in a jiffy...'

Jiffy? This guy's worse than me!

'... I'll even throw in some legal advice, too – you look like you might need some.'

And then, the whole reason I collided with the side of the road in the first place races up to me and punches me on the nose.

'Bloody Joe!' I say before I realise I'm thinking out loud. 'Running off to the Balearic Islands with his pregnant popsie, cutting all child maintenance, leaving us destitute in his wake...'

'Excuse me?' James butts in. 'Did you say *cutting* all child maintenance?'

'Yes I did – can you believe it? Some father he turned out to be.'

'I think it's actually illegal to cut off all maintenance.'

'But he said he'd had advice and they said he didn't have to pay anything because he'd be in Spain. At least, I think that's what he said.'

'We'll soon see about that,' says James, suddenly looking rather attractive – despite his spew-spattered trainers. 'First things first. Let me drive you home; we can have a chat and I'll see what I can do.'

'I can drive myself!' I say, like a petulant five-year-old. 'I'm not a bloody invalid, you know!'

'All right, all right!' He pats the air down in front of him. 'But if you could give me a lift to my chambers, I'd be grateful. Can't see myself running home in these things now.'

He takes off his trainers and socks and chucks them in a hedgerow, while I consider his request.

'I won't be able to pay you – for the legal advice or the panel-beating, I'm afraid.'

'Not to worry – I'll put it on account,' he smiles, revealing lovely straight, white, clean-looking teeth and, I suddenly notice, a very kissable mouth.

Which might have something to do with my decision to give him a lift home. I'm still a bit shaken, but I'm not going to add to the 'pathetic, boozy damsel with ulterior motives in distress' rep I've got by letting him drive *me* home. God knows what the local curtain twitchers'd make of that.

I take it slowly while I fill him in on the latest from Joe.

'We'll have to move fast on this, then,' he says.

'Damn straight,' I agree, 'he's leaving for Spain any minute now!'

'It's people like him who give divorced dads a bad name,' he tuts. 'I mean, what kind of man wants to wriggle out of paying for his children?'

'A selfish one,' I say, 'who's as tight as a gnat's chuff, with all the morals, integrity, compassion and basic decency of a... a...'

'Fox,' says James.

'Hmmm, I was thinking more of—'

'No!' James yells, grabbing the steering wheel. 'You're going to hit *that fox*!'

The tyres screech as we veer to the right-hand side of the road and then veer left again, just in time to not only miss the fox, but also an oncoming lorry carrying a forest's worth of logs.

'Bloody hell, Annie!' He puts his palm to his forehead. 'Keep your eyes on the road!'

'I was!' I tell a tiny fib – for I was actually, surreptitiously, sneaking a sideways look at James and his big violet/indigo/Elizabeth Taylor eyes, his small but not insignificant nose, his full, cherry red lips and his slightly dishevelled brown hair and burgeoning beard.

I do like a man with a beard, I think to myself. A *man*, that is.

'I was just, um, thinking about... do you know anywhere in Old Stoke that does electrolysis?'

Oh, Christ – what ARE you bibbling on about now?

'You've just crashed your car, your ex-husband's running off to Spain, cutting off your maintenance, you've got two kids to clothe, feed and house and all you're thinking about is… *electrolysis*?' James asks, incredulous.

'No! Well, yes, sort of…' My left hand instinctively darts up to my chin, my fingers desperately trying to hide the hag hairs that must be long enough to plait by now. 'People act weirdly when they're going through trauma. My friend Ash, for instance, found out her husband was having an affair and the first thing she did was—'

'Go for a mani-pedi?' James offers. 'In Spain? From a woman who's carrying your ex-husband's child, with loads of money behind her business – money that should be going to *your* children so they can be kept in the manner to which they should be accustomed?'

'All right, all right,' I say. 'Keep your Y-fronts on.'

'Listen, Annie,' he says. 'If men like Joe are allowed to get away with this vile behaviour without being brought to book, then the whole of society's… then people like me… men like me who are trying to do the right thing are going to get tarred with the same irresponsible brush and before you can say decree absolute, our lives will be ruined by nasty village gossips who mark you down as a booze-hound husband, a deadbeat dad and a shit solicitor to boot.'

'Is that what…?'

'Yeah,' he says as we go past a ludicrously posh boarding school. 'My ex-wife was on the board of governors… at that school, in fact.' He points to the impossibly green, luxurious hedge that goes on for miles.

'She did a lot of volunteer work with the elderly, she worked on the council – she had real clout, real sway in the community. So when she wanted to get out of our marriage, but didn't want to be regarded as a scarlet woman, having an affair with at least one other man, her reputation potentially in tatters, she went on the attack and began a successful smear campaign against me, claiming I was an alcoholic and citing unreasonable behaviour and irreconcilable differences. Before I even knew what was happening, clients were deserting me, I was getting dirty looks from everyone in the street and the bar staff at The Zebra refused to serve me.'

'Ooh – that's the worst, isn't it? When you can't even get a pint?'

'Don't be facetious,' he says. 'Actually, the worst bit was when my kids started to believe her lies. They were – *are* – the apples of my eyes, but they refused to speak to me for years. Not a day goes by that I don't worry about the huge emotional damage we've done to our kids. I wanted them to live with me, but she wanted full custody of them, saying I was a drunk and couldn't be trusted around them. She didn't want them with her, either, mind, so she sent them to that boarding school we just passed, Friar's Fields.'

'God, that's so sad,' I say.

'I know.' He shifts in his seat to face me. 'They're great kids, growing up to be super men. They're starting to thaw a bit now, wanting to see me more – but I'll never get those earlier years back. You're the lucky one, really, you know. You get to see your kids grow, be a party to their lives, really enjoy the day to day...'

I don't know about that, I think to myself, with one a smart-mouthed narky pre-pubescent and the other one the tantrumming champion of the world... I don't know whether enjoyment comes into it much, but I don't say anything to him, lest I sound cold-hearted and remind him of his wife.

We drive in silence, digesting the enormity of everything he's just said. And by the time we get back to Old Stoke and I pull up in front of his 'chambers' (AKA the room above the butcher's in the high street), he tells me of the plan he's hatched: he's going to alert the investigators at the Child Maintenance Service and the HMRC to get onto Joe immediately; he's putting out a stop on Joe at all air and sea ports and he's even thinking of paying Joe a little visit himself later on.

'You know, you don't have to do any of this for us, James,' I say as he steps out of the car, closes the door and leans in through the window.

'How much money do you have left in your account as of now, right this minute?'

'Um, I dunno.' I hum and haw for a bit. 'About one hundred or so pounds. One hundred and fifty, tops. He's supposed to be putting in fifteen hundred in – oh!' I gasp.

'Right,' his voice goes down an octave. 'So I do have to do this.'

I nod slowly and then start to panic.

'Oh, shit! What am I going to do about the weekly shop? One hundred and fifty pounds won't even cover half a Waitrose basket!'

'Go to Aldi then,' James says as he straightens up to go. 'Like all us poor divorced bastards do.'

Of course, of course! Why had I not thought of that before?

'Oh,' he bends down to the window again, 'and by the way, you don't need electrolysis.'

'You're joking, aren't you?' I glance in the rear-view mirror and see myself blushing. 'I look like Wolverine!'

'You've got far more pressing matters to contend with,' he smiles lopsidedly, looking to my mind like a cross between Indiana Jones and Hugh Jackman.

Just as he's walking away and I'm staring after him, panting ever so slightly, my tongue hanging out the side of my mouth only a tiny bit, I try to work out whether I'm still feeling woozy from the crash or whether this is what swooning actually feels like. Then he looks over his shoulder and says:

'Anyway, I've always found Wolverine to be the most attractive of all the X-Men.'

—

Three reasons to be cheerful:
- I just survived a (minor) car crash.
- There's an Aldi sort of near us in Reading and I'm quite excited about the thought of a cut-price supermarket.
- That James is rather nice, isn't he?

—

October 15 – Annie Small

You know you're in a bad way when the highlight of your day/week/year is a trip to the supermarket.

But in all fairness, Aldi is no ordinary supermarket.

Mind you, not even this fantastic discovery is enough to completely lighten my dark mood. It goes some way towards it, though, considering the whole week's groceries only set me back £60.

James was right, Aldi is a godsend. Talk about the divorcée's saviour. Aldi, that is – not James. Although…

If he can somehow force Joe to continue paying the maintenance, we'll be fine. But if he can't and that slippery eel gets away with it, then I have no idea what we'll do.

This sudden descent into the doldrums makes my head hurt even more – and Roofie's endless barking isn't helping, either.

'Awwww,' I whine at Roofie. 'Do I have to? Do I have to suffer the slings and arrows, the unbearable indignities you heap on me time after time in the pursuit of being the perfect dog owner?'

Roofie looks at me with those eyes, starts furiously wagging that tail and sets about shredding my long White Company cardi with those sodding teeth.

'Get OFF!' I yank the once-sophisticated, once-soft merino lambswool cardigan from his unfeasibly strong jaws and inspect the tears, dripping in slobber. I want to cry.

'I'll take that as a yes,' I huff as I roughly put the lead on his collar. A nanosecond later, I've just opened the front door a tiny crack when he nudges it wide open with his snout, launches himself off the front doorstep and gallops down the driveway out onto the footpath.

I manage to slam the front door shut before he drags me after him, nearly in tears with the frustration and hellness of it all, pleading ineffectually with him to stop or at least slow down.

'Just hold on a minute or I'll… I swear it, Roofie, I'll… STOP, will you? Roofie! NOOOOOO!'

He totally ignores me and pulls on the lead with such force from his neck, he nearly chokes himself, his throat making these horrible, raspy sounds.

'ROOOO-FI-II-II-II-IE!' my voice bounces as he tugs me along.

After two minutes or so, I remember that resistance is futile, so I give up trying to sound masterful and in control and let him run while I follow after, legs pumping like chubby little pistons – sausage links on speed.

The inexhaustible and possibly untrainable Roofie leads me down a snicket to the fields behind the Co-op. We pass mansion after mansion, enormous acreage after enormous acreage and I beg him to stop.

Eventually, he obliges. Well, he stops for long enough to do a seventy-three--second wee (I actually counted) in a grassy patch near the little bridge over the river Little Chalky.

Ah, maybe that's why he was so keen to get out of the house so fast – he was desperate for a wee. In which case, I can hardly blame him – I mean, God knows we've all been there before, right? Amelie once peed on the steps of Charing Cross Station while we waited for a taxi because she was busting for the loo, so I get it. You know, needs must.

When he's finished, he calms right down and wanders by my side to cross the bridge when we come to it.

It's a tiny bridge – in fact, 'bridge' is far too grand a word for it – it's more like a few planks plonked over a puddle. But there is a railing, just high enough for me to lean on, lead handle around my wrist, faithful hound at my side, while I stare into the mud beneath my feet and contemplate the shit situation we're in.

God, you know – you think you're fine and over your ex and you're moving on with your life nicely, thank you very much, happier than you've been for yonks –and then, all of a sudden, WALLOP! Out of left field, he comes at you, punches you in the face and pulls the rug out from under you.

It may be a stained rug, smelly with the remnants of botched toilet-training attempts, gritty with the un-popped corn left over from Family Friday Fun Movie Nights, dark with the detritus of muddy walks and spilled cups of Yorkshire Tea, but it's *your* rug. A fifty-pound fake from IKEA, you betcha – but *your* fifty-pound fake, *your* symbol of new beginnings, *your* bold statement of courage, integrity and independence.

'Oh, where did it all go so horribly wrong?' I ask the ether.

When we got Roofie?

I look down at him and see his luxuriant mahogany-coloured coat, the thick, wavy fur on his chest giving him a decidedly leonine look. His right paw is poised as if pointing at something in the near distance, his head close to the ground, his nose twitching madly, like the net curtains in Old Stoke.

Well, yes, obviously he was a massive mistake and I was a fool to think I could ever handle training a wilful wood-sprite of a puppy and two recalcitrant kids. Perhaps I should seriously consider re-homing him. But he is beautiful. Camouflaged so well by the reds and ambers of the autumn leaves all around us. And when he finally tires of biting into your flesh and rests his gorgeous snout on your lap, well, it's just lovely.

When we moved to Old Stoke?

The jury's out on this one. I mean, we had no choice but to come here. And it's really rather pretty when the sun shines and you're not vilified by the entire village. Also, when – *if* – we ever have enough money to fix Audrey's house up, it'll be just perfect with some roses round the Farrow & Ball-painted front door, a loft conversion so I actually have a bedroom, a hand rail that's actually attached to the wall so that walking up or down the stairs isn't akin to scaling the north side of the Eiger...

Sending the kids to school in Thistlebend?

Once again, we had little choice in the matter. Clearly Izzy hates it and Ben is just about tolerated there – but they look so good in their uniforms! And I never would have met Charlotte and Willow and got the gig as Agony Aunt on *Chilterns Today (Forever in your heart)* if it weren't for Thistlebend and The Pantry in the school car park. So swings and roundabouts on this one.

'Curse you prosecco and your infernal warm fizz!' I raise my fist to the sky and shake it like the mad woman I am fast becoming.

Maybe it all went tits-up when we got divorced.

Nah. Now that *is* mad! Getting *married* was our first mistake – we should have stayed friends. Without benefits. And now it's too late: he's acted like too much of an arse for us to ever be amicable. I probably have too, let's face it. But now we'll never be able to agree to disagree and be friends – even for the sake of the kids.

And I'm not sure I believe Amelie anymore, when she says getting divorced is the best thing that could ever happen to you. So far, it just seems to have opened up several different Pandora's Boxes of troubles, worries and disasters.

I dunno. It was going well, but now? Now it all feels hopeless.

I can't even muster up any positive thinking inspirational quotes to cheer me up – all I can do is gaze down into the brown goo below as a wave of helplessness and despair crashes down on me. We'll have no money, I'm unemployable, everyone hates me and the kids will be taken off me.

It's all gone to cock and it's all my fault. As per bloody usual.

Maybe everyone would be better off without me. Maybe I'm the fly in the ointment who just mucks everything up. If something happened to me, the kids could always go and live with their dad in Magaluf. They'd probably love being with him there, with all that sunshine and trampolines and Nerf guns and computer games coming out of their kazoos... Finally everyone would be happy, free to get on with their lives without the human handbrake on fun and good fortune that I so clearly am.

The tears sting my cheeks and I blink hard, trying to stem the flow. I rest my forehead on the handrail, dark thoughts lumbering about in my head like black clouds heavy with rain as I watch the teardrops slide off my face and plop into the puddle below.

It takes a few plops, though, before I realise it's not my tears falling at all – it's big, fat blobs of rain. Typical, I think. Of *course* it would start raining now.

The words to 'Why Does It Always Rain On Me?' by Travis come to mind and while I sing them, inadvertently blowing bubbles as the rain mixes with my saliva, Roofie jumps up on me, licking my face and pawing at my hair.

My thinning, split-ended, badly in need of highlights, frizzy hair.

'I know, Roof,' I cry. 'Why did I think I could do this?'

As if he's telling me to shut up, get a grip and pull myself together, his head whips around to stare down something that's moving in the bushes just downstream.

Through the curtain of rain, I can see his eyes get that hard look about them, like he's sizing up his target, waiting for the optimum point to strike.

His right paw slowly rises to that pointing position again.

'No, Roof,' I say gently. 'No, darling, don't... no – no, Roofs, leave it, don't... leave the poor little BUNNNNNNNNNNNYYYYYYYY!'

He darts under the handrail and leaps into the puddle. He pulls hard, my right arm lurches after him and I bash my head on the railing as I go down, letting go of the lead and coming to a halt, landing face-first in the muddy puddle. I don't move. I can't move. I seriously consider drowning myself right then and there. And re-homing the hound is a definite.

But the puddle's too shallow for that kind of caper. Well, of *course* it is. Can't even do away with myself properly.

'Ah, Annie,' booms a deep, creamy voice from somewhere behind me. 'Sloshed again, are we?'

Even though I know I've stacked it on over the last few months, when the man offers me his hand and pulls me out of the mire, my heavy morass of despond, I feel as light as a toothpick.

My head's hanging low, but I manage to sneak a peek at my knight in shining armour as he pulls me out of the mud.

It's George. Gorgeous George. Gorgeous Gentleman Farmer George. The good old GGFG.

'You're looking well,' he says, the dimples down his cheeks carving themselves into his skin. 'Better than the last time I saw you, anyway.'

'Yeah,' I mutter, unable to think of anything else. 'Sorry about that.'

'Your forehead's bleeding. Here, lean on me. I live nearby, at the farm hidden by the hedgerow just over there. Can you walk?'

He pulls my arm around his neck and tries to help me walk, but as soon as I put all my considerable weight solely on my left foot, I scream.

'Woah,' says George. 'Watch the eardrums.'

'Sorry,' I sniff. 'But my ankle's killing me.'

He nods, bends down and scoops me up, one capable arm at my back, the other under my knees.

I feel like the helpless heroine to his manly hero. My Debra Winger to his Richard Gere in *An Officer and a Gentleman*, my Dilys Price to his Fireman Sam. Or the fire chief, old what'shisname. Oh, you know who I mean.

'But… but…'

'Shh,' he shushes me. 'Zachariah, my wire-haired vizsla, will round your dog up and bring him home, don't you worry.'

I wasn't worried about bloody Roofie – haven't given him a second thought since he tore off after that rabbit. No, I just thought George might not be able to lift me, considering all that sugar I've been mainlining lately.

But he has no trouble whatsoever, literally sweeping me off my feet while for the second time in one day, I wonder whether this is what it feels like to swoon.

–

I'm in the luxury guest bathroom at George's, having a bath. It's one of those uber-expensive claw-foot baths, that has the gold taps and shower head in the middle instead of the end.

I've chucked my White Company cardi and all my other gear except my battleship-grey t-shirt bra into a plastic Waitrose (of course) bag and with no GHDs or even a hairdryer in sight, I'm going to have to let my hair dry au naturel. Which isn't such a bad thing – it could do with a break from all that murderous heat damage.

I gingerly hop out of the bath and dry myself off with the super-soft sage-green towels that've been languishing on the heated towel rail and catch sight of myself in the mirror above the his 'n' her bathroom basins.

I gasp. For not only have I piled on the pounds, but my thighs are now covered in cellulite.

George has very kindly lent me some caramel-coloured corduroy plus fours, some natty Argyle socks with a matching Argyle sleeveless sweater-type thing, a pin-striped man's business shirt with a button-down collar and a pair of cotton M&S boxer shorts.

I put the boxers on and my God, they're comfy. Strangely liberating, too. I don the rest of the clothes and feel like a country gent in a Bertie Wooster novel, almost waiting for Jeeves to knock on the door, letting me know that tea will be served in the drawing room when I'm ready.

I'm so lost in my daydreams, that when someone *does* knock on the door, I nearly jump out of my skin.

'Hello?' I call out, looking at the door.

'Hot chocolate's in the kitchen when you're ready,' says George. 'No rush, take your time.'

'Thanks, George,' I reply. 'Be down in a sec!'

What a thoroughly decent chap, I think to myself as I pull on my wet, ugly bra and finish getting dressed.

'Do I look ridiculous in these plus fours?' I ask as I join George in the vast kitchen downstairs.

'No,' he says. 'They fit you perfectly. Length-wise, anyway. But they're breeks, not plus-fours — country walking trousers that stop at the knee — for the more discerning gentleman.'

'Or country walking trews that stop just below the ankle for the shorter, more dis*ast*er-prone lady…'

'Yes,' he looks me up and down as I clamber up onto a high stool at the breakfast bar. 'Quite.'

'Do I look fat in this?' I say, sure I sense some approval when he looks me up and down.

'No, you look completely charming. Like Annie Hall.'

'A short, fat Annie Hall…'

'Short, yes — Annie Small.'

'Ha!' I laugh, abandoning the idea of the bar stool — too bloody tall for short-arses like me to scrabble about on.

'So how did you pitch up after the awards?' George pours my steaming hot chocolate from a cast-iron Le Creuset milk pan into a big polka dot Emma Bridgewater mug.

'I was — and still am — embarrassed beyond belief by my performance. Half the village won't speak to me anymore, the other half never did and I just feel like running away, to be honest,' I say, my face in my hands in an attempt to hide my shame.

'You? Run away?' He raises a bushy eyebrow. 'What happened to all that "Beaton by name, not by nature" guff you were giving me at the awards?'

I snort with derision.

'Honestly, I don't know what got into me. I don't drink at all anymore, but somehow I got swept up in the moment, carried along on a tide of excitement. And now I'm paying for it. Everyone in Old Stoke hates me!'

'Not everyone, surely,' he says, his voice rich with warmth and… richness.

I go on to tell him how we were doing really well, moving to the country, living the dream, but that now, after just one night, we're living a dystopian nightmare. Of biblical proportions.

'Not one to exaggerate much, then?' He puts a plate of shortbread biscuits in front of me.

'Honestly!' I'm just warming up. 'It's like pitchforks at dawn out there!'

'Go easy on the dumb country oik references, Annie,' he says, taking me a bit by surprise. 'That's exactly the kind of prejudice we're trying to do away with.'

'Well, you're the one who put the piece of straw in the business-suited statuette's mouth…'

'It's called irony, Alanis.' He doesn't look up from the probably real marble kitchen counter.

'Oh?' I widen my eyes. 'I would've thought you oiks would find that offensive.'

'Not as offensive as being called hayseeds. And anyway – you're one of us, now, aren't you? You're a hayseed too.'

'I am? Well, yeah, maybe…' I mumble.

'Yes, it was a good do.' He pours water in a giant Mason bowl and puts it on the floor just as his obedient vizsla and my delinquent dog come bounding through the stable kitchen door. 'Great turn-out and a good time was had by all. Tell me – did you get enough for the feature?'

'Hmmm?'

'For the *Chilterns Today (Forever in your heart)* story? That Charlie wants to run in next month's issue?'

'Buggeration!' I blurt out. 'I completely forgot I had to write it up! And the agony column's due any minute now, too…'

'Might be the perfect place for a public apology,' he says, raising both bushy, salt-and-pepper eyebrows at me. 'If, you know, you wanted to make amends.'

'That's not a bad idea, George,' I say, looking around the kitchen, breathing in the understated opulence and classic country charm.

'So did you buy all this stuff online? I seem to remember you said you were into e-shopping or something…'

'I don't *shop* online,' he laughs, 'I build online shops. So, if you wanted to start a business selling, say, slogan t-shirts, my company helps you do it without having to keep stock in your shed, without having to pay extortionate overheads on premises or staff, without you having to source fabrics, manufacturers, printers etc – and you'd make a packet. All from your living room while you're in your PJs working on your lap top.'

'It's that easy?'

'Easier.'

'I'd LOVE to do that… make slogan t-shirts, greeting cards, put words on mugs and mouse mats and welcome mats and—'

'If you've got something to say, I can help you say it and monetise the hell out of it.'

'Really?'

'Yup,' he says, confidence radiating from him. 'I've been selling polo gear lately and it's the easiest money I've ever made.'

'What? The mint with the hole in it? How on earth can you make money out of selling Polo mints merch?'

'Oh, Annie,' he sighs. 'You are a one.'

I don't really know what that means, but I can tell by his grin that it's something good.

'Polo as in princes, ponies and mallets? Jodhpurs, riding boots, hats? There's the new playing field being built in Ufson Downs and business is booming. I'm able to provide quality merch for a fraction of the price. Rich people are very canny with their money – which is why we manage to hold onto it so well.'

'You mean they're skinflints? Tight as gnats' chuffs?'

'No.' He looks at me with his disarming blue eyes as one might regard a naughty puppy. 'Not tight, more like careful – able to spot a bargain at a hundred paces.'

'Of course, of course,' I tut, as if I know full well how toffs operate and I'm only teasing him, pretending not to know how money works.

'What's more, with e-commerce, no one gets hurt in the process, no one gets exploited – talk about win– win. Of course you'd have to get onto Facebook, Twitter, obviously Insta…'

'But I'm a total dunce when it comes to e-anything. Especially computers and technology – I can barely figure out how to turn my laptop *on*, let alone set up shop on it...'

'I know what you mean – my daughter taught me how to do everything. I could do it for you?'

'How old is she?'

'Lucy? Sixteen.' He looks into the distance and exhales loud and long. 'Going on eighteen. What about yours?'

'Izzy's nine. Going on thirty-nine. Got any other kids?'

'Seb, my son,' he says. 'He's twenty-one. Big fan of polo, actually. And parties...'

A grey shade of sadness crosses George's face at this point as he fiddles with the jars of hot chocolate and coffee. Those jars... they suddenly look familiar to me even though I'm sure I've never seen the brand before. And then it comes to me.

'Is that Aldi hot chocolate?' I can hardly believe my eyes.

'Nothing but the best,' he grins.

I nod excitedly and tell him about my trip there. He doesn't seem particularly impressed.

But he does crack a smile and ooh, those dimples – they're divine.

My heart skips a beat and I have to look away. God, he's *gorgeous*.

'I must say,' I cough a little bit, suddenly feeling quite hot. 'It's rather fortuitous bumping into you today as I just so happen to be looking for a way to make money fast, now. Being, as we are, in the shit. As it were.'

I don't know why I'm speaking like this – like Hugh Grant in a Richard Curtis film – must be having a hot flush and feeling nervous at the same time.

'Well look no further Annie,' he says. 'I'm your man.'

God! I wish he'd stop saying things like that! I'm coming over all unnecessary as it is!

'E-commerce is the future.' He gets all serious and sips his coffee dramatically. 'And the future is now.'

'Sounds amazing,' I beam, suddenly feeling more optimistic.

I look around some more, drinking it all in. Then my eyes settle on a humungous clock on the wall above the six-seater tartan corner couch in the snug part of the kitchen. It's got massive Roman numerals on it and I'm struggling to figure out what the hell the actual time is. I'm crap at numbers at the best of times – but when they're in a foreign language? No chance.

'If I can help in any way, just let me know,' he says.

'You can tell me what the time is for starters...'

He glances at the clock and says, quick as a flash, 'Five to three.'

'Shit! I'm going to be late to pick the kids up! I've got to run, now, George – where are my boots?'

I hobble to the front door, which is approx. five miles from the kitchen, sit on the stone floor with not so much as a passing thought for the potential for getting piles sitting on such a cold, hard surface, and squelch my muddy boots onto my beautifully soft Argyle sock-clad feet.

As I limp on out of the house, down the long gravel driveway, past a Range Rover and a nifty-looking cream MG, I shout back at him:

'Thanks for everything, George! See you soon!'

'Sure you don't want a lift?' he yells back.

'I only live just up the road,' I say, even though I'm not sure where I am in relation to our house. 'I'll be fine!'

'Don't leave me,' I'm surprised to hear him say. 'Don't leave me!'

'What?' I turn around.

'Don't leave me with your dog!'

Oh. That makes more sense.

'Could you hang onto him for me for a bit? I'll be back to pick him up as soon as we get back from Thistlebend. 'I wouldn't ask, normally, but—'

'Just GO!' George says as he shoos me away. Nice guy, I think to myself as I limp down the country lane, writing my apology column and t-shirt slogans in my head as I go.

Several minutes later, when I get to the end of the lane, it dawns on me that I haven't a clue which way to go now. Raindrops start falling and I realise I'm completely and utterly lost, never having been up to Old Stoke Heights before.

And then, just as I'm about to burst into tears, an enormous four-wheel drive pulls up beside me. The passenger door flies open, revealing two dogs barking insanely in the back. Well, one dog barks insanely (Roofie, natch) – the other, Zachariah, George's wire-haired vizsla, just looks a bit scared, to be honest.

'Your carriage awaits, m'lady,' George says in what I think is a Parker from *Thunderbirds* impression. Hard to tell in this rain.

I step up into the exceedingly posh car, get a whiff of the all-leather interior, see the walnut dash and gently lower my enormous arse onto the extra-wide seat.

I practically melt into it.

'Oh. My. God. Do these seats have bum warmers?'

'Standard,' George says matter-of-factly as the door automatically closes.

And as we float silently towards Thistlebend on a cloud of luxury, the rain stops and I swear we actually drive through a rainbow.

–

Three upbeat positives to counteract the countless negatives:

- I caught sight of my hair in the side mirror of George's car and I didn't hate it. It wasn't frizzy, but it was really quite curly. In a good way.
- We drove through a real-life rainbow – how *up* is that?!
- Still no sign of any unicorns, but how about that George, eh?

–

October 29 – To Whom I Have Annoyed

A small cardboard box is sitting on our doorstep this morning when I get back from drop-off. And when I open it, there's a mug inside.

It's a lovely big cream-coloured mug, with huge black letters on it saying:

Always Beaton by name
Never beaten by nature

The note tucked inside the mug says:

Dear Annie Small

Don't be a mug, be a millionaire mug seller!
Ask me now, I'll show you how.
G xx

That George. That gorgeous George. Could he be the man I've been looking for all my life? Clever, handsome to the nth degree, possessor of weapons-grade charm and loaded beyond all reason... He *is* being awfully nice to me, despite the fact he's so clearly way out of my league. And class. But he *is* acting like he might fancy me, isn't he? Or maybe he's just after some positive coverage in *Chilterns Today (Forever in your heart)*.

But his sister *owns* that magazine – he doesn't have to creep up to me to get a good write-up.

Of course, he might just be a naturally nice person, encouraging a fellow entrepreneur in her e-commerce endeavours, nothing more, nothing less.

Although that just seems so unlikely in this day and age.

He is a bit older than me, though, so perhaps he grew up in a more chivalrous time: a time when you wooed someone by being nice to them, flirting gently and finding out about them and all the things you have in common.

As opposed to the time I grew up in, when a boy registered his interest in you by gobbing at your feet.

Not that I'm romantically interested in George or anything. Ours is a strictly business relationship. I haven't got time for romance and chivalry and all that old-fashioned gubbins – I've got to look after my poor, confused kids and make our fortune by pick-up this arvo!

I open up the laptop and check my emails and see there's one from Audrey, deep in the heart of the Amazon. Who knew they had wi-fi there?

Annie!

What are you doing? What have you done? My reputation in Old Stoke is apparently in tatters! If money's the problem, as it so very often is, don't worry about paying the rent, just you do what you have to do to make things right.

Make amends, my darling – life's too short for disagreements and misunderstandings. Make your apologies and get rid of any bad blood.

Sort it out, sweetie – or I'll come home and sort it out for you. And the last thing I want to do is cut short my amazing adventure. I've just met the most wonderful man and I'm staying at his place in Rio. I think I'm about to get a really good ROI…

All love to you and the bairns,
Aud xxx

So my ignominy has gone global. I feel absolutely rotten, having tarnished Auntie Audey's good name – even if she has no idea what the hell ROI stands for. Or maybe she has. Urgh. I don't want to know.

Next, I see one from James Raphael. I eagerly click on it.

He addresses me as Wolfie (short for Wolverine), sending a tingle down my spine. Which is, hopefully, not what it feels like to sprout a new crop of hair on one's back, but what it feels like to fancy someone again. God knows, it's been so long, I wouldn't have a clue.

It's highly unprofessional for James to be so familiar, obviously, but it's also kind of sweet. As soon as I think that, James appears in my mind's eye, throwing his revolting trainers into a hedgerow and I tilt my head to the side, sighing.

Of course, like I told myself mere seconds ago, I'm not up for any emotional attachments – I've got my hands full on that front, what with the kids and the dog... And I'm still reeling, in one way or another, from the divorce, so I haven't got the time, the energy or the wherewithal for any of that slushy stuff. Not at the moment, anyway.

But gor! Who knew the country would be littered with so many lovely men?

I shake my head and cough.

Back to the business at hand, Annie – focus!

James's email says he's got the CMS and the HMRC on the case and he's waiting for them to get back to him. He says Joe will have left a trail as big as an autumn snail's, so it won't be long before he has some more concrete info for me. And, hopefully, some money.

Next there's a message from Charlotte. Or Charlie as her twin brother calls her:

> *Annie*
>
> *Where's your copy? Make something up fast. In-tray me ASAP.*
>
> *Despite your antics at the awards, I'm going to keep you on. And offer you my sincerest congratulations — you're the first person to have caught G's eye and captured his imagination since That Woman left him.*
>
> *Keep up the good work.*
>
> *All best*
>
> *Charlotte & Willow*
>
> *PS Hurt my brother and I'll kill you. Not personally, of course — I wouldn't want to risk*

getting blood spattered on any of my time-
less, classic pieces. Do you have any idea how
impossible it is to get blood out of camel cashmere?
No? Well it is. But I digress. What was I saying?
Oh yes. I can't hurt you personally — but I know
a man who can. Several, in fact. I think it's
important you know that about our family. X

So he *does* fancy me! And even though Charlotte's email might make a lesser woman gulp, thanks to its sinister, menacing, downright *threatening* tone, I have no intention of embarking on anything lovey or, indeed, dovey with George or anyone for that matter, therefore I am in no mortal danger whatsoever.

Perhaps I've lost weight lately. And I thought the only thing getting thinner was my hair! Nah, I couldn't possibly have, not with all that secret Twix-scoffing I've been doing when the kids are at school. Maybe with the stress of everything I've lost a little excess poundage? Unlikely. But why, then, do two good-looking men, both friendly, neither clinically insane (as far as I know) or beset by cataracts seem to have the hots for me?

Maybe they don't. Maybe I'm getting carried away on a wave of optimism, positive thinking leading me up the garden path straight back to Fantasy Island. Maybe James is just using my case to put right his sullied reputation and strike a blow for decent divorced dads everywhere. And George? Well, he's just exceedingly well brought-up, isn't he?

An email from Amelie pops up. I click on it slowly, my left hand over my eyes, fingers splayed so I can read the screen.

> *What the actual fuck?????*
>
> *When are you going to call/text/email me????*
>
> *I hope you're okay. You were such a mess! I don't know – you look after your best friend for years and years and this is the thanks you get? You can apologise to me in person soon, though – Tom and I are coming down to Old Stoke for Bonfire Night. Although we're staying at Tom's this time – that dog of yours creeped us out. It's hard to shag un-self-consciously when a red setter's standing next to the sofa bed, staring at you, pointing at you with his bent paw and panting. I think he might have tried to join in and hump the arm of the sofa at one stage.*
>
> *Anyway, I have SOOOO much to tell you about me and Tom. It's like it was meant to be. It's like two hearts beating as one. It's like love!*
>
> *See you soooooon!*
>
> *Tam xxx (That's Tom and Am together – Tam! Get it? Tom and Am? Cute or what?!)*

–

Poor Roofie. No wonder he's behaving so badly. I'd be scarred for life too if I'd seen what he has. Talk about night terrors.

Speaking of best friends, I wonder how Aisling's doing. And if Amelie and Tom – sorry, *Tam* – are coming down for Bonfire Night, maybe I'll ask Ash and Pete, too. I'll send her a text later. Right now, though, I've got to get on with my apology.

I take a sip of excellent Aldi Earl Grey tea out of my new favourite mug and begin work:

–

Q: Dear Auntie Annie,

My family and I recently moved to the Chilterns and everything was going swimmingly until a few weekends ago when I got unceremoniously trollied. I can't remember what I did or said, but a friendly neighbour filled me in and now I'm mortified.

Apparently, I made passes at my friends' husbands, kissed a total stranger and made a friend flee in tears when I let loose a torrent of wholly unwarranted abuse at her.

To make matters worse, I'm nearly fifty-one, so I really should know better by now. I'm so ashamed. It's all a total disaster.

I'm actually a really nice person, but my behaviour the other night would suggest otherwise. Can I make amends? And, if so, how?

Also, there doesn't seem to be anywhere to get facial hair lasered/waxed/torched around here – any suggestions? Word on the street says your face is as hair-free as a Veet factory. Just how do you do it, Annie?

Please help – I feel such a (hairy) fool!
Yeti-In-Waiting

–

A: Dear Yeti,

I feel your pain. Strange as it may sound and hard as it may be to believe, I, too, have found myself in your unenviable position once or twice. But there is light at the end of the tunnel, let me assure you.

It's one thing growing old disgracefully – but quite another thing getting so drunk you make a total tit out of yourself like you did when you were twenty-five. Only now, you can't handle the hangover, the shame or the consequences. Now you can't laugh it off and blame youthful exuberance on your behaviour – I mean, you're fifty-one, for God's sake!

I'm not trying to make you feel any worse, really I'm not. I just think it's time for some tough self-love. Because when you're nearly old enough to be getting your bus pass, letting yourself get so out of control like that can be devastating. A real blow to the morale. When things are hard e-bloody-nough already.

Far be it from me to go around dishing out platitudes like cups of tea, but what's done is done, it is what it is and, as they say in the classics, you are what you are. (Answers on a postcard to the usual address, please, if you have even the faintest clue what any of that actually means!)

Anyway, as I see it, you have two options:

1. *Brazen it out. Go about your business as usual and pretend nothing happened – or at least nothing you should be ashamed of. This approach is favoured by those under twenty-five and really tricky to pull off when you're in your fifties.*
2. *Apologise. This is the big girl approach – face up to your wrongdoings, admit them, say sorry and move on. Time heals all wounds and this is the fast track to getting over it.*

You can't turn back time to change events (more's the pity) and everyone knows what you did so you might as well accept it and apologise for it. You're human after all and we all make mistakes. Which is, incidentally, exactly how we move forward, learn and – dare I say it – grow.

Which brings me to the wisest bit of my answer: you may have upset your friends, but you've done more damage to yourself. Because the biggest casualty of this drunken debauchery, I'd wager, is your self-esteem and confidence. You say you're mortified by your own behaviour and that's no way to live, is it? Killing yourself softly on the inside for something that you can't change, and had no control over?

The only way to boost yourself up again is to stop berating yourself now, take back control and get yourself a copy of Kick the Drink... Easily! by Jason Vale.

In your defence, no one's perfect. In fact, we're all struggling in our own ways, with problems peculiar to us. It's often a completely different story behind closed doors to what we see out in public. We all wear a mask of some sort or another, all have our favourite narrative about ourselves, trotting out the same old lines, choosing carefully what we let others see. And there's nothing wrong with that – sometimes it's the only way we can cope, the only way we can survive. I mean, look at Facebook! It's all a load of self-aggrandisement, PR BS. So much so, it's now known as Fakebook.

So in a nutshell, if I were you, Yeti, I'd pick myself up, dust myself off, apologise to everyone (including yourself) and get on with your life. And stay off the sauce!

And what better time to show compassion, kindness and goodwill to all men (and women AND YOURSELF) than right now? Because let's face it, it's all about forgiveness in the end – and how can we move on, be our authentic selves, live our best lives without letting go of old arguments and scars, scattering them to the four winds as we make way for rejuvenation and rebirth? We can't, that's how.

So let's throw off those heavy chains of judgement and let's get on with living a good life and spreading some joy. Starting with letting up on ourselves a bit, seeing wins where we might previously have seen nothing at all, success where we may only have been able to see failure. Let's rewrite our stories in a positive vein. Because this confidence and self-esteem malarkey is often merely a matter of perception, really: whether you think you can or you think you can't, you're right.

And while I've got your attention (Oi! You up the back – wake up!), here's my favourite Christmas cracker joke of all time:

Q: What's Good King Wenceslas' favourite pizza base?

A: Deep and crisp and even.

Sorry.

Anyway, thanks for reading – and if you got this far, congratulations. See you at Chilterns Primary on Bonfire Night, everybody!

All my love,

Annie xxx

PS Apparently there's a lovely little beauty boutique in sunny Fugsham. Word on the street says it's a must for any woman battling a beard.

–

I send it off and hear back from Charlotte within the hour:

> God you bang on – had to give you two pages! Best bit? Good King Wenceslas. Maybe it's time you started getting paid. How does £100 a month sound? And I won't see you at the bonfire night, no. But Georgie will…

Three positive take-aways:

- All the positive thinking and asking The Universe for stuff seems to have worked. I mean, not only have I managed to keep my job, I'm going to get paid for it soon, too!
- James will make sure Joe won't get away with skipping out on his responsibilities – it's become his own personal crusade.
- Two hot men – count 'em, TWO – might fancy me.

Chapter Thirteen

November

November 5 – Avast Ye Landlubbers!

In the name of research and not frightening the horses at this evening's bonfire night, I go to Fugsham, as advised, to get my face waxed.

Which is all well and good, but after years of furious plucking around my chin, there are loads of ingrown hairs (little black, immoveable dots) and the beautician has to pull out the big guns and use Hot Wax on me.

'I thought it was all hot wax?' I say, feeling anything but beautiful.

'It's weird – all wax is warm, but the Hot Wax is really thick and super-strong. So it can pull out, you know, the tougher, more reluctant hairs.'

Great. Not only have I got two recalcitrant kids, I've also got tough, rebellious hag hairs, too.

Still, looking on the bright side, as is my wont these days, they won't stand a chance against the nuclear wax.

'Let's give it a go, then!' I chirp and close my eyes, gripping onto the sides of the gurney I'm lying on.

The beautician goes for it and as she smears the goo onto my chin, I can feel it's thick, sticky and heavy. It's almost quite relaxing and soothing until—

THWACK!

She rips one strip off.

'Ber-limey!' I say.

THERRRIP!

Another one bites the dust.

'Jesus!' I yelp.

'Just... one... more and you'll be—'

SSCRRRISH!

'CHRIST ON A BIKE!' I screech.

'There.' The beautician rubs some sort of cream into my burning face. 'That's better. Smooth as a baby's bottom.'

'What have you come as?' Amelie gasps when she sees me. 'Blackbeard?'

I run my fingertips over my chin, but can't feel anything. It is, as the beautician said, as smooth as a baby's bum to the touch. What's she on about?

'Here.' She pushes her compact mirror onto me. 'Look like tiny blood blisters to me. Let me guess... Hot Wax?'

Now it's my turn to gasp. There are about a million tiny black dots all over my chin area and it looks like I've gone berserk with a Sharpie, trying to give the impression I'm a pirate with a three-day growth.

'Ahoy there,' I grumble at my reflection.

'Driving Home For Christmas' by Chris Rea strikes up suddenly. And even though it sounds super-tinny coming out of the school tannoy system, it somehow serves to ramp up the festive feel that's making everyone a bit giddy tonight, and I promptly forget all about my chinny chin chin.

We make our way through the playground, the smell of frying onions teasing our tastebuds and catching in the backs of our throats as we pass the hamburgers and hot dogs stalls, dodging and diving, ducking and weaving through the huge crowds milling about the cupcake stand.

Finally we make it to the bushes near the entrance to the school oval – the best vantage point for the fundraising fireworks do, apparently, and where we're meeting our friends. I know! *Friends*.

Jane's the first to see us and yoo-hoos, jumping up and down, beckoning us over.

When we get to her, I introduce Amelie and Tom as separate entities, even though they insist on being called 'Tam', and Ben and Izzy come alive, their faces lighting up with the Catherine wheels illuminating the sky and the idea that next year this will be their new school.

Jack's sitting on John's shoulders, sticking his tongue out at Ben; Sue's son is sitting on her husband's shoulders and Liz's son is sitting on her shoulders – she's way taller than her bloke, so her little boy will have a much better view sitting on her.

I look over to 'Tam' and wonder whether Tom would mind playing Daddy for a bit and scooping Ben up onto his shoulders.

But Tom's face is currently being eaten by Amelie, so I dismiss the idea. Ben won't let it go, however, and tugs at my coat, whining about the fact that he hasn't got a dad's shoulders to sit on.

Curse that Joe.

And so, feeling strong and brave (I am woman yada yada yada), I crouch down and indicate to Ben to climb onto my shoulders.

But for the love of all that's gracious and holy he's heavy! I slowly manage to just about stand fully upright, creaking and groaning as I go, when Jack, sitting on John's shoulders, leans over and pushes Ben's chest. I lose my footing, my back concertinas under the weight and I call Izzy for help, reaching out for her just two seconds too late as we crash down into the tangled emperor-sized bed of nettles behind us.

'Ow, OW, OWWWWW!' cries Ben.

'Hold onto my neck.' I push myself up from the stinging, vile vegetation and hover over Ben.

He does as he's told and I run with him, cradled in my arms, to the first aid unit in the school library, where we stay for the remainder of the fireworks, rubbing Savlon into our skin and cursing the cruelty of Mother Nature.

—

'2000 Miles' by The Pretenders is jangling out of the jukebox when we walk in to the front bar of The Zebra.

Jane and John, Sue and whatshisname, her husband, and Liz are standing by a long, medieval feasting table by a roaring fire and wave us over to join them. Well, Jane and Sue wave – Liz is still giving me the hairy eyeball every chance she gets and I swear I heard her sniggering when Ben and I fell into the nettles.

My kids yelp and run over to their kids and when we descend upon the table, Tom and Amelie still barely able to keep their hands off each other, I'm greeted by hugs and kisses and directed to the roaring fire.

'God, I love a proper, open fire,' I sigh.

'Me too,' says Sue. 'Shame this one's gas.'

'Really?' I'm amazed. 'But there's that unmistakeable smell of woodsmoke in the air…'

'Pumped through the ventilation system.' Jane leans in. 'Same way the smell of freshly baked bread is pumped in on a Saturday morning, the smell of roast lamb at lunchtime on a Sunday…'

'It's all synthetic, you see – nothing but a façade,' Sue confirms.

'The cheeky buggers!' I say. 'I thought this place was so country, so charming, so authentic…'

'Well, appearances can be deceiving,' Jane smiles.

'Yeah,' Sue joins in, 'we all have our masks, our own preferred personal narratives, don't we?'

I take this as acknowledgement and acceptance of my apology which must have already come out in the latest issue of *Chilterns Today (Forever in your heart).*

Which reminds me. I've made a card for Liz. It's a prototype for ones I hope to sell in my e-shop. I figure Hallmark cards are so outdated, something we need right now is cards that will help us find the right words when we're navigating the choppy stormy seas of awkward adult social relationships that go beyond 'with sympathy' and 'sorry to hear you're leaving'.

My cards will have cute drawings on the front, done by the kids, and things like 'Congratulations on your Divorce!', 'Wishing You a Merciful Menopause' and 'Phew! Thank God you got your Period – Teen Pregnancies are so not Trending Right Now' on the insides.

But for now I take my entrepreneurial hat off and look Liz in the eye as I hand her the card.

It's got a badly drawn sad face on the front (I've always been rubbish at drawing), with the words: *Sorry I behaved like such a dick* over the top of the faux-emoji.

Inside I've written:

Dear Liz,

I'm sorry.

I guess I was so caught up in the minutiae of my own life, constantly gazing at my own navel, I didn't stop to think about what fresh hell someone else might be going through.

I'm so sorry.

Can you ever forgive me?

Annie xxx

Liz takes it, reads it and bursts into tears, leaning down towards me and wrapping me up in the biggest, warmest hug I've had in a long time.

'I'm sorry too,' she sobs. 'I judged you harshly the minute I saw you. But I was so wrong. You're not a social pariah, responsible for all society's ills, are you?'

I'm a bit bowled over by the question and don't have a chance to answer before she starts up again.

'No, of course not! What a load of old bollocks. I'm glad to know you, Annie – because even though you're short on stature, you're awfully big on heart.'

Which makes me well up. I mean, I think that's possibly the nicest thing anyone's ever said to me.

And so, feeling relieved and almost a part of the gang, I offer to get eggnog, mulled wine and hot chocolates for everyone and slope off to the bar, despite the fact I can't remotely afford it. But the desire to be liked and accepted is too strong to resist at this point. And anyway, drinks are bound to be cheaper in the country – and if I pay by my card I won't even have to admit to myself that I've spent anything at all! Genius.

The landlord (or 'local treasure' as Jane and Sue refer to him) is a gruff piece of work and I don't see him smile once as he makes the drinks, even though he must be making a fortune with the bar full and the insanely marked-up booze flowing.

'Here You Come Again' by Dolly Parton strikes up on the jukebox, the steel guitar twanging sadly as Dolly's sweet voice tells the tale of some guy returning to woo the woman he's wronged.

I love this song, so I sing along as I carry the drinks back to the table. And when I bend down to put the tray on the table, I suddenly realise that my right knee's hurting. Actually, it's bloody killing me, ripples of pain emanating from the joint that feels like it's grinding itself further and further down with every breath I take.

Must have jarred it when we fell in the nettles.

Now where the hell did I put my knee support thingy? I rummage about, but it's not in my rucksack, despite the fact that just about everything *else* I own is – folded-up flyers for food delivery companies, school photo order forms (so that's where they are!), broken hair clips, unused (thankfully) dog poo bags, empty perfume bottles, etc. That's annoying – it must be at home, buried somewhere underneath the mounds of clutter that seem to rush to any clear space that ever appears on our front room floor.

I sit down, rubbing my knee, surveying the scene and wondering where it all went so right.

It'll be my birthday in week. A full year has passed since my fiftieth and what a contrast! I mean, here we are in a beautiful village, in the local boozer with our new friends, the kids playing nicely (ish) with each other, ruddy-cheeked and red-nosed – just how kids are supposed to be in a country winter.

I seem to have been forgiven my misdemeanours by Jane, Sue and Liz, which is a major relief – and I don't feel like such a village outcast anymore, me and my kids tossed onto the scrapheap of rural life before we've had a chance to have a really good crack at it.

George, he of the twinkly eyes and lush guest bathroom is talking with James – and they're both looking over at me every now and again. Which makes me a bit self-conscious, actually. I touch my hair and realise it's been well over a year since I had a cut and colour. I look down at my leggings, muddy Fly London boots that I can't zip all the way up because of my chunky calves…

What. A. Dag.

What are you saying, Annie? If you can't say anything nice, don't say anything at all.

I catch sight of myself in a mirror on the wall. I squint and suddenly, somehow, see more clearly. Actually, I tell myself, my hair's not as bad as I'd have thought, considering it's been left to go curly. And I swear my legs don't look quite as sausage link-y as they did a few months ago. Even those cool boots are much closer to being zipped up all the way than they were and if you don't look too closely, you can't see any of my Long John Silver stubble, either.

I quickly look away before my tentative grasp on that silver lining is lost and storm clouds start rolling in.

I tell myself that when the money starts raining down on me from *Chilterns Today (Forever in your heart!)* and the mug/t-shirt/greetings card business, I'm going to treat myself to a new hairdo and some cool country clothes – maybe even hit the equine outfitters at the local riding school. I'll grab some Dubarry boots, a couple of tweed hacking jackets, some tight, cream jodhpurs (after I've lost a stone or three), anything *at all* from the Celtic & Co. catalogue…

Even Roofie seems to be happy, play-fighting with Zachariah, their wet coats drying fast near the huge roaring (fake) fire.

We've come so far, I think to myself. When we first bowled up in Old Stoke, we had no idea how we were going to handle life as a family of three. Things were tough, no doubt about it and it's still a work in progress. But that's life, isn't it?

And obviously I've had indispensable help along the way – Mum and Dad, Auntie Audey, Jane, James and George – even the kids, after a fashion, giving me a purpose. But now I feel so much more steady on my pins, able to stand on my own two feet, I'm ready to rescue myself. Be my own hero, if you will.

Because now I get it. Failure or success, it's all a matter of perspective and perception. It's all in your head. And if you can find the positive – no matter how minuscule or seemingly irrelevant – it's a win. If you can notice the little things, it'll make a big difference. And that's not some cringey platitude or a nonsensical navel-gazing line, it's a *fact*.

A warm feeling washes over me. Happiness? Contentment? Incontinence? Whatever it is, it's kind of comforting and reassuring. I feel safe and secure. Like, I *know* that no one's going to come and pull the rug out from under me. At least not in the next ten minutes. And even if they do, and I tumble to the floor, falling flat on my face, so what? I'll laugh, pick myself up, brush myself down and just get on with it, I suppose, as we all do. Time after time after inevitable bloody time.

I smile as I look around and wonder if maybe there really is something to this positive thinking lark, after all. And even if there isn't and it's just an illusion and all us poor positive thinkers are deluded beyond all reason, at least we feel more confident, more open to possibilities and more able to tackle another day. Which has to be a good thing, right? A major positive.

Don't get me wrong, it's not like I'm oblivious to unpleasant truths, in denial of disasters and blind to calamities looming on the horizon. It's not like I think you can cure cancer with happy thoughts and I suddenly believe in unicorns and fairies or anything – I mean, I haven't lost my mind *completely*. Yet.

It's just I've got this niggling feeling that maybe, *just maybe*, I'm exactly where I should be.

Annie and Amelie's Ten Commandments
for the Divorced Single Mum

1. **Thou shalt not badmouth thine Ex**
   Or at least not in front of thy kids. Yes, even if thine Ex hast been a bit of a dick. Fear thee not, the truth willst out when thy kids art older.

2. **Thou shalt give it thy best shot at being friends with thine Ex – even if thou canst not stand the guy**
   Bite thy tongue and think of thy kids. And thy maintenance payments.

3. **Thou shalt not let the superior, sneery judginess of others get thee down**
   They art probably jealous of thy comparative freedom, after all, stuck in their small lives of quiet desperation as they undoubtedly art.

4. **Thou shalt not give a rat's arse about thy so-called friends who let thee down when thou needst them most**
   Thou findst out who thy real friends are when thou becomest an SM and thou'll be surprised by the ones who fall by the wayside when the shite really hits ye fan.

5. **Thou shalt not eat thy feelings – particularly if thy feelings are made out of Lindor Balls**

Or at least not every night. And anyway, family blocks of Cadbury's Fruit 'n' Nut art loads cheaper and go some way towards thy five a day.

6. **Thou shalt rest assured this fresh hell of half-term shalt, too, pass**
School holidays can be a tough time for ye olde Single Mums – but also prime fun time for McDonald's, duvet days and *SpongeBob* marathons (which thou canst easily snooze through, no worries).

7. **Thou shalt be proud and revel in thy new-found status as A Single Mum**
And thank thy lucky stars thou gotst out of thine own crap relationship, because now thou canst really love and look after those kids properly without some pretender moaning and droning on in ye background about how tired/poor he is.

8. **Thou shalt resist temptation to compare thyself with other mums**
Thy kids will doest enough of that for thee. And it won't be pretty. So give thyself a break and remind thyself how utterly marvellous thou art – thy kids are still alive!

9. **Thou shalt almost *expect* married maters at thy school gates to mistake thee for a threat and eye thee with suspicion**
They do this because they can't imagine anything worse than being a Single Mum – but thou knowst better (and have they *seen* their husbands lately?! Ha! As if!)

10. **Thou shalt think of ye perks of being a Single Mum when life at ye coalface gets tough (from approx. 6:30 am–8:30 pm daily)**

    Throughout the tears and tantrums (mostly thine own, obvs), thou willst maybe get a sec to think about the movie/cake/bath/bottle of gin thou willst immerse thyself in when thine Ex takes the kids off your hands for a couple of hours.

11. **Thou shalt get in amongst it on thine own local dating scene when – and, indeed, if – thou art ready and feeling up for 't**

    Elite Singles ist apparently fantastic for meeting like-minded potential love interests. If, however, 'tis only a quick bunk-up thou art after, try Tinder.

12. **Thou shalt embrace ye sisterhood of Single Mums**

    And bin thine own prejudices. For united we stand, divided we fall etc.

13. **Girl, thou shalt put thy records on regularly and play thy favourite songs**

    Show thy kids how in charge thou art by playing great songs about strong, cool women. 'I Am Woman' by Helen Reddy springeth to mind. Great for defusing tension, breakfast kitchen dancing and helping thy kids' feminist principles and musical tastes develop correctly (i.e. mirroring thine own)

14. **Thou shalt accept thou did playest thy part in the split**

    Thou art big enough to take half the responsibility – thou art a grown up, after all. But don't bang on about it – he was worse. And he started it – so there.

Oops – went up to fourteen. Maths never was our strong point. Still, you get the picture... And so, armed with these handy commandments, you and your no-doubt gorgeous kids can live Happily Ever After, unfettered by social stigma or handbrake husbands. Now let thy joy be unconfined!

Annie Beaton found these really useful:

A Year of Positive Thinking by Cyndie Spiegel
    (Althea Press)
The Six Pillars of Self-Esteem by Nathaniel Branden
    (Random House)
Kick the Drink… Easily! by Jason Vale (Crown House
    Publishing)
Stop Smoking in 2 Hours – a FREE and brilliant app by
    Jason Vale
Feel the Fear and Do It Anyway by Susan Jeffers
    (Vermilion)
The Secret by Rhonda Byrne (Simon and Schuster)

A Letter From Mink

Well hello there! And welcome to the wonderful world of Annie Beaton. Although, of course, when I say 'wonderful', what I actually mean is chaotic, cluttered, messy and more often than not, completely and utterly disastrous! You know, like most of us from time to time – or at least a *leetle* bit like us every now and again. But even if your path doesn't take the testing twists and turns that Annie's does, I do hope you can still relate somehow... and let me in on your secret!

Mind you, I guess it's the mishaps, misfortunes and miscommunications which beset Annie – and her reactions to them – that make her so much fun, in the end. I mean, she brings so much trouble on herself, what with her impetuous nature and inflated sense of how much she can really handle, doesn't she? And she still manages to keep smiling. For the most part, anyway. Silly old moo.

Obviously, years and years of extensive research went into the creation of Annie and her brood and I really hope you enjoyed dropping in on her. If you're that way inclined and feel like posting a review somewhere, please do! I'm super-keen to know what you think – especially if Annie's tale of overcoming adversity made you feel better about your own challenges and/or made you laugh.

Because if you don't laugh at life's little setbacks, you cry, don't you? Not that there's anything wrong with having a good old blub or anything – it's just that laughter releases feel-good hormones whereas crying releases, well, a load of salty tears and bubbly snot, really. And who *isn't* an ugly crier?! Laughing's just so much a better look in the long run.

Like Annie, I'm a bit of a technophobe/Luddite, to tell the truth – so all I've managed to set up over the years is a Facebook page and a Twitter page/spot/whatever.

Still, do get in touch if you want to talk about Annie or writing or relationships or kids or crazy dogs – anything at all, really. Just say hi and let's have a chat!

So anyway, thank you so much for your support on this, Annie Beaton's 'journey' (a word she may once have struggled saying, but now trips off her tongue almost as easily as a swear word) and I look forward to letting you in on more of Annie's misadventures in the country soon.

In the meantime, I wish you and yours all the best – may your Tunnock's Tea Cakes come by the truckload and be completely calorie-free!

Lots of love,

Mink x

Facebook – Mink Elliott Books

Twitter – @MinkElliott